THE **WILDEST** ONES:
Hot Biker Tales

Edited By
M. Christian

D1722223

A STARbooks Press Release

Published in the United States
FLF/STARbooks Press
P. O. Box 711612
Herndon, VA 20171
Printed in the United States.

Cover photography reproduced by permission granted by David Lewis. Mr. Lewis may be contacted by email at davidlewisimages@aol.com or feel free to visit his website at www.davidlewisimages.com. Many thanks to graphic artist, John Nail for his enthusiastic collaboration on the design of *Wildest Ones'* extraordinary cover. Mr. Nail may be reached at: tojonail@bellsouth.net.

First Edition Published in 2005
Library of Congress Control Number: 2005928606
ISBN: 1-891855-55-7

PRAISE FOR EDITOR/AUTHOR
M. CHRISTIAN

"M. Christian speaks with a totally unique and truly fascinating voice. There are a lot of writers out there who'd better protect their markets—M. Christian has arrived!"
—*Mike Resnick, Hugos and a Nebula award winning author of more than 40 novels, 200 stories, 12 collections, and editor of 30 anthologies.*

"M. Christian is a sick fuck: the best reason I still read erotica."
—*Shar Rednour, author of* The Femme's Guide to the Universe

"M. Christian is one of the most powerful voices in today's erotica. With a voice that ranges from edgy to lyrical, from heart stopping to heart pounding, M. Christian is an amazing talent. Truly, one of the most important erotic writers we have. Speaking Parts is one of M. Christian's finest works to date."
—*Cara Bruce, editor of* Viscera, Venusorvixen.com, *and* Best Bisexual Women's Erotica

"M. Christian is today's premiere erotic shapeshifter, with too many stories to tell to be fenced in by only one gender or identity. Reading these tales is like climbing on for a sexual magic carpet ride through different times and places, diverse bodies, and infinite possibilities."
—*Carol Queen, author of* The Leatherdaddy & the Femme

"M. Christian is one of the finest living writers of erotica. Between these covers is a wealth of imaginative, well-crafted, smoothly written fiction that sings with joy and savvy queer sensibility. It's yummy."
—*Patrick Califia-Rice, author of* Macho Sluts, Melting Point, Doc and Fluff, *and* No Mercy.

ACKNOWLEDGMENTS

If this book is dedicated to anyone, it's to all these wonderful authors. I'm just the editor; they are the ones who've written a memorable book. I'm also eternally grateful to Jill, my light and my love, for all the roads we've traveled and will travel in the future.

Special thanks go to Michael, Paul, and the other great folks at STARbooks for this fantastic opportunity to put our kick- stands up, jump on the throttle, and head out to parts unknown.

TABLE OF CONTENTS

THE **WILDEST** ONES:
Hot Biker Tales

—To our bitch and master:
The open road

INTRODUCTION
M. Christian

On The Allure Of The "Outlaw Biker" Mythos As Adolescent Domination/Rebellion Fantasies Utilizing Exaggerated Paternal/Discipline Figures As Idealized Machismo Role Models Embracing Homosexual Sadomasochistic Fantasies: A Conversation Between "Big Daddy" McKenna, Treasurer Of The Nevada Eagles Motorcycle 'Gang,' and M. Christian, Ph.D.

It does not take an unusual amount of examination, documentation, and analysis to enable a thoughtful researcher to draw the parallel between the so-called 'Outlaw Biker' lifestyle and adolescent fantasies of power and freedom from responsibility and parental/societal expectations. But what is less frequently investigated is the appeal of how the 'biker' archetype is similarly a reflection of homosexual dominance and submission role play, yet the signs and signatures of such a connection are more than evident when viewed in that context. Examples abound: the structure of a typical—if such a word could be used to describe the id-driven dynamic among the members—outlaw motorcycle 'gang' is rife with sexual actions designed to establish a hierarchy, as well as reinforce the members' separation and, from their perspective, their superiority over society at large.

To help shed some light on these sexual dynamics and so form a clearer connection between the rituals and activities of outlaw biker society and homosexual domination and submission fantasies, I've asked a member of such an organization, "Big Daddy" McKenna of the Nevada Eagles, to join me in a brief discussion of his experiences. Mr. McKenna, you hold the title of 'Treasurer' in your 'gang.' Can you please take a moment to explain how you came to have such a title and what your duties within the 'Eagles' involve?

"BIG DADDY" MCKENNA: Fuck if I know. Guess I don't lose the fucking beer money, not like some other fucking asshole shit-heads do.

M. CHRISTIAN: Quite. But was there some kind of special form of initiation into the responsibility? Something beyond your normal activities within the Eagles?

"BD" MK: Shit no. 'Course I hadda kick the fucking shit out of Grease Monkey to get the fucking wad. That fucking asshole. I gave it to him good, too—broke a couple of his fucking ribs, then poured my brew over his fucking head. Fucking asshole, he had it coming.

MC: Ah, so you physically defeated your rival for the position of inter-organizational authority then deposited a beverage on him. Very... primal, but not exactly suitable for the purposes of my thesis. May I ask why you did not, for example, sexually assault him while he was vulnerable? From what I've learned, that also would have established you as a dominant male just as effectively, if not more so.

"BD" MK: Fuck him up the fucking ass? Shit, man, that fucking asshole likes that kind of fucking shit. Why the fuck should I do that?

MC: In other words, because what would be a humiliating and thus submissive act for others—forced anal intercourse—is pleasurable for "Grease Monkey," you denied it to him and instead sought out another way of effectively lowering his standing in your group. Very interesting. How else did you cement your position of authority within your 'gang,' or was simply defeating Grease Monkey sufficient?

"BD" MK: That fucking did it. Just needed to know who the fucking boss was. Fuckin' A.

MC: But would it have been 'correct' behavior within the confines of your organization to demonstrate your superiority in other ways, including the previously mentioned anal intercourse, or perhaps by forcing this other member to perform fellatio on you, isn't that right?

"BD" MK: Suck my dick? Shit, I like the knob to get jobbed like the best but Grease is the shit for sucking. Got this pissy small mouth on him, he has. Good for fucking, Grease is, but you sure as shit don't want his gob on ya.

MC: So it was simply a sexual preference that led you to only beat and not sexually utilize this member of your tribe. But what of other members of the Eagles? If there was, say, a conflict with another 'brother' would you then use sexual dominance to establish yourself as the alpha male of your own nomadic, motor-vehicular pack?

"BD" MK: You mean fuck someone up the ass 'cause they fucking pissed me off? Shit, I guess so. I mean I like to stick the dick in whatever moves, you know, but...shit...don't want no asshole sticking theirs up mine so I don't want to make no...whatchacall it, 'president.'

MC: Do you mean 'precedent'?

"BD" MK: Whatever. I guess. I mean, Grease is a fucking asshole and fucking got what he deserved but I really bust his balls and he ain't gonna cover my ass when it fucking needs it, right?

MC: I believe I understand your sentiments with regard to the need to preserve a well-ordered structure within your society. By preserving the dignity of one member you create a situation where this individual is kept in a position of subservence by not only the threat of this unpleasant action but also by being indebted to you for not following through with it. This is all very interesting.

"BD" MK: Yeah, fuck. Whatever you said there. Hey, you got any beer?

MC: I'm sorry, I don't. But I have some mineral water if you'd like.

"BD" MK: Fuck that. You said there'd be beer, man.

MC: I'm afraid you must be mistaken, Mr. McKenna. Now, back to the structural procedures that comprise your group of motorcycle-sporting individuals. You mentioned previously that Mr. Monkey was not someone you would utilize for fellatio. Am I correct in assuming that there would be others within the Eagles whom you would force to orally pleasure you, say to establish yourself within the hierarchy?

"BD" MK: No fucking beer. Shit. Fuck you, man.

MC: For instance, I would speculate that periodically a motorcycle tribe such as yours would enter into a phase where the currently dominant individuals would need to re-establish their position within the group through the use of, yes, physical force, but more importantly by utilizing sex as a means to subjugate and humiliate rival males vying for the privileged leadership positions. Now among other primate cultures, such as baboons and chimpanzees, activities such as forced anal intercourse or fellatio are used to dominate others by forcing them into the recipient or 'female' posture, though how that would relate to members of an all-male group such as yourself I have still to investigate. Perhaps you could shed some light on the process, Mr. McKenna, as you are the closest thing we have to an expert. Pondering the situation myself, it first comes to mind that this sexual aggression would very well serve to push the social climbers into a less-desirable status within the group, one that is viewed as simply a sexual object, always the recipient rather than the initiator, in other words.

"BD" MK: Fuck you. Get my fucking ass down here, then not have any fucking beer. Fucking asshole.

MC: Or maybe there is an extension in those forced into submissive roles to the rest of the world as viewed by the troop as a whole. That would make a large degree of sense as the entire 'gang' sees itself as the aggressor in many situations in dealing with those not of the tribe. By using aggressive sex, particularly anal intercourse and submissive fellatio, certain members of the troop would force upper hierarchy interlopers into a position of being not only below their strata but also too close to being 'beyond' the troop, on the outside....

"BD" MK: Fuck you, you fucking asshole. I'll fucking show you not to fuck with me—

MC: Please, Mr. McKenna, sit down. I just have a few dozen or so more questions to ask you then you can go have all the nice, delicious beer you'd like.

"BD" MK: Fucking prick. I'll show you fucking anal intercourse you motherfucking asshole.

MC: Mr. McKenna what are you doing! Put that thing away this instant—

TAPE ENDS

MEDUSA
Alexander Renault

Who sees inside from outside?
Who finds hundreds of mysteries
even when minds are deranged?

See through his eyes what he sees.
Who then is looking out from his eyes?

—Rumi, c. 1250

I have always had a penchant for cleanliness, crisp white collars, and orderliness. My sister's boyfriend Rob was like the guys in high school and college that I hated—carefree, uninhibited, cocky, the kind of men that are good at sports and got off on locking smaller guys like me in the gym lockers. I can't act too superior because at least he was employed, even if it was menial labor—something about boat engines.

I was also trapped at home with my parents, between jobs. You could always hear him coming from a mile away coming to pick up my sister on that bike. Can't you put a muffler on a motorcycle?

Rob always seemed to smell kind of weird. I think he usually stopped in on his way home from work, and of course he smelled of exhaust, gasoline fumes, and motor oil. Whatever gunk guys like that usually had stuck to their bodies. He had this hideous picture painted on the side of his bike, a woman with glaring, ugly eyes and snakes for hair. Probably a photograph of his mother.

My parents didn't like him either. They thought Rob was too old for my sister, a divorced man in his early forties paying out probably half his paychecks for child support. He was the type who never really grew up. Or shut up. He razzed me terribly about my clothes, my haircut, anything he could sink his teeth into. Asshole.

I have this problem with blushing and when I get angry or upset it is often difficult to hide. Rob took to calling me Peach, which I hated, and I think it was a nasty way of making fun of my fair complexion and reddish hair. He was a real class act straight out of the gutter.

"Hey, Peach, whatcha doin'?" he asked walking up the front porch steps. He was dressed as usual—disgusting, shredded jeans, a grimy T-shirt, black work boots.

"What does it look like I'm doing, Rob?" I replied, holding up my copy of a book while I sat on the front-porch swing trying to cool off in mid-July. "See, this is what people call a *book*."

"Oh, you sure are a card, little man!" he snorted, showing his large teeth, his slack jaw edging slightly to the left like an old dog. He always had tobacco stuck between his teeth and I could never imagine what Gina ever saw in him. He was absolutely *creepy*.

It was yet another endless horrifically humid summer day in North Carolina and I had just gotten out of the shower after trying to cool myself off when I heard the motorcycle pull in at the side of our house. Everyone was at the beach for the afternoon and I didn't relish the idea of having to deal with him alone.

I felt like an idiot spying out my bedroom window. I had planned on just a quick glance but there he was, just starting to tinker with his bike after taking off his shirt. God, it was like a silly scene out of the movies they rented out of the backroom of that Charlotte video store.

He was a sight, all right. White hairy torso, tanned arms, neck, and face. People like him gave the South a bad name.

The strangest thing about Rob's body was his beer gut. It wasn't really big—he was a big guy so he didn't look fat or anything—but I started to find myself wondering what the hair on it felt like, all swirled in dirt and oil. I immediately squelched my disgusting thought.

"Peachy!? Oh, Little Peach, would come out here a minute?"

He was wiping his filthy hands on his T-shirt while his arm muscles bulged. As I walked down the stairwell in our house I began to think, "I pledge allegiance to the flag of the United States of America, and to the Republi—" It was the same trick I used all through school, repeating something simple and innocuous in my head to clear my mind, redirect my energies, to ignore the tortured embarrassment of my own hardness. Sometimes I hated myself.

"Peach, would you go fetch your Uncle Robbie a beer, boy?" he asked before loudly passing gas.

I supposed getting him a beer was better than having a conversation with the Neanderthal so I got him a bottle and opened it carefully over the sink. I couldn't stand the smell of beer and did not want any of it to get on my clothes. The white linen shirt and slacks cost a fortune.

As I held out the bottle at full arm's length, Rob said, "Don't you worry, I ain't gonna bite ya." That made me smile a little but I was unnerved by the look he gave me as he swilled his initial sip. With the head of the bottle hidden between his lips and the hair of his moustache and beard, he looked me directly in the eye as he swallowed, one, two, three, four gulps. I just turned and walked back toward the porch.

"Hey, where's Gina?" he called out to me.

"She and the folks are at the beach. They won't return for a few hours so you can come back later," I said too abruptly.

"Get me another beer, will ya, Peachie?"

I felt myself turning red. "I will get you another bottle of beer if you promise to stop calling me that name," I said indignantly.

Rob put one hand over his heart and the other in the air as if taking an oath. "I hereby swear to never call you Peach again if you satisfy me with just one more beer."

I felt a little knot form in my stomach as Rob moved his hand over his chest, rubbing the sweat and oil together. It began to look as though he was trying to rub the grime directly into his large, extended pectoral muscle.

I felt my own hardness, and I was mortified after I returned with another bottle of beer and realized that I had a visible…*indiscretion* in my lower area.

"Aren't you gonna have one with me?" Rob asked with a toothy, sardonic grin.

"One what?" I asked before I caught myself. "Oh, a beer? No, I don't like the taste of beer. I don't like how tends to make people uncivilized."

Rob walked closer to me, holding out the bottle, but the way he moved made me feel strange. It was kind of like a swagger you would see in a pirate movie, only not fake. His jeans were tight. He was such an ape and I could not believe this man had ever procreated.

"Come on," he said gruffly, "It ain't gonna kill ya to loosen up a bit."

I tried to be nonchalant as I took a nice big chug, but some of it slipped into my nasal cavity and I choked horribly. Rob kept laughing at me while I coughed it up and I quickly paced back into the house, choking on the disgusting concoction of stomach acid and beer. Beer— white trash champagne.

Humiliated, I went to my bedroom and took off my shirt. It smelled of beer and sweat. Perhaps the heat was just getting to me so I stripped down to my underwear and lay down. Once the sun started going down later on it might cool off some. I only wished I hadn't left my book on the porch.

I involuntarily jumped when my bedroom door opened, the type of violent spasm when you jerk your arms and knees toward the center of your body, the primitive brain gearing up to survive a lion attack or to run from a bear.

"Whoa, whoa, *whoa!*" he said with what appeared to be an instantaneous look of concern in his watery eyes, and more than a little fear. "I just wanted to say I'm sorry for laughin' at ya."

My eyes would not move from his powerful body. He was not in shape like the jocks at school, but was meatier, a slab of earth. Something about the salt-and-pepper gray hair of his chest and his strangely healthy stomach were hypnotizing. We have all grown so tired of the perfect bodies in the media. Rob looked real. Filthy, but real.

I did not utter a sound. As Rob moved closer to my bed, I sat up and could smell him. Without unlocking his gaze, he gently kneeled onto the edge of the bed, cupped the back of my head with his hand, and drew me to his nipple. It grew rock solid between my sucking lips and I grew faint from the moment. Rob was moaning, "Oh, baby... Suck your mama's tit, boy. Suck it good, little bitch."

The smells of his body were pungent and I almost passed out when he forced my face into his armpit. Sweat, dirt, and pheromones attacked my brain as I breathed him in. After stripping he fell upon me.

He removed his boots and socks; he unbuckled his belt and peeled off his pants in an amazingly quick set of jerky movements. What were supposed to be basic white briefs were hidden during daylight hours underneath his jeans. Rob's were dark and stained, oil soaked into the waistband.

I felt faint and inadequate at the sight of his crotch in those briefs. He must have had the hugest balls I've ever seen (on a human being, anyway) that jiggled and moved when he made the slightest motion. It was like his genitals had an independent life, bouncing and moving of their own accord.

Then Rob did the strangest thing—he put his boots back on. Then he swiftly pushed me down flat on my bed and smeared his greasy body against me, face-to-face. My white underwear, my sheets, my pillow were all stained with him and I felt him grinding his pelvis into me. I felt his slime all over me, his mouth sucking at the nape of my neck, the smell of his greasy hair.

He reached down and I felt his hard meat against my thigh as he quickly sat up and yanked off his underwear. I moaned—I could not help it—just before Rob took his filthy underwear and stuffed a large part of it into my mouth. I could taste the musky saltiness of his vile undergarment and could smell him, the odor seemingly permeating every neuron of my brain.

Rob reached down and grabbed his shirt with one hand while the other ripped off my briefs. I felt elastic cut the insides of my thighs near the base of my tiny buns as I heard the cloth tear. Before I knew what was happening he rubbed his T-shirt against my ass and I could feel the burning of used motor oil invading me while he fingered my virgin hole.

The pain was almost too much to bear, his thick long fingers reaching into me as if to pull out my heart. One, two, three fingers. I said, "Stop!" but only I knew what the word was. For Rob, it was just me moaning, gagged by a mouthful of his soiled underwear.

Far from a scene from a movie, I grimaced in pain as he slid what had to have been three fingers in and out my asshole. There was a dreaded moment of silence and I sensed it coming, with loathing that I only now realize was actually anticipation of my deflowering.

I saw how his boots were rubbing dirt into my bedspread. How strange he looked, leaning back, his massive erection embedded in the blackest bush, so dark it matched the leather of his boots. He was all hair grease, his ape-like body ready to violate me, a pearl of ejaculate at the tip of his penis. His foreskin seemed thick.

All of him was on me. My legs jerked into the air, I automatically put my hands on his chest to keep from being suffocated but he just knocked them away and ground his pelvis into me. With my hands now across his back, I marveled at how the muscles bulged with his excitement, the sweat gathering at the pool of his lower back. Then I felt the head of his cock pop through my anal muscle barrier and I tried to cry out. He stuffed his underwear deeper into my mouth, then began rubbing the painful raw slits at the base of my butt cheeks where the elastic had cut into me. It hurt but it drew my attention away from the agony of my hole being stretched by the cock of this sweating, grunting pig raping me in my own bed.

After the pain began to feel more like pleasure, I grabbed hold of his buttocks and felt the strong muscles of his rump, this animal's pumping ass cheeks, the thick hair of his crack undulating to what grew to be an almost hysterical rhythm.

My silly mental theorizing quickly faded as Rob bit my neck, plunging his cock into me harder and harder, sometimes releasing an involuntary beer fart that filled the room with more bizarre odors. For a second I imagined I was Gina, or some woman desperate to trap her man by getting pregnant. There was no room for rational thought within the fuck. I was this smelly pig's bitch, this disgusting animal's whore, and I needed his seed.

In a vicious circle, I found that the louder I moaned, the harder he fucked me. Through the squeaks of bedsprings, my sounds and his farting, I was lost in a swirl of a place I'd never been.

After what felt like at least 20 minutes of solid pumping, I knew he was close when he started speaking to me through what sounded like clenched teeth, his head buried into the nape of my neck.

"Take my cock you good-for-nothing, pansy-ass faggot."

The more he spoke, the more I felt the head of his meat expanding as it stretched me open wider.

"I know you want this, you little bitch.... Peachy faggot...little... worthless...*cocksucker*—"

With those words I felt him empty himself inside me, his dick pulsing out his seed, marking me his bitch from the inside. He writhed, grunted, and pulled at my hair. I do not think he meant to hurt me but his violent jerking tore at my scalp with both of his hands while he kept coming and coming.

When he was finished he withdrew from my asshole and collapsed next to me, on his back. I looked down at us, at him, a mixture of elixirs, and I could just catch a whiff of the traces of my shit rising from his thick cock.

After about five minutes, once his breathing became normal, Rob quickly got up. I almost laughed at the picture of him—a hairy as atop thickly muscled blue-collar-worker legs with him still wearing those black boots. He looked brutal.

Rob pulled up his pants and while his back was turned I slipped his underwear from my mouth and stuck it down between the mattress and bedroom wall. Rob quietly and quickly slipped away.

We never spoke of it again but he stopped teasing me and calling me names. He never knew how I pulled his underwear over my head every night for weeks, the back of the cloth directly over my nose, breathing in the precious scent of his asshole while I jacked off over and over again until even his odors dissipated from the cloth. I must have been quite a sight.

Air became my enemy as I kept Rob's filthy underwear sealed in a freezer bag, under my mattress. I could not get enough of his smells and jacked off to his scent for as long as it lingered in the cloth. It wasn't long before I had to just throw them away, the life sniffed out of them forever.

Whenever Rob came to pick up my sister his bike reminded me of a secret anger. Seeing the seething woman with her hair of snakes painted on the side of his motorcycle, I realized the nature of her wrath.

THE MILD ONE
Chris Bridges

Bull Manson tried to count the number of beer bottles on the table in front of him, but they kept moving. He gave up and settled for peeling the label from the latest addition. It came off in his fingers with the ease of long practice, and he leaned back in his chair to slap it onto the bare ass of the man lying on the bar behind him, who jumped.

"Jesus, Bull!" he yelled, laughing. "Gimme some warning!" He twitched his butt away from Bull's smirking face and settled back down again. He was nude except for boots, leather cap, and enough beer labels to completely cover his hairless body. Well, almost completely—his nipples were peeking out between the logos and the gap between his cheeks was invitingly open. He braced for Bull to follow through but Bull was already twisting open his next conquest, so he laid his head back on the thigh of the other guy on the bar.

The rest of the place looked as though a hopped up and out-of-control biker gang had charged in on their bikes, and torn up the whole bar in a drugged and drunken orgy that turned into a no-holds-barred fight, and then back into an orgy, which had more or less been the case. Bull looked out over his domain and saw that it was good.

Bull's lieutenant, a burly gentleman named "Shit," who resembled nothing so much as Bigfoot's half-crazed stunt double, lay sprawled over the jukebox. His pants had failed to make the distance; currently his half-erect penis was rising and falling with the beat. Angelnuts, one of the newest gang sluts, was sitting cross-legged in the wreckage in front of him, hypnotized by the movement. One of Angelnuts' hands was moving very, very slowly between his legs, and Bull calculated blearily that at his present rate of speed Angelnuts should be ready to orgasm in about a week. All three of The Beeyatch Brothers were asleep in the corner, their shared slut still attached at both ends. The bartender and a few of the slower bar patrons were tied up and stacked up behind the bar. The rest of the gang were scattered across the room in various states of nudity, consciousness, health, and arousal. It had been a pretty good Friday night, apparently.

A nagging thought prodded at Bull's sodden mind. Coke? Ass? Cops? Cops! That was it. They'd be coming soon, one of the escaped barflies prolly called 'em. Someone always did. Getting so a man could hardly have any fun anymore, goddamn police state.... Better start rousing the boys, he thought, and balled his fists in preparation.

Then he sat back in his chair to fully appreciate what had just walked in past the shattered door.

The apparition in the doorway was over six feet tall, and his appearance was like seeing a daisy growing on a battlefield. He was dressed in impeccably pegged light tan slacks and a golf shirt that hugged his muscular chest and flat stomach like Saran Wrap on a fat girl. His hair fell in artful blonde waves to his shoulders, and Bull's experienced eyes observed something stirring in what appeared to be a sizeable package.

He lowered his sunglasses just enough to peek over them and around the room, lingering for a moment on Shit's waving baton, and then stopped at Bull. "Excuse me," he said, smiling, in a voice of honey and molasses. "Is there a men's room here?"

Bull's expression remained stone cold as he jerked his thumb over his shoulder. "Thank you," the man said. He walked past Bull, not getting too close but not avoiding him either. After he disappeared around the corner the label-covered guy on the bar sat up, with a sound like someone bending a Christmas present.

"What the fuck was that?" he said. "I swear, there's so much sugar in that boy you spill water on him he'd fucking dissolve!"

Bull stood up, his drunkenness burning away in the grip of a different, more powerful need. "Happens I have a sweet tooth this morning, Slitch."

"Watch your ass, Bull. You don't need another rape charge, and we ain't got bail money."

"I don't never rape anybody," Bull said with a snaggly smile. "I'm just real convincin'. Hey, start getting everybody up, we gotta blow this pop stand."

His knuckles cracking were gunshots in the silence. "I'm gonna go pick me up some to go."

He left Slitch to sift through the bodies and he ducked around the corner, positioning himself against the bathroom doorjamb just as he heard the flush inside. He waited impatiently during the sink sounds, and the sound of the towel dispenser rattling. The door opened and the new meat stepped out, stopping with a little jolt before he ran into Bull's barrel of a chest. Bull smiled at him, the same smile he always used to bother the guards.

The new boy lowered his eyes and started to slide past but Bull shot out an arm like an iron bar to block him. New boy's hair smelled like strawberries and cream, a definite improvement over Bull's usual conquests (which generally favored vomit and Valvoline). He looked up. "Excuse me, sir, but I need to get by."

"I know just exactly what you need," Bull said with a practiced sneer. "And I'm here to give it to you."

"Really? And how did you know what that is?"

Bull leaned closer, menacingly. "I got what all men need, bitch, and twice as much as you've ever seen."

Any second now the new meat would start trembling and get that wonderful look of preppie innocent girlie terror that was all Bull's eager boner was waiting for. Any second now...

Instead, he stepped forward, with a noticeable lack of shrieking terror, and grabbed Bull's crotch in his hand, squeezing tight. Bull watched in shock as he smiled with even white teeth and said, "Hmm, this feels like about half of what I need. I hope you've got more somewhere."

Caught completely off guard, Bull started and almost tried to pull away. The new guy stepped closer and kept squeezing, never losing eye contact. "Oh, wait, it's starting to come see me, that's better. Is there more?"

The wail of approaching sirens cut through the air. The new guy let go, patted him once, and smiled ruefully. "Oh, darn. I didn't get the chance to find it all. Here," he said, rummaging in his back pocket and whipping out a card. "Call me." A final grin and a wink, and he walked away.

An hour later, back in Shit's house, the scene resembled the one they had just left, only here the sleeping bodies were stacked more neatly. And there was more debris. Slitch had delabeled himself, whining about his body hair the whole time, and was sprawled on the couch watching television. Shit was asleep in his bedroom with two of the boysluts and one of the Beyatch brothers. The other two were awake and arguing over the best way to rebuild the carburetor that had been spread across the coffee table for the last two weeks. Next to them, Bull sat in the single recliner, staring at the snowy white card in his hands. There was a picture of the new meat, and the name of a local realtor, but the rest of the card was a snowy white that stood out in stark contrast to the rest of the room. The urge to defile it was overpowering, but it also held the blond's name, address and phone number, and a reckoning was in order. Behind him several fist-, foot-, and head-sized holes in the drywall bore crumpled testimony to Bull's frustration.

"Let it go, man," Slitch said. "Rich bitch goodie-good, you don't need that. You need someone just as nasty and dirty as you are."

"He pissed me off."

"So? Everything pisses you off, that's why you're in charge. I seen you punch out a priest because you said he was a cock-teaser."

9

"He was eyeing me! No, this is different. This is way different. This guy fucking challenged me! Me! Little skinny goddamn flower-smellin' tooth-brushin' tight-assed bitch!" Bull stood up. In a remarkable display of learned survival behavior the other members of the gang instantly drew away from him, even the unconscious ones. Bull kicked back, sending the heavy recliner backwards into and partly through the wall. A half dozen beer bottles skittered across the floor. "He was gonna make me punk for him! Every other bitch I've grabbed dropped to their knees right away! Tough guys, big guys, made men, they all dropped for me! You dropped for me, right?"

Slitch, who in fact would drop for anybody and had, just nodded fearfully.

"And you!" Bull stomped on the coffee table and smashed it to flinders before grabbing Buford Beyatch by his throat and lifting him off the couch. Buford, who tipped the scales at 315 and had once bitten the exhaust pipe off a truck, hung in Bull's grasp and tried very hard to remember how "Hail Mary" went. "I barely had to kick you before you spread for me, right?" Bull screamed.

"That's right, Bull," Buford wheezed. "I loved every minute of it." He had, too, since he had just seen what Bull had done to the poor guy next to him, who hadn't. That memory still kept him up, some nights. He crumpled when Bull let go. Next to him his brother Bennie concentrated on holding very, very still. *Hail Mary, really faced...*

Reaching into the storm, Slitch put his hand on Bull's knee, above the chains. "What is it, Bull?" he asked, not unkindly. "Does he represent an innocent, wholesome world to which you've always aspired but have never dared approach due to your non-conformist attitude and unfortunate upbringing?"

Bull looked at him strangely, breathing hard, before hauling off and slugging Slitch in the face. "No, I just want to fuck the shit out of him," he said. "I'll be right back."

He strode outside, kicking a few bikers on the way, and jumped onto his bike. Inside, Slitch crawled back up onto the couch and sighed. He looked down at Buford, whose face now closely resembled a beefsteak tomato.

"That poor guy. He's going to get his balls broken, I just know it."

His name was Kyle Hanson, and he lived in Ashburn Heights. The good end. Bull roared into the driveway at the end of a long contrail of thick black smoke that was already settling on the perfect gardens and coughing pets of the surrounding houses. He stormed across the front yard, going out of his way to stomp on the beautifully landscaped flowers before stepping onto the porch and raising a boot to kick in the inlaid wood front door. Just as he kicked forward the door swung open and he flailed, off-balance, to land in a heap on thick, soft carpet. He looked up to see the blond holding the door.

"You made it! I'm so glad," the blond said, and he held out a manicured hand. Bull tried to muscle him down but he was stronger than he looked and had better leverage. Bull found himself pulled roughly, but politely, to his feet. "Come on, I'll get you a drink."

Bull followed him, walking slowly to look around. Even to his brutish eyes, the surroundings looked perfect. It was a comfortable, welcoming room with plenty of bookshelves, artwork, and electronic equipment everywhere. He decided to begin by throwing the over-stuffed armchair into the plasma flatscreen TV, but first that drink sounded promising. He could use a bottle or two.

Kyle met him coming into the kitchen and handed him a tall glass. He downed half of it in one draught, spilling some of it down his beard, and then losing most of the rest when he coughed. "What the fuck is this shit?"

"Iced tea. Let me get you some more."

"I don't want this horse piss, I want—" Bull stopped, because he suddenly saw exactly what he wanted. Kyle had walked into the kitchen and reached up to grab the box of tea bags on a high shelf. His shirt rode up revealing smooth tanned skin, well-defined abs, and a slim waist that disappeared into his belt and promised more goodies below. Bull's fingers twitched involuntarily and he stepped forward to jam his hands under that shirt. Kyle spun around and made a moue, putting his hands on his hips and cocking his head to one side.

"Oh, look at those hands," he said. Before Bull could stop him Kyle grabbed his fingers and held them out for inspection. Bull looked down. Nothing unusual there, two big strong hands. His nails were chipped and coated with engine grease, and there were the scars, of course, and the words "FUCK YOU" tattooed across his knuckles, just like always. He had to admit, they looked very out of place in this white, surgically sterile kitchen. Kyle stepped forward, still holding his hands, so that the two men were face to face and their hands were pressed firmly between their chests. "You'll go and wash them, won't you?"

Bull's mind swam—all he could feel was a firm, muscular chest pressing against the backs of his hands. A chest that would arch and stretch and twist beneath him. His mouth began to water.

Kyle stepped back and Bull, who had killed people for no other reason than because Sunday afternoons are boring, actually felt a moment's shame at how his golf shirt now had dark smudges on the front. "Down the hall, first door on the left. Scoot!"

11

He was standing in the overpoweringly pink bathroom, suds down to his elbows, before reason returned. "What the fuck am I fucking doing?" He grabbed a towel and viciously scraped at his arms, and then yanked the towel rack off the wall and smashed the sink to pieces with it. "Yeah!" Two good kicks sent the toilet over and water gushed from the pipes. "That's more like it! Fuck!" he bellowed, and put his fist through the shower door. "Goddamn cocksucking bitch's got me all twisted up!" He kicked the bathroom door open. "That's it, I'm going in there and ramming it right up his—"

Bull stopped dead at the dining room entryway. The table was set with a lavish dinner—thick steaks, baked potatoes, garden peas, a huge bowl of salad, and what appeared to be a Dutch apple pie cooling in the middle. Kyle was lighting candles. "Just in time! Have a seat, and would you be a dear and open the wine?"

He sat, numbly, and reached for the bottle. It took an act of will not to break the neck off and drink deeply from the contents, but Kyle looked so happy he couldn't think of disappointing him. Instead he sat down and glared.

Why wasn't the punkass bitch afraid? Shouldn't he have lunged for the phone by now? But instead Kyle just beamed at him like a joyously reunited lover, and piled food on his plate.

Bull wasn't used to spending any time with someone who wasn't either part of his gang or appointed by the court, and it confused him. He snapped open his knife and dug the cork out with eight or nine smooth movements, and poured both their drinks with the grace of a palsied steward. During dinner he even struggled to use silverware, and made an effort to avoid shoving more of the steak into his mouth at one time than could actually fit. Kyle kept up both sides of the conversation, but Bull was more than happy to let him, since it meant he could just stare at a firm jaw line and sensuous mouth. Also because it kept Kyle from noticing the spreading pool of water coming from the hallway.

Finally he couldn't take it any more.

"Why haven't I raped you yet?" he demanded.

Instead of being shocked, Kyle smiled as if he'd been waiting for the question. "I'm what you want, Bull."

"No shit! I came here to throw you down and fuck you 'til you puke, but every time I try you smile at me and I feel like planting flowers or some shit."

Kyle shivered a bit, the first time he'd shown anything besides amusement. "Really. Wow. No, you misunderstand. I'm what you really want, and you want to earn me. You could just take me, we both know that. But you're a fighter, a competitor. You're used to beating any foe, and winning any prize you see, and you know, deep in your gut, that raping me isn't winning me, it's stealing me." He stood up and ran his hands down his body. "Your men are dirty, tattooed, rude, crude, and more like animals than something upright." He smiled proudly, confidently. "I'm not. I'm unblemished. I have no tan lines, tattoos, bruises or scars, and I always wear underwear. I'm the pinnacle of the world you can't have, and somewhere deep inside, you want to see if you can win me because you deserve the very best, not because you're strong enough to take it."

"What the fuck are you talking about?"

Kyle smiled a hungry cat smile. "Your secret wish is to be the strongest man around, in every arena. I could tell that when I saw you." He stretched out a hand and lazily ran a finger up and down Bull's inseam. "And up until now you have been."

His fingers coaxed hardness to life and stroked it to its full, thick length. "My own fantasy is to have a tiger in a suit. I want a man who looks normal, but has a wild, untamed streak inside. Hidden below the surface, a predator waiting to spring out and feed. Now," he said to Bull's confused stare, "I could find some good-looking schmuck and make him fierce, but it's much tougher to tame a wildcat than it is to excite a pussycat, and I love challenges as much as you do.

"You want me, you can have me. And I'm the best you'll ever have in your life, I promise you that. But you'll have to earn it."

Breathing heavily, Bull stood up. "I can whip any three men, armed or unarmed. Bring 'em on!"

"Oh, this will be much harder than that, Bull. You're going to do what you've always secretly wanted to do, but never dared. You're going to take a walk on the mild side."

It took hours, and almost cost Kyle his furnishings. The wreckage of his dresser drawers and the smoke still seeping out from the bath- room bore vivid testimony to the time and diplomatic effort necessary to get Bull to submit to a simple manicure, and he still wasn't sure how he was going to get rid of Bull's stiff and stinking clothes without precipitating a public health emergency.

But finally Bull was staring at himself in a full-length mirror, and marveling at what he saw.

He was clean, inside and out, for the first time that he could remember. Shaved, hair cut short and combed, skull earring replaced with an elegant diamond stud. His leathers were gone; he now wore tooled leather shoes and a charcoal gray Armani suit that stretched across his broad shoulders. Fierce dark eyes glared out of a surprisingly distinguished face, and as he looked himself over he realized that the only signs left of his biker self were the FUCK YOU tattoos on his knuckles. Part of him, reacting to old and well-worn instincts, wanted to beat the shit out of the guy in the mirror, but that part had been getting smaller and smaller, quieter and quieter.

He looked smart, and held himself with quiet dignity. But the danger, the ferocity was still there. He was a pirate in a suit, a barely-controlled torrential rage that silk and wool couldn't—quite—conceal.

It had been a long afternoon, and Bull was still tingling with the constant intimate touches the blond had given him at every step. Kyle had bathed him, massaged him, and coaxed his lanky body into cool silk clothing. Fortunately Kyle had two full baths, and Bull had sheepishly turned off the water in the first one and helped pile the wreckage into the tub before allowing his host to lead him to the master bathroom. Now Bull stood tall and proud, looking like a bank manager and feeling like James Bond. The Connery one.

They had stopped once for a quick snack and he had spent the entire time talking and making Kyle laugh with his stories, all the while looking deeply into his eyes. He hadn't spoken so passionately since his last parole hearing.

"I look damn good," he said now, and immediately regretted his language. He turned to apologize and found Kyle lying across his bed, looking up at him like a starving man. Kyle has been incredibly patient during the ordeal, but Bull couldn't help noticing that the more upright he became, the wilder Kyle had seemed.

"You sure fucking do," Kyle said now in a new, gruff voice. His eyes were glittering with lust, and his pants twisted like there was a cobra trying to get out. Bull walked over, a panther in gray, and sat carefully next to him. "You are absolutely perfect. You're perfect," Kyle said. He ran his hands over Bull's thighs and moaned as he felt the tailored cloth slip sensuously under his hands over cabled muscles. The smell of crisp new cloth filled his nostrils. He rolled over to free an arm and reached out to grab Bull's cock, mighty and stiff, surrounded by silk and summer-weight wool, and he let himself fall back to the mattress with his legs spread.

"Now fuck me," Kyle gasped. "C'mon, fucking rape me you bastard!"

Bull ran one gnarled (but clean) hand over Kyle's twitching hip, then stood up. "Nah," he said.

"Hold me down and ram…what?"

"It wouldn't be polite," Bull said, with perfect diction and not a little satisfaction. "We barely know each other." He walked over to the mirror and adjusted his tie.

Kyle sat up, panting and red-faced. "What the fuck do you mean we barely—"?

"I just think we should wait before taking our relationship to a physical level."

"You what? I washed your dick, you son of a bitch! How much more physical can you get?"

Bull turned to face him with a smile and no small amount of satisfaction. "I think we should date a few times first, get to know each other. Besides, I don't have any condoms with me, and that's just irresponsible. Don't you agree?"

Kyle watched, furious and frustrated, as Bull walked away. He jumped up and followed, throwing his arm out to block the doorway. "Oh, no. You're not going anywhere until you fuck me, Bull."

"Brian."

"What?"

"My name is Brian. Pleased to meet you."

Kyle stood in front of him, breathing hard, hair tousled, shirt wrinkled and wet, his straining erection pushing at the lines of his slacks. "I don't give a fuck what your name is! You're going to throw me on the ground and fuck me 'til I puke! Now! I busted my fucking ass for this, I'm the lion-tamer that controlled you and you're going to turn on me and fuck my brains out!"

Brian looked down at himself and the finely tailored creation that had been wrought, and looked back at the wild-eyed creature in front of him. "I think I prefer my men more cultured, thank you," he said, and he gently moved Kyle, and his hard-on, aside to open the door.

Kyle watched, helpless in his fury and lust, as Brian gingerly wiped off the motorcycle seat and carefully climbed on. The biker didn't leave immediately, though, and when he got back off the bike and came back towards the door, Kyle's lust flared higher and hotter and the pounding of his cock threatened to burst his heart. Breathlessly, gratefully, he braced himself for the ferocious and unstoppable onslaught and thus was completely unprepared when the former biker stuck a card underneath his nose.

"Here," he said. "This might help you out." And the Biker Formally Known as Bull left, driving carefully under the speed limit.

Kyle looked down at the card. It was his own, but on the back was written an address and the name "Shit McNavery." Underneath that was written, simply, "Good luck. B."

As happens for some people, especially people who wear tailored clothing; things seemed to always go right for Brian from then on. He became a pro golfer, bought a house in Westchester, voted Republican, dated his tennis instructor, and lived a perfect life—except for one unfortunate run-in years later with a biker gang who, utterly failing to recognize him, beat him to whale shit on general principles.

SPIT
Greg Wharton

The first time Dodie spit on me my gut reaction was to punch him. Or maybe I'm remembering it from a far more butch attitude than I possibly could or should. Perhaps I wanted to just pull my head away in disgust. Or yell out: Nooooo! Or maybe push Dodie's hovering fuck-slickened body away in time.

It doesn't matter really. I didn't react that way. I didn't punch him. And I couldn't have anyway. My arms were firmly tied to his bedposts. My head grasped tightly in his warm wide hands. My mouth was held open by his salty thumbs, just seconds before sucking first one than the other as if they were as delicious as his cock, which they were.

If I had managed to move my head to the side his glob of spit and phlegm would have landed on my face anyway. So I simply watched as the spit left his mouth to land on my outstretched tongue and lips after first taking a long slow stringy trip in between.

But maybe that wasn't the first time anyway.

Maybe that was earlier in the evening.

Or was that yesterday?

I was leaving the Eagle. I hadn't actually been leaving but had just gone out back for a pee. My friends hadn't shown up yet and I had been downing beer. The bathroom was way too crowded and I didn't really want to join in on the party nor pee on the already wettened boy in the trough. So, I left and headed out to the lot behind the bar, a parking lot full of motorcycles lined up, past my baby, a glimmering new candy-green Harley Low Rider that made my cock harden in pride and planted a solid grin on my face—despite the fact I had gotten it second-hand and cheap thanks to a friend of a friend's unfortunate recent financial situation—to the end of the line-up of bikes.

There stood a tiny baby-blue Vespa, conspicuous and shiny and out of place among all the real bikes. Maybe it was my sense of superiority at now being a real biker at a real biker bar when faced with such a sissy ride, or maybe it was the four Michelob Lights I'd quickly put away while waiting for my friends to show up, or both, I don't know. But I unzipped anyway, pulled out my half-hard cock, and after a few strokes up my length that could have quickly become a full-on jerk-off—maybe afterwards, I might have thought, focusing on the tiny little-engined squirt of a sissy bike—I took aim and sprayed my beery piss all over the rear tire, the frame, and then seat of the Vespa.

I don't remember giggling, though I probably was at marking some macho territory on the inferior bike, and therefore, biker. I couldn't wait to go back inside to try and scope out which fag owned it and dared to pretend to be a real biker. Or that's what I remember thinking...before that biker found me.

"What in the fuck do you think you—and your skinny white ass—are doing?"

The last of the stream of piss dribbled down onto my beat-up black Doc Martins, not that that mattered. They'd seen much worse than a little pee in their time.

My fugue slowly cleared and I imagined what he might look like: small-framed, red hair maybe, and glasses. Definitely glasses. Converse tennis shoes, or maybe sandals. A bookworm, a student. That would explain it. A nerd on a Vespa. I might even have slowly stroked my half-stiff prick as I thought this. I shifted my head to give my best glare over my shoulder, giving him my trademark butch and kinda-crooked toothed smile, at this point not even bothering to do anything about my half-uncovered ass and fat cock still dribbling piss over his Vespa. I slowly turned—

"I said, what are you doing, you stupid drunk motherfucker?"

He was only a couple feet away. Dodie was easily several inches taller than my 5' 11" frame. And though he was clearly angry, his voice was calm, commanding. I was startled, and probably didn't appear as calm, caught with my dick out and a stupid smile on my face, clearly surprised at the vision that had caught me. How had I missed him in the bar? He was a sight. Built like a linebacker, Dodie was tall, dark, and amazingly handsome. A vision of flaming beauty. His deep-brown skin shined as if oiled, most of it showing, covered only in a tiny pink baby-doll T-shirt that was cut off mid-belly, and the shortest and tightest white cut-offs I'd ever seen packed on a man.

At least a man his size.

One quick glimpse at the tight puckered bellybutton then down the trail of fur to the pooch of barely covered and what looked to be very fat cock, and I surprisingly relinquished my alpha-male mode to him.

"I, uh—"

"You, uh, what? Thought you'd show off your big dick by way of messing up my transportation? I am so tired of you tired old butch white boys thinking you and your bikes make the man!" And with this, he gripped me by the back of my neck. "Look what you've done! Mm, mm, mm... You are going to take off that skanky cheap shirt right now and polish by bike..."

And I was on my knees, jeans still undone and barely covering me, my now extremely hard cock pointing to the sky, my naked pale ass cheeks glowing white with the moon's reflection.

"Then you're going to suck my cock. Then and only then we'll think about how you can try and make this rudeness up to me! What's your name?"

"Ke—eee!" His grip on my neck tightened to the point of pain.

"Key? What kind of asshole name is that for the man who'll soon be opening up each and every hole for this queen's pleasure?" And then he released me.

What's going on here? My cock was so hard it hurt. The leaking piss was now replaced by an urgent stream of pre-cum. I looked up into his big brown eyes and timidly said, "Kevin. My name's Kevin."

And somehow my shirt was off, his Vespa dried off as well as it could have been done in the dark with a cheap polyester shirt, his spit all over my face, neck, and chest, and his very stiff—and yes it was very, very thick—cock in my mouth.

And he laughed and laughed and laughed.

Or was that later in the evening?

Besides having my arms bound way too tightly to be able to move much, Dodie had my legs pulled back, his strong palms now forcing my knees down onto my shoulders, feet straight up into the air, pointing to Jesus just as I'd done to other faggots many, many times before, and his amazingly thick gorgeous cock forced all the way into my asshole.

He was fucking me like I've honestly never been fucked before— well, in fact, as I've never been fucked before even though I have but when it had happened I hadn't admitted to it anyway since all my friends thought I was a stud and I didn't want to be known as effeminate—turning my insides into one big jumbled bunch of electric nerves. He fucked me hard, then harder, ramming in and out, in and out, each time hitting my—oh my God is that my prostate?—as it had never been hit before.

All negative reactions to the sight of his spit leaving his body in route to mine died away when I felt his cock harden even more inside me and I saw the light burn even brighter in his eyes.

Was this the first time he spit on me? Does it matter?

"You like that, huh, my little butch bottom?" he said with a wet sneer that was a dangerous mix of sexy and downright scary.

"Fuck... unh...fuck—"

"Yeah, bitch!" He pounded me faster and I liked it. Oh, yes, I liked it!

"I...unh...unh...unh..."

19

And he spit on me again.

He made me follow him back into the bar after he was done with me trying to make it up to him, my sore but still unfulfilled big pink cock tucked uncomfortably back into jeans, my pee-wet shirt tucked into my back pocket, my chest and face a mess of his come and spit, to wait for my friends and let them know I wouldn't be spending the rest of the evening with them.

They still weren't there, and Dodie didn't intend to wait. Who knows what they would have thought? Maybe nothing. Or maybe they would have thought—assumed—I was leaving to fuck Dodie's fag ass all night long, though I doubt it since he was halfway out of the bar and I was running after him like a puppy. Real tops don't run after men like puppies. For some damned reason I didn't really care. I left with Dodie, or, right after Dodie, following him out of the bar, around back and through the lot where he had first caught me.

Good puppy! Fuck, what was wrong with me?

Still not sure how a big flaming queen such as Dodie could top me, but knowing nonetheless that there was little else I wanted right now as much as that very pleasure. I obeyed Dodie when he made me leave my Low Rider in the lot and climb on the back of his Vespa, clinging to him like a virgin schoolgirl out for her first ride, my arms wrapped tight around his waist as if I feared I'd fly off, my face shoved into his back as if ashamed that anyone would see me.

And they did. No one I knew—that I know of—but Dodie and I were quite the sight riding through town to his flat: a big flaming black fag with a killer smile and sparkling glitter mascara, skin barely covered by his baby-doll tee and daisy-dukes, and a slightly scared new-born butch bottom, pink skin a-flushing with humiliation as he hung on for life to the waist of his new top like he'd never been riding before.

Or maybe that's just my twisted memory of it.

Maybe it wasn't quite like that.

Maybe I enjoyed the ride, Dodie defiant and proud and beautiful on his flaming sissy-blue Vespa, making his way through the streets with a new butch boy-toy at his back, a boy-toy feeling somehow free and exhilarated.

Either way I was definitely excited.

I knew that Dodie was going to fuck my skinny white ass crazy.

And I knew that he knew that was just what I wanted.

"Fuck. You are the most beautiful piece of ass I've ever had. Come on, baby, show me how you come." And he shifted his shiny body back, my knees pushed back to either side of my head, his cock still lodged deep inside of me, and grabbed my aching cock in his grip.

Dodie had come twice already, once in my mouth and once up my ass. Just twice? Or was that three times? I'm pretty sure he shot all over me earlier—last night?—in the parking lot. So Dodie had come two or three times but I hadn't been allowed to yet. And I really, really wanted to, needed to, come.

"Mmmm...Dodie..."

"Damn, look at that cock, Kevin. That is one beautiful big pink cock."

"Ah...Dodie...I really want to come...."

"I've always heard that it was so. But now. Whoo! Ah-ha... Now, I know it's true. The bigger the dick, the bigger the bottom!"

He smiled at his so-true joke and his eyes, his bright brown eyes, drilled into mine for just a second before focusing on my aching cock, then another great wad of his spit was released and my cock was wet and he was jerking me hard and fast and I was going to come and his cock felt so good inside me and "fuck me Dodie fuck me oh my god fuck me harder!" and he did fuck me harder and I swear I could feel his cock actually growing I could feel him coming again and again and "oh my god, Dodie, oh my god!" and I came and came and he came and we both laughed and laughed and laughed.

Or was that later?

That next morning—or was it afternoon? It was sunny anyway. Dodie dropped me back at the Eagle's parking lot. I was tired and sore. Tired because we had been up all night. Sore because he had been up all night fucking me.

Hard. Then harder. Then again.

I had left my clothes at his flat. At his instruction, and with relatively little resistance, considering, I was now wearing the white cut-offs he had been wearing the night before. No shirt. No boxers. My boots were also still at his flat. In their place I was wearing a pair of silly pool flip-flops, pink and yellow striped, with big daisies that fanned over the top of each hairy foot from their grip over each big hairy toe.

Did I feel like a big fag? Yes. Did it matter? Well, yes, it did matter, damn it! But there was a chance that Dodie wouldn't pick me up later like we had planned unless I did what he said.

And I did want more of him later.

Or was it already later?

"Go on, Kevin. Collect your big-man bike. I'll pick you up here at 8:00, hon."

My asshole burned, and I was naked but for his daisy-dukes and sandals that should only be worn by some tacky, old, leather-tanned, Miami Beach widow. What a mess I was. Sticky and stinky, and now dressed like a queen. It was enough to make me cry, but I honestly felt more like laughing at myself.

I slid off the back of Dodie's Vespa and leaned in to kiss his sweet mouth. "Thanks, Dod—"

"And leave last night's macho attitude at home, girl! Relax a little."

He gave me a passionate wet kiss, then slapped my ass and pointed me towards my Harley with a hearty laugh. And he laughed and laughed and laughed, and I laughed too until I realized why he was laughing.

Dodie pulled away, his tiny engine managing to spit up a cloud of gravel and dirt in his wake, his laughter still loud enough for me to hear as he sped away. The miniature desert storm subsided as I sat down on the sticky seat and let the bright sun warm my face, then I squinted my eyes down at my hairy white toes wiggling under the big plastic daisies.

Wouldn't you know it? Someone had peed all over my Low Rider and I didn't even have a shirt to clean it with.

And I laughed and laughed and laughed.

THE BIKE RIDE
Jay Starre

I hovered just inside the doorway, certain that the husky biker had seen me. I waited silently with my hard-on throbbing under my chaps and jeans. Blake, my Boss Man for the day was busy, and I wasn't about to interrupt and incur his wrath. Besides, the show was unbelievable.

Perched on the seat of a gleaming hog, a mostly naked blond was grunting and writhing under a vicious anal assault Blake was in the midst of perpetrating. On his knees with his face pressed to the leather seat, the victim's ass was in the air, a large dildo crammed up between his squirming buttcheeks. The blond wore a black hanky tied around his neck, and a black leather jockstrap outlining his muscular asscheeks, but that was it. A black dildo glistened with grease as it thrust in and out of his crack in the gloved hands of his assailant.

I shivered, even though it was warm out. My own butthole twitched in sympathy as I stared at that ass being violated so viciously. Blake wasn't holding back. I could hear his low laughter as he pulled the dildo almost all the way out, about a foot of fat rubber, and then twisted and jabbed as he forced it back in. The blond victim grunted and humped back toward that fat invader as if he was more than happy to get all that rubber up his butt.

Blake himself was not really tall; I had an inch or two on him at 6' 1". But he exuded a nasty kind of power, especially with that evil-looking black dildo in his hands. I noticed the two vivid tattoos that snaked over his forearms and biceps, accentuating their muscularity. He was stocky, with a big butt and thighs perfect for hugging the sides of his hog. I shivered again as I imagined those big legs spread over that bike as it thundered alive to tear off down the highway. All that power, and Blake was busy demonstrating it as he continued abusing the blond quaking before him on the back of his motorcycle.

"Let's see if I can pull a load out of the little piggie."

I heard that deceptively soft voice for the first time as Blake reached under the blond's crotch and began working on his cock. I could see the long bone jutting out from the fly of the black jockstrap, pink and pulsing. That black-gloved hand yanked on it, while the other gloved fist gripped the base of that greased dildo and gutted the poor sucker with it.

He cried out. His ass rose up as it took almost all that dildo up it.

Suddenly his cock was spurting a spray of milky goo all over the bike seat. Blake was laughing. He pulled cum from the poor dude's dick like he was milking a cow, then he let it go and yanked the dildo out of his ass at the same time.

"Clean up that mess. Lick it up before you get the hell out of here."

That silken voice again. But there was a whip behind it, apparently. The trembling blond rose immediately and then toppled from the bike to kneel beside it and begin lapping up his own sticky cum from the leather seat. I stared at the blond's shaking asscheeks. They were wide apart, and his crack was open. I could see his asshole, swollen and red with grease glistening all along the violated rim. The center pouted outwards, spasming with flushed emptiness.

I trembled myself. I had little doubt that my own asshole would be looking just like that before the day was out. I was Blake's for the day. I did not know what he was going to do with me, but I had just witnessed his proclivities. My limbs were weak and my asshole throbbed, but my cock was stiff as a board.

Blake ground the blond's face into the leather seat viciously and laughed. The young dude's tongue lapped obscenely over the seat picking up sticky cum until it was completely clean. Then Blake gripped him by the neck, pulled him to his feet and smacked his naked ass with the flat of his hand.

"Get out of here. I got business to take care of."

He turned to me as the blond glanced my way and grinned sheepishly before trotting from the garage into the back yard.

"I see you're here, Matthew. A fresh bitch for the day, how sweet. What can we do with your ass?"

We faced one another just inside the doorway of his garage and checked each other out. He wore a navy-and-red handkerchief knotted over his scalp, which made him look just a bit like a pirate. An evil one. His face was square, outlined by a short auburn beard that framed a pair of pursed, lush lips. There was a scar on the upper lip, pulling it up in a partial sneer. His nose and eyes were symmetrical and near perfect. There was no question that he was handsome in a scary way. His amber eyes were pools of unreadable darkness.

He was a loner. He belonged to no club, or gang. He loved to ride, and he loved to fuck, and he loved to be on his own. That was his reputation, Blake the hard-ass loner. I shivered again as our eyes locked.

But then my eyes slid from his as I looked down. A simple black leather vest was unbuttoned, revealing a powerful chest with swirls of dark hair across it. I saw a flat stomach just above a heavy black belt cinched tight around his waist. His jeans were worn and faded but his chaps were dark and supplely polished. His thighs were massive.

"You're a cute fucker. Tall and lean and young. Are you gonna do what you're told, or am I going to have trouble, bitch?"

He spoke quietly in a matter-of-fact tone. I noticed how straight and white his teeth were as I stuttered out a reply. "My club nominated me to be your bitch for the day. We intend to honor out debt to you. I intend to honor our debt to you. Sir," I added the last as his hand whipped out and seized my wrist in a painful grip.

"You bet you owe me big time. I got your sorry-ass club out of a jam with the pigs. You could be in jail instead of bending over for me."

Blake was dragging me by the wrist over to his bike. I recalled with vivid accuracy what had just occurred there. That greasy black dildo was gone, and so was the swollen asshole it had been stuffing, but the memory wasn't.

"I think we'll go for a ride. How's that sound? A nice, long ride. Let's get ready."

Blake's voice did not rise, but his grip on my wrist was shouting at me to obey. That reputation of his claimed he was mean as hell. So far he seemed nasty, but not really mean. I would soon find out.

"Strip, bitch."

"Yes, sir!" I replied with feigned enthusiasm. I wasn't reluctant about the sex, in fact I was hard just standing beside him. It was the fear of the unexpected that had my gut churning.

He released my arm so I could remove my clothing, but I felt the imprint of that vicious grip still burning. His eyes watched my every move with appraising sharpness as I removed my cap and the club handkerchief around my neck, and dropped them to the floor. My hands were quaking as I took off my vest and then lifted my arms to pull my T-shirt off over my head. My hands were tangled in my sleeves in the air when I felt fingers suddenly grasp my nipples and yank on them.

"Sir!" I yelped.

"Bitch," his quiet voice replied.

Those fingers twisted and tore briefly while I untangled my arms and tossed my shirt aside. He was grinning as he released my nipples and continued watching me strip. My nubs stood out from my shaved chest like two pink towers, burning from that harsh tweaking. I was quick to unbuckle the belts of my chaps and jeans and shove them down as I lifted one leg and kicked off my boot. I struggled to keep from falling as I removed my boots, socks, pants and chaps.

Blake's hand came out to steady me, his gloved fingers clasping my waist more gently than they had my wrist. But then they immediately tore at my underwear, yanking them down over my ass as I hopped around in the act of stripping. His hand rudely probed into my asscrack as I bent half over. I was shaking and flushed with embarrassment, but not about to object. My ass was his, and there was not a damn thing I could do about it.

"We'll plug that butt before we go out. I know just the thing to stretch it out and make it feel good and stuffed."

What was he talking about? Was he going to fuck me before we took off? Or was he going to shove that used dildo up my butt? I finished stripping as he walked over to a bench on the wall and rummaged around in it. I was totally naked when he turned and came back. My eyes zeroed in on what he held in his hands. It was a big, black butt plug.

He smirked at me as he rubbed grease into the blunt sex toy and approached. "Put one knee up on the bike so your ass is open. This is going up your sweet little pussy and staying there until it's time to fuck you with my cock."

I flushed at his lewd suggestion, but obeyed without hesitation. The plug was large, but not dangerously so. I could take it if I relaxed. I was shaking as I stood beside the big bike and lifted one knee to place it on the seat. There was still a wet spot where the blond had shot his load and then licked it up. My knee slid in it as I felt air on my butt and Blake's eyes on my ass. A moment later the blunt tip of that greased plug was pressing directly against my hole.

"Yeah. You have a sweet butt. I like a hard butt, all muscle with dimples in the sides. I like it shaved too. I like to see those pretty little buttlips as they spread open. You like that? You like the way that rubber feels stretching open your hole?"

His voice lost some of its evenness as he began to work the rubber up into my butt. I could tell he was getting excited. That was enough to allow me to relax and accept the growing girth of that big rubber. It was liberally greased, and he was pumping it in and out slowly enough so that my asslips had time to accommodate to the increasing width of it. I grunted at the pressure but could not deny the pleasure as well at the sensation of something rubbing and probing at my sensitive buttlips. I grunted again and arched my back, well aware of how I looked with my ass up and my balls hanging down—and that black plug being forced up my asshole.

My cock throbbed as my asslips pulsed. It felt good, very good. The steady, jabbing pressure was just painful enough to be pleasurable as the same time. He seemed to know what he was doing. But then the plug only got larger. I strained to take it, pushing out with my asslips and humping up with my butt. He pulled out slightly as I grunted out, and then pushed deeper. I gasped and felt my prostate ache with added pressure. How much of that thing was up my ass?

"That's it. We just about got it. Open up that tight cunt. Yeah!"

His silky voice did the trick. I shivered and thrust backwards over the invading rubber. Suddenly it was sliding deep into me and my asslips were clutching the narrowing base. It was up my butt! I shuddered as I felt the square flange nestle up into my crack and my buttlips seize the base in an unrelenting grip. How was that thing ever going to come back out?

"Now get dressed. We're going for a ride."

I staggered to my feet, my legs wide apart. I could really feel all that rubber up my ass and I could barely close my thighs. He was grinning at me. "What should I wear, sir?" I managed to ask.

"Your helmet, boots and chaps will do. It's plenty warm out today."

I obeyed, slowly pulling on my chaps over my naked thighs. The supple leather felt good against my flesh, a sheen of sweat making a slick lubricant between it and the chaps. I felt my ass open and vulnerable hanging out of the back of the chaps, but guessed that was his intention. Bending over to pull on my boots, I felt that plug shift and penetrate deeper into my guts and gasped out loud. He reached out and smacked the base of the plug, which elicited a startled wail out of me.

"Get on the bike behind me. Let's go, bitch."

I was putting on my helmet just as he was. I felt exposed with my ass hanging out and that gross plug protruding between my buttcheeks, but the feel of the hard helmet encasing my skull was reassuring. He was straddling the bike and suddenly it was roaring to life. The sound of the engine sent an exciting tremor through my guts. I lived to ride, and with a surge of rising lust and anticipation, I leaped up behind him, half-naked with a butt plug up my ass.

I settled into the seat, the plug digging into my guts and prostate as I felt Blake's taut butt and thighs against me. He was revving the engine as he engaged gears and suddenly we were turning in a circle and aiming for the doorway. The garage door clanked open automatically as the thunder of the powerful engine reverberated in the room and I felt its vibrating power in my ass and guts.

I was so exhilarated when we roared out into the open air; I momentarily forgot that my ass was exposed to anyone who followed us. Blake expertly swerved out onto the highway from his driveway in the spring sunlight. The rural road was far from town, and thankfully no one spotted us as we headed for the desert.

It was early spring in Nevada. The afternoon temperature was in the low 80's, which was just perfect. The wind raced around our bodies as we thundered down the empty highway. I embraced Blake tightly, my hands on his waist and my thighs pressed against his. We were one body as he swerved from side to side down the road and geared up for a screaming race into the desert emptiness.

He knew where to find the nothingness we needed. A few turns and we were alone with the sky and the flat expanse of bare desert, a few wildflowers and tumbleweeds relieving the emptiness. The plug up my butt vibrated constantly with the rock and roar of the bike's engine. I felt as if I was flying, my ass full and my cock hard and all fear at bay.

It wasn't long before one of Blake's gloved hands reached down to seize one of mine. He pulled my hand from his waist to his crotch. I felt the thick bulge there, and knew what he wanted. I used both hands to unsnap his leather chaps and then his jeans. With the scream of the wind in my ears, I slid my fingers into his hot crotch and felt the steel of his fat cock. I pulled it out, leaning over his shoulder to stare down at it. The fucker was huge. Purple, with a deep piss slit dividing the massive cap, it jerked hungrily between my fingers and oozed out a big drop of glistening pre-cum. I used my fingers to smear the slick goo over his cockhead while he geared up and increased our speed to a gut-churning 80 miles an hour.

I stroked and pumped his cock as we raced along. The big thing jutted out from his fly in drooling arrogance. I pressed my own hard cock into his butt and squirmed my ass down into the leather of the seat, forcing that plug deeper into my guts as I imagined his big pole up there reaming me out.

Sweat soaked the leather seat under my bare ass. I rubbed around in it, fucking myself with the greased butt plug as I pumped Blake's stiff prong and we roared along the abandoned highway under the blue sky.

It was a timeless moment of intense passion. I felt that big cock in my hands as I felt that big plug in my butt and that powerful engine between my thighs. The roar of the bike and the scream of the wind drowned out any other sound. We were in an echo chamber of screaming silence.

But then Blake slowed. He geared down and the race of the wind died. I pumped his cock and squirmed around in the seat, fucking my own hungry ass but that did not deter him. As my passion rose, the bike slowed to a stop. We pulled off the side of the road and parked.

"Get on the front. I'm going to fuck your greased ass while we ride the day away."

The echo of that screaming ride was still in my ears and I heard him through a numb passion that made it almost impossible for me to release his hard cock. But he was in control, and he bodily shifted me as he got off and then straddled the bike behind me. He placed my hands on the handlebars and then dug around in my ass to grab hold of the butt plug implanted there. I grunted and stood in the pegs as he twisted and tugged on that big black rubber. It stretched and tore at my asslips as it began to come out. But then it suddenly spurted out and he was laughing as he tossed it into the desert for some startled hiker to discover later. My asshole throbbed emptily and I shivered from head to toe. Blake was still laughing as he fingered my greasy hole with squishy intimacy. I bent over and closed my eyes, all my attention on those gloved fingers rooting around deep in my guts. I ached and gasped at the rough intimacy, but too soon he pulled his fingers from my hole and then gripped my bare ass. Then he pulled me down to squat over his lap. That big cock worked its way up into me like a red-hot branding iron.

"God, I'm fucked!" I gasped out.

He was laughing as he reached up to roar the bike back into life. The vibration in my guts matched the slow thrust of his cock. He shoved us off back onto the highway and suddenly we were flying again. I felt the wind on my bare arms and chest, spread wide across the front of the bike. His hot crotch shoved into my ass, his burning rod poking up into my steamy bowels. It was unbelievable.

We flew along the empty highway. A few cars passed, and even another hog, the rider waving and nodding, unaware of the heavy fuck going on right out in the open daylight. I nestled back into that hard cock, riding it as I rode the powerful bike between my spread thighs. My prostate sang to the tune of the revving engine and the thrusting cock up it. My asslips squished and mushed around that digging boner.

I rubbed my own hard cock into the leather seat, fucking it as I was fucked. It was an endless delicious ride of blue sky and faded desert and cock up the ass. The shriek of the wind in my ears became the shriek of orgasm as Blake's steadily thrusting cock finally ignited my trigger. I spurted into the cup of my chaps as Blake sprayed into my ass. We came together as the bike swerved and glided over pavement in a flying roar.

Blake pulled over to the side and halted. The noise ceased, along with the vibration and the thrusting pressure up my ass. He dismounted and stood beside me as I sprawled on the bike with my thighs apart and my scummed ass drooling jizz and grease.

I lay there both exhausted and exhilarated. Blake had not turned out to be mean, just nasty. Even nastier than I had thought, I realized as I felt his hands lifting my butt up into the air. I crouched expectantly over the bike with my asshole quivering and my jockstrap full of jizz.

Then his tongue was stabbing up into my fucked hole, and his lips were clamping over it as he sucked his own scum from my slot.

Right out in the open. He ate my ass while I moaned like the biker slut I was. The only thing I could think about was the ride home and what he could possibly do to me then.

WAI
Moses O'Hara

He had a pubic tattoo—the burning bush. Flames shooting up his abdomen, blue eyes and a silver buzzcut. Drunk and sunburnt. Welcome to Maui.

"Sorry, man. I'm stoned."

He pissed on me. He actually fuckin' pissed on me. And I couldn't decide whether I wanted to punch him or fuck'm.

"Lucky you're wearin' jams"—and he smiles. He fuckin' smiles. Clown.

"Yeah, I was feelin' lucky."

He belched.

I turned to him. Figures. "You know—you've got sour cream all over your chin."

He seemed surprised. Then he took his tongue and licked it off. Only—it was obscene. Fully. Trust me. I've seen some obscene. And this guy had a total friggin' man tongue. He grinned.

Licked clean.

"I'm impressed."

"Wanna bite?"

"No. I don't want a bite of the fuckin' burrito you've been eating while you take a piss at the public urinal." I smiled. "—but thanks."

Then I put my dick back in my lucky jams and went on my way.

"It's vegetarian."

We met at the luau-style chocolaty-chip nuptials of "V-Man" and "Princess". Local beach, Ka'anapali—catering by Maui Tacos and Anheiser-Busch. I have no idea who the fuck "V-Man" was…some biker. But "Princess" and I went way back, several names at least.

Cheryl De Rosa, Mrs. Danny Sloan, Cherry—which was the name she stripped under which is when she started sellin' pot on the side which is when I met her—Cherie Sykes (her porn name), Mrs. Kurt "The Club" Morales, according to her driver's license: Sheila Darnell, "Chloe" briefly when she was trying to get a fresh start and finally—

"So am I supposed to call you 'Princess' now?"

She shrugged. "…Like I give a fuck."

—ladies and gentlemen, the blushing bride.

We bumped into each other on Front Street in Lahaina Town a coupla nights before. I was gathering up supplies to bring back on the ferry to Molokai and she was doin' body shots over the second floor railing of Moose McGillycuddy's. She gave me the wolf whistle.

"Yo, Moses!"

I looked up and she shouted. "What the fuck are you doin' in Hawaii?!"

And that was the last I saw of the ferry.

"Are you having a good time?" She came up behind me in the surf and caught me off guard. "I can't believe you came to my wedding."

I turned around. "Of course I came." She had on a white leather bikini and frosted lipstick. "You're a trip."

She smiled. "…And you look very handsome in your lei."

"Amazing what a string of white orchids can do for a guy."

"Any guy in particular?"

"I thought we were talking about me."

"So did I."

"Okay. So who's the guy in the 'Kill Whitey' T-shirt?" Nothing. So I scanned the beach. "Playin' horseshoes."

She squinted over the top of her sunglasses—and gasped. "Match?!" Then she looked back at me and smiled a very particular sort of smile. "Jeez, Moses. I had no idea."

"What?"

"Nothin'. You crack me up."

"What?"

"Nothin'. MATCH!!!"

It was deafening. The skin peeled back on my face and my eyeballs rattled. Seagulls fell from the sky.

"Oh my God, what the fuck are you doing? Don't do that. Don't *call* him."

"I'm getting another drink—What is your problem?" She lifted her beer bottle into the air and started waving it. "Match!"

"I swear to God I am gonna fuckin' kill you."

"Please. I could beat the shit out of you." She could also put out a cigarette with her bare foot. "What is he, fuckin' deaf?"

No such luck.

You could see him sit down in the sand, take off his motorcycle boots, then he reached back over his shoulder and pulled off his T-shirt—single-handedly. It's gotta be one of the sexiest things a guy can do. And I'm thinkin' to myself…what the fuck did I just get myself into?—I hope. And then he grabbed a coupla beers from the nearest cooler and started trudging into the water.

"He's our vet."

"Your vet? He's a veterinarian?" I had to let it register. "I heard him talkin' about 'fixin' the cats on Molokai'? I thought he was tryin' to have someone whacked."

She looked at me for a second and then she shook her head. But not in a good way. And then she ran up to him and whispered something in his ear—for a really long time. And then she turned to me and *winked.*

"Nick Matulitis—I'd like you to meet Moses..." She had absolutely no idea. You could tell.

"O'Hara."

"*Really?*" She made a face.

He went to shake. "You know you got a great ass."

Wow. Maybe these really were my lucky jams. I shook his hand. "Don't believe a word she says. She's delusional."

He didn't let go. "I'm gonna pull your pants down."

"I beg your pardon?" It was like living in the Twilight Zone.

"You'd better start runnin'." He tightened his grip. "'Cause I just decided—I'm gonna pull your pants down."

"I think I'd start runnin' if I were you." Fuckin' Cherry.

"Three, two—one." And I took off.

So now I'm tearin' down the beach, shin-deep in water with this friggin' mental case linebacker right on my ass, plowin' through the waves, and mothers grabbin' their kids and everyone's tryin' like hell to get out of the way and I'm about this close to screamin' like a punk when all of the sudden he's just airborne. Like somebody fired him out of a fuckin' cannon—and he's on top of me.

Crushed. We musta hit the wet sand going about sixty. And skidded.

He flipped me onto my back. "Pull your pants down."

"Are you fucking crazy?" I couldn't even breathe.

"Pull 'em down." His chest was heaving and water dripped off his face. "You can do it—or I can."

He stared down at me a second, lifted his weight a little and yanked 'em down.

Fully checked me out. And then collapsed back on top of me.

"I wanna fuck you."

My dick sprang up stiff and slapped against the inside of his thigh. So much for playin' hard to get. He closed his legs around it and brushed his lips just barely against mine. "Lemme fuck you."

"Damn. What the fuck did she *tell* you?"

He grinned. "Ask me to kiss you."

Deep crow's feet and this kinda beat-up face. "Kiss me."

He wrapped his hands around my wrists. His breathing slowed. He kissed me. And then he kissed me. Full-on fuckin' no-holds-barred-

33

tongue-down-my-throat-hands-down-my-pants—if I were wearing any. Physical domination. Size may not matter but it sure as fuck makes a difference. He let go of my wrist and I wrapped my hand around the back of his head. He kissed me—gently on the lips.

"See. Was that so hard?" He smirked.

"What are you doing?" Some Cindy-Lou-Who-wannabe flower girl floating by in a pair of bright pink water wings and the bottom half of a hula-girl bathing suit.

Match looked up. "We're wrestling."—without missing a beat.

"Why are you wearing long pants in the ocean?"

"I'm cold."

She looked over at me. "Why is his face all red?"

"He's embarrassed." Then he shook his head and smiled. "Because he's not a very good wrestler."

Clown.

He paid a bunch of the local kids fifty bucks to keep an eye on his bike—so he was the big hero. They all came rushin' around him as soon as we got out of the water. Hangin' off his arms. He looked back over his shoulder. "Remember. You're with me now."

And I mean, what the fuck was that supposed to mean? But I liked the idea of it. His. So I figured what the fuck.

Cut to the cake.

"Would ya just cut the fuckin' cake." Ah, the lovely Princess Cherry.

V-Man kept squeezin' her boob and hammin' it up for the photographer instead of takin' care of business. The photographer in this case being his mother—Potsy, who also contributed several hundred dollars in illegal fireworks and a Day-Glo brown Jell-O mold to the happy occasion.

"Smile!"—and he finally knifed the thing.

They danced to a bootleg copy of Kid Rock and Pam Anderson singing a duet of 'Something Good' from 'The Sound of Music'. Tiki torches, Chinese lanterns and a wedding-bell piñata—everybody welcome. Aloha. And everybody was cooked.

"Get your stuff. We're leavin'." He pushed his groin against my ass. It seemed like Nick (notice I call him Nick now) never took his hands off me—which was both disarmingly alien and oddly comforting all at the same time. He patted my stomach then slowly slid his hand up to my chest and started playin with my nipple. "Now."

He bit the back of my ear.

I turned to face him. "I gotta go get my shoes and backpack outta Potsy's R.V." Potsy loved me. I devoured her Jell-O mold and went out to get her Winston's—twice. Guess I was everybody's bitch that night. He whacked my butt. "So go."

Conquered—or at least explored. It musta been the atmosphere. There were several couples dancing, if you count the ones that were passed out, and the air smelled like gunpowder. I snagged a big corner slab of wedding cake and headed for the parking lot.

I've never been a particularly social animal. It's not that I don't like people. It's just that I generally like to experience them at a slight distance. That is, of course, unless I want to fuck'm. In which case—all bets are off. I scanned the sea of Harleys trying to spot his bike by description. Classic '79 Electra Glide, loaded with chrome—lotsa custom work. Useless.

And you know I'd never go out lookin' to fuck a biker. It just wouldn't even occur to me. Too specific—among other things. But my mistake. A bottle rocket whizzed by my head. I think I liked the licentious attitude.

I arrived at the somewhat front door of Potsy's Dodge Sportsman motor home and wiped my bare feet on the welcome mat before I went in. Very homey. I put down my cake and picked up my backpack—figured change clothes, down some water, go to the bathroom and I'm outta here. Then I ended up helping myself to a joint...and some Kool-Aid.

The entire front of her refrigerator was covered in shit. Magnets and crap. Articles on acupuncture. The recipe to her Jell-O mold on an old stained postcard. Turns out the secret ingredients were bourbon and grenadine—no wonder the flower girl took her top off. A seriously yellowing picture of "Johnny." Black Flag T-shirt giving the finger. Johnny. He definitely looked more like a "V-Man." I opened my water and gulped down like half of it and then I dropped my jams.

The whole camper rocked to one side.

"You shouldn't a made me come lookin' for ya." Nick. He locked the door behind him. "Now I'm gonna have to fuck you in Potsy's R.V."

No shirt, jeans hangin' open and that friggin' tattoo scorchin' up his torso—he took a swig of beer. "I'm so fuckin' into you it scares me." And I meant it.

He dropped his pants. "So prove it."

I wanted to jerk off.

I'd been thinkin' about havin' his dick in my mouth all day and now there it was—all fuckin' thick and aroused. He tugged at his balls. Hairy as a motherfucker and I like that in a guy. Hairy balls—and a good solid handshake. I smiled. "I am gonna blow your mind."

You can never go wrong masturbating a guy while you give him head. The combination of wet tongue and a firm grip—he forced his dick up through my fist and into my mouth, fuckin' my throat for a minute, until I could taste the pre-cum and he knew he'd better back off. "C'mere." He fell back onto the bench seat and spread his legs.

I walked up to him, dick droolin', and now I really did want him to fuck me—in case that was ever in question. He reached out, closed his hand around the base of my cock, got hold of my balls and pulled me closer. "I said, c'mere."

I leaned forward and he sank his tongue into my mouth, wrapped his arms around my waist and pulled me down on top of him.

Intensely makin' out with a guy and then havin' him suck on your dick has gotta be one of the all-time most pleasurable things in life. If you're so inclined. He lapped up my rectum and it was like havin' a cow lick my ass. Not that I have any idea what it's like to have a cow lick my ass. But—"Fuck, man."

He plunged his tongue way deep into my asshole and then started fuckin' me with his fingers. Christ. Kinda gentle at first but then with considerably more intent. He was gettin' ready to fuck me with his dick, you could tell—and I don't get fucked all that often.

He came up with a big schemer of something, I don't even want to know what the fuck it was but all of the sudden he was greased.

"Hey Moses. Look at me."

I looked at him and then I looked away. I don't know why. And then I looked at him.

"You know, from the first time I saw you I thought—that snotty little prick. I wanna fuck him." He smiled. "I wanna fuck him so bad."

He rubbed the head of his dick against my asshole. "You're fuckin' beautiful."

I grinned.

"You are." And he pushed himself into me, just slightly. "And now I'm inside you." Full penetration. "And that makes me so fuckin' happy."

His dick felt massive. And now I'm total pussy for this guy. I woulda done anything. Turn over. And you could feel the jism building up in his balls. Fucked like a dog on all fours and I was lovin' every minute. He licked the back of my neck and started jerkin' me off—which was just about more than I could take. Major gusher—cum all over his hands, fingers in my mouth and he's still fuckin' me.

"Holy shit." He reared up, grabbed onto my hair with his free hand and then blew his load so fuckin' deep inside of me that I bet it's still in there. "Fuck..." He kept pumpin' into me. "Oh, fuck."

"I wanna go to sleep with my dick in you." And he held onto me so tight it was like he was afraid I was goin' somewhere.

Cool.

"Hey, maybe we should head up to Haleakala for breakfast." I was looking at his hand and just sorta drifting in the afterglow. "We could take your bike."

"Can't. David'll be back by then."

"Who's David?"

"My boyfriend."

Oh yeah. Me too.

Spell Broken

I woke up about forty-five minutes later. The 'Apocalypse Now' effect. Several small explosions in the distance and you could still see smoke hangin' in the air. Roman candles. And a wedding. I grabbed my stuff—my backpack and shoes and shit and ducked into the bathroom. Quietly.

I looked in the mirror. Nice work, Moses. Then I splashed some cold water on my face and took a piss and pulled up my lucky jams and took a coupla Potsy's Vicodin—just 'cause that's the way I can be. And then I left her twenty bucks in a cup by the kitchen sink 'cause I also took a handful of sparklers.

I looked at Nick—experience complete. And I decided to leave him my wedding cake. He deserved it. Then I stole one of the roses off the top. Cheryl De Rosa. And I ate it.

He'd definitely remember me.

Beautiful night. Potsy was sittin' in a lawn chair lookin' up at the stars—and I figured maybe I'd pool-hop my way back down to Black Rock, grab a complimentary breakfast at the Sheraton and then catch the morning ferry back to Molokai.

"See ya, Potsy."

"Not if I see you first."

And then I left whistlin' that fuckin' song from "The Sound of Music"—just like some kinda sap.

SHELTER
Barry Alexander

Brodie fought the rain for a couple more miles, but the sky opened and dumped half a ton of water on his head. His breath fogged the visor of his helmet making the gray, drizzly afternoon even grayer. He knew he was going to have to pull over or risk running his bike up the ass end of a semi. Cars still roared past, making no concession to the heavy rain or decreased visibility. Hell, some of them didn't even have their lights on. The wash from a semi splattered his windshield, temporarily blinding him. He fought to steady the big Harley Softail as the suction from the semis threatened to pull him in.

Once Brodie got the big hog stabilized, he started looking for a place to pull off the interstate. The last town was twenty miles back. He knew he should have stopped, but he was so close now, he'd wanted to ride straight through.

There was no sign of shelter. If there were farmhouses, it was getting too dark to see them. Stubbled fields of corn, the last of the winter's snow frozen to the broken stalks, alternated with huge expanses of yellow-brown pasture. Muddy water swamped the ditches. Mud—the first sign of Iowa spring, Brodie thought with a grin.

When he saw the exit sign, he slowed down and watched for the overpass. At least, it would give him some cover from the cold rain. He finally saw the slash of concrete across the horizon and rolled down the throttle. The revs died down and he glided up to a controlled stop on the shoulder. Silence roared in his ears like it always did for the first few minutes after he shut the engine down. He swung his leg over, kicked out the stand, and leaned the heavy bike. His balls still tingled from the heavy vibrations of the V-twin engine. Straddling the big hog always gave him a huge hard-on. He grabbed his heavy shaft and squeezed gently. Might as well take care of it while he waited out the rain.

Brodie took off his helmet and ran his fingers through his short brown hair. It still felt strange, having so much hair again. He kept it cropped for the last three years, but hell, he had to let it grow again if he wanted anyone at home to recognize him. His mom would have a heart attack, if she'd seen what he'd looked like out in San Francisco— cropped hair, queer radical T-shirt, pierced nipple and ears. She'd never see the tats or the piercings, he thought with a grin, then sobered as he remembered what brought him home.

He sat down on the concrete spillway, and leaned against the slope. It wasn't the most comfortable place to jerk off, but at least no one could see him. Brodie dug out his swollen cock and stoked it while he looked around. There wasn't much to see. A row of concrete columns separated him from the edge of the interstate. Late afternoon had slid into evening; it was so dark now he couldn't make out the opposite side of the divided highway. Rain gurgled down the gutters and sluiced down the edges of the cement slope. The curtain of rain falling from each side of the overpass concealed him from the oncoming traffic. The hollow rumble of cars passing overhead and the growing darkness made him feel like he was in a cave. Brodie jumped when he heard something move. He looked up and saw a row of draggled pigeons fluttering between the ridged beams. Nothing like a little company on a cold, wet night. Well, it sure as hell didn't look like it was going to let up any time soon. He might as well get comfortable. Brodie resigned himself to spending one more cold, lonely night on the road.

He left his dick hanging while he unpacked his bedroll and spread it out. It was still tumescent but no longer as hard as it was. He worked it for several minutes after he got settled, but he just couldn't get into it. Maybe he was too keyed-up from thinking about how close he was to home. It felt weird going home again. It was hard to believe that only five years ago, he'd traveled this same road to California. Even the name had seemed a golden promise of paradise. California—sun, and sand, and unbridled sex. A place where he could be openly gay for the first time in his life.

The freedom went to his head. Too many parties, too many drug-hazed days. Three years had passed in a blur of pleasure, then he'd met Scott. If it hadn't been for Scott, he might still be there, an endless party of dope and sex. The parties stopped when Scott got sick. He still felt guilty that Scott had been the one to get sick—Scott wouldn't even try drugs and hated anonymous sex. Brodie hadn't gotten him into bed until their fourth date.

Sitting by Scott's bed, Brodie had had a lot of time to think. Scott's mother hadn't even come to the funeral. She couldn't bring herself to accept a gay son. Maybe if she had seen what a sweet guy Scott was, that he had made something of his life. Maybe, if there had been time. They could have made up. Scott had tried, but she just wouldn't listen. "I gave her a chance," he said sadly.

Standing at Scott's grave two months later, Brodie knew it was time to go home. Without Scott, there was nothing to keep him in California. He'd never even tried explaining things to his parents. When they yelled and ranted, he'd walked away and never looked back.

A semi roared past blaring its horn. Its lights flashed on something bright on the other side of the highway. Had to be another biker, Brodie decided. A car wouldn't have that much chrome. He decided to introduce himself instead of finding a visitor stealing his wallet while he slept. Most bikers were decent sorts, but Brodie liked to play it safe.

Brodie tucked his neglected cock into his jeans. He crossed the road, his boots thudding on the wet concrete. He caught another flash of chrome as he got closer and grinned. The bike was bristling with polished aluminum and chrome. The guy must have decked it out with every piece of chrome he could find. It glittered like a Christmas tree, reflecting the red taillights of the receding truck.

Just as he was about to say hello so he didn't startle the guy, he banged his shins into something, pitched forward, and landed in something prickly. "Damn it to hell!" he roared. He'd forgotten the metal guardrail. He wriggled around, trying to get out of what turned out to be the dried-up carcass of a Christmas tree

"Who's there?" The voice sounded young, but Brodie couldn't see much more than a vague silhouette in the darkness.

But there was nothing young about the 12" inch-hunting knife in the hand of the guy standing over him. Brodie hadn't seen a knife that big since he'd watched *Crocodile Dundee*. It looked like a movie prop, but he had a sinking feeling it was very real. He stopped thrashing about and lay very still.

Light flickered from the polished blade, and Brodie realized the hand holding the knife was shaking. The realization did not reassure him. A scared kid with a knife was more likely to act first and think later.

"Take it easy, man," Brodie said in his friendliest tone. Cautiously, he started to sit up.

"You hold it right there, mister." The kid's voice was shaking as badly as his knife, and he sounded like a very bad John Wayne imitation, but Brodie didn't feel like laughing—not until he got rid of that damn knife.

"Hey, come on. At least, let me get out of this damn tree—the needles are poking me right in the balls."

"First, you tell me what the hell you're doing here." Brodie thought he detected a slight relaxation in his tone.

"Same thing as you. Raining too damn hard to be scooting. I saw your wheels and came over to check it out."

"What are you riding? I've got a 96 Bad Boy with 13" ape bars, full floating rotors and a bad set of pipes. Wait until you hear it. Man, those porkers sing."

Brodie grinned and stood up. Worked every time—ask a man about his ride and he'd fall all over himself telling you.

The next thing he knew he felt the knife whip past his ear. "I didn't say you could get up yet."

Brodie had enough. Before the guy could recover from the near miss, Brodie slammed the guy in the right shoulder, snaked his hand up his arm, and grabbed his wrist. Brodie kneed him in the crotch. When he doubled over, Brodie hooked his leg around the guy's ankle and followed him down. His breath went out of him with an *oof* and Brodie wrenched the knife away when the guy's grip loosened.

Brodie straddled the guy, pinning him to the ground. It was too dark to see much, but he could feel the slender body trembling under him. He was also wet; Brodie could feel the dampness from his jeans soaking into his.

"What are you going to do?"

A little scare might teach him some manners, Brodie thought. "I could do anything I wanted," he snarled, leaning close to the pale blur of the guy's face. "And there's not a damn thing you could do to stop me." He paused a moment to let that sink in. The guy squirmed underneath him and Brodie was startled to feel a new hardness between them. The guy was getting a boner!

Brodie felt an answering surge of blood to his own cock. He was tempted to do something about it right there. To reach down and touch that stiff cock poking into his balls. To lean in and taste the lips so close. To explore the slender body trembling under him. It'd had been months since he'd been with another man. Even before Scott died, he'd been too sick to be interested. There'd only been that one night—when Brodie had been so horny, he'd called an escort service for simple relief.

"Are you going to hurt me, mister?" He sounded very young and very afraid.

Brodie pulled himself together. He got up and pulled the guy to his feet. "No, of course not. I just wanted you to remember this. You could really get hurt trying something like that. Never pull a knife on a guy unless you know how to use it. Understand?"

"Sure. I'm sorry mister. I didn't mean nothing."

"What's your name, kid? I'm Brodie."

"My name is Chris, and I'm not a kid damn it, I'm twenty."

"You're soaked. Didn't you have any rain gear?"

"Didn't think I'd need much where I'm going. I'm heading out to California. San...Fran...Cisco! He said it as proudly as Lancelot must have announced his search for the Grail.

" What about blankets or towels?"

"I've got a sleeping bag. Don't need much else. I'm traveling light."

41

"How long you been traveling?" Brodie asked dryly.

"All day. Started out from Galena. That's in Illinois," he added helpfully.

"Look, I've got some dry stuff on my bike you can use. It's too cold to sleep wet. Grab your sleeping bag and come over. I think I can even promise you a cup of hot coffee."

There was a long silence. "If I'd have wanted to try something; I'd have done it when your boner was poking me in the crotch," Brodie said quietly.

"I was hoping you wouldn't notice."

"It's a little hard not to notice something like that, especially when it's not so little."

"You really think so? You're not mad are you? Because I'm…"

"Gay? It's OK to say the word, Chris. No, I'm not mad. I've been on the same trip you're on."

"You've been to San Francisco? Wow. So what are you doing back here?"

"Come on, let's get that coffee and get you dried off."

Brodie picked up the Christmas tree and drug it behind him as they crossed the interstate. The overpass had kept it mostly dry. He broke off several branches and started a small fire. The dry needles caught quickly. He filled the small kettle from his canteen and set it on the fire.

"The fire won't last the night, best get out of those wet clothes while it lasts."

Brodie couldn't see much as Chris got undressed. Chris stood carefully out of the firelight; his body hidden by the deep shadows. But he could hear. The creak of his leather jacket. The metallic jingle as Chris loosened his belt. The snap as he opened his jeans. The slow, ratchety scritch of his zipper sliding down. The wet drag of fabric over bare skin. He was glad Chris couldn't see his own arousal, probably scare the kid out of his wits, he thought with a grin.

He caught occasional glimpses of bare skin as a car or tuck would pass, their headlights briefly strobing on Chris's slim body and long legs. But before he could focus on what he wanted to see, the vehicles were past, their taillights casting red spears on the wet pavement.

He handed Chris the soft towel he kept for polishing his bike. Their hands touched for a moment, and Brodie thought he felt the cold fingers tremble.

"I can't wait to get out there and get out of this hick state." Chris's voice bubbled over with enthusiasm as he dried himself. "I've heard about San Francisco ever since I can remember: Castro Street, The Eagle, the bars, the baths…. Imagine—you can actually walk down the street with your arm around another guy, or kiss him, and nobody thinks anything of it. I can't wait".

"You have to pick your street. Do that on the wrong street and you can get the shit beat out of you in San Francisco just as well as in Red Neck City.

"I'd love to get in one of those videos, you know? Everyone says I have a great body." What do you think?"

"It's a little hard to tell in the dark," Brodie said, dryly.

"You can touch me if you want."

Brodie hesitated, not sure how much more Chris was asking. He wanted to touch him very much. But Chris's earlier modesty left Brodie a little unsure—no point in getting himself all excited if he was going to back away. He ran his hands over Chris's shoulders and across his chest. His fingertips touched a small tight nipple, and he felt Chris suck in his breath. He drew his hands back before they were tempted to reach lower.

"Yeah, you have a nice chest." Brodie's voice was unexpectedly hoarse. He draped a blanket around Chris's shoulders. You'd best put this on so you don't freeze."

"What's it like?" Chris asked, as they sat on the sleeping bag and waited for the coffee to heat. "San Francisco must be just packed with porn stars, at least according to the magazines. You could be just walking down the street and run into Joey Stefano."

"Joey Stefano is dead, Chris."

"Yeah, but what a great life—getting paid to have sex! Can you imagine? You ever meet one?"

Brodie couldn't resist a little name-dropping. "Just one—Joe Star. We went out once."

"Ohmygod! You dated Joe Star! I would just die. Tell me," he asked, his voice low with hushed awe, "What's he like? What's he *really* like? Is he really as gorgeous as in the videos or is it just makeup and lighting?"

Brodie knew what he wanted to hear. "Just what you'd expect— totally gorgeous. Hot and hung and hunky." And it wasn't a lie. Joe was all of those things. "Actually, he was kind of sweet." He was also strangely shy and very unsure of himself, except for his sexual prowess.

"I knew it," Chris said in a tone of satisfaction. "Did you ah, make it with him?"

"Yeah."

"Sooo? How was he?"

"Very talented." Chris wasn't about to tell him the rest of it—about calling the escort service and getting the surprise of his life when Joe Star came to the door. Or the guilt he felt after having sex on the bed Scott would probably never come home to. Afterwards, Joe had just sat there and held him while he cried, and didn't even charge him for the extra hour.

"God, you're so lucky!—I'd love to have that gorgeous cock up my ass."

Brodie just let him babble. He didn't tell him it that it was his own ordinary 6-inch cock that had plowed Joe's backfield. It was the least he could do for Joe—help him keep his carefully nurtured image.

Chris looked at him differently. Brodie could almost feel the speculation in his eyes.

"Brodie, you wouldn't want to ah…that is…"

Brodie reached out and pulled Chris in, covering his mouth with his own. His tongue plunged down Chris's throat. He was startled by his own hunger. Chris didn't mind. He rolled on top of Brodie and ground himself against the hard ridge in Brodie's jeans.

Brodie pushed the blanket off Chris's shoulders. His hands slid down the smooth muscles of his back to cup the small globes of his butt. He cupped them, his fingers sinking into the fleshy mounds as he pulled Chris closer to his aching cock. His fingertips brushed the back of Chris's scrotum and the boy groaned as he tried to climb inside Brodie's skin.

Chris practically ripped off Brodie's shirt in his eagerness. Brodie pulled it the rest of the way off and tossed it over the Harley. Chris's mouth sucked its way down Brodie's throat, licking and lapping and tasting. He nuzzled through the thick mat of chest hair and whimpered like a puppy when he finally found what he was looking for. His lips tightened around the distended peak and his tongue played with the little bar that pierced Brodie's left nipple, pushing it back and forth and making the nipple harden even more. He caught it in his teeth and tugged. Brodie groaned. He loved it when guys did that.

Chris opened Brodie's jeans and burrowed his hand inside. His fist closed around the base of Brodie's cock and squeezed. Another dollop of precum oozed out of Brodie's cock and soaked into his damp briefs. He took his hands off Chris's rump long enough to force his jeans over his thighs. Chris abandoned his nipple. His hot mouth moved down Brodie's torso. Then Brodie remembered.

"I don't have anything," he warned. "How about you?"

"A whole box on my bike."

Brodie groaned and stood up to pull up his jeans. "I'd better go get them. You're not exactly dressed for a trip across the street."

Chris knelt up and caught Brodie's hips to stop him. "I also have a handful in my jacket pocket. I'm going to San Francisco, remember? I'm damned well going to be prepared. But we don't need them yet. I've got something else in mind."

Chris rubbed Brodie's shaft over his face and took a deep hit of Brodie's ball scent. His tongue reached out and touched the base of his sack. Brodie shivered as the warm tongue lapped upwards. He loved having his balls worked. He was beginning to think Chris was a lot more experienced than he had thought. He felt Chris's lips press against his furry pouch for a second, then his lips parted and he sucked in one fat ball. Brodie had to grab his shoulders for support.

He slid his hands over Chris's shoulders and caressed the smooth, taut skin on his chest. He brushed his fingertips over the flat nipples and felt Chris's gasp tickle his balls. He squeezed the tiny points gently and Chris began to suck furiously, his tongue lashing over the captured ball. Chris kept his hands busy, his fingers stroking the sensitive area behind Brodie's balls. Brodie's cock swung back and forth bumping against Chris's forehead and leaking copious amounts of precum in his hair.

Chris's finger slipped up the moist crack and gently circled the closed ring of Brodie's anus. "I can't believe Joe Star's cock was up here." Brodie was going to correct him then thought why bother? Let him enjoy his fantasy.

"You are so lucky, man. It must have been fantastic."

Brodie wasn't surprised when Chris asked him to lean over the bike. He'd half expected it. He hadn't anticipated the intensity of Chris's reaction—the almost reverent way he gently parted Brodie's cheeks, the hesitant, shy little licks along the sides of the deep divide as he prepared to rim Brodie, to worship at the shrine anointed with Joe's seminal offering. He acted as if Brodie's ass was a kind of reliquary, precious because of its former contents.

Brodie felt his tongue drive deep inside, searching for…what? Some trace of Joe's phantom presence? The secrets of the universe? Brodie had never expected his ass to be such an object of worship. Maybe he thinks there's a trace of ectoplasmic semen up there that emanated even through latex, Brodie thought.

Then he stopped thinking. The hot, wet tongue scouring his inner walls was driving him out of his mind with pleasure. Brodie braced his forearms on the leather saddle of the Harley and widened his legs. Chris's chin ground into his ballsac as he tried to drive his tongue even deeper inside. Brodie squirmed with pleasure. He'd never had a rim job like this.

"If you want to do anything else, you better do it fast. I'm just about ready."

Chris pulled his mouth away. "Can I…you mean you'll let me?" he panted, his warm breath huffing against Brodie's damp skin.

"Sure, but hurry up—it feels awfully empty up there."

Chris scrambled to find his jacket. Brodie heard him rip open a packet and shivered in anticipation. In seconds, Chris was back, his hands on Brodie's hips as his cock pushed against the ready hole. Brodie reached back and ran his fingers gently over the shaft, then across Chris hip. He felt the thin layer of latex and relaxed. He'd learned long ago to always check.

The fat head pushed easily into the well-lubricated opening, but Brodie still felt a twinge of pain as his passage widened. He hadn't been on the receiving end for a long time. Chris didn't give him long to get used to it; he was too eager to get inside. He pushed hard and lodged half of his dick inside. A couple more hard thrusts and Brodie knew he had every inch. Chris's bush scraped his cheeks, but the warmth of his groin felt wonderful in the cool night air.

Chris humped and pumped and pounded as enthusiastically as if he were trying out for a porn video. And he just might be pretty good at it, Brodie decided, as his fat cock plunged again and again inside him. He didn't seem to tire; his hips slammed against Brodie's butt, powerdriving every hard inch. What he lacked in style, he more than made up in speed and stamina. Brodie's cock swung enthusiastically in tempo with the rhythmic thrusts. Brodie wanted to pump it, but he needed both hands on the seat to keep his balance. Chris was pounding him so hard he was in danger of knocking bike and man over. He knew he was leaking precum over his Harley, but he didn't care.

Chris leaned closer, his bare chest warm against Brodie's naked back. He reached under and caught Brodie's swaying cock. Brodie moaned as the fist wrapped around him and started pumping. He bucked forward to drive more of his cock into the fist, then back again to get more of Chris's hard meat inside him.

He was getting damned close, when Chris let go. Brodie was about to protest when Chris grabbed both his hips and started jackhammering him. A torrent of "oh, shits" and "fuck, yeah's" escaped from Chris's mouth. In seconds, Chris was there. His hips stopped and his body shuddered as he pumped his load into Brodie's ass.

Brodie was afraid Chris was going to leave him hanging. He pulled out and whipped off the used condom. He dropped to his knees so fast it must have hurt. He plugged Brodie's empty hole with his hot tongue. Brodie was wide open and Chris was able to get deeper inside him than anyone ever had. He had to have had the longest tongue Brodie had ever felt. When he felt the hot tongue flick against his prostate, Brodie let go. Torrents of hot cum splashed all over his Harley. Waves of pleasure rippled through his body. Chris plunged his tongue all the way inside, and Brodie felt his guts clamp around it. He didn't think he was ever going to stop. They were both gasping when it was finally over.

They squeezed into the same sleeping bag, but they didn't get much sleep. Chris had a hell of a lot of stamina. Brodie couldn't remember when he fell asleep, but it was morning. The rain had stopped. Chris's body was pressed tightly to his in the sleeping bag. Every muscle in Brodie's body ached from sleeping on the hard surface, but he didn't want to get up. He wanted to savor the heat and touch of the young body next to his for just a few more minutes. He knew he didn't dare. It was still dark, but already it was clearing in the east. Already he could make out the shape of the Harley sitting beside them, waiting. In a little while, drivers would be able to see them. He didn't fancy spending his first day home in jail on a morals charge. It was time to get up.

He nudged Chris awake. Whatever had drawn them together was gone. Chris was eager to get on his way. He looked very young and very vulnerable in the morning light. Brodie thought of all the things he'd like to warn him about—the dangers of too-easy sex and too-easy drugs. But he remembered how he had been at that age. And he knew he couldn't tell him a damned thing.

In minutes, they were both dressed. Chris hugged him briefly, then dashed across the interstate ignoring the semi that blared his horn at him. He quickly started his bike and revved the engine several times so Brodie could hear the staccato thunder of the bike's song.

Brodie waved and straddled his own machine. For a moment, he was tempted to swing the bike around and head west again. Going home seemed like the scariest thing he had ever done. But he knew he had to try. Brodie glanced in the rearview mirror. Chris and his bike receded into the distance, blending into the landscape Brodie had left behind.

Brodie blipped the gas, and the Harley roared into life between his thighs. He paused to wipe the wetness from his eyes, then settled the helmet on his head. Damned morning sun always did hurt his eyes.

SPLASHBACK
William Dean

It's the whip that gets me—and the rarity. It just don't rain all that much west of L.A., out on the coast. But that's when I'm hitting my groove, when those big splashes come pounding down and my bike's clipping through them. Well, what can I say? It's like running through a shower of cum. Or like I'm Mistah Speed Sperm hauling ass down the throat of the world. Yeah, I love the rain and that hooking stretch of road up the coastline: nothing but gray beaches, tossing surf, and wet asphalt. Sometimes, I just gotta pull over and rip off the helmet, you know? Punch down the kickstand. Let the rain wash over my bare face like the Big Upstairs Man is cumming all over me. It's a good splash. I was taking it all, just grinning up into the black clouds up on the Trancas Road when this SUV roars past and damn! Deluge. Water fucked. Tsunami. Fuck me!

Okay, so I got hot. Who wouldn't? Purple-eyed anger. I swear steam must have been sizzling off my leathers and I was shaking with it when I see the red lights flash. In a heartbeat—a loud one, too—I'm off the Harley and running. Every step, I'm bloating with muscles and rage and by the time I'm at the driver's door, I'm ten feet tall and ready to rip up some shit.

"Motherfuckin' prickhole sunna-bitch, get your ass out of there cuz I'm gonna fuck you up!"

And the window slides down with a low buzz and suddenly I'm literally staggering. I swear to God, the face is like something you see in museums and that. Michael-what's-his-name, you know? Round glowing face, eyes big as coffee mugs, nose with a little tweak and bump, lips like ass cheeks you just want to spread and devour, hair tightly curled as pubes, but long and urging you to pull it. Well, hell, I'm thinking. All that fire and rage just sinks straight down past my belly and rushes into my cock sayin' "Hello!"

"Jeeze, I'm sorry, buddy."

"Huh?"

"I'm really sorry. I didn't see you until…I mean, it was too late to slow down and I…" His eyes were that kind of blue that pull you right into them. "Hey, hang on, I got a towel in the back."

He pops the door open and climbs back into the van and no shit, he's even bending over, butt my way. "Do I wanna?" my brain is shouting. I tell my dumbass brain to shut the fuck up and climb up inside, pulling the door behind me.

"Shit happens," I tell him with a grin, wiping the towel over my head. "You got me good though, ya know?" I toss the damp towel on the floor between us.

"Jeeze," he says again. "I'm real sorry. Do you...do you drink? I think I've got..." He opens this little cabinet and pulls out a pint of JD. "Might warm you up." He hands it over and slumps that bubblebutt down. I'm eye-raking his body as I take a healthy gulp. Oh, yeah. Loose shorts and I can just see the shadowed head of his cock up the leg hole. Old one-eye is staring right at me and under my leathers I can feel my own staring right back.

He coughs into his hand. "Umm. Do you know if...I mean." He glances out the side window. "I wouldn't want to get a ticket, but..." He tilts his head.

Then we hear it. Like the wind is suddenly whipping the rain against the road. Whoosh. White light hits the windows and he flinches and freezes. It's like lightning has frozen on his skin, washing away all the color. Whoosh again and the wind rushes past us, rocking the SUV in an earthquake one-two punch. The light is gone again.

"Could have been..." His lower lip is hanging loose. "A cop." The words finally stumble out of his mouth.

I take another long drink of the JD and wink. I waggle my thumb. "I'm up here all the fucking time. Naw. The deputies hunker down in this kind of weather unless they get called for an accident."

"Really?"

I pass the JD back and he takes a good pull. He kind of chokes as I follow his eyes and he's definitely checking out my meat. Which at this moment is trying to set some kind of tolerance endurance test against my leathers. I'm harder than a fucking I-beam.

His eyes drift back to the window. "So, you come up here a lot?"

I nod and run my hand along my thigh, up over my cock. The tight wet leather is outlining it pretty good. I hold up my palm and we both look down at the beads and streaks of water. In the dim light from his dashboard, the drops are glowing and pearly like cum on sweaty skin.

I look over at him. "I come a lot, yeah." I flash him some teeth.

He laughs, that soft kind, you know. "I guess I splashed you pretty good." He picks up the towel and starts folding it. His hands are soft and fluttery. Each time he makes a fold, he smoothes out the cloth, pressing it tight and then turning the towel around. I can't help thinking maybe I oughta just pop this guy with my fist and split. He's pretty enough, but damnit he splashed me and now he's making like he wants some action. Or is he? Maybe he's just a tease queen. Or acting all shy-shy. Screw it. I reach over to the door.

"Hey! Ummm." He looks up from the towel and points to the bottle. "There's still a little left and…." He holds up the towel and all his careful folds come undone. "You oughta wipe those down if…if you're going to sit here a moment," he says. His voice gets even softer. "Or I could. I mean, as an apology, sort of…."

"Yeah. I guess a good wipe-down'd be in order."

Okay. Now we're getting somewhere. I mean, I was starting to wonder if he wants to play or just flirt with a bad biker and then run home to whoever pays the bills. I nod and pick up the JD again for a nip.

While I'm tilting it back, in a flash, he's on his knees in front of me, face hovering inches from my cock and he's barely moving the towel. I mean, like a millimeter every heartbeat, up and down like he's trying to find the rhythm of the pulse. He just looks into my eyes and smiles. Mona-fucking-Lisa.

He's just dabbing at the rainwater on my pants, like he's trying to soak up each drop separately. And I'm starting to get antsy. Is this guy just teasing me off or what? He's still got this silly smile on his lips, spacing out.

Whoosh. Another car comets past us and I hear its tires clipping some big puddle. Splash against the side of the van. The guy's still down there, patting away at my knee with his little towel, still inches away from my throbbing cock. I close my eyes because all I'm starting to see is red. Okay, so for a minute there I was lost in it, you know? But now I'm remembering that if this fucker hadn't splashed me in the first place, I'd be long gone up the coast. I'd be out in the whipping rain, hitting my groove. I look down at the guy and then out the window. Who knows how long the rain's gonna last. At the rate he's moving, it'll be a fucking hour before this guy is wiping on my dick. One more look at him is all it takes. His eyes are closed and his head's back and he's just smiling that fucking Mona Lisa smile up at me, like he's waiting for Prince Charming to kiss him or something.

I ain't really a thinker. I ain't some guy goes around judging other guys, but shit! What the hell is in this guy's mind if he's expecting to find Mr.-Right-for-Romance by mud splashing him in the middle of the night?

"Fuck this!"

"What?"

I'm reaching down and flicking open my buckle with one hand and sliding my other hand up over his face into that sprawl of his curls.

"Oh," he says, "but I…."

I've got my leathers down now and start pulling his head forward. I'm gritting my teeth and hissing words. "Suck it, bitch. Suck Daddy's cock. Make it good for me."

"Wait!" He's squirming in my grip. "Kiss me, first."

"Kiss this!" I'm rubbing my cock against his mouth, but he's trying to turn his head away.

Oh yeah, he's playing little Missy Virgin Mouth, keeping his lips tight, you know, but his jaws open, so it feels like my cock's plowing into virgin ass. Half the head is in and already his tongue is working. But I like pulling his hair and holding him back.

"Kiss my cock."

I pull his head back and his lips kiss the tip.

"That's right, bitch."

I shove the head all the way and I can see he's smiling, lips around my cockhead, every time I call him bitch. He's grooving on it. "Wipe me down real good, little bitch. Apologize to Mr. Cock with that tongue. Tell him how sorry you are."

"Ahh...sowwy...ah...sowwy."

I push another two inches into his mouth. "Not with words, you fucking bitch. With licks. With sucks. Apologize with some suck."

Now he's gurgling and I'm thinking Oh, shit, maybe this is virgin throat, virgin head, or maybe I'm just bigger than he's used to, but it don't matter because it's getting to me either way.

"You want Daddy to splash you back, bitch? You want a big wave of Daddy's cum to rain on you? You want me to rain down in your belly?"

His eyes roll back and then he closes them as I'm pushing deeper between those tight lips. His cheeks are puffing in and out like the bag of a vacuum cleaner turned on and off. Fuck, I'm getting close to shooting. It's like fucking the mouth of one of those fucking angels painted on church ceilings or something. I can feel his cock humping against my leg and he's shaking all over and my body starting to jerk around. I know I'm going to get him, get him good and suddenly I'm there.

The moments slow, like they do sometimes when you're buzzed all to hell. I can feel my cockhole open up and the flood surge of my cum splashing against the roof of his mouth like a geyser. It's too much for him. Another big jolt and I ease up to feel his teeth sliding along my shaft, snagging on my cockhead. I look down and just start laughing as the globs of pearly cum start dribbling out of his mouth, down his chin.

"Bitch!" I shout and put both hands in his hair and shove my cock all the way to the balls into his mouth. It's surprised the fuck out of him and he's gagging. Or maybe just mock-gagging for the show of it because suddenly his cock is shooting, too. Little watery spurts up over my knee—watching them drags the last bit out of my balls. I let go of his hair and he's falling backward. My last shot of cum hits him right between the eyes. And I'm still laughing as it splits apart into two dribbles running down both sides of his nose.

"Shitshitshitshit!" He's muttering over and over.

"Splashback's a motherfucker, huh, bitch?" I'm still chuckling as I haul up my leathers and toss back the last of the JD.

He's wiping the cum off his face and glaring at me. "Fuck you. I thought...I...."

"Yeah, I know, bitch. You thought I was gonna tickle my tonsils with that little prick of yours, too? Maybe next time when your Daddy's not still pissed off. See ya around, bitch."

I'm strolling back to my bike when I hear the screech. He's pulling away. Into the rain. Yeah, the rare, sweet coast rain, west of L.A. And sitting on my bike, before I slide my face behind the helmet plate again, I just got to rear back and laugh like a loon and let it wash me clean.

STRANGER DANGER
Rick R. Reed

A ll Bradley Sheffield knew, as he steered his beat-up red Corolla into Kleeson Memorial Park, was that his emotions were at war. Lust, dread, want and need combined, battling for dominance, making Bradley's forehead sweat, his palms slippery on the steering wheel and his entire body tremble with need. What Bradley Sheffield didn't know, as he maneuvered around potholes and ruts, was that he risked never driving out again.

Kleeson Memorial Park, in western Pennsylvania was known for its hills, abundant oak and maple trees, picnic grounds...and cruising. The park had been called "The Woods" far longer than "Kleeson Memorial." And Bradley knew The Woods well, knew the paths that twisted down hills, stopping at small clearings where one could kneel and suck a stranger's cock or bend over and feel the snug fit of that same cock sliding into one's ass. Knew the signals. Bradley even knew many of the other guys who regularly cruised the park...and for whom to watch out.

For example, Bradley knew to avoid the White Corvette (Bradley named most of his tricks for their cars). The White Corvette was in reality a large black man. Deep voice, sharply defined pecs, a full six-foot-four of hard muscle. He was the opposite of Bradley: china doll pale with a shock of straw-like blond hair, while Bradley was wispy, almost ephemeral, a cloud of yellowish smoke, light enough for the wind to carry away. The White Corvette had set Bradley's heart to racing when he first spied him, had aroused in him the predatory instincts which had become as natural as breath. Bradley had followed him deep into the woods.

Rough trade had been exactly what Bradley had been looking for: perhaps someone who would pull his hair as he went down on him, slap his face, force him to take it all....

What he got instead was nothing.

The White Corvette seemed to like to play the game, to become the elusive prey, but when it came time to stop playing, to bring on the real thing, White Corvette was more interested in studying the trees.

Bradley had hoped for a more sexual type of intercourse, but even social intercourse didn't happen: White Corvette wouldn't even speak, let alone touch, or be touched, or suck, or....

Another time, after spending more than three hours in the park, Bradley was ready to concede defeat when he saw the '72 Blue Nova. When desperation pressed its cold hand to Bradley's heart, certain men suddenly became "adequate." Blue Nova was "adequate." Mid-40s with a pot belly and teeth going to yellow, Bradley wouldn't have considered him two hours ago, or even an hour ago, but suddenly Bradley's libido was pointing certain things out to him: how sexy the man's salt-and-pepper mustache was and how that Harley Davidson belt buckle drove him wild. When they got into the woods, Bradley pulled Blue Nova's jeans down to find a dick that was "adequate" but covered with small scabs. "Go on, boy, suck it," Blue Nova whispered, "Them sores ain't gonna hurt you. It's not VD." Right. Bradley had hurried away, not looking back, even when Blue Nova called him a "Fuckin' faggot."

So Bradley knew. Who was good and who was not. And Bradley loved nothing more than making a new friend. So when he saw the motorcycle and the blue-jeaned guy astride it, alarms went off and Bradley whipped the Corolla to the side of the road. Just behind him, Motorcycle waited, straddling his Harley. Wearing a black T-shirt and tight Levis with the knees worn out, Motorcycle caressed the bulge in his crotch. Bradley swallowed, noticing the size of the bulge and how it pressed against denim so faded Bradley wondered how it stayed in one piece. The summer air stilled as Bradley gazed into his rearview mirror. Behind the reflection of his own pale-blue eyes, Motorcycle was climbing down from the huge bike. Bradley's heartbeat picked up as Motorcycle crossed the road, heading onto a path leading into the woods. Woods that practically told Bradley's sexual life story. His dick swelled, pressing hard against the liner of his nylon running shorts as the tight ass disappeared into the trees. "We're gonna have some fun today," Bradley whispered as he set the parking brake and hoisted himself from the car. Once on the path, Bradley followed its course to the big maple most guys found provided enough privacy for whatever it was they wanted to do.

Motorcycle was not there.

For a moment, Bradley panicked. Maybe he had misunderstood; maybe this hunk was straight; maybe he went into the woods to take a piss. C'mon, Bradley. An image of Motorcycle's black-leather-glove-clad hand rose up, caressing the faded denim of the man's crotch. The stare. Bradley had been coming here for ten years—since he was fourteen. He spoke cruise better than he spoke English.

Bradley trudged onward, following the path's descent. The air was thick; gnats dove for the moisture in Bradley's eyes; mosquitoes buzzed in his ears. Maybe the guy wasn't worth it.

Then Bradley recalled the tanned arms, roped with muscle, the hard outline of his pecs through clinging black fabric. And up ahead, Bradley saw him. Motorcycle looked back and paused, making sure Bradley was following. In spite of the heat, Bradley shivered. "Why doesn't he take off his helmet? Why doesn't he take off those gloves? What's he hiding?" Bradley pictured small purple lesions on the guy's face, his hands. For a second, anyway, Bradley considered turning back. Motorcycle was going too deep into the woods and hot as he was, Bradley wondered: is he worth dying for? But Bradley was not one to ask questions in the face of hot cock. He would be careful, he told himself: "No exchange of bodily fluids." It was worth the risk, he decided, watching the taut ass lead him deeper into the privacy of the woods. "I really will be careful this time," Bradley whispered. But even as he said it, his asshole twitched, eager to be forced open.

There was another turn in the path and Bradley watched Motorcycle disappear into a copse of oak trees. "Christ!" Bradley slapped away a mosquito.

"What's he need to go in so deep for?" He giggled, thinking of how deep he'd like Motorcycle to go. But really, they were so far from the main road now, Bradley knew if he screamed, no one would hear. There had been stories of fag bashings, even a killing a few years back. Maybe this guy... "Nah," Bradley told himself, "I've been coming here ten years." Still, something cold fluttered in his gut as the path gave way to brambles and Bradley looked down to see his ankles scratched and bleeding. He had never been this deep into the woods. Motorcycle was far enough ahead that Bradley could turn and run back to the safety of his Toyota and not be noticed right away. But that faded denim crotch bulge rose up before him and his mouth watered. Bradley trudged on.

Finally, Motorcycle stopped at a place where a tree had fallen and the land leveled off. He didn't turn to look as Bradley struggled down the hill, grasping tree branches for support and wiping the sweat away from his pale forehead, tossing blond hair out of his eyes.

Motorcycle faced away, staring off into the woods, one hand at his crotch, rubbing.

Bradley stumbled once and then was behind him. He closed his eyes; the width of the tan shoulders, the tight ass, the small waist; his nervousness vanished. Coming up behind him, Bradley slid his arms around Motorcycle's waist and reached for his crotch.

Even through his jeans, Motorcycle's cock felt enormous, so hard Bradley could feel the blood pulsing inside. One of Motorcycle's arms shot back and drew Bradley close to him. Bradley was afraid he'd shoot in his shorts as the man pulled him against him. He let go of Bradley and turned; the visor was too dark to see his face.

"First time I've seen you here…I think," Motorcycle said.

"I wouldn't know if I'd seen you here before or not." Bradley pointed to the wind visor obscuring the man's face.

Motorcycle laughed, his deep voice sounding strange, too loud here in the quiet. Bradley paused. The man grabbed him again, so tight the wind rushed out of him and Bradley thought his ribs would break. "Spank me," Bradley whispered into the helmet, pushing down his nylon running shorts.

The leather thwacked against Bradley's bare ass, not hard enough. It was never hard enough. Even when they left welts.

Bradley dropped to his knees, struggling with the buttons on Motorcycle's Levi's. Above Bradley, the black helmet tilted down toward him, a ridge of hard muscle pushed out against the black cotton fabric of Motorcycle's T-shirt.

And then it was in front of him. Bradley gasped. In the movies, in the stroke mags, the guys always had huge cocks. But Bradley usually found average guys when he pulled down their pants. Six, six-and-a-half, seven inches tops.

But this dick was every boy's fantasy. Purple veined and actually throbbing, it jutted out from a thatch of black pubic hair. Eleven inches, twelve? Too thick for Bradley to wrap his hand around. Pre-come oozed out of the piss slit, which yawned almost open with the tumescence of Motorcycle's erection.

It looked dangerous.

Bradley took a breath and went down on it. Black gloves sank into Bradley's blond curls, pushing. Bradley opened his mouth so wide he feared it would rip at the corners, yet he met Motorcycle's upward thrusts without gagging.

Retreated. And went down again.

Motorcycle yanked Bradley's hair with one hand, slapped his face with the other. Bradley's eyes watered as the huge dick rammed against the back of his throat again and again. He wrapped his tongue around the shaft, exploring its blue-veined ridges with his tongue. In turn, Bradley took each of Motorcycle's balls into his mouth; spit and pre-come ran down his chin. Bradley groaned, tasting the pre-come, savoring Motorcycle's musky odor, spawned by the heat and humidity of the sweltering August day. He hoped that later Motorcycle would fill his mouth with piss, growing delirious with the prospect of that hot, salty warmth, resisting his efforts to gulp it down even as it cascaded down the front of his mesh shirt. Bradley flashed on the words 'bodily fluids' and remembered his earlier promise to be careful. "Just this once," he thought, "won't hurt anything. I want to slurp up his come, drink his piss...now." Bradley moaned again, burying his fears with images of hot piss. But he was getting ahead of himself. Bradley slowed to take Motorcycle's sex in his hands, tonguing it up and down, licking the piss slit clean. Taking the dick in his mouth about halfway, Bradley looked up at Motorcycle.

Sun glinted behind the black helmet. Even without the back-lighting, it would be impossible to see a face.

Motorcycle slapped Bradley's left cheek and then both hands grabbed his ears, holding Bradley's head still as he slammed his rigid sex deeper into his throat. Deeper, until Bradley could no longer see: the tears flowing. Black pubic hair chafed against his lips, balls slapped against his chin.

Bradley hoped this day would never end.

The tightening. Balls jumped up near Motorcycle's body. His cock stiffened beyond possibility. Erupting. For one second, maybe less, Bradley started to pull away. But then, closing his eyes, he gulped as hot bullets of semen shot deep, slamming into the back of his throat. Not wanting to lose a drop, Bradley moved his mouth up to the head, so he could better taste the starchy erupting cream. Motorcycle's head went back and a moan, loud, deep and full of virile pleasure escaped his lips, his black helmet, filling the emerald air with his cries. Bradley's cheeks billowed out with come; he hoped Motorcycle would never stop pumping; pumping with such force it was almost painful.

Quivers shot through Bradley, electric, and he looked down as his cock. Without so much as a touch, it pumped out his seed, staining the front of his running shorts dark.

Motorcycle yanked Bradley's head away, just far enough so that Bradley could reach out with his tongue and lick away the drop of come poised at the tip of his dick. Head pulled back, Bradley cried out in pain and pleasure as Motorcycle began slapping him back and forth with his sex: cheeks, nose, mouth...hard enough to start a trickle of blood at his lips.

And then the piss...yellow stream, wide, strong-smelling, began. Covering Bradley's face. With a grunt, Motorcycle pulled him forward, hard enough to pull out a hunk of Bradley's hair, and forced him down. He drank, gulping, not having time to savor its salty heat, but knowing just the same that nothing tasted more satisfying.

Piss ran down his chin and just as he had imagined, covered his mesh shirt, the smell of it growing stronger, causing Bradley's cock to harden again. When Motorcycle was done, his cock stood at half-mast, heavy and reddened from the force of Bradley's sucking. It was then Bradley noticed the purple lesion on Motorcycle's left thigh. He shuddered, tasting the piss and come at the back of this throat. Hadn't he read somewhere that one exposure didn't have to mean infection? Hell, he thought, lifting the heavy cock with his hand, it's probably just a blood blister.

Motorcycle's voice, bass, came out of the helmet. "Now, little faggot. Let me give it to you. Give it to you...." Motorcycle laughed. He grabbed Bradley with so much force under the armpits, Bradley screamed. Spun him around, ripped the nylon shorts from his body. Bradley's eyes opened wide as Motorcycle slammed him over the dead tree, his erect cock crashing against the bark. "Thank you," he whimpered. Across the mossy bark of the fallen tree was a smear of Bradley's blood, crimson on the green lichen. He felt certain he would come the moment Motorcycle entered him.

Motorcycle was poised at his ass. Bradley whispered, "Please, let me see you."

Bradley turned, reaching out toward the smoked glass visor. Motorcycle slapped his hand away.

Bradley swallowed hard. "Just this once," he thought, "I've come this far." He lay again face down across the tree.

There was no sound. No wind. No birds. No insects. Bradley reached back and spread his ass cheeks, rotating them in a slow motion come-on. "Please sir," he said, speaking to the tree beneath him. "Don't hurt me."

JUST UNTIL LEATHERMORN
Jason Rubis

Merle heard the shit start going down right as he was taking the grease-stained paper sack from the guy at the counter. Somebody outside was squalling like a lunatic, and from the voice, that somebody was Snake.

Well, that wasn't good. True enough, Snake and the word *lunatic* weren't what you'd call incompatible, but in Merle's experience he generally wasn't a screamer, even when he was getting a nut. Tucking the sack under his arm, Merle grabbed his drink (extra-large cola, good and cold in its big-ass paper cup) and 'scuse-me'd his way through the gawping, muttering lines of straights to the door.

Out in the Burger Rustler's parking lot the Texas sun was burning down on his and Snake's bikes and a mass of straight cars with American flag bumper stickers and BABY ON BOARD signs in the windows. Snake was ass-down on the hot concrete, eyes bugging out like a couple of ping-pong balls. Made him look kind of like the zombies in *I Eat Your Skin* (damn cool flick, that one; one of Merle's A-1 favorites). He had some pink-colored thing gripped in one fist. Merle couldn't quite make out what it was.

A girl was holding a gun on Snake from a couple of yards away, pointing the barrel right at his balls. She had her legs spaced widely apart and her arms outstretched straight in front of her, holding the pistol tight in both hands, like she knew exactly how to use it.

Thing was, she wasn't a she; Merle saw that as soon as he got close enough. What you had there was a boy dressed like a girl. Twenty-one, twenty-two, maybe. He wore a black leather jacket over a baby-blue bikini-top and a short denim skirt that showed off his long, tanned legs. Longish black hair, looked Japanese. Strappy high-heeled sandals on his bare, red-toenailed feet. Real cute-looking, actually…but not cute-*acting*. Not now, anyhow. He looked seriously pissed, was the truth, and that gun wasn't cute at all.

"Give her back!" the boy shouted. His voice was thin and nasal; he was talking to Snake, and he meant business. "I swear, I'll shoot you right in the nuts if you don't give her back!"

"Merle!" Snake wailed, catching sight of his friend wiggling on the lot like a whipped dog. Most un-Snakelike, that wiggling. It did Merle's heart some pain to see his buddy wiggle like that.

"Hey," Merle said softly, walking up to the boy with a slow, easy stride, like he just wanted to ask him the time. You had to handle these things a particular way, especially when your guy's family jewels were on the line. "What's goin on here?"

"He took Lysandra," the boy told Merle, speaking through gritted teeth.

Merle took a closer look at the thing in Snake's fist. His shoulders slumped. "Snake," he said wearily. "What the fuck you doin', man?"

"Merle, I was just…"

Merle raised the paper cup to his mouth, got the straw in his teeth and sucked him down a good long draught of cola. Man, that was good. Hot weather like this, good cold pop beat the living shit out of beer. "Give him the doll back, Snake."

"I toldya, I was just…"

"Yeah, I know you were *just*. You like your balls, Snake? Come on, man, that ain't cool, fuckin with a guy's doll." Sounded funny, saying it that way, but Merle guessed it was nothing more than the truth.

Glaring, Snake tossed the pink thing out onto the asphalt with a quick jerk of his hand. The boy crouched and reached for it, not taking the gun off Snake until the doll was safely in his hand. He kissed its little face and cooed at it.

"Poor Lysandra! What'd the bad redneck do to you, baby?"

Snake scrambled to his feet and backed off towards his bike. "Redneck?" he spat, hustling his balls like he wanted to check they were still there. "You put that gun away, Mary, I'll show you 'redneck.' Show you a big red cock right up your pink little *ass*, is what I'll do."

The boy didn't hesitate for a second. He thrust the doll into a pocket and his pistol into his skirt. "You want some of me?" he shrilled, crouching and beckoning to Snake with his red nails.

Merle, still sucking on his pop, swiveled his head around, taking in the crowd of straights gathering around them. Big old mommas and some even bigger poppas. Fat guts, but muscles like Popeye, every damn one of 'em. Not a good bunch to mess with.

"He took that li'l girl's doll," one of the mommas told Merle. "I seen him."

Snake's eyes bugged again. "Little *girl*?"

"Be cool, Snake."

"Yeah, *Snake*," the boy smirked. "Be cool."

"Aw, Merle! Lemme just pinch his head a little!"

"Relax, man," Merle said, shaking the sack. "Come on, now. I got you those jalapeño-cheesy things you like. We're just leaving," he told the straights, spreading his hands in a calmly beneficent gesture. "My buddy didn't mean any harm. Just a little joke got out of hand."

Merle's act worked. It always did. The boy sneered, but the crowd, satisfied that the gentle-voiced fellow with the Jesus Christ hair and beard had things in hand, began to move back towards the restaurant.

Merle had just begun to relax when the Japanese dude showed up, a little old gray-haired guy in a sharp black suit. He just kind of appeared, taking the place of a particularly large and irritable-looking momma.

"Alicia," he said, his voice quavering but stern. "What are you up to now?"

The boy didn't move. He had the doll back out and was completely focused on stroking its long brown hair.

"I apologize," the man told Merle, inclining his head slightly. "My niece and I are traveling, and we stopped here for refreshment. I did not realize she would get into trouble while I was inside."

"Niece?" Merle blinked. "*Alicia?*" he added, glancing at the boy, who promptly stuck his tongue out at him.

"That was what I said," the man said, not so much as blinking. "Should I perhaps speak more slowly?"

"No sir," Merle said judiciously. "I guess there's no need for that."

"He's yours?" Snake demanded, jerking his chin at the boy. "Hey? Why you wanna give that little bitch a gun for, man? He's freaking unstable!"

"I did not give Alicia the gun. She took it. From my glove compartment, this time. I always try to hide it, you see, but it's no good. She *likes* guns."

"Boom," Alicia grinned, running a hand down the front of his skirt. "Bang-*bang!*"

"We-ell now," Merle said quickly, "I guess all's well end's well, right? Nice meeting you all, but my friend and I should really get going..."

"May we speak together?" the man asked suddenly. He sidled off a little, and when Merle followed he kept right on sidling, until they were—in Merle's view—a dangerous distance from Snake and Alicia, both of whom were now growling audibly at each other.

"Do you like her?" the man asked, his voice low and confidential. Merle blinked. "Like her?"

"Do you," the man said, one eyebrow raised high, "*like* her? Alicia. Would you like to take her with you? She's very good. You know what I mean, I think."

"Oh, now see...I don't think we're exactly on the same page here. My friend and I aren't..."

"Please don't do me the discourtesy of lying to me. It is hardly necessary, you know? Your answer, please."

Merle slurped at his pop, buying time while he figured out how to handle this. "But he...I mean, she...she's yours...isn't she? Why would you...?"

"I'm not a young man anymore," the man said, hand on chest. "Taking Alicia on was foolish. I thought I could handle her, but...my heart. You see what I'm saying. You are a gentle man. Patient. In control. You are what Alicia needs."

"But I..." Merle was all set to tell the guy he just wasn't interested. Kinky was one thing, but buying a drag-princess with a gun-fetish in a burger-joint parking lot was kind of on the excessive side. Besides, he and Snake were on their way to an event where Miss Alicia would be as seriously out of place as she was out here. More, maybe. They didn't go for femmes at LeatherMorn any more than they did at Burger Rustler.

Then the money came out. A lot of it, from a fat wallet that gave up the bills without looking appreciably thinner. They were big bills too, none of them under a hundred. Merle almost dropped his sack.

"Of course, I wouldn't expect you to take Alicia on without proper funds," the man said smoothly. "She is accustomed to a certain style of living, even when living...rough. There's enough here for that, and also to provide very generously for any trouble your friend and yourself are put through on her behalf."

Merle was trying to talk without his mouth falling down onto his chest. "But...he...she...won't he...I mean, she'll..."

"Oh, she'll go with you, no problem," the man said wearily, shoving the wad of bills into Merle's jacket-pocket. "She's tired of me. If you don't take her, she will *pick* someone. Perhaps someone not as kind as yourself. If you take her, I will at least sleep well."

"Well," Merle gulped, casting a none-too-willing eye back at Snake. "I guess a man's got to sleep."

"Particularly at my age," the man nodded. "Take my word for it."

It felt good being back on the bike—even after a short pit stop. The wind whipping your hair back that way like long, tender fingers, kissing your face raw...that was the way. For Merle, there was no other, hadn't been since he got on his first bike, years and years ago.

Of course, having a pretty something's arms wrapped around your waist during the ride wasn't bad either. Sex with Snake was a kick in the ass (and you could take that literally or not, as you chose), but Snake wasn't the kind to hold you tight, like you were the one firm foundation in his universe, someone big and strong who'd protect him.

It had been a long time since Merle had been with someone like that. He hadn't realized he'd missed it.

Then again, Alicia—tight grip and all—wasn't exactly the ooh-aah-you're-so-strong type.

"There's another one! *Get* it!" Merle had no trouble hearing him, even over the roar of wind and engine.

"Honey, that little rabbit ain't hurtin nobody," he shouted. Alicia pummeled one-handed at his shoulder.

"I said *get* it! Smash it *flat!*"

Merle steered deftly around the jackrabbit that had frozen stock-still in the middle of the road.

"We coulda had that for *supper!*" Alicia howled, slapping the back of Merle's head. Merle sighed and glanced over at Snake, who was sitting bolt-upright on his Yamaha several yards ahead, eyes fixed coldly on the road as he tore on. Even if he had been able to hear Alicia fussing, Merle knew what his response would be: you bought the bitch, you take care of him.

Except Alicia hadn't been bought, she had been...well, what *did* you call it? Snake hadn't been impressed by the money, Merle knew he wouldn't. For Snake, money was something that came along when you needed it—or didn't, in which case you just did without. What Merle did counted in his eyes as a perversion, much more so than anything they would encounter at LeatherMorn.

Speaking of which, they weren't all that far away from the campground now. By morning they'd be there, and then their Alicia problems would be over. Merle had it all figured out. He would take some time out from the festivities to play matchmaker—find the little dudette a nice stable Daddy to go home with. He'd been thinking about Burt Foster for that. Burt was just a weekend rider, but a good enough old boy. Had a real nice place up in the hills around Lake Travis, close enough to the lights and action of Austin to keep Alicia happy for a while. Merle would give Alicia most of the money and just say Sayonara.

Yeah, that's what he would do...assuming they got through the night without Snake and Alicia killing each other.

Not that Merle was taking any bets on that.

"Shit man, that's her, that's Onadera's bitch, you see her, man?"

Chile was naked except for his jacket and eye shadow—and the raggedy-ass feathers he wore braided into his hair, of course. He never took the damned things out. He was standing on the ridge, hopping from one bare foot to the other, cock and balls swinging as he steadied the binoculars.

"I don't believe it, but it's her, for real! Hangin with these two dudes, real rough-lookin! They're goin' off somewhere together...ow! Fuckin rocks hurt my fuckin feet, man! Here, *you* look!"

Banzai-Man ignored the binocs thrust into his face. He was Doing Sword, which could mean a number of things at any given time. At the moment it meant cleaning and polishing. He loved the way the steel gleamed as he slid the bunched cloth up and down over the blade. Like jacking off, but better. *Everything* about the Sword was better than anything else.

Obasan had given Banzai-Man the Sword just before he left Cali, when his name was still David. It was funny; *Obasan* was from the old country. She should have been way more conservative than his parents. Banzai-Man would have thought she'd be right on his ass with them when he got caught fucking that guy. But in the end she had turned out to be so cool. The Sword proved that. It had belonged to her grandfather, who had been some hot-shit general back during the War. On the Japanese side, of course.

"You like him," she had whispered to him that morning. Banzai wondered for a minute what that said about Gramps, but she went on: "Warrior. *Samurai*." Nothing in the world since meant more to Banzai-Man than that whisper...except for the Sword itself, of course.

"Banzai, c'mon man, *look*." Chile's voice went soft and pleading, like it was real important that Banzai-Man look at Onadera's bitch, camped out beside the highway with whatever two feebs Onadera had picked to play bodyguard. Banzai didn't need to look. He stood and feinted with the Sword, struck a pose, pulled back slightly, the hilt gripped firmly in one hand. Badass. Just like his man Toshiro Mifune, or that other dude, who played in the *Lone Wolf & Cub* movies.

Chile gave it up and sat heavily down on the tattered blanket Banzai-Man had laid out for their camp. He pulled one foot into his lap, rubbing the sole, watching his friend's stylings with wide, appreciative eyes. "You so hot, bro," he whispered after a while. "How 'bout you do me now, huh? That a good idea? Huh?"

He rolled over on the blanket, hiking up his jacket so his ass showed.

Banzai-Man sighed. Chile was a good bitch. Half-Indian, half-Mex. Getting kind of old now—twenty-eight was old for a bitch on the road—but he had aged really well. He was always able to score for whatever they needed whenever they needed it. And it was hot having him around. Sure, he got on your nerves with his yang-yang all the time. But tearing up that round little ass of his was just like eating candy.

Still, it was getting dark, and they had work to do. Yoshi wasn't paying them to fuck, he was paying them to pick up Onadera's bitch. Banzai-Man didn't know why Yoshi wanted her...maybe just to piss off Onadera. The two of them had been rivals for years, since before Banzai-Man had been born, which struck him as seriously cool. Two old warriors, plotting against each other for decades. Now they'd taken their fight to the States, which was where Banzai had come in.

Banzai-Man liked working for Yoshi. It made him feel like a real old-school samurai, working for an actual Japanese *yakuza* instead of the small-timers who usually hired him.

On the other hand, there was something about having your bitch show you his ass and beg you to take it.

Banzai picked up the bottle of oil he'd used on the Sword and tipped it over Chile's backside. The contents dribbled out, running in clear rivulets over and between his cheeks. Chile hissed in a breath and wriggled all over. He knew this was an honor. That damned oil didn't come cheap.

Banzai-Man crouched and thrust his hands under Chile's jacket, kneading and rubbing. Chile was good and tight all over, slight but muscular, good to hold onto. Chile purred and kicked his feet, impatient for dick.

Banzai always challenged himself to do the deed as quickly as possible; not because he didn't enjoy it, but because that just seemed cooler. He unzipped and went to work, one hand bracing himself, one reaching under him to maneuver his cock into place and ram it home.

"When we go down there in a minute," he said, wincing a little as he got into rhythm, "and take those fuckers, I want you to be naked, just like you are now, right? With my come dripping out your asshole. Show them you're...my bitch. Show 'em."

Chile moaned, and Banzai-Man, thrusting, grinned.

Yeah. That was just how they'd do it.

"He's watching us, Merle. God-dammit...."

"Shhh...." Merle got his arms under Snake's back, pulling him upward to meet his mouth, willing him to relax. They kissed—plenty of teeth and tongue and beard—and Merle pushed his face into the place where Snake's throat met his shoulder, breathed in, bit him there. Softly at first, then harder. Fucking out here on the rocky ground seemed to inspire a certain roughness. You couldn't really let go, though, the way you could in a room, and really whale on your buddy...but that little bit of forced restraint seemed to make the whole thing hotter, at least to Merle's mind.

"Come on." Snake made to turn over, but Merle touched his cheek. "No, I wanna see your face. Come on, guy, get those legs up."

Snake did. Merle spat in his hand and got himself ready, then went in with a low grunt and closed eyes. Snake's bunghole was relaxed enough, but the man himself wasn't happy. Merle couldn't really blame him. Alicia was out there, crouched by the fire, probably playing with his doll—or maybe something else small and pink. Though he hadn't said a word since Merle had nodded to Snake and led him out into scrub, the boy's presence couldn't be ignored.

"Shhh," Merle said again, hissing it. Damn, what was it about Snake? He just never got tired of him...felt like he could go all night.

"Shush nothing. I'm gonna have enough fuckers watching my bare ass tomorrow morning without that little cunt...*hey!*"

The pebble hit the ground a good three feet beyond where they lay, but it nearly took a chunk out of Merle's ear as it whizzed by. Another one hit Merle square in the kidneys. It hadn't been thrown hard, but Merle had stripped, and it felt like there was a good-sized dent in his back now.

"Merle..." Snake caught the momentary grimace of pain on his friend's face, and his eyes caught fire.

"Just ignore him, buddy." Merle had known that fucking in front of Alicia was a seriously bad idea, but neither of them had gotten a nut in two days. It had taken them long to reach a spot isolated enough to do something about it. Waiting even till morning just wasn't an option.

"Just relax. He's just a spoiled brat, he don't mean no harm. Now, give it up for me, okay? Just lemme..."

A small, sharp explosion of pain flowered in Merle's right butt-cheek. He yelped and straightened his knees, pulling out of Snake just as his load came. Over by the fire, someone got the giggles.

"*Alicia!*" Merle stumbled back to the campfire with clenched fists.

"Just ignore him, man!" Snake said, actually laughing a little. "He don't mean no *harm*, man! Peace and love, baby!"

"There's a time for peace and love," Merle grated. "And there's a time for switchins."

Alicia stood crouched by the fire, laughing at him. He threw a last pebble at Merle's bare feet, then shrieked and ran off, making for the stony ridge that flanked the highway.

Merle wasn't in any hurry; Alicia still had his heels on. But the kid was far more agile than he'd suspected. Merle could just make out Alicia's pale form in the dying light, scrambling up over the top of the ridge.

Damn. Merle didn't fancy going up that ridge himself, not bare-assed naked. By the time he got his boots and jeans on, the boy could be long gone. If he took it into his mind to spend the night playing hide-and-seek with Uncle Merle and Uncle Snake, they'd *never* reach LeatherMorn.

"Alicia!" Merle roared. "Come on back here, there ain't nowhere for you to hide up there. Come on, you know what you did. Face it like a man!"

Shrieks from the top of the ridge—and one of the voices definitely wasn't Alicia's, though it sounded kind of similar. Then someone else with a much deeper voice was yelling, sounding royally pissed-off.

As Merle stood watching, Alicia came charging down the slope like sixty, still laughing and screaming like he was on a ride in an amusement park. Seconds later a guy in biker's leathers and boots came down after him. His long black hair was tied in a topknot, and he was carrying—Jesus Christ, Merle thought, was that a *sword?*

It sure enough was. By the time the guy reached the bottom of the ridge and came stomping over, there was no doubt about it. The guy had a long, curving blade in his hand, the kind of sword you saw in samurai movies.

"Hey," Merle said. He held up both hands, high-stepping it backward. "Whoa now...."

"I saw them *fucking!*" Alicia shrieked, digging his nails into Merle's shoulders. "He was fucking this sissy in the ass! Just like you and Snake!" He broke into a crooning singsong:

"Oh-hh, it's a night for lov-ers!"

"Alicia..." The guy had stopped short a few paces away from Merle, breathing hard and glaring. The guy looked Indian...or maybe half-Asian; it was hard to tell. He was young—twenty-four, Merle made him—with a scruffy little half-formed beard.

"Look man, I'm sorry if my friend here disturbed you." Playing peace-maker again. Damn, but that shit was getting *old*.

"S'alright." The guy turned his wrist so that the sword pointed away from Merle and Alicia. Merle had the idea that this was meant as a gracious gesture, but he still didn't like it.

"Your 'friend' actually saved me some time. I would have had to come get him sooner or later. We can get this over with right now."

Merle frowned. "What you mean come get him?" He didn't like the way that sounded.

A second somebody was half-running, half-sliding their way down the ridge, cursing and whining the whole time. Under his leather jacket, this one was as naked as Merle himself. He was skinny, with long black hair hanging around his narrow shoulders. Definitely femme. There were feathers in his hair, like he was trying out for some kind of Native American drag-act. But he looked a lot angrier than Mr. Samurai.

"Fuckin *twat!*" he hissed, making for Alicia. Merle moved quickly, keeping himself between the two. Alicia seemed happy to hide behind him.

"You disrespected my *man* up there!" The black-haired guy shrilled.

"Yeah, well, your *man* sure has a little dick! I saw it!"

"Yeah, well, I guess you're used to little dicks, all those Japanese dudes you've been fucking!"

"What do you know about that, Pocahontas?"

"I know everything about you, whore!"

"Who's a whore?"

"I know a ugly damn whore when I see one, honey, and I'm lookin at one right now!"

"Bitch!"

"*Bitch!*"

Mr. Samurai thrust a couple of fingers into his mouth and whistled piercingly, loud enough to echo. The two femmes shut up and stared at him.

"Quiet! Both of you! You," he said, gesturing at Alicia with the sword. "You're coming with us. Chile, take him up there. You," he told Merle, "you just do yourself a favor and go back to your bitch, okay?"

"Now hold on there, buddy…fact number one: I don't like your tone. Fact number two: you ain't taking Alicia anywhere."

"Fact number *three*," Mr. Samurai growled, swinging the business end of the sword up so that the tip of the blade hovered an inch under Merle's nose. He didn't elaborate further.

"Merle, don't let 'em take me! They work for Yoshi, Merle, please!"

"Yoshi?" Merle demanded, staring cross-eyed at the sword-blade. "Who in hell's *Yoshi*?"

"Onadera warned me about him!"

"Onadera?"

"Enough talk," Mr. Samurai growled. "Chile…"

While Merle stood trying to figure out what in hell he was going to do, Mr. Samurai's boyfriend grabbed Alicia. "Gonna shave off all that pretty hair of yours," he hissed. "Make you bald."

"*Eeuuuw!*" Alicia wailed. "*Merle!*"

Something hit Mr. Samurai's sword, ringing off the steel with enough force to turn the blade aside just for a second. It was enough time for Merle to grab Mr. Samurai's wrist and get his arm around the guy's throat. The two of them did an awkward, shuffling dance, Mr. Samurai cursing like a demon, Merle trying like hell to hang on. The additional effort of keeping his naked flesh out of the way of the wildly

68

swinging blade didn't do anything for his grip. Alicia took advantage of the confusion to break away from Chile and begin a slap-and-scream contest with him.

"Snake? That you threw that rock, Snake?" A crazy part of Merle was thinking that this business of grappling naked with a sword-swinging wildman might actually be really hot...under very different circumstances, of course. "Don't be shy man, come on join the party!"

Snake—never one to miss a cue, old Snake—stepped out of the shadows, hefting a fresh rock in one hand. "Took a little lesson from Prissy-Britches back there," he said. "Why don't you just drop that fancy-ass toad sticker, man?"

"Cut your *ass* up with this!" Mr. Samurai howled, still dancing with Merle as Chile hopped and screamed encouragement, looking like some kind of mutant cheerleader. "Go on, throw it! I ain't scareda no damn *rock*!"

Something to Merle's left made a loud *click*. "You scared of *this*?" Merle, Snake and Mr. Samurai all twisted their heads around, and saw Alicia holding a pistol on Chile, who was backing away and hissing.

The gun's barrel turned slowly. "Freeze," Alicia said. Everyone did. Merle took few seconds to wrest the sword out of Mr. Samurai's hand. Even with the gun on him, the guy didn't want to give it up. It was like his fingers were welded to the hilt. When Merle finally got it, the guy stared at him like he would have killed him for a nickel.

"Alicia...how in hell'd you get that gun? I thought you gave it back to...well, to your uncle."

"Got it back. Right before he left. I told you, like guns. You know what *else* I like? I like handcuffs and rope. Funny thing, I found a whole bunch of both in your bag, Merle. Why don't you bring our new friends back to camp? We'll all play."

"Is it just me," Snake muttered, "or does he sound different?" It was true, Merle realized. Alicia's pose echoed the way he'd held the gun back at the burger-joint parking lot: cool and very much in control...but now his voice matched his pose. No shrilling and lisping for his dolly now. Chile and Mr. Samurai stood by watching with cautious eyes. They, at least, didn't look at all surprised by Alicia's transformation.

Snake tossed his rock aside and started walking. Alicia moved the gun slightly in his direction. "Not so fast, cowboy. We're all going back together."

"Now wait a minute, whoa, just hold on one *second*," Merle cried. "I thought we were all on the same side here, princess...what're you holding that piece on Snake for?"

"I told you," Alicia smiled. "We're *all* going to play."

Gaman. Had to have *gaman*, endure whatever the bitch dished out.

The tip of the feather Onadera's bitch had ripped out of Chile's hair slid lazily over Banzai-Man's balls, tracing their outlines before moving up over the underside of his cock to dab at the head.

The bitch's voice was silky. "Like that, baby?"

Banzai-Man's longed to jerk his head up and tell the bitch to go to hell, but he knew that if he stopped gritting his teeth for even a moment, he was going to majorly dishonor himself. His cock had already betrayed him by rising up and pressing itself hard and fat against his naked belly...but that was what cocks did. It was their nature to betray their owners at inopportune times. The thing Banzai-Man promised himself he would *not* do was moan...or still worse, laugh. His balls were ticklish as a motherfucker. So was the rest of him, but luckily the bitch hadn't paid much attention to anything but his nads so far.

Chile hadn't been so lucky. Like Banzai-Man, he had been stripped upon their arrival at the camp, cuffed and tied up tight, wrists locked behind his back, ankles bound together with rope. Forced to lie on the stony ground and wriggle like a crippled rattler. Onadera's bitch had ignored Chile's cock, but every time the poor little bastard opened his mouth...

"Let my man alone you fucking stinky-ass bitch *whore*, you don't touch his cock, that's my—*aaahahahaaaa!*"

"You know," the bitch smiled, crooking a finger and tickling Chile's twitching soles with a single red nail, "if I was a tenderfoot like you, I don't think I'd be mouthing off right now, Miss Thing."

"*Eeeee!* Banzai! Make her stop, bro, *please!*"

"Aww, he ain't gonna stop me, honey. He likes hearing you giggle. Makes his dick hard, just like it does mine. See, we're all just having so much fun here. So now..." The bitch pulled his legs up under him and sat running the feather again and again over his palm. "Now we're going to have some more fun. You two are going to tell me all about Mr. Yoshi."

The feather's edge ran swiftly over Banzai-Man's toes. "Aren't you?"

Banzai-Man hissed and bared his teeth at the stars, concentrating on ignoring the feather. It wasn't just that this tickling crap was so baby-sit...it was fucking *disrespectful*. But the bitch had overplayed his hand now. Ordering Banzai-Man to betray Yoshi was the best possible way to get him to marshal his *gaman*. It wasn't just that the man had his loyalty; Yoshi was ice, and reputedly a very creative motherfucker when pissed. If you betrayed him and he caught you...oh, man. It would make this sissy-ass so-called "torture" look like a day at Disney World. No *way* was Banzai-Man going to talk....

The feather meandered over the tops of Banzai-Man's feet. "Tickle, tickle..."

No way. No way in *hell*...

The bitch began scratching lightly at his soles with sharp fingernails....

Oh shit.

"*Ahhh!* Unnghh...haaaa..."

"Tickle-tickle! Aww, that's tickling him, isn't it? Big strong man got the giggles? Oh, poor little Chile's jealous! Here...let's do *both* of you at once!"

"Merle!" a voice called from somewhere a million miles away. "Merle, what in hell's he *doin* to them? Tellin 'em jokes?"

"He's tickling their feet, Snake."

"Well shit, *I* don't know, I'm just asking. I can't see, way he's got me."

Onadera's bitch had tied his two former buddies up back-to-back over by the remains of the fire. Banzai found little comfort in the fact that the bitch had turned on them as well. *They* weren't being tortured, of course not. The dumbfucks didn't know anything. All they could do was jabber at each other, while Banzai-Man....

"Let my fucking feet alone, Jesus, cut it *out*!"

"Okay. You don't like it on your feet? Here."

As Banzai-Man lay sweating and gasping, the bitch got on top of him, creeping up on him inch by inch until his denim skirt was rasping against Banzai's cock and the two of them were nose-to-nose.

"Keess me, you fool," the bitch whispered, and planted a little peck on Banzai-Man's pursed lips before going to work on his naked sides with all ten fingers.

Chile, predictably, was furious. "Hey, get offa him, I mean right *now*, what the hell you think you're doing? Get your own man, you cunt!"

"As if. I like yours just fine, honey. And he likes me. Don't you, lover?"

"Kill you..." Banzai-Man managed. His ribs...he never could stand it on the ribs....

The bitch stopped tickling and caressed his cheek. "Why all the drama, baby? Just tell me where Yoshi is. That's all I want to know. I won't tell him you talked. You think you're the only toy gangbanger he's got out on the road looking for me? Ha! Onadera and I spent all last week dodging them, practically. Why you think he set me up with those two nice men over there?"

That startled Banzai-Man, just a little. Of course Yoshi had other guys working for him, he had a whole army, practically…but this was *his* job. A memory of Yoshi sitting in the hotel flashed back to him, resplendent in a black suit, sipping straight Suntory and talking about trust, duty, loyalty…all the things that got Banzai's latter-day samurai's dick hard as steel. Light from the room's window flashing on Yoshi's glass, his lined face solemn and beautiful. He had sent *other* guys out after Onadera?

"So tell me, cutey. Tell me right now, or I'll…"

Fingers crept through his hair, steadying his head. When Onadera's bitch locked lips with him, Banzai was still in the hotel with Yoshi. Too late to repel the kiss, too late even to form the thought that he *should* be repelling it. The bitch was excited, Banzai-Man could tell that from the way his crotch in its sissy skirt was grinding against his own. The way his wet mouth with its fine, barely-there mustache rasped against his. The way he breathed, whispering "Yeah, you're hot. You know you are. I could fuck you to pieces right now, lover, split you up the middle, put you in my mouth and *swallow* you…."

Banzai-Man's mouth fell open in a split-second moment of weakness. The bitch's tongue entered it and took up residence for what might have been five full minutes. During that time, Banzai-Man's *gaman* went flying out the window. He couldn't help it. He was exhausted, his whole body aching from the ropes and rough ground, tingling from the bitch's fingers. His cock betrayed him once again, doing the old one-two-one-two against the bitch's denim.

But that was okay. It was just a little dry humping, just…keeping the bitch busy, that's what he was doing. Distracting him until he could figure a way out of this mess, get the Sword back, and then…

"He's in Dallas!"

The bitch's mouth separated from Banzai-Man's with a loud, moist *smack*. "Say again, pussy-cat? I was a little busy there."

Banzai-Man went cold all over. Then he was screaming, jerking against his ropes and cuffs and his captor's body. "Chile, I'm gonna beat your ass black and blue!"

But Chile went on, snarling the words like he was willing poison into them. "Yoshi's in Dallas, *alright*? He's staying in some hotel, *all right*? Banzai-Man's got the address up at our camp in his bag, just get *off* him, leave him alone, I'm sorry, Banzai, I couldn't stand it, bro, I couldn't…watching him…" Chile's voice dissolved into a soft, shamed mumble.

Banzai-Man's rage fell from him. He shut his eyes while Onadera's bitch got off him. He was deaf to Chile's whining apologies, to the bitch's triumphant chatter. It was all over now. Finito. Done. Despite his best efforts, his boss had been betrayed, and now he was a dead man.

"He gone?" Snake asked.

"You heard the bike, didn't you?" Merle said, squirming as he got his jeans zipped. Alicia had slipped him the handcuff-key before taking off up the ridge. By the time he had managed to get himself and Snake loose, the roar of Banzai-Man's bike starting up had sounded from the top of the ridge, then slowly faded to silence. Yeah, Alicia was gone.

He had taken Merle's face gently in his hands and kissed him. "Take care of yourself, Daddy. You know, I kind of wish I could've tortured *you* a little. Maybe next time, huh?"

Merle hadn't known what to say to that, really. One of those things. He knew he'd have a million pissy-ass replies perking up in his mind later on that day. Stuff about people who used other people. But that was for later. He shrugged his jacket on and stared at the sky. Morning was coming, pale and somehow weary-looking. Well, it had been one hell of a night, after all.

"So...give me this again," Snake frowned, rubbing at his wrists. "Alicia was working for that Japanese guy all along?"

"Onadera, yeah. Looks that way. Guess he must have thought he'd get a jump on that Yoshi dude quicker if he sent Alicia out with us two. And Alicia went along with it."

"So what'll he do now? Where's he going?"

"Shit, I don't know. Go help Onadera with his *yakuza*-wars some more, I guess. Whole thing's beyond me, buddy. Right now all I want to do is head out. We can still make LeatherMorn before noon, get some sleep there, start fresh tonight. Put this whole mess behind us."

"What about them?" Snake asked, jerking his head at Banzai-Man and Chile. Chile was shaking all over, whimpering again and again about how sorry he was. Banzai-Man said nothing. He just lay there.

Merle sighed.

"Hey," he said, going over and giving Banzai-Man's leg a kick. "You dead or alive, buddy?"

Banzai-Man shrugged.

"If I let you up, you gonna be trouble?"

Another shrug. Merle decided to untie Chile first. The little queen sat hugging his knees, sobbing like his heart was breaking. When he got Banzai-Man loose, the guy didn't do a thing, just folded his hands on his chest and lay there. He said, "It don't matter, bro. None of it matters now."

"Aw, come on. Alicia said he wouldn't tell Onadera."

"Maybe. Maybe not." Banzai-Man got up finally and slowly dressed himself. When he went over and picked up his sword from where Merle had set it down the night before, he looked so dog faced that Merle didn't have the heart to stop him. He looked at the blade and said, "Should just off myself now and get it over with. *Hara-kiri.*"

Jesus, Merle thought. Friggin' drama-queen.

"Got laws out here about littering, man," he joshed. "Hey, how 'bout you two come on out to LeatherMorn with Snake and me? We could double-up on the bikes. It's usually a pretty good time."

Banzai-Man shook his head.

Chile flung himself onto the ground at his boots, wailing and shrieking. Reminded Merle of an old Mexican lady he'd seen once in a church in El Paso. Banzai-Man pushed him away with one foot, not roughly, but not particularly gently, either.

"I'm going," he said.

"Well, here," Merle said suddenly, taking Onadera's money out of his pocket. "Guess you can use this better than Snake and me. Maybe help you get settled someplace. Get you a new bike, anyhow. Didn't bring us much luck, I guarantee."

Banzai-Man stared at the money. He peeled off a few bills, nodded at Merle, and started walking, the sword over his shoulder like a hobo's bindle.

"Hey, what about your buddy here?" Merle called.

"She's yours. She didn't bring *me* much luck."

"*Mine*? Now wait a minute, man! This is twice in one day somebody tried to saddle me with his boyfriend. I'm starting to get abandonment issues!"

But Banzai-Man was walking, headed for the highway. Looked somehow like he knew where he was going. Merle couldn't argue with that.

But Chile...he was a different matter. He hadn't even bothered to put his clothes on. Come to that, his clothes didn't amount too much more than his jacket. Merle hoped he had more back up on the ridge.

Chile rolled up into a sitting position, sniffling and wiping his mascara-streaked eyes. "You gonna take me with you?"

"Oh man, I don't know." He snatched a glance at Snake, who was over by the dead campfire, obliviously rolling up their unused sleeping bag.

Merle's attention was turned forcibly suddenly back to Chile, who was hugging his legs and kissing his knees. "Please, bro! I got nowhere else to go. I'm a real good bitch. I'll suck your dick, cook for you, whatever you want…."

"Hey, hey, that's alright," Merle said, patting awkwardly at Chile's shoulder. "Just…jeez, just *relax*, babe!"

All right, yeah. Just till they got to LeatherMorn. He doubted Chile was completely helpless, but he couldn't very well leave the little queen out here by his lonesome. Wouldn't be right…

"Hey Snake," he said, forcing a jovial note into his voice. "Hey buddy, come on over here…*got a little surprise for ya!*"

THE COMFORTING EARTH
James Williams

"It occurred to him that he ought to ask himself why he was doing this
irrational thing, but he was intelligent enough to know that since he was
doing it, it was not so important to probe for explanations at that
moment."
—*Paul Bowles, "A Distant Episode"*

Darren woke up feeling as if he had spent the weekend fighting his
way out of a phone booth full of thugs who were working him
over with rubber truncheons. It wasn't just that he ached—for ache he
did, from top to toe and limb to limb, inside and out and everywhere
else—but that he ached so *assiduously*: every muscle he could identify,
every bone, ever joint, every organ, his mouth, his nose, his eyes, his
balls, Christ, even his *hair* hurt, everything hurt.

He lay still in the semi-dark to keep the pain at a distance, and
considered. The noises he heard sounded like traffic on a two-lane
blacktop not very far away. He smelled hay—that would be alfalfa,
probably, still a wet green, nowhere near ready for cutting and baling,
but certainly enticing to a hungry cow—and motor oil, gasoline,
leather, iron, darkly tangy copper. He tasted the copper, too, and his
tongue had access to someplace in his mouth where he knew a tooth
should be. The evidence was starting to become ominous. He
experimented placing his hands in different places without moving
them too much because they hurt too, and he felt the kind of harsh
vegetative growth urban dwellers refer to as "weeds" growing in thick
tufts and stalks between patches of bare earth interspersed with rocks
too big to be pebbles and too small to be stones.

Satisfied that his hands had done all right with the ground, he tried
moving them farther. They got to his face, which was a good sign, but
he was not encouraged by the dull-wet stickiness they felt there, like
blood— very much like blood, in fact—that had not quite dried. But all
the pieces of his face appeared to be where they were supposed to be,
so *Yay*. Several conclusions were possible from what he had learned to
this point, but only one seemed likely.

He opened his left eye slightly and with difficulty because the
lashes were gummy and the light his lids admitted was tinged with red.
That would be probable in conjunction with the blood on his face, but it

was another not-good sign. Carefully, he let his lid prise the lashes up, and, without moving his head or neck any more than necessary, sent his shaded vision on a scouting mission. As he had suspected, he was lying on the ground, and his bike was lying a couple of car lengths away, apparently in one piece. Darren felt this would be a good time to go back to sleep, but first there was the matter of that other guy with greasy hair wearing really ratty leathers sitting in the shade of a gnarly old oak tree smoking a cigarette like some apparition from a bad alternative TV commercial of the mid-late 20th century. He expected he should have to deal with him. He opened his right eye, too.

It was about all Darren could do not to groan loud and long as he rolled onto his side and levered himself up onto one aching elbow. His shoulder seemed to shriek inside his body and he was uncertain it could prop him up. His head felt as if it were hosting a thunderstorm that had blown in from over Lake Michigan, and he could only hope his synapses wouldn't be struck by lightning. Breathing was an art he found he had not perfected: ribs, lungs, shoulders, back, no part of him seemed amenable and yet he willed it so: in, out; in, out; inspiration, expiration; create, destroy; live, die. He pushed himself further and got up onto his hands and knees. For a passing moment he felt like death in a bad mood in some cheap imitation Ingmar Bergman movie and thought he'd probably vomit up a whole set of black and white chess pieces, but like all other things, this too passed. From hands and knees to knees alone should have been an easy step but his hands were so cut up and the bones so bruised he felt they were twirling in tight vats of broken glass. He saw that they were leaving fresh blood wherever he put them and shook his head dispiritedly. He was just not having a good day, and it seemed he had already been working at this standing up business for a couple of years so far.

"Hep yup, brother?"

What?

"Hep yup?" Hep yup. Help yup. Help you up.

Darren angled his head toward the greasy haired man outlined against the white-blue Illinois summer sky. One of his long, dirty hands was extended down to Darren, who thought he could nod agreeably and then nearly fell into his Samaritan's knees while grasping for his paw.

"Luklak yewbee hort?"

"Looks like," Darren agreed.

"Wyntchew jeslah steeluhmint."

Darren didn't think he wanted to lie still a minute; he didn't want to relinquish the gains he'd made, but the planet had speeded up enough in its eccentric rotation that he was having trouble swaying upright, so he took the greasy man's advice and fell back to the comforting Earth.

"Lemme hepyewgit cumfbitul." The man bent down, and with a few very fast, strong twists, his spidery arms and crafty fingers split Darren's jeans and chaps and hauled them both down to his knees. The ripping denim stripped a piece of hanging skin off Darren's thigh, and the pain that tore his attention from the man's behavior also kept him from doing anything to protect himself.

"Sheeitmayn," the man exclaimed with glee, "yewdungohnan crappedchuseff!"

Already the length of the man's filthy leather pants was clamping Darren's neck to the ground so tightly he could hardly breathe. His wiry legs pinned Darren's arms to his sides, his bony knees clamped Darren's head like a steel-spring nutcracker, and the man bobbled his stinking, long, thin, coarsely-veined cock back and forth along his victim's lips. The funky smells of moldy leather, coffee piss, and ancient cheese told Darren the man must not have bathed in weeks, in months. He started to gag, but the man leaned hard on the pantsleg tourniquet and cut off the blood to Darren's brain. "Suhkmahdik," the man said softly through a playful smile obscured by spittle. "Suhkit lawngenzlow."

Battling to breathe, Darren obediently opened his battered lips and the man let up on his neck and began to fuck his face. "Suhkit, suhkuh, suhkit lawngenzlow." Darren took in air then closed his lips around the cock and started to suck it, thinking *long and slow, long and slow* as the dirty man dragged and dribbled across his bloody gums, long and slow to the back of his rasping throat, long and slow down his gasping gullet, long and slow, in and out, long and slow looking peacefully all around him at the sky and birds and occasional distant traffic, long and slow like a man without a care in this world or the next, long and slow the dirty man rode him, rocking long and slow on his face like a jaunty cowboy out for a ride on a dimestore pony going nowhere in the saddle long and slow. The man seemed in no hurry to come, and even slowed himself down and held himself back from Darren's lips now and then as if deliberately trying to prolong his ride. Long and slow he pumped his fuck, long and slow, and when he did come he caught Darren wholly by surprise, speeding up his movement not a whit but his head and shaft just filling up further on a single draw like a rush of air into some meaty balloon and then spurting all over long and slow from back to front and filling Darren's mouth in one, two, six, ten, a dozen separate, deliberate, salty, slow-motion bursts of thick, bleachy come and paying no attention whatsoever to Darren or the way he writhed.

"Oooaaahh," the man sighed in a slow satisfaction, milking himself of his very last drops into Darren's waiting mouth, "Oh yeaaahhhh."

He climbed off Darren, taking his leathers with him, and casually stood nearby pulling them on one leg at a time, with no haste or concern. He looked around and found his cast-off boots, battered black and scarred with use, covered with muck, and one with a flapping sole.

Dressed, he drew a cigarette from someplace in his beaten jacket and put it to his mouth. He fired it up with some piece of spark and left it in his lips. Smoke curled up from the end of the cigarette and ruffled the air all over the front of his stubbled face each time he exhaled. He stood over Darren and put out that hand again.

"Lemme hepyup now."

Darren put his hand in the man's hand and felt himself yanked to his feet. His jeans and chaps were still clumped around his knees. In a single swift motion the man tossed Darren up on his shoulder. He walked over to the fallen bike and set him back on the ground, pushed down on a shoulder till Darren sank to his naked knees.

"Nowyewgo," he said. "Wantsum hep?"

"Yeah," Darren nodded, looking up at the man.

"Spraydum."

Darren moved his thighs apart and started to work on his very hard meat. He was already at the edge. The dirty man smiled almost kindly, almost fatherly, and even though Darren knew about what to expect he took Darren by surprise with the speed and placement of his swift, sure kick.

Darren felt his balls erupt and the dirty man kicked him again. The third time Darren shouted and came, falling back to the Earth as he threw his hips into it, fucking the weeds, the dirt, the rocks, then more slowly, slowly, emptied, nothing. After a couple of minutes he felt shaken by a long, slow breath, and gradually he came back to himself. He rolled over and there was the dirty man, still standing and the cigarette smoking in his face without his hands.

"Yokay?"

"Yeah. Thanks."

"Kinyagetcher bayk?"

"Yeah. Thanks. Thanks again."

"Sokay. Seeyattuhbar." The man turned and sauntered away. Over behind the oak tree he climbed on a bike of his own, all highly polished black painted metal, shining tires, and chrome gleaming with care that roared to motorcycle life as if it had been just waiting for its rider. He straddled his bike as he had straddled Darren's face, pulled on a pair of sunglasses, and with the briefest of waves, rode straight up the grass embankment, onto the road, and off toward the westering sun.

Darren wiped himself off as best he could, stood up, and pulled his clothes back together. He stretched and tested his body, but nothing except his tooth was damaged even though he'd hurt for a couple of days. He stood his bike up and checked the few scratches: nothing he couldn't fix this evening. He'd go get a beer with Smitty and talk over the scene. Still, he wished there were some easier way to get what he wanted than this.

THE ROAD KILLERS
A. F. Waddell

The Road Killers roared the American West from desert to valley to redwood forest, conquering space with vibrating metal wedged between their leather-clad thighs. Adventurers, outlaws, philosophers, chefs, they were men loving men, men fucking men, telling the world to get fucked if they couldn't dig it.

On the road were raccoon and 'possum and rabbit and more, little fellas and mamas knocked shitless by sport utility vehicles and mini-vans and Cadillacs and more. The creatures were sometimes clipped and knocked roadside. They were sometimes hit and rolled under the vehicle, bouncing from tire to axle to tire to exhaust, as in some perverse pinball game. The occasional coyote and deer were seen, in various stages of post-kill bouquet and stickiness. This was where the art of staging came in. A good Road Killer could tell if the meat was edible, knew how to cook it over an open fire or in a Dutch oven, and how to complement various meats. 'Waste Not, Want Not' was the Road Killer credo, emblazoning their leathers and T-shirts.

The Road Killers had a growing rep. They'd kicked a big bunch of mean redneck ass at a bar outside Tulsa. They'd been minding their own business, having brews and a dance when the Okie opened his big mouth. "'Waste not, want not'? What kinda sissy faggot shit is that? Y'all one a' them anti-litterin' groups?" A melee broke out, a mix-master of pounding fists, cracking teeth, and cracking heads. Road Killers wiped the floor with Okie trash that night and split before heat showed. They'd discreetly camped in the desert that night, not even building a fire. The next day they'd boogied the back roads, popped over the Kansas line before heading West, then South, New Mexico bound.

Outdoorsmen, they occasionally hit the cities, cruising the generica of strip malls before hitting the Radisson or Hilton to rent a suite, dig room service, pay-per-view, a hot soak, and soft beds. Hotel squares and straights at the desk were often leery until Henry whipped it out: they'd feast their eyes on his big bills, his colossal cash.

They copped cash dealing weed and organic herbs and spices. The sensimilla was super. The tarragon thrilled. The rosemary rocked. The sage sizzled. Fragrant nights around a popping fire seemed of another time, a shared spirituality, a racial/genetic memory of wandering cowboys who rode and slept hard. Cicadas, mockingbirds and coyotes cried in the background of fire-lit dark. The mens' physicality completed a circle. Flying white-hot, human cries juxtaposed that of wildlife. The animals became wide-eyed and quiet, upon hearing an eerie human call of the wild.

Cruising South through New Mexico, Henry led the pack in scattered formation, followed by Jack, Chuck, Tony, Steve, and Rico. He likened their grouping to the instinctive V formation of large migratory birds; the group becoming seemingly one, a simple yet complicated functional unit, voicelessly communicating though a system of hand signals and head movements.

Motorists gave Road Killers the eyeball. A black woody PT Cruiser with whitewalls passed them: suburban kids from Santa Fe, smoking dope and chugging beers. Beer cans and lit cigarettes flew from the windows. Aluminum popped Henry's hog. *Goddamn bozos*. Road hazards were many. Flying objects tossed by clueless motorists, road junk falling from truck beds, and oil slicks were a few nasties that could spin a rider into road pizza.

A red Jeep Cherokee passed. Long hair blew atop tanned shoulders. Jeep Jockettes with coy bumper stickers were phenomena. The woman turned her head towards the group, licked her glossy lips, smiled and throttled. Pussy could be amusing, Henry thought. Doll-like women presumed to rule the world by flipping their manes and licking their lips. Henry and the boys sometimes loved to toy with them, before dropping a bombshell of disinterest and unavailability.

From a gray Ford Windstar minivan a couple gave them the fish-eye. From the back seat a young boy's face directly, moistly pressed glass, making faces, mouth wide open; another impassively stared. Henry almost shuddered at the thought of contained energy: car vibes of children and parents. In Henry's mind the vehicle flew through space, its inhabitants little planets unto themselves, throwing off pieces of molecular energy, which orbited their bodies. Car doors needed occasionally opened to avoid explosions. Henry read lips. "Justin, Trevor, be nice, don't make faces at the motorcycle men. Be nice!" was the motherly gist.

Supply runs were haphazard. The Outpost on 64 sported less-than-pristine merchandise: dusty cans of Vienna sausage in congealed fat, menudo, and beef stew. Snack bars with greasy chilidogs also provided incentive for The Road Killers to cook. They really cooked.

"Where you boys headed?" winked the smiling, heavily coiffed blonde cashier. Didn't she know that blue eye shadow and dark red lipstick were outré? That heavy foundation was unbecoming? That floral print polyester wasn't happenin'? She cracked gum. Henry's pet peeve. It tweaked his ears and nerves and induced murderous fantasies.

Crack. SNAP. Crack. Henry started to slightly tremble. *The GUM, dear GOD, the gum. Hands around her throat! Squeezing till she SPITS it OUT! "LOSE the GUM!"* Jack stepped in, touched Henry's arm, and spoke.

"We're headed west Now what do we owe you?" Jack paid for bottled water, potatoes, carrots, onions, aluminum foil, matches, and beer.

A north turn accessed an unpaved road. They turned left towards the San Juan River.

Preparing to make camp, they parked and unpacked sidecars. Chuck prepared a fire. The cook pit was a stone-lined depressed U shape with the tallest stone at the top. A portable grill would lie across the stones.

Tony popped a CD into the boom box.

"Hey man! I HATE that shit. Let's put on some real music!" Steve rifled the small CD collection and replaced The Village People with Santana's *Abraxas.* Steve, Tony and Rico stripped, passed a joint, walked the riverbank of willows and cottonwoods, and waded waist-deep into the water.

"Aiiiiiiiii! It's fuckin' COLD!" Tony yipped.

"Don't worry about it. It's wet, isn't it?"

After a long hot ride, water and Dr. Bronner's Liquid Peppermint Soap proved invaluable. The San Juan was chilly. Its depth varied. There was a drop-off point that caused a sudden and frightening descent. There was contact with other living creatures.

"Man, what the fuck was THAT?" Tony yelled. "I HATE it when swimmin' things touch my legs and nibble! Can snakes bite underwater do you think?"

"Yes." Rico smiled. "Water Moccasins can."

Chuck started dinner a little while before dark, giving lessons to the group. "There's no shell on the underside of an armadillo, see? Cut the stomach skin loose from the shell. Gut him. Start cutting him out of the shell by holding the knife next to it. As you cut start rolling him out. Cut and roll till he's out. Trim off the fat. Cut the meat into chunks, like for a beef stew. Season and brown with salt, pepper and chopped onion, then add liquid and vegetables and boil till it's done. The meat will have the texture of pork." He tossed the meat chunks and onions into a large cast-iron pot with olive oil. He stirred as they sizzled and browned, releasing their aroma. He poured in water, a little burgundy, and added potatoes and carrots. Organic Italian Blend topped it off. He covered the simmering pot.

"Wow, isn't this cool? A picnic table!" Strategically placed candles and lanterns lit the night as they sat and looked into their steaming plates.

Tanned faces with crow's feet shone in flickering light; glistening pink lips wolfed food and guzzled beer. Their eyes took a softer tone; the pace of their consumption slowed. Tony rolled joints, lit one and passed it. Steve took it, put it to his lips, inhaled, and passed it on.

Steve was suddenly talkative. "Listen now, I have a little story!

"Two guys are house-sitting in Marin County. A rustic little place in Larkspur. Great location. In the woods. Isolated...

"The decor left a lot to be desired, but what could they do? It wasn't their place....

"Plaid upholstery, rust shag carpet, cheap dark wood paneling. Black velvet paintings of Elvis and bullfighters. Of dogs playing poker. Oh, the horror, the horror...

"One night they're sitting on the couch reading, and begin to hear noises outside. Bumping, scratching, and rustling noises resound near the house. They investigate, walking out onto the deck. The noises stop. They go back inside. The noises start again....

"One guy goes back outside and says 'Hey! Is anyone there? Don't fuck with us. I have a gun!' he lies. No response. He goes back inside....

"Back inside, they resume reading, when...

"Thump thump THUMP THUMP go footfalls up the steps and across the deck! The front door flies open! A tall long-haired man sports a chainsaw! 'What have you DONE to this place?' he screams. BBBBrrrrrrr Bbbbbrrrrr! He cranks his tool and swings it, bisecting a doily-clad plaid recliner. 'The style was minimalist with neutral colors! What have you DONE?'

"'It wasn't US! I swear it! We didn't DO it!' The men scream in terror as he hefts his Husky. bbbbbbbbBBBBBBBRRRRRrrrrrrrrrr!

"Police found demolished furniture and body parts. Investigation revealed what is now known as the case of the Interior Design Chainsaw Killer. A disgruntled, deranged former homeowner, the remorseful seller of the property, has a psychotic break and returns to his former home. True story.

"I'm turning in now. Sleep well, my friends." Steve smiled.

The tired, wasted men mentally replayed the horror. *Chainsaw killers! Plaid!*

Henry and Jack lay in a double sleeping bag. The group used no tents, sleeping in the open.

"Did you hear that noise?" Jack whispered.

"It was only coyotes. Or wolves. Don't worry about it."

"I thought I heard a chainsaw."

"Silly. Pot always make you totally paranoid. Relax. You're safe."

Jack moved atop Henry, face-to-face, chest-to-chest, belly-to-belly, cock-to-cock, then down. Henry held the sides of Jack's head; it seemed a velvet-tunneled magical orb, hovering over him, sending a warm energy. Henry's prick sprung up: like a fat stalked mushroom from a dark grassy patch, a snake poking its triangular muscular head from the grass. It offered its sweetness: like an all day lollipop, a candy cane, a big spoon dripping cake-batter love. Jack's fingers circled its shaft; its head flared over his grip.

Jack worked Henry, their energy crossing boundaries of skin and nerve and brain. Sucking seemed an eroticization, a maturation of an infantile desire for satisfaction, a primal devourment. Taking his cock more deeply Jack mentally reiterated Blow Job Etiquette: Lips together. Teeth apart. Lay down a tongue cushion. Tongue on the sensitive frenum underside. Relax the throat.

Henry's force was delicious, insistent, inevitable. Jack accommodated him; he worried about hurting him, biting him, as Henry wildly moved in and out of his face. He relaxed his throat muscles. Henry's orgasm began; he drove deeper into the back of Jack's mouth, into his upper throat. Tension and expectancy preceded the throbbing and pumping of his semen, a cell raging burst of pearlescent milk white against pink. Warm and heavy, it splashed against the back of Jack's throat. *Swallow. Quick. More.* Come had a unique taste; Henry had a unique taste. Some connoisseurs considered semen to be an acquired taste. The taste allegedly derived from the producer's diet. As in cannibalism, vegetarians allegedly tasted better. The taste of semen was described with difficulty: to Jack it was salty, slightly pungent though pleasant, an exotic food of sorts. The texture was like comfort food: thick and rich and filling. Soon after he swallowed it, he was certain that he could feel it intermingle with his own body essence and chemistry, Henry's cocktail dosing him, feeding his cells.

"How about a swim?"

"Sure."

Carrying flashlights, they walked toward the river.

"Jack, what's the difference between a BMW and a porcupine?"

Jack smiled. "I don't know. Tell me."

"With a BMW the pricks are on the inside!"

The men's laughter echoed as desert creatures seemingly joined in. Big owl eyes and slitted coyote eyes twinkled as the animals hooted and howled.

DIONYSUS REDUX
Jeff Mann

Don's late, as usual. Five minutes after I've taken the roll, he strides into class, his boot heels resounding on the floor. He places his motorcycle helmet carefully on an empty desk beside him, then settles into his seat. His dark eyes meet mine, hold my gaze for a second, and then he smiles, drops his eyes and opens his notebook.

Today in freshman English I'm holding forth about the fearsome pitfalls of dangling participles, but I'm also studying Don, as I have all semester. Don's about twenty-five—older than the rest of these students—and very tall, easily six inches taller than my six-foot height. His eyebrows are thick and black and meet over his nose: a sign of lycanthropy, according to the folklore I've been reading lately, wild mix of man and beast. His long hair's just as dark, pulled back into a ponytail, loose strands falling over his face. His ears are pierced: silver hoops. He shaves rarely, his jaw almost always shadowy with beard stubble. He dresses as if he can sense my silent and carefully concealed appreciation: torn jeans, tight muscle shirts or tank tops that show off his prominent pecs and gym-hardened arms. Today it's a dingy wife-beater beneath a leather vest. And, always, he's wearing boots and carrying that black motorcycle helmet.

Don looks like I wanted to look when I was his age, a decade ago, when I was still single, still a little wild. I wore a lot of leather, I had a closet full of scuffed boots with mud-caked treads. I hit the gay bar of that West Virginia college town looking for sex, sex that, when found, was never quite rough enough. And I really wanted a motorcycle. That never happened: couldn't afford it, plus my family nay-sayed like crazy, pulling out all the statistics about fatalities, brain pans broken, and so on.

Now I'm gainfully employed, a quiet academic in yet another pissant college town, this one in the mountains of southwest Virginia, and I've got Tod, a sweet-tempered husband who loves to cook and keep up our little home. I'm happy, I think. But whenever I look at Don, well, it's difficult to discourse about grammar and, at the very same time, furtively study the black chest hair smoking over the top of that wife-beater, the tattooed black swirls on the left shoulder, the barbed-wire armband on the right upper arm.

Today, late September, it's especially hot in here—no air-conditioning in this building—and about the time I shut up and let the students form groups to critique one another's rough drafts, Don shucks off the leather vest and I can see, plain as day, the imprint of two heavy nipple rings through the off-white fabric of his undershirt. To avoid getting hard, I tug my eyes from the muscled curves of his chest and stare out the window. It's been a dry summer, and the oak leaves are wrinkled brown at the edges. I count them as they fall outside the screen. Torn and scattered tatters of a rough draft that just didn't work.

"Professor?" Baritone growl. Don at my elbow. The smell of him, like curry somehow. Or resin. Some question about his paper. I stare at his shoulder tattoo: dancing octopi, or a thorn bush bursting into flame. I clear my throat, breathe him in, and try to compose a reply without stammering. Why is it that we spend our lives struggling not to do what we most want to do? Talk about civilization's discontents. I want to bury my face in his musky armpit. I'm damned tired of being civilized.

Mid-October, midsemester. A lot to grade today. My office is small, crammed full of file cabinets and books on composition and literature. I'm marking freshman comp papers—"choppy sentences," "misplaced modifier," "paragraph unity?"—which means my mind's restless and wandering. After work, I've got to hit the grocery store to pick up the items on a long shopping list Tod handed me this morning. Tonight's TV lineup will be fun, especially after a few Manhattans. Maybe we can have Bill and Rick over for dinner this weekend. Maybe Tod and I can order those new blaze-orange guest towels. Maybe I can finish Nietzsche's *The Birth of Tragedy*.

Then there's Don's paper on the top of the pile. He may look like a big, dumb, muscle-bound biker, but the guy can write. Too bad, really: intelligence just completes the package. The inaccessible package. Our cat dropped a dead mouse on the doorstep this morning, and I couldn't help but envy animals, envy any appetite free of ethics.

Yesterday, as I drove off campus, as I waited at a red light, Don came up alongside me on his motorcycle. I watched the muscles of his thighs move beneath his jeans as he dropped one foot to the pavement. I studied the bike: a black Honda Shadow. When I was his age, I used to collect ads for the Honda Nighthawk. I wanted that bike almost as much as I want Don now. Just as the light changed, Don turned and caught my stare. He grinned, waved, gunned the bike, and we parted ways. I took my usual right towards the condominium complex, he took a left onto the road leading out of town and into the mountains.

Now, seeing little to mark on his paper, I'm trying to imagine Don shirtless, trying to imagine the pitch-black fur swirling over his big gym-thick tits. I'm trying to imagine riding that bike behind him. I haven't been on a motorcycle since that first time, when I was twenty, that summer down by the reservoir, when we college boys home from school used to drink cheap, sweet wine, lie around in the backs of our pickup trucks, shoot the shit and cool off in the lake. I can't remember the name of the boy who offered to give me my first bike ride, but I remember it was a Harley, and I remember that he had a half-shirt on and I could feel the wisps of hair on his belly as I clasped him around the waist and the vibrations of the bike gave me a hard-on.

Today I want to burn these papers and all these books. I want to tip over the desk, break my pens in half, toss my laptop out the window. I want to be up in the mountains with Don, out in the Indian summer sunlight, cruising down country roads afire with October-orange maple leaves, feeling his belly hair beneath my fingers and his hard back bare against my own bare chest.

Instead, I've got in my hands his freshman comp essay, which he held in his hands only hours ago. Over his typed name I run my tongue. Paper tastes like nothing.

Rising stiffly, I lock the office door, then reach for a Kleenex. I close my eyes, take one fur-rimmed nipple in my mouth, unzip the front of his jeans, pull out his cock, then mine.

"There's a scruffy one for you." Tod's always mocking my taste in men. Friends had warned me that you never end up with your type, and they were right. After years of romantic disasters, here I am, settled down at last. With a man I really, truly love, a man who treats me better than anyone ever has, a man who wears coats and ties and makes a corporate salary we both benefit from.

Still, even after several years with Tod, I can't help staring at the rough-looking ones, bearded rednecks like the guys I grew up around down in Summers County, the thick-muscled mountain men, the tattooed bikers like Don. Tod knows: he's caught me looking so often, he knows exactly what I like.

"When sexy boys turn to skank," Tod sighs disapprovingly, as I stare at another goateed guy, this one with a shaved scalp, huge arms, and an oil-smeared undershirt. Tod doesn't mind me looking, but he's made it pretty clear that I'm not to touch. "Don't even think about it," is the unspoken message. His Southern Baptist background has given him pretty strict standards of conduct.

Funny thing about marriage. All those years I was alone, searching for someone interested in more than a quick fuck, I just knew that once I found the right man I'd be a monogamous homebody. Instead, settling down has just highlighted the wild in me. But every time I talk about getting a tattoo or a nipple piercing, Tod presses his lips together and shakes his head. He's not much into kink, either, which more and more is what infuses my fantasy life. Pretty soon, if he has his way, I'll be as domestic as he is.

Today we're in Lowe's, shopping for a gas grill, a carpet, and a new reading lamp. As usual I manage to maneuver Tod down the aisle where the ropes and chains are kept. Picking up a length of clothesline, I grin at him and arch one eyebrow, wrapping the end of the rope around my wrist. Hope springs eternal.

"You have enough of that stuff already." Tod rolls his eyes and tugs me towards the carpets. "Come on. Let's find a throw rug that'll look good in the den."

We've got a new gas grill roped securely into the back of my pickup truck and are heading home, following the road along the river, when we approach the new Buffalo chicken-wings franchise and I almost wreck. There's some sort of biker convention going on, according to the sign, and, sure enough, I can see the sleek gleam of motorcycles lined up in the parking lot. On the front deck is a crowd of bikers. I can pick out leather jackets, dark glasses, black beards, tattooed biceps. And—I swear it's him, damn, I wish I weren't driving so I could see better—Don, leaning against the deck railing and sucking on a plastic glass of beer. Cheap beer, I'm guessing, not the expensive microbrews Tod and I drink. It's the last of the warm days of autumn, and he's as shirtless as he is in my jerk-off dreams. I get a vague glimpse, a glimpse smudged by 40 miles per hour: huge brown shoulders, a torso matted with fur as black as a country night, the ubiquitous beard stubble. Then he's gone.

"Christ, Allen!" Tod yells. "Red light!"

I slam on the brakes, and the grill bumps against the back of the truck cab. We come to a stop about a foot from the car ahead of us.

It's snowing on the last day of class. Don's without his helmet today, and I can't help wondering what he drives in inclement weather. Probably a pickup truck like mine: he seems like a country boy. It's been chilly since late October, and I've missed seeing his bare arms, his tank tops. Lately, along with a new goatee, black as India ink, he's been wearing dirty sweatshirts and a heavy black leather motorcycle jacket, but I still can't get out of my mind the sight of nipple rings outlined against his undershirt, or the maddening mat of chest hair I saw in passing on that warm afternoon at the biker's convention along the river.

Today I hand out teaching evaluations, bid the students farewell, and then leave them to fill out the forms. As I close the door, I can see Don's long dark hair, freed from its usual band, falling about his face as he bends over the Scantron sheet. Little likelihood I'll ever see him again. Hell, I never even got to shake his hand, much less suck his cock.

Tod's home early, leafing through seed and bulb catalogs. "I'm going to take a turn on the punching bag," I say, heading for our cramped basement gym.

"All right," he murmurs. "Remember, you're supposed to bake bread for tonight. And later, I want you to look at these daffodil varieties I want to order."

The punching bag sways crazily beneath my blows. I don't really know what I'm doing—never did get a change to take a boxing class—but it feels good anyway. I slam the bag till I'm gasping, switch to some bicep curls and some bench-presses, then head for the bedroom to undress.

Naked and sweaty, I sit on the bed's edge. I tug open the bedside dresser and run my fingers over neat coils of rope, a ball gag, nipple clamps, clothespins, a cock ring. Stuff I've collected for years, stuff I never get to use anymore. "Sick," was all Tod had to say when I confessed my leather predilections. He's so good to me otherwise; how can I complain?

In the shower, in this particular daydream, Don's soaping up my hole and tugging on my tits. I'm bent over, grunting through the wash-cloth he's stuffed in my mouth. By the time Don's all the way inside me, Tod's shouting, "Allen? What about the bread?" and I've shot all over the faucet.

I carefully wash the evidence down the drain. I towel down, rub lots of deodorant on—unlike me, with my passion for musky armpits, Tod detests body odor—I wrap myself in a towel and pad down the hall. "I don't want to bake tonight," I say apologetically. "Too much trouble. Let me grab a bourbon and I'll defrost some cornbread." Tod looks up, a trifle annoyed, before returning to his seed catalog.

Bikers are everywhere today, along the West Virginia Turnpike. I've left Tod with his laptop and his conference calls, and I'm driving up to Charleston to attend a composition conference. It's mid-April. The cruelest month, as T.S. Eliot puts it, and today I'm convinced it's cruel because, after the long gray-swaddled winter months, bikers and joggers and all the other sexy young guys I can't have are pulling their shirts off in this warm sun. The mountains are green-gold and painted with redbud and flowering dogwood, the air is crystalline, and bikers pass me right and left. Every other one I think is Don, coming up behind me in the rearview mirror. It never is, but, for just a few seconds, there's that sick, excited roiling in my stomach before the bike tears on past with someone else astride it.

I try to imagine how free those guys feel, with the spring wind in their faces, but my comfort-flaccid imagination just can't make that much of a broad jump. Every day this semester that I've passed a parked bike on campus, I've had to stop and stare and yearn. Occasionally, I've furtively stroked their seats, their roll bars, their fenders; I've tried to imagine what hot man's ass and thighs have straddled them. Now that I have a decent salary, I might be able to afford one of the cheaper varieties. But Tod's laid down the law, just like my family did a decade ago, just as he has with the piercings and tattoos. "Guess you'll have to find somewhere else to live," he says, a joke with an edge, every time I openly contemplate buying a motorcycle.

What a litany of names—Harleys, Goldwings, Valkyries, Shadows—the bikes I've seen on campus, the bikes that pass me today on the turnpike, loaded with the kind of guys who look like they'd hurt me exactly the way I want to be hurt and then some. Sun's pouring over my face, Don Henley's "The Boys of Summer" is playing on the tape deck. I unbuckle my seat belt and slow down long enough to struggle out of my T-shirt. Now the spring's rushing over my bare chest, and my nipples are getting hard. I roll one between my fingers till it hurts. The patch of hair between my pecs is speckled with gray.

I don't go to the Shamrock very often. Tod doesn't like to go out, but tonight he's on a week-long business trip in Chicago and it's a hot Thursday night in July and I'm restless, so I've stopped by the town's only gay bar for a beer after a dinner with friends. Since I'm fairly out on campus, I don't care who sees me here, though I do feel like someone's Daddy, considering how young most of the clientele are tonight.

The jukebox is blaring Pat Benatar's "Promises in the Dark"— whoever selected it must be at least as old as I am—and I'm a little dull on my third beer. One look around the bar full of twinkies convinces me that a hot affair while my husband's out of town is not very likely. These boys look like their definition of a rough time in bed is a night spent sleeping on a pea.

Benatar's about to finish up—*on the edge is where it seems it's well worth the cost*—when someone nudges my elbow. I look up, expecting that gay colleague in history who's bored me here before, then suppress a gasp.

It's Don. His hair is down, a black forest-cascade about his shoulders. He's grinning at me. The dense darkness of his bushy goatee reminds me of how much gray my own beard is already sporting. The muscles of his shoulders and arms remind me of how much I need to be getting back to the gym. The jagged designs of his tattoos remind me of how fucking tame I've become.

"Howdy, Professor." I try to look at his eyes, not at the shelf of pecs he's displayed so nicely in a black tank top. "Glad to see you here," he says. With that, he squeezes my shoulder and heads on by, a few more young leather-toughs following in his wake.

I down my beer in one big gulp and head for the door.

"Wanted to pick up my comp papers, if you still have 'em." The very next afternoon, and Don's leaning in the frame of my office door, that familiar black helmet hooked in one finger, a red helmet grasped in the other hand.

I'm worn out today. Couldn't sleep last night. Too busy wondering about why Don was in that bar, too excited realizing that he might be gay, too busy jerking off. As I stand and force a smile, a drop of sweat makes its slow way down my side, beneath my neatly pressed dress shirt.

Fumbling through several semesters of student papers, I've finally find his folder when the scent envelops me, a scent I remember. When I turn, Don's standing right in front of me, ripe in this heat. He smiles, slowly scratching one armpit, as if to release more pheromones, and drawls, "Found 'em?"

I've always been mute around men this hot. Nodding, I hand the folder to him, trying to suppress the nervous quiver running down my hand. Instead of leaving, Don shuts my office door. He sets the folder of papers on my desk. He places both motorcycle helmets on the folder, drops into a chair, crosses his long denim-clad, black-booted legs, and smiles at me in the lengthening silence.

It's hard to meet his gaze. Instead I'm staring at his big chest again, staring at the circular imprint of his nipple rings beneath another grimy wife-beater, staring at the silver chain disappearing into his storm-dark cleavage. Hair tufts out along the edges of his undershirt, curls over the top of it like ocean waves a few seconds before they break. He cups his hands behind his head, gives me a good long look at the wild bushes of his armpits, another good whiff of him, and he smiles some more.

My knees are shaking now, so I sit down, trying to think of something to say. Resting one hand atop his helmet, I ask, voice as steady as possible, "So what kind of motorcycle do you drive?"

Don laughs. He fumbles with his ponytail, loosens the leather band, and lets his black shoulder-length hair fall down around his shoulders. "You go to the Shamrock a lot?"

"No, my…partner isn't really into bars." Am I whispering, or are my ears just too full of my own panicked heartbeat?

"So why were you there last night?" Don asks gently, leaning forward till our knees almost touch, propping his bushy chin in one hand. His eyes aren't brown or green or hazel. They look black, as if they were all pupil. As if someone had carved them out of volcanic glass.

His knee bumps mine. Once, then, negating any possibility of accident, twice, and then a third time.

"Uh. Tod's out of town. Till next Tuesday. He's away at a—"

"You want me to kiss you?"

It's as if all the laws of physics were suddenly suspended. As if rain rose, not fell; as if lawn grass were indigo and the sky chlorophyll-green. When pigs fly? How about a Vietnamese pot-bellied pig with a wingspan the size of a condor?

"What, what did you say?" I stammer, just before Don's mouth is on mine, black goatee to graying beard. It's only mid-afternoon, but he already tastes like beer—maybe he's knocked back a few just to get his courage up for this outrageous and unexpected come-on. His tongue pushes inside me, and I respond—God, how could I not? I've been fantasizing about just such an impossible occurrence for months. I'm tonguing his lips and the soft bush of his goatee. His strong hands grip my shoulders, and my fingers run along the curves of his pecs, linger on those hard circles of steel embedded in the stiff and prominent nubs of his nipples.

Then I realize where I am and start pulling away. We might be caught, Tod will kill me. As soon as he senses my reluctance, Don's hands slip from my shoulders to my wrists. "Keep still," he commands, pressing himself against me, gripping my wrists and forcing my hands behind my back. He bites my lower lip, then shoves his tongue into my mouth again. I try to tug my hands free from his grasp, but he's as strong as he looks. His erection grinds against mine, then he pulls his face away, licks his lips, looks down into my eyes, and whispers, "We're gonna go for a ride. You'd like that, right?"

Only a fool would say no to a miracle. I nod slowly, then lean my head against Don's tattooed shoulder. He releases my hands, and now we wrap our arms around one another. He laughs softly and nips at my ear. He hands me the red motorcycle helmet, slips a finger beneath my belt buckle and tugs me towards the door.

The pulsing shimmers through my thighs, spreads through my groin and up my spine. Bikers must have perpetual hard-ons, I think. My stiff dick is pressing against Don's ass, my arms are wrapped tightly around his lean waist. It's terrifying, really, this close to the skull-shattering pavement, flying this fast through the air. I'd have a bellyful of bugs if it weren't for my helmet. The jade-green mountain landscape streams by as if the whole world were a wind tunnel. As if we were flying backwards into the past, or forward into a future without rules and without logic.

It's hot as hell today, and despite the 60-mph wind, we're both sweating. I can't smell Don at this speed, but I can feel the sweat matting the back of his undershirt, moisture beginning to meld with the sweat staining the front of my Oxford shirt. I reach up to tug on one nipple ring, he pushes his beefy pec against my hand, and my dick gets even harder.

Only a few miles on the interstate, and then he pulls off Salt Pond Road and heads up a tortuous country road I've never been on before. It only now occurs to me that I don't know where we're going, I don't know if I can trust him. He is, after all, a hell of a lot stronger than me. But isn't that what I've been wanting? To be out of control?

Near a covered bridge, Don pulls off onto the gravel berm, near an abandoned trailer. He lifts off his helmet, then tugs his wife-beater over his head before replacing his helmet. Half-turning, he mutters, "Take off your shirt." Those black eyes, like two onyx rosary beads, fix me unblinkingly. He seems used to telling men what to do.

I obey. I unbutton my professionalism and hand it to him. He stuffs both moist garments into a side compartment of the bike and we're off again. My naked skin's pressed to his as tightly as the laws of physics will allow, tight as the seam of the distant horizon, where sky and ridge-top meet and melt in a haze.

We ascend for miles, following the narrow road, looping around the mountain's flanks. High-summer pastures come and go, blue-green Appalachian vistas, the scent of honeysuckle. Then the tangle of wild grapevines, the shady archways of trees. Don may be the embodiment of wildness I've been looking for, but he's sensible nevertheless, taking the sharp curves with care, leading us further and further up the side of this mountain, the shabby white houses finally falling away until there's nothing but forest corridors and his wet lats against my chest, his impossibly thick belly hair beneath my fingers. I want to run my tongue down his spine, but the helmet visor's in the way, so I settle for squeezing his hard-on and feeling his nipples grow stiff between my fingers.

Don veers off onto an even smaller road this time, and now it's pure woodland, not a trace of humanity save for this thin band of asphalt that arcs up and down like an electrocardiograph print-out among gray temple-columns and leaf-canopies of maple and oak. We climb one last slope, and suddenly the trees fall behind, the road ends and we're here, this flat open space atop the mountain.

Don slows the motorcycle to a stop, cuts the engine and flips down the kickstand with his big boot. After a good hour's worth of mechanical roar, I'm stunned by the silence. There's nothing to hear up here but the wind, which is cool at this height, even in midsummer. The view is enormous: 360 degrees of mountains like distant surf frozen in the act of shattering, or shattering so slowly in the inevitabilities of geologic time that they appear to be static. The space is treeless, about twenty yards across, covered with flat rocks and low grass. There's this little muddy spot where folks have clearly parked before, and a blackened firepit, where earlier visitors have had their campfires.

I wonder if Don's ever brought a man up here before, to fuck by a fire. I'm guessing so. It would be cold by dewfall, even in summer, and two men would have to nestle close in a sleeping bag to keep warm. I haven't slept on the earth, beneath stars, for a decade.

Don climbs off the bike and stretches. He turns to me and smiles. The sun's slanting with late afternoon, and it glitters in the wet thatch on his torso, glitters on his nipple rings, on the hoops in his ears.

"C'mere," he says, still helmeted, and I do, slipping off the bike and standing before him. He grabs my bare shoulders, gently nudges my helmet with his, then drops his fingers to my chest and starts to work. I return the favor, stroking the steel in his tits, these tits I've been yearning to touch for so many months, flicking the pebble-hard nubs. In response, his touch intensifies on my nipples, and soon we've got a contrapuntal torture going, both of us grunting and hissing with appreciative pain beneath the helmets as each man squeezes and twists, digs his fingernails into flesh.

"Wuhhff!" Don moans. He pushes me away, tugs off his helmet, then mine. He strides over to the bike, opens one of the side compartments, then looks at me and raises one eyebrow.

"This all is what you wanted, right?"

My grin is so wide it must look idiotic. I nod, grasping my cock through my Dockers. The wind picks up, soughing past my ears. Now I'm unzipping my pants.

"So, how rough you want it?" Don pulls a coil of rope from the side of his bike, fashions a slipknot, and repeats that quizzical look. Over his shoulder, the sun's just disappeared behind a purple-gray cloud.

Suddenly I'm scared. And more aroused than I've ever been in my life. I drop my eyes to the grass, look up at the rope, tug my dick out of my pants, drop my eyes again. I can't seem to speak. This must be what the pop psychologists call shame.

95

Don's clearly had some practice dealing with confused kink-buffs who are too shy to ask for what they want. He's on me in a heartbeat. Suddenly he's grabbing my arm, pulling me towards him, shoving me belly-down over the bike, and pulling my hands behind my back.

"Whoa! Hey! Wait a minute!" I shout, squirming in his grasp. Sure, I do my best to struggle—well, not my best—but those long hours he's spent at the gym have paid off, and Don's got my hands tied in about thirty seconds. Another skill he must be well practiced at.

I'm about to continue the confused pleas I made as he tied me, but Don doesn't give me the chance. Instead he spins me around and presses my face into the midnight forest between his pecs. His skin is so hot it feels as if a lava field flows just beneath the fur. He smells like the forest, like new leaves and old earth. "Suck," he commands, shoving his right nipple into my mouth, and I do so greedily, slurping and licking, biting down, taking the salty ring between my teeth and tugging till he groans.

Don pushes me to my knees and takes out his cock. He rubs it against my forehead, my bearded cheek, teases my lips with it, then pulls my head back with a handful of my hair and shoves it into my mouth like a warrior sheathing his sword.

He's proportionate. It's more meat than I've ever managed, and I'm choking and slobbering and trying to steal breaths as he pushes himself in and out of me, holding my head in his hands. I deep-throat him as best I can, kneeling there in the mud. Mouth stuffed full, I look up at him, over the dark savanna of his belly, the spruce-dark hills of his pecs, steel tit-rings swaying and glinting like drunken moonlight.

Don's looking down at me as he rides my face, smiling gently, vaguely. He lifts his head to gaze out over the mountain vista I can no longer see, then closes his eyes and sighs, leaving me to look up at this beautiful vista of my own. I try to figure out what I'm feeling—other than ecstasy—as he rocks my head back and forth along his cock and his pubic hair tickles my nose. The only word I can think of is reverence. I've seen bodies like his in picture books—barbarian warriors, Greek statuary. He's the kind of man I always wanted to become.

He's tensing now, and I start swallowing his dick even faster, ready to feel him spurt down my throat, but he abruptly pulls out, shaking his head. "Not so fast, Professor," he whispers, seizing me by the shoulders to keep my eager mouth at bay. "I got some other things planned."

With that, he lifts me to my knees, then helps me off with my shoes, pants, and boxers. Now I'm standing here naked—in the middle of the forest, on this mountaintop—with my hands tied behind my back and my hard-on bouncing in the breeze. Completely at the mercy of this huge biker. Exactly where I want to be.

"Time to take a break," Don announces. He rustles around in his bike's saddlebag and pulls out a Mason jar. Grabbing my erect cock, Don leads me over to the scattered stones edging the overlook. There's a kind of natural seat here, a few feet from what looks like a steep drop into treetops. He leans back against the rock, then gently pulls me down to sit on the ledge between his legs, my back against his chest. The sandstone is warm beneath my bare ass; his torso's even warmer against my back. Don unscrews the jar and takes a big swig.

"This'll relax you," he whispers in my ear. He lifts the jar to my lips and I sip. I've had moonshine before, and this batch tastes like a cross between the surface of the sun and a bushel of Georgia peaches.

I gasp, the liquid tearing at my tonsils. Don takes another gulp, smacks his lips, and lies back with a sigh of satisfaction.

"Franklin County moonshine. I helped my Daddy make it. Pretty tasty, huh?"

I nod, take another proffered sip, then a gulp, before I feel the first symptoms of a buzz already starting up in my skull.

"Yeah, Professor, relax," Don mutters dreamily before knocking back another snort of whiskey. He tips the jar to my lips yet again, and again I take a big burning mouthful. A few yards from our feet, a hawk soars by. "You gotta relax if I'm going to fuck you," he says casually, his hand softly stroking my hair.

I stiffen. With Tod, I'm the one who usually does the fucking. No way I can take a cock that big. And with that fear, the thought of other unpleasant consequences rushes in. What would Tod do if he knew? Are these ropes around my wrists going to leave telltale bruises? Don'll split me open.

Panicked, I jerk away from Don, but he just laughs. With exaggerated care, he places the near-empty jar on the rock, then roughly pulls me back against him and folds his legs over mine, pinning me down. I manage "Hey, look, I don't think I can take—" before his big hand's suddenly clamped over my mouth.

"Oh yeah. Oh yeah, you can. I been wanting to ride your ass since the first day in class last fall." His other hand lightly brushes my silvering chest hair and starts in on my nipples again. They're already sore from our earlier co-tugging, and his present brutality only excites me more. I wish they were pierced, so Don could tug on the rings till I screamed behind his big hand.

When he drops his hand to my cock and starts stroking it, I buck and shake, just this side of shooting. He can read the signs, because he immediately desists. Don waits till I've cooled off a little, then ruthlessly starts in again, alternating between my aching tits and my bobbing cock, bringing me right up to the edge and then letting me down again. By the time he's done this six times, I'm begging against his moist palm, begging for release.

"So now I'll bet you're ready for me to fuck you, right?" he says slyly. Don pulls my head back till it's wedged against his shoulder and I'm looking up into his eyes.

"Right?"

My eyes widen. He kisses my brow. Once, then twice.

"I won't hurt you any more than you can take, all right? Any more than you want to be hurt. All right?"

Beneath his hard grip I muster a weak nod.

The seat is smooth leather, cool against my belly. I'm bent over the bike, legs spread, hands still tied behind my back. Don's stuffed a rag in my mouth and sealed it in with a band of silvery duct tape. There's no one this far out in the woods to hear me, but I figure Don just likes the muffled sounds I make, since he keeps saying, "Go on. Make some noise for me!" when he doubles over his belt and beats my ass till it burns. At this point—having dreamed of a scene like this all my adult life—I'm starting to like the taste of the gag, the way it fills my mouth. I'm starting to like the stifled grunts I'm making now as Don's goatee brushes my belt-sore butt cheeks and his long, pointed tongue works its way up my ass.

Beneath me in the grass, tiny blue flowers I can't name are blooming. When I lift my head and groan—Don's pushing a lubed finger inside me now—I can see the sun setting over the Alleghenies. Behind me, behind Don, as he greases up a second finger and opens me up a little more, the first stars are appearing and darkness is descending like a slow summer rain in the east.

Rustle of jeans being unpeeled, falling down around boots. Rip of a condom packet. He's on top of me now, whispering in my ear. Sweet words, endearments, reassurances. I can feel the chilly metal of his nipple rings against my shoulder blades, the head of his cock bumping at my hole. He kisses the back of my neck, rubs his beard over my cheek—his beard, moist with my ass-musk—and pushes the first couple of inches in.

Polka dots, glowing paramecia fill my sight. I bite down on the rag, determined not to sob. I can take this. I can take him. Tears are gathering in the corners of my eyes. I look out over the blurry valley, out at the blurry horizon. The sky's turning indigo, and the evening star has appeared.

Don gasps as the head of his prick pushes past my last resistance. I moan into the gag, tears run down my cheeks. I stare at darkening tree-tops as the rest of him slides in, on and on and on and on, till at last he's all the way in, his belly is rubbing my back and his breath is warm in my ear.

"How's that feel?" God-sent mixture of brute force and gentle concern, he's keeping perfectly still, letting my ass adjust, and slowly, slowly, the agony ebbs.

One big hand reaches up and wipes the salt water off my cheeks. "Baby, you feel so good." He tousles my hair, pulls out, then very slowly slides inside me again.

"Yeah, you're startin' to like that, aren't you?"

What can I do but nod? He's right. I pull at his belly hair with my bound hands, then grind my ass against him

"Okay, lover, here we go," Don growls. He wraps one arm around my heaving chest, claps another hand over my taped mouth and starts pounding me like Ragnarok's scheduled for tomorrow.

Don's come twice, across my ass and across my back. I've come twice, across the smooth leather of his motorcycle seat.

The moon's out, a sickle moon, a new moon. Don's foraged for some fallen limbs in the surrounding forest, and we're lying beside the fire he's started up in the rock-ringed fire-pit other lovers have used before. Crickets are chirping all around us in the dark.

We're both naked now, curled together inside this sleeping bag he's unpacked from his bike. I'm still bound and gagged. In fact, after he finished fucking me, after we lay side by side in the grass, heartbeats slowing, before he headed off for firewood, Don tied my feet together, then reinforced the rope around my wrists and ankles with the same duct tape he's used over my mouth. "I like you trussed up like this. Plus I don't want you getting away." As if I could get down off this mountain and walk back to town in the dark. As if I'd ever want to leave him now.

"You were real sweet, Allen. I been lookin' for someone like you," he murmurs against the back of my head, goatee soft against my scalp, one big tattooed arm draped over me.

"You all right this way?" His finger traces my eyebrows, taps at the tape over my mouth.

I nod. My shoulders and wrists are aching, but I don't much care.

"I'll let you loose in the morning," he says, voice trailing off. "Might want to fuck you again tonight.... Wake me up if you need to piss."

His cock's soft now, finally, and I can feel it snuggled against my ass, the ass it so recently savaged. My buttocks are still burning, and I'm pretty sure they're welted or bruised after the beating Don gave me. I have no idea how I'll explain those marks to Tod. I have no idea what I'm going to do about Tod.

Not long till Don's snoring. I'm pretty drowsy too, wrapped in the arms of the wilderness, here by a dying fire, an owl hooting somewhere. I test my bonds just to relish my own helplessness. I look up at the stars, that processional of mythological beasts, those supposed drivers of destinies. I look at the moon, a polished target moving over the black humps of the mountains. I study the tiny flowers in the grass beside me, the broken wings of maple seeds. I watch the rich carbon all fire ebbs into, the black earth and gray-white bones that flame always leaves behind.

WHAT MIGHT HAVE BEEN
T. Hitman

Often in my thoughts and memories, and sometimes in my dreams, I am there again before things turned bad. My hand is on Danny's stomach, freshly exposed with a yawn that pulls the tails of his old navy-blue T-shirt out of the tops of his jeans. At forty-three, the tips of his flattop have gone silver, but the crisp, thick pelt that covers the sculpt of his muscled abdomen remains a rich, dark color. Coarse, like wheat, it resists my intrusion. But now, as that one time in his apartment, Danny doesn't. My hand glides lower into the tangle of hair jutting out of the exposed elastic band of his white briefs. Inches below, hidden in his pants and underwear, waits the object of my search, Danny's cock. Like then, just to think about it draws all the moisture from my mouth and distorts the elements that surround me. I am on my knees, and my hand inches steadily lower. Getting there seems to take forever.

Fast forward to twenty minutes later and I'm on my stomach bent over his nasty harvest-gold couch, being fucked for the very first time in my life, a mere twenty-six years at this point. The incredible taste of Danny's come and the rancid dregs of his piss burn on my tongue. My humiliation has now reached its second phase. *Fuck,* to be there again, beneath him. My virgin hole stretched and no longer resisting his invasion, my belly filled with the dark communion of his male fluids, I imagine myself with that lost smile on my face. Foolishly, naïve, for an instant I remember myself thinking, *it will always be like this, this good...*

Good? This is the best I've ever known and perhaps ever will. The days ahead, I muse, are full of possibilities and what ifs, just as my asshole is filled with hard ex-soldier Biker dick.

I think about his rugged, thick tool inside me, sliding up and down, in and out, the human version of the pistons in his Harley, lubed and raw and loud. I get loud, too. I call out Danny's name, momentarily forgetful that there are windows open in his apartment. He yells at me to, *"Shut the fuck up!"* A moment later, and not breaking his stride, he shoves something into my mouth. I gag on the cottony invasion of one of his white socks. I see it briefly through my pain and excitement before it goes in. The toes are damp with a breathtaking afterimage of grime and sweat, his own version of the Shroud of Turin, powerful in its own magnificent way. Danny's feet stink the way a real man's are supposed to, musty and magical, the toes sour with his perspiration. I bite down on the stale sock in my mouth and suck on the moist cotton toes as he rams in harder.

Fuck me, I attempt to beg through his sock and my clenched teeth. *Tear into me the way you race down that fuckin' road on your Harley. Fuck me, you fuckin' cock-knocker! Love me...*

The words never fully emerge. The slap of his fat, swollen balls against the cheeks of my ass, the heady taste of his toes and the phantoms of his piss and sperm overwhelm me. I come into the itchy, dirty fabric of the couch cushion without touching myself, my cock road-burned into shooting by the near-violence of his fuck thrusts and the sensory overload of knowing, at long last, I've had Danny. He's mine. He will be mine. We'll become *we*, no longer just *he* and *I*.

The world erupts in a supernova of exploding stars as I travel too close to that prominence. Danny breaks his own rule, grunting loudly as his full, sweaty balls unload for a second time. His shouts, tribal and primitive, trail to whimpered cries as he readies to squirt hot gasoline up my butt. Before I can finish coming fully, he pushes me over the edge again into that most unbelievable of sexual myths, a multiple male orgasm. The hand around my waist, holding me tight against him and an anchor for his thrusts, pulls away, shocked by the geyser that sprays the back of his fingers. His other hand hits the couch palm-down in an attempt for balance. He's still inside me, hard and wet and on the verge of shooting. Danny whips out and pulls me off my back and onto the floor in front of him, and as he makes me take his load again, makes me taste myself on his wet dick, he huffs out an exasperated laugh. I look up at his face, his handsome, handsome face, blessed with those cold, blue eyes, that incredible full mouth, and the ring of that perfect, prickly goatee that's started going silver, and for an instant, I see him smile.

His ice age is over, and like the late spring day outside the apartment complex, he's found rebirth. It's all thanks to me. That excitement burns even brighter around us and inside me than the fire of his dick forcing its way past my sphincter, the scrape of his toned, hairy legs against mine, his foot odor and piss and masculinity that stink up the air and stain my flesh with sweat in the presence of such raw power.

Danny is smiling, reawakened from the frost, and the possibilities of what lie ahead for us seem so endless, so good.

I still think of Danny when I hear the roar of a motorcycle. I still remember him when I hear the sound of sirens.

The early November Friday morning I moved into the garden apartment complex on Lewis Lane in Atkinson, New Hampshire, was the last day of that year's Indian summer. My reasons for living momentarily blurred into the mountain range of boxes that clogged the apartment from front to back. Overwhelmed and facing the sudden silence of being alone again, I fell into the comfort of the lone easy chair sticking out of all that cardboard and closed my eyes.

This was what wanting more out of life had gotten me, the square box of a garden apartment in the middle of the woods. A front room at the front, a bedroom at the back, and a tiny kitchen and bathroom sandwiched in between. Breaking up with Jeff had landed me in a remote wooden apartment house set on the slope of a hill, with willow trees and hemlocks at the back, and facing 300 acres of conservation land across the lawn at the front. My dumpy car sat alone in the parking lot, gathering leaves from the giant willows that towered over the property. The silence was maddening, a stark reminder of what I'd left behind.

For two years, I'd lived with Jeff. The sex was silent and lame, the passion nonexistent. The most energy I could ever remember us exchanging was when he'd slammed the door following my last trip out with a cardboard box in my arms, and me tearing out of the driveway, leaving black tread marks in my wake. This wasn't what I anticipated when I accepted the fact that I was a true-blue cocksucker and could either live with it or go crazy in denial.

My ex wasn't much of a man, certainly not the kind of man I wanted to be with, needed to be with. I wouldn't miss him. My anger was for the years I'd never get back, years that I could have spent pulsating with someone else, engaged in the sweat-drenched, raw sex I craved, which had so far eluded me.

Pissed off and tired, I forced myself up out of the chair and pushed open the front room's sliding glass door, which looked out over the main staircase at the front of the building. A wall of warm air swept in. I'd fully intended to open boxes, organize, clean, *anything* to distract me from my unhappiness. I turned away from the curtainless sliding glass door and its view of the willows, the woods, and the small pond across the street, but as I did, I heard the distant roar of a motorcycle.

The rumble built steadily, until the entire house quaked with its power. I moved to the front door and gazed out to see a flash of chrome glinting in the afternoon sun, the unmistakable form of a Harley roadster, grumbling as it decelerated to a turn into the driveway below. The glint of sunlight on metal temporarily blinded me, but somewhere in that nimbus, I made out the raw, rugged shape of the man riding on the back of the hog. Dazed by the lingering afterglow, I caught a look at him, starting at his feet, perched on the pedals in large, black combat boots, worn and tightly-laced, showing a hint of white sock at the top, faded denim blue jeans, a black T-shirt tucked into his pants, and the black metal dome of his helmet. What I was able to glean about his body, the strong, hairy muscles of his upper and lower arms, his big hands, the trace of fur at the neckline of his T-shirt, stole my breath.

He stepped off the bike, stowed it into place on its powerful kickstand, removed his helmet, and marched across the lot and toward the house. The apartment complex had two sets of wooden stairs, one at each side of the building, but he took the main staircase, ascending it to the second-floor balcony, his steps set to the cadence of silent drumbeats. Stars still filled my eyes, making it impossible to see his face clearly, but I did make out the silver tips on black hair of a military flattop as he clunked past my apartment and plodded to the corner unit two doors down.

Each of his heavy footsteps on the balcony walkway made my heart quicken its pace. I caught myself unintentionally drawing in a deep breath, not only because I suddenly had trouble breathing, but more in the hope of catching his scent on the warm breeze swirling in from the open slider. My lungs filled with the warmth of the day, and to my shock, I realized I'd gotten hard.

This god was my neighbor.

I remember thinking then that my new life on Lewis Lane was suddenly looking much brighter. Unable to fight the urge, I stripped down completely, leaving a trail of clothes between the front door and my bedroom, and stretched across the bare mattress on the floor, I jerked myself to the most powerful orgasm I'd had in weeks.

I was still stroking, coaxing myself to climax for a second time, when I heard the roar of my neighbor's Harley, just shy of three in the afternoon. Glistening with a sheen of fresh, clean sweat and drops of drying come, I peered out the slider to see my car sitting alone again in the driveway. Later that night, as I lay in the darkness and silence of the house, secretly burning beneath a single sheet, he came back, his return heralded by the raw and powerful clarion of his roadster's engine.

Sometime before the dawn, I shot awake in my bed, crying out, soaked in sweat, sure the room had caught fire around me. Every inch of me tingled with the itch of imaginary flames. I was still orgasming into the sheet beneath me when I realized I had, in actuality, been humping the mattress and had teased myself into shooting due to my first wet dream in fifteen years.

I had to have my neighbor, the biker guy. I had to know that kind of sex, no matter the cost.

When I remember what sex was like before my move to Atkinson, I fall into a cold and numbing temporary void. The tastes and smells go bland, like Jeff. Worse, I remember his pitiful, shaved-hairless body lying on his back, a woman in every way except for the small knob of his penis. I remember his lisp, his persona, and the boredom of coming with him and his high-pitched yelps when he did. This was not what I wanted and I fled it.

Men, *real men*, have a certain quiet radiance, a strength, a smell—and not always a clean one—that is unique. Real mean are simple. White socks on their feet, soap and shampoo, beer, and rough, rugged sex. And some of them ride motorcycles.

Over the next week, while unpacking boxes and organizing my new apartment into something of a new life, I mentally took note of my neighbor's comings and leavings. The clunk-clunking of his old Army boots thundered along the balcony past my door and down the stairs routinely every weekday around three in the afternoon, only to return like a storm each night near twelve.

A few nights during my first week following the move, I'd turn out all the lights in the apartment and crack open the sliding glass door, just enough to let the gust of the cool November wind into the front room. I'd sit on the carpeted floor dressed only in a loose pair of boxers, pulling the leg aside and freeing my dick to hang hard at its full seven electric inches in anticipation of the attention I would inevitably give it.

I'd masturbate, fantasizing about meeting my neighbor in the parking lot, kneeling in front of him in the shadows of his Harley. In my mind, the smell of the motorcycle's still-hot engine mixing with his odors came clearly to my senses, raw, mean, and merciless. Stroking my cock, I'd imagine popping open the button fly of his blue jeans one snap at a time to reveal the slightly sweaty pouch of his crisp, white underwear beneath. His crotch reeked, in my mind, of the ripeness of his nuts, which had just ridden the leather of the Harley's seat down immeasurable roads and highways. In my fantasies, he ordered me without words to service him. Since I hadn't yet heard his voice in the real world, in my mind he only snapped his fingers, and that idea excited me more. He was a force of nature. He didn't ask. He just did like any other hurricane, earthquake, or big bang. He took.

While working my finger to the second knuckle into my cherry asshole, I dreamed of being bent over the leather seat, which in my fantasies was always still hot from his ass and balls. I imagined having his thickness in me, plowing me with the same motion he'd no doubt fucked plenty of women in his past. There were others, a whole cadre of them: Me on my knees between his spread, hairy legs and big feet as he sat on the toilet, sucking him off while he read the Sunday paper; Me licking the stink from between his toes after removing his old combat boots and stale white socks; Me on my knees, him urinating onto my face, into my open mouth, me swallowing his liquid gold; Me on my back like the choicest piece of pussy he'd ever bred, him staring straight into my eyes and not looking away, focused only on me and what I meant to him, tender when he needed to be, tough the rest of the time. A real man.

For several nights, I sat in the shadows just across from the open slider, dreaming these things but never allowing myself to cross beyond and come, until the distant roar of the Harley's engines made it impossible to hold back. Usually, by the time he pulled into the driveway, I was howling, unable to hold back, though the thunder of the Harley smothered my cries. When he was on the stairs, a dozen feet away, I'd gnash my teeth, trembling as the room altered from shades of obsidian and gray to burning tongues of red before my eyes. And when he walked past, his incredible body a yard from where I hid in the darkness masturbating to thoughts of his greatness, the world—and I— erupted in a blinding effulgence of stars colliding and universes being born from flame.

Then it would end with the sound of his door closing two apartments away. Soaked in sweat and spent, suddenly aware of the cold in the air, I'd pick myself up and shower and try to sleep, though thoughts of the kind of sex he made often crept into my dreams.

Once, a few days before I met Danny on a snowy, gray afternoon, I caught myself sleepwalking. Had I not bumped my hip in the kitchen table, I probably would have walked right out of my apartment and straight to his front door, my hard dick metronoming between my naked legs, my body, mind and cock possessed by his incredible beauty.

The day of the snowstorm—about a week or so after the move—I bumped into my neighbor on the balcony. There wasn't anything accidental about our first introduction; knowing his schedule, I intentionally waited until a few minutes before three o'clock that afternoon to get my mail.

The day had started as one of those bright, white mornings where the sky was opaque with towering, overcast layers and gradually filled in with dark storm clouds that threatened to drop the first snow of the late fall. My hands filled with forwarded mail, I marched—slowly—up the steps dressed in a decent pair of faded blue jeans, nice sneakers, a tight T-shirt bearing the name of our hometown Football team, and a light jacket. As I slowly fumbled with my keys, hoping to draw things out just long enough, I heard the sound of my neighbor's front door groaning open. Out he stepped, dressed in his military-issued boots, blue jeans, black leather jacket zipped up to the neck, and black leather gloves on his big hands, one of which clutched his helmet.

A few breathless seconds later, our paths officially crossed for the first time.

I glanced up at him, and for a brief and startling instant, time somehow slipped out of focus. My neighbor marched toward me, his head slightly bowed, the heavy, plodding clunks of his footsteps magnified by the distortion. He approached me in slow motion, and finally, I was given an unobstructed, clear, close-up view of his stunning features.

He was handsomer than I'd guessed before that moment. Not male-model perfect, with his unshaved, leathery neck, the grimace of his hard, angry face, and the visible scar on one of his cheeks poking out of the perfect ring of his goatee and mustache. But his eyes were the bluest I'd ever seen, and I couldn't be sure if my heart had sped up or stopped as he drew nearer to me, apparently lost in a miasma of thoughts I couldn't begin to guess at.

"*Hey,*" he grumbled.

Time came speeding back into sharp clarity. "Sup," I asked, doing my best to appear cool on the outside, even if my insides had ignited with the spark from his single word. I now knew what his voice was like: deep, heavy with secret pain. He barely made eye contact on his way past me and down the stairs.

Turning away from the open door, I said, "Nice bike." Later, I realized how stupid I'd sounded, how desperate.

"Thanks," he said over his back.

He cut across the front lawn to the parking lot. With the backdrop of his black leather jacket as a canvas, the day began to paint him with flecks of snow. I watched, mesmerized, as he mounted the Harley and pulled on his helmet. Flakes of snow landed on his shoulders and clung, intact, before melting under his body heat to roll down the dark slope of his torso. I, too, was melting and dissolving in my lust for him. He was all I could think about, all I wanted.

That night, I waited naked in front of the sliding glass door as I had on many nights. Only this time, I left on the light. With the snow still falling and my heart in my throat, trapped between the late November cold and the insane fire burning inside me, I waited and listened, listened and touched myself, fingering my asshole, playing with my dick for the fourth time since our meeting on the balcony that afternoon. Midnight came and passed. I wanted to shoot my load, turn out the light before it was too late and go to bed. Maybe, I wondered, the snows had made driving difficult, slowed him down from returning home. I willed myself to climax, begged my hand to move and not stop until my stomach was covered in come. I'd eat it, I told myself, and pretend the load was his, like I always did. But then, I began to imagine other reasons for his lateness. It was Friday night—maybe he'd scored some snatch and was, at that very moment, licking around it, eating it deeply, scraping its sensitive perimeter with his rough, unshaved face while sucking on its clit, making its owner buck and squirm. He was a cuntmaster. I thought of him, his cock rock-hard and pushing out horizontally from his unbuttoned blue jeans, his nuts loose in their sac. That sac, I was sure, was hairy and pungent, male-smelling and magnificent after eight hours of work. Every time I wanted to come and turn off the light, the fantasy of him about to fuck that faceless, nameless woman prevented me. I put my own face on her body. I wanted to be there, beneath him, I wanted—

The roar of distant thunder suddenly rocked the still, snowy night. It grew steadily louder.

Turn out the light, quick-!

I half-closed my eyes and resumed jerking on my tortured dick.

The Harley's noise crescendoed. A few seconds later, the clunk-clunking of combat boots registered through the chaos of my thoughts.

He's on the stairs! Don't do this—what if he sees you? What if—

A wicked smile broke out on my face. I leaned back until fully supine on the carpeted floor, in clear view through the open sliding glass door. I couldn't stop, wouldn't have had I given myself the choice. Unclenching my teeth, I stroked my cock to the cadence of his footsteps up the stairs and onto the balcony. And when he was right outside, I let out a breathless gasp, a wild, deep howl, and shot my load as his shadow passed by me.

Through still-slitted eyes, I gazed beyond the haze of the fire consuming me out onto the balcony to see him as he marched past my apartment. Both horrified by what I'd done and more turned on than I could ever remember being, some unaffected part of my consciousness realized he'd walked by the same way he always did, head slightly bowed, eyes locked straight ahead, completely disinterested in me or the world that surrounded him. My bold, insane act had gone completely unnoticed.

The coldness of the night struck me twice as hard, cooling the liquid on my belly and making me shiver. I closed the door and shut out the light and knew things would be different from that moment forward. To my neighbor, I was invisible, and my behavior had bordered on addiction, on insanity, on danger.

I slept that night without tasting myself and trying not to think of him, and woke the next morning to find everything changed. The winter had arrived, and as if to seal the end of the Indian summer, the end of the heat, when I went to get my mail the following afternoon, I noticed the Harley was gone from the lot. It was now parked under the building's overhang with a tarp thrown over it, and a beat-up black truck was parked in its place out in the driveway.

I channeled the fire inside me for my neighbor into my work. No more late nights and certainly none spent at the door; what I'd felt, craved, was now a lump kept repressed somewhere deep inside me like a cramp—constipated, unconscious.

I moved my desk into the front room where there was more light, and though I was aware of my neighbor's movements past the big glass sliding door, I rarely acknowledged him anymore.

On an overcast Tuesday afternoon there was a knock at my front door. One simple knock, like, I imagined, the sound of a bird flying blindly to its death against the house. I glanced up to see a person's silhouette on the other side of the front door's powder blue Cape Cods. The darkness outside and the soft incandescent lamp light inside had drawn a tangible line through the day. I crossed through the region of pale, photoscoping gold and turned the doorknob. A rush of cold air invaded the front room, sweeping up to meet me, infused with the clean smell of leather and approaching snow. Standing on the other side was my neighbor, the biker dude.

"Hey," he said.

All moisture drained instantly from my mouth, and for a second, I couldn't respond. Then I imagined myself standing there, looking stupid with my jaw dropped. The cool, confident façade returned to my face.

"Hey, man," I answered.

"You got any beer?"

In something of a daze at his request, I remembered there was a six-pack of the light shit in my refrigerator, along with precious little else. A wave of icy-hot excitement rippled through my insides, telling me my lust for my neighbor wasn't as dead as I'd thought, just dormant. I could feel it waking, stretching, hungry to be fed, a sudden, aching emptiness inside me.

"Come on in," I said, stepping back from the open door, extending a hand that I'm sure must have been shaking.

And just like that, Daniel Frederick Mosier stepped into my life.

"...*Gregory*," I said, meeting his shake with my one free hand. "Nice to meet you, dude."

Danny's grip was rough and electric as he responded with his name. I shook back, trying to match his strength, hoping to prolong our contact. Time again seemed to slow as I imagined the fingers of that hand gripping the bars of his Harley, more, gripping his cock when he pissed and when he masturbated, using them to pleasure himself or his partner or to scratch at his nuts or pick the sock fuzz from between his sweaty toes. Hot coals filled my mouth, and after handing him the cold can in my other hand, I returned to the fridge for a beer of my own. I needed that drink now. I heard him pop the lid behind my back. Retracing my steps, I saw him knock back a swig, his hairy throat knotting under the influence of a heavy swallow.

"You got nice things," he growled, looking around my apartment. He scanned the stack of papers on my desk, the still-uncapped blue fountain pen, the idle computer whose screensaver shifted between images captured by the Hubble Telescope.

"I don't own a Harley," I joked, taking a sip of the cold-piss beer.

Danny didn't pick up on the thread, and instead continued with his original statement. "I don't own shit. But I've never been broken into since I moved in here."

"How long ago was that?" I asked.

"Few years ago." I nodded and commented on it being a good thing. And then, between sips of cold beer, he said, "I see you sitting there at that desk sometimes. What are you doing?"

I shuffled from one foot to the other and shrugged. "Writer. I'm a writer," I said.

Danny's face muscles flexed the slightest as he registered the information. I expected him to ask the next standard question—*What do you write? Novels, articles, short stories, screenplays?* But he didn't. His interest began and ended with the clenching of his rugged jaw.

"You?" I asked.

"Shit job," he said. "Work second shift in a factory. It fuckin' sucks."

He offered no more than that, and instead knocked back the remains of his beer and set the empty can on the desk beside my notepad and pen. "Thanks for the beer," he growled. "And welcome to the neighborhood."

He checked the place out one last time with an absent glance and headed for the front door.

"See you around," I said. "Come again sometime."

He stepped from the light back into the shadows on the other side of the door. The beer in my empty stomach quickly soured, and I was aware of the mildly painful itch from the erection I'd popped snagging in the elastic waistband of my underwear.

But I didn't touch it.

*

There are times when the memories come so clearly—

I see myself standing on the balcony, watching Danny walk away from me, and I can see with haunting clarity the back of his scalp, freshly buzz-cut, the pink of his skin visible through the neat patterns of hair.

I see his eyes, flaccid with defeat, barely noticing the world around him as he walks through a dark winter day wearing invisible blinders that guide his steps.

All winter long, the Harley hibernated under the balcony overhang. Danny and I had a few more encounters in the real world, nothing special or memorable. But the ones we had in private, in my fantasies, proved explosive.

Winter's cold faded and the days grew steadily longer again, warmer. And when spring returned, so did the heat inside me, the lust for him that still controlled me.

One warm Saturday morning, feeling lonely and horny and miserable, I plodded down the stairs to get the mail and saw that Danny was removing the tarp from his motorcycle. The Harley glistened and glinted in the direct May sunlight. He knelt and bent and stood beside it, checking connections, inspecting for damage, toying with it, completely oblivious to my presence.

That entire day and into the early night, I walked around half-hard, shaking nervously, unable to focus on anything. My behavior was irrational. There was no way to reason why I did it, why I bought a six-pack and, with it hanging from my shaking hand, why I walked from my apartment to Danny's later that night. It was around nine in the evening. A raw, muggy sheen of mist hung over the world.

I knocked on Danny's front door. The glow of the TV behind the thick curtains of his sliding-glass door shifted with the movement of a shadow. I heard his footsteps approach the door. The door opened, and Danny appeared, looking gruff and tough and slightly pissed by my invasion.

"Heya," I said. I held up the six-pack for him to see. Danny's amazing blue eyes shifted to the sextet of aluminum cans. "Thirsty?"

"Yeah," he said. "Come in."

I walked for the very first time into Danny's apartment, and in so doing, crossed a line from which there would be no returning.

Danny's apartment was physically identical to my own, but with marked differences. An ugly couch with dirty harvest-gold cushions sat jammed between his slider and a kitchen table. The table was covered in mismatched plastic containers, cups, half a loaf of bread in its bag, a cooking pot, and a few empty beer cans. A pile of clothes, his discarded boots, and a toolbox sat on the floor near Danny's TV, which was tuned to the Saturday night baseball game. I noticed a pair of dirty white socks in that pile. My eyes darted down to Danny's bare feet, big and perfect and magical. The only other elements in the room were a scarred leather chair, an ugly lamp, and a crude watercolor painting hung by a thumbtack on the wall above the couch.

A musty, stale odor infused the air, raw and male, yet not unpleasant. The apartment was a mess. With the dark heavy curtains barely stirring in the humid night breeze, it felt more like a cave. Danny's cave.

I sat on the couch. Danny took the old leather chair and grabbed a beer from the ring of cans. I almost choked on my first gulp of suds. A nerve-wracking silence settled over the room. I settled back on the couch's ugly, smelly cushions and drew in a deep breath of the masculine stink in the air. Was it always this quiet here, this somber?

Nonchalantly, I studied the apartment, whose core had plagued my fantasies for months. It was darker, dingier, danker than I'd imagined. My eyes rolled back to Danny, to his big, sexy bare feet. In the poor light, I detected the small lines of dark fur on his big toes and the trace of leg hair above his ankles, poking out of the cuffs of his blue jeans.

My cock swelled at that image. I found myself breathless, drank more of the smell in the air than the beer, oblivious to just about anything except my desire for him. Shaking my head, unsure how to broach the subject of my seduction, I stammered, "This is sad."

The leather chair creaked slightly. Danny tipped his furrowed gaze in my direction. "Huh?"

"It's Saturday night and the two of us are sitting here watching baseball instead of getting laid."

A sarcastic smirk broke on Danny's face. I distinguished it instantly from a true smile. "Getting laid? What's that?"

I fought the urge to think of how many times he'd laid me in my masturbation fantasies. "Been so long, I can't remember," I chuckled. The conversation again fell to silence in the tenebrous confines of his apartment, my comment about sex as overlooked as my comment about writing and my performance six months earlier at the open sliding glass door on that long-ago November night.

"So what about you?" I asked, an invisible hand choking my throat.

"What about me *what?*" Danny grumbled.

"You know," I said. "You dating anyone? You getting any?"

"Naw, not really," he said. His eyes remained glued on the television, but I sensed he wasn't really watching the baseball game so much as he was avoiding the truths I was digging at. I couldn't help but ponder the pain he must have known in the past, the heartache and heartbreak that had left so handsome and desirable a man little more than a zombie, a shell of his former self.

A sad, sinking feeling formed in my stomach, an invisible ball of rusted nails and broken glass.

I'll save you from this, Danny, said a voice in my head. *I'll give you the kind of sex no woman before me has ever shown you—if you give me what no man yet has...*

I felt my lips twitch with the words, feared I might actually speak them and reveal my true reason for being in his apartment.

Let me suck your dick, Danny. Let me save you from your loneliness and in so doing save myself from mine. We could be so good together. You're everything I've ever lusted after, ever loved in a man, from head to toe. Fuck me on your Harley, Danny. Just fuck me!

My mouth was hanging open when he said, "There was this one chick. She gave me that—" He aimed his left fuck-finger above my forehead. I twisted around to see the paint-by-numbers landscape tacked to the wall.

"Was she any good?" I heard myself ramble.

"She was okay. Fuckin' bitches, they're all the same." He burped and finished off his beer. Then he stood, shuffled past me and his discarded combat boots on his way to the table for another. As he passed, I caught the side profile of his cock, hanging full and meaty in the crotch of his pants. The room around me ignited in a blinding display of temporary stars.

"Big stud like you must get all the pussy he wants," I joked, the words flying automatically from my mouth.

"Naw, not since the Army, and that was a long time ago," Danny answered with his back turned toward me.

I studied his ass, square and perfect and muscular, less than a yard from my face, the curve of his back, his large, hairy arms, that region of pink skin at the back of his skull visible through the clip-pattern of his buzz cut. I drank the last of my beer, sure I'd pass out at any second. This was it. I had to come clean and let him know how I felt.

"I know where you can get some. At the very least, a hell of a blow job."

"Yeah?" he grumbled, no change or excitement in his tone.

Without blinking, eyes burning, and my tongue suddenly as leaden as his feet when he walked, I confessed, "Oh, yeah."

Danny revolved and approached the leather seat. Halfway there, he stopped and stretched, an action that exposed the taught, hairy sculpt of his stomach from the bottom of his T-shirt. Before I could stop myself, and not sure I would have if sanity had prevailed, I reached out, placed my hand on the hairy warmth of his muscular abdomen, and swept it down toward the meaty fullness of his groin.

It was the only instance in my life, to date, when I somehow found my consciousness removed from my actual body. An astral projection, a waking dream. Suddenly I was outside my skin, watching the scene unfold from across the room. There stood Danny, caught in a stretch, momentarily lost in his pose, with me on the couch, one hand gliding down the topography of his fur-covered stomach. I saw it all clearly, and somehow even felt it, even though I was two separate entities—the warmth of his skin, the ripple of his muscles jerking away from my violation.

My hand cupped Danny's cock.

"I'll suck you off, man," my physical self said.

I squeezed Danny's manhood, and he let my touch linger there.

At least for a second...

I see it all so clearly, still, six years after that May night in 1997.

I see him, shocked out of complacency by the invasion of a hand to part of his body no other man is ever supposed to touch.

I see me, desperate, in danger from having gone too far.

Danny knocks my hand away. His eyes are wide and focused, showing the most life I've yet seen from him. He looks so pissed I'm scared, and yet, in this disconnected state, I'm even more conscious of the fact that I've actually touched his cock. I've felt his nuts roll under my palm. I've felt his dick, thick and meaty, twitch in response to my touch. At long last, in a manner, I've had him!

Then the truth of the situation strikes, and I realize what I've done. Danny knocks my hand away and bellows, "Don't fuckin' do that, dude!"

And my two halves collide, becoming one disoriented creature again, seated at crotch level before him.

"Come on," I plead. "You like head, don't you? I'm totally into giving it. You knew I liked guys, right?"

Danny goes silent, but still hovers menacingly over me. I think about reaching for him again to cement the point, mostly to feel that incredible thickness of his for a second time.

"It could be perfect," I say instead. "You and me. I could be your cocksucker, dude. You could use me to service you, make you feel good, feel like a man, any time you want—"

"Get out," he snaps. He turns his back to the baseball game and sits in his old leather chair.

"Danny—"

"*Get out!*" he bellows. The anger in his voice shocks me out of my paralysis. "Leave the beer."

I leave the beer and stagger out the door and back to my place two apartments distant. Sweat soaks my skin, and I'm on fire internally. Part of me wants to cry in the face of his rejection. But my heart races. I've touched his cock. *I've touched Danny's cock!* So I masturbate instead, knowing I'll surely cry later. First, though, I have to come.

I come three times before the night is over.

And then I weep.

The next day is warm, too, but a sultry May breeze sweeps in from the windows. I'm sleeping when a loud thump rocks the silence of my apartment.

Naked, nervous—my heart would race for days following these events—I stagger to the front door. I push the Cape Cods aside to see Danny standing on the front step. He's come to punch me out, to murder me or at the very least fuck me up real good for grabbing hold of his dick last night, I'm sure.

"*What...?*" I call through the door.

"Can you help me with something?"

I choke down the invisible knot in my throat and crack open the door. "I'm in bed, dude. What do you need?"

Danny's gorgeous blue eyes lock with mine. "The battery on my bike's dead. Can you give me a push so I can pop it and get it started?"

The request catches me completely off guard, leaving me as surprised as Danny was when I felt him up twelve hours earlier.

"S-sure," I say. "Give me a few to get dressed, 'kay?"

Danny nods. His cold blue eyes travel up and down, but saying nothing more, he clunks past my sliding glass door in the direction of his apartment.

For the next hour, I sit on my bed and debate my offer to help him, unable to fathom why I let life lead me to this place. The weight of his rejection presses fully on my shoulders, the guilt of my violation against him, on my conscience. Sure, I'll help him push an 800-pound hog up the slope behind our house so he can pop the clutch and start the engine. Fuck, though, what if that's not what he's really planned. Maybe he does want to hurt me. He could. He's ex-military. He's tough. What if he wants to take me up on my offer? He could do that, too. Dump his nut-juice on my face. Shove his big, hard soldier's dick up my virgin pussy.

While contemplating what to do next, I hear Danny tinkering under the overhang, and I remember seeing him down there fiddling with the

Harley's plugs and gauges, testing the tires, cleaning the chrome. He just wants a jumpstart. I can give him that. I owe him that.

And yet—

Part of me refuses to give up home, refuses to think he is so far away from happiness that he's only staring into an abyss of incredible sadness. Maybe, just maybe, he's spent the night considering how good it would be to agree to my offer, to use my mouth, to not be so alone. A mix of fear and excitement fills my body. Tense, I pull on a pair of light blue sweats, no underwear, a pale green T-shirt, white socks, and my sneakers. The day, I am sure, will end with either heartbreak or complete happiness, nothing in-between. Little do I think it will embody both extremes.

I exit the front door. Danny isn't at his bike, beneath the overhang. I look down the balcony to see his front door slightly ajar. My heart drums in my ears as I head toward that beckoning portal, lay a hand on the door, and push it open. Like a trap leading to the underworld or an invitation to enter Heaven, the door quietly opens, releasing the familiar, musty smell of the apartment's interior.

"Danny?" I call weakly.

"Yeah," I hear him grumble.

I step inside the door, enough to close it behind me. I hear the click of the latch falling securely in place, sealing us in together. Danny is kneeling near one of the open toolboxes, giving me his back. Unconsciously, hungrily, I study the firm square of his ass, showcased to perfection in denim, a hint of a white sock at the top of one boot, that region of pink scalp at the back of his head. I draw in a deep breath of the male-smelling stink in the air and feel the corners of my mouth twitch into an appeased smile. How could I be here again, so powerless in his presence, wanting him so desperately?

"*Danny,*" I repeat, this time louder.

He stops fiddling with his tools and stands, his eyes aimed at me harshly. I sense he really isn't look at me, but through me. I step closer and say, "About last night."

"What about it?" Danny snaps coldly.

"What I said…what I did—"

"So?" he grumbles.

Part of me wonders if he's somehow forgotten the whole incident, of if he's so disconnected with reality, with life, with humanity; was he even paying attention when I fondled his cock? Worse, am I the disconnected one? Did I imagine the whole thing?

"So…what I did…" I stammer.

"You touched my prick, dude. That wasn't cool. You're a cocksucking faggot," he says.

The words slice through me, figuratively and physically. Anger rises inside me, brought to the boiling point by his insult, his frigidity. But as I stare at him, horrified and momentarily speechless, I realize how relieved his words have left me. He's stripped away all pretense, all bullshit. He's somehow freed me from the cage my lust has built around me for the last six months. I'm free.

"Yes," I say clearly. "But I'm the cocksucker you need right now to help you." His eyes narrow. "Danny, in the whole time I've lived here, I've never seen one person enter this place. Not one visitor, not one guest. You don't have a single friend on this planet except *this cocksucker*, and if you want me to help you push your bike, you're gonna have to be a friend back and listen to me. You're gonna have to consider that I could be the best thing that ever happened to you."

My outburst shocks us both. The room again falls quiet. I face him, and this time, it's me who doesn't blink.

"Danny," I continue in a softer voice. "When I look at you, I see perfection. You are so handsome, all I can think about is how badly I want you, to suck on your cock, to let you come in my mouth. To make you feel good, better than any woman ever has. I want you so badly it's all I can think of."

"You want to suck my cock?" he growls.

I nod. "It would be so good for both of us. Can't you see that? My mouth, your dick. I'd give you anything." I drop to my knees in front of him. His mean, narrowed eyes follow me. "Won't you just consider it?"

The space between us, no more than five or six feet total, becomes a gulf. The silence in the room grows strangulating; the air seems to double in weight. Danny's rugged, brutal good looks take on the pallor of granite, cold and primal. I look at him and I fear him, fear the rage he's bottled behind that stony façade. Like a volcanic mountain holding back the pressure of magma, Danny's face turns a shade of red, crimson, explosive. I recognize the danger I've willingly placed myself in, the all or nothing of where he and I now stand due to my confession.

Danny shuffles closer, closer yet. Another footstep puts his crotch right in front of my face.

A shudder trips down my spine, pitching the world temporarily out of focus. Just when it stabilizes, Danny throws back his head and stretches, sighing out a deep, exhausted breath. The navy-colored T-shirt tucked loosely into the top of his blue jeans rises up, exposing the crisp, dark fur on his muscled stomach, and he says, "Suck my cock, cocksucker…"

Hands shaking, I work to free Danny's magnificent cock from the prison of his pants, and then his underwear. His jeans go down past his knees with a savage yank that bares the incredible contour of his solid, hairy legs. Danny's scent is released, a mix of soap and testosterone and clean male skin along with the heady natural musk of his balls.

I take hold of the elastic waistband of his tight whites but hesitate only long enough to press my nose to the meaty bulge in his underwear. I take a deep whiff of his heavenly smell, and then another. Soon, I'm intoxicated.

"*Cock-lover,*" Danny growls above me. He shuffles in place. I fear he'll back away from me and deny us both the joy that's sure to follow. I place a hand on his powerful quads to steady him and marvel as his leg's fur scrapes beneath my palm.

"I love *your* cock," I whisper, breathing in the fumes from his package.

Somehow, I get him out of his combat boots. His funched-down pants follow. I sniff his feet and find them every bit as wonderful and smelly as I've hoped. The stale, masculine stink of his toes nearly makes me come without touching myself. Slowly, I peel off his socks. How I've wanted to lick Danny's big, handsome feet. Now I do. His scent marks my face. I can smell it now, taste it, his straight man's musk has claimed me as his property.

Slowly, seeming far slower than the actual few seconds it takes, I tug at Danny's tight, white briefs. The thickening tube of his meat does a logroll down with his underwear before popping out into view, flopping half-limp, half-stiff over the swollen, hairy come-tanks of his nuts. Danny's cock is fat at the center. The head is shaped like an arrow and scored with pink concentric lines that all converge at the bull's-eye of his pee-hole, which is closed tightly, and perhaps has been for some time, flexing open only to piss. His shaft is pockmarked with bumps and grooves, scars and imperfections, the way a man's cock is supposed to look. To me, it is the most perfect thing I have ever beheld.

Danny's nuts hang loose in their hairy sac. A dense pelt of dark fur encircles all.

"Suck it," he orders. There is no mercy in his voice.

Licking my lips, I lean in and open wide. Through my disbelief, some still-functioning register in my mind records the events in every senses-stirring detail. I suck on his fleshy pole, feel it bone at its center and push back against my tongue. I smell the maleness of his bush, his balls. I taste salt, something else—sweat? The unshaken, now-dried residue of his last piss? Sperm?

As fast as I suck him into my mouth, I spit out Danny's cock for a taste of those hairy nuts. I see the clamped-shut piss-slit on the head of his dick winking back at me, wide, wet, happy. He is now fully erect. I quickly suck one of his nuts into my mouth, give it a gentle tug using my throat muscles, and then release it for its slightly fatter twin. I lather the back of his ball-bag with the tip of my tongue, lick at the smelly patch of skin where his nuts bang against his asshole, and steal a taste of his most-private, forbidden place before Danny orders me back to suck his dick.

I take his cock between my lips and focus on giving him the kind of sex, of a quality he's likely never had prior to this breezy, warm May day. I have licked the stink of his foot odor from between his toes. I have sucked on his balls and tongued a taste of his asshole. I've touched his hairy legs, his stomach, taken his cock into my mouth. None of my fantasies can compare to the real-deal!

Glancing up, I see him, harsh but handsome Danny, too beautiful to be believed, and for one moment, with his stiff cock pistoning in and out of my face, the barest trace of a smile cracks his angry expression. This is how I want to remember him, smiling like that, eternally happy in that moment as if he, too, can see the potential joy in the days that lie ahead of us. He even unfolds his arms, places one of his rough hands on my shoulder. He strokes his stomach with the other.

I nurse on Danny's incredible cock and he rewards me for my worship. I sense it coming in his grunts, no longer angry but vulnerable with passion, and the way his low-hanging sac of bull-nuts draws up tight around the base of his shaft. His cock turns to steel on my tongue. This is it. This is what I've dreamed of, obsessed about, his come—

Danny huffs, *"Fuckin' cocksucker!"* through clenched teeth. I suck harder. The first blast of his gasoline ricochets off the roof of my mouth and splatters over my taste buds, bitter, sour. Four more scalding shots of nut-juice blast into my mouth, filling it as he has only done to cunts before this afternoon. His come is so gamy, the kind of load that has fermented in a man's balls too long without release. But to me, it's ambrosia.

Danny has saved me, and I've saved him, I believe.

I hold his come on my tongue and savor its bitterness before swallowing it. I grip him by the root of his cock, begin to back away from it, release it to clean off the drops of spent load with my tongue. But Danny grips the back of my head suddenly, unexpectedly, forcibly.

"No," he growls menacingly. "Keep it in your mouth."

I do as he tells me, confused. And then I hear him grunt, feel his body tense. He lifts to the tops of his bare toes and moans.

Danny floods my mouth, only this time, not with the contents of the balls that have banged my chin for a solid fifteen minutes, but the contents of his bladder.

The first raunchy jet sprays my mouth. Unprepared, I gag. Danny holds onto my head, leaving me powerless to resist him and unable to escape. His piss tastes mostly like his come, manly, sour, nourishing. I guzzle it down to keep up with him and to stop from choking. I swallow, one gulp after another, losing count. This is the beer we drank together that previous night. It burns in my throat, fills my belly. I swear I can smell its stink, but that's not possible—Danny has my face pressed right to his crotch. My mouth has made a perfect seal around his dick, which is half-hard now and squirting piss like a fire hose gone wild under its own power and the pressure of the liquid jetting through it.

Danny chases down the come in my mouth with his piss. I swallow every drop of his nectar and catch myself smiling, too.

In my memories of that day, some of them distorted by the past seven years, what happens next does so quickly, not more than a minute or two later, I am sure.

Danny finishes urinating into my mouth. He pulls his cock out, its liquid popping sound the only noise in the apartment. He milks the last few drops of piss onto my lips. I lick them up and notice he's stroked his cock back to its full stiffness. I lap a stray drop of piss off his balls before taking him back into my mouth. I only get a few sucks of his reawakened dick when Danny yanks it out of my mouth and grabs hold of one of my shoulders, hauling me up from my knees. I start to question him. He shuts me off and rips down my sweats. My cock tick-tocks up, almost into his face, and for a second I wonder if he plans to reciprocate, to suck on it with the same reverence I've shown to him. However, that would make us more than what we are, a real couple, when we are only the slave and the master, the cocksucker and the cock-sucked. No, he has other plans.

He gives me a shove onto the couch, onto my stomach. The stink of those harvest-gold cushions imprints on my psyche. My stomach, full of his piss, shifts uncomfortably, threatening to send its contents back up, but it doesn't. My dick, rock-hard and one conscious stroke shy of squirting, grinds into the dirty velour fabric. I moan something, the weak ramble of an argument that dies, smothered in the cushions of the couch. Danny responds by yanking off my sneakers and then the sweats already down around my ankles. He launches a mean, forceful, "*Shut the fuck up!*" I feel the words and the warmth of his breath on the sensitive, virgin flesh of my asshole and inhale the pungent stink in the air, all protestations ending.

"*Danny, fuck me,*" I gasp.

"I'm gonna," he huffs.

The lick I quiver in anticipation of, and the scrape of his perfect goatee on my butt never come. Instead, he hawks up a wad of spit onto his hand and rubs it over the arrow-shaped head of his dick. The wet, slurping noise as he strokes it in his hand makes my mouth water for another taste of his manhood. I run my tongue over my teeth, revel in the bitterness that infuses my mouth. I beg him to let me suck his cock, to get it ready for penetration. He ignores me. I sense him over my shoulder, a tall, ominous shadow. He releases his cock and grips the cheeks of my ass, one in each hand, spreading them. A lone finger tickles the sensitive skin near my hole. Without warning, the finger stabs into my ass-lips, forcing its way in. I buck on the couch and cry out.

"*Shut up,*" Danny orders.

I whimper and shake my head. He takes no prisoners, gives no quarter. He goes deeper. A second finger joins the first just as brutally. I try to push open my asshole to accommodate. It feels like I'm being split open, pulled apart, like a fresh, sweet, ripe Summer peach. But the idea of Danny's fingers inside me supersedes my discomfort. He fingers me like he once only fingered pussy. This is what I wanted, more than anything.

"*I love you,*" I think I say. With all that's happening, it's possible I only think it. Still, I feel it. He has given me real, raw sex for the first time.

I love you, Danny!

His fingers fuck me deeper, teasing my cock from the inside. I'm so hard now, I'm too stiff to actually come. Fingers, though, aren't enough. Not for me. Not for him. We are in synch. He withdraws his invading fuck-touch, but only to replace it with his cock. I feel it slide along my crack, the wet head of his dick teasing me with probing strokes before catching in the ring of my asshole. There is no preamble or preparation for what is to come next. I push my asshole open as he shoves in, sparing myself some degree of agony. On my stomach on the smelly, harvest-gold couch, I let out a deafening scream. My own voice rings in my ears as the world turns shades of blood red before my eyes.

"I said shut the fuck up!" I barely hear Danny demand through the echoing resonance of my shout.

The next time I cry out, he'll shove one of his stale, stinky white sweat socks into my mouth. That moan will be one of joy, for the pain at his plundering of my virginity will shortly turn to pleasure.

The head of his cock will tease my prostate.

He'll breed me the way I've always dreamed.

I'll come into his sofa and almost lose consciousness when I ejaculate a second time, right after the first, attaining a mythological, male multiple orgasm.

Danny, he'll start to come up my ass, shooting his seed into me, and still squirting, he'll pull out and make me drink the rest of it down and lick the taste of my own asshole off his cock.

And then he'll go cold again, quietly turning away to wipe off his crotch with the same discarded sock he'd earlier shoved into my mouth.

I'll think this is only the beginning for us, for what will come as we dress in silence, never once suspecting it is really the end.

I feel Danny's seed and sweat between the cheeks of my ass, hot and slimy. Staring at the wall of his back, the back turned my way, I help him push his motorcycle around the building and out onto the driveway. From there, using all our strength, we stagger the Harley up the incline of the hill behind the garden-apartment house. This leaves us both drenched in sweat. Saying nothing, we pass the stands of spruce and hemlock that shield the house on one side of the road, up toward the sweeping branches of the willows on the other side. Sore and on fire and still horny for him, I can't wait for this to end. *Start the damn bike. Do what you have to do, then fuck my hole again, Danny!*

Eventually, we reach the top of the hill. Danny moves the Harley into position and mounts his bike the same way he mounted me back in the apartment.

"You gonna give me a ride if this works?" I ask playfully.

"Go fuck off," he says. His words hold no humor. He readies to go, to push off and ride the hill, pop the clutch, jumpstart the dead Harley's heart. My voice momentarily stops him in place.

"Hey, Danny, you want to come over to my place later?"

"Sure," he says.

He kick-starts the Harley down the hill. There's a sputter, a choke, then an eruption of sound and noise and energy. The motorcycle comes alive, just like I foolishly think Danny has.

He rides off and out of sight, leaving me alone on the slope of pavement behind the house. He never comes over that night. As I sit licking my lips, reliving his taste, aching for the feel of him inside me, I realize things will never be the same again for either of us.

In the hot summer months that followed, I realized what Danny did. He did it to create an ending, not a beginning. Somehow, I found the ability to put him out of my mind and mostly out of my heart, and liking the raw quality of the sex he gave me, I sought and found several other men of his caliber. Some, I dated. Others, I blew. A few, I got to know deeper than the basic act of sex. However, I never forgot the taste of forbidden fruit we shared on that May day in 1997, even if Danny apparently had.

The most Danny and I exchanged after that was a few grudging hellos in the driveway. He stopped climbing the main staircase and passing my front door, instead opting to use the private stairs at the side of the house to enter his apartment. Me, I started getting my mail after he left for work. We'd entered that place where we went out of the way to avoid each other.

The heat of Summer waned to the coolness of September and then October beyond that, and while the roar of Danny's motorcycle often sent my heart racing as the days grew shorter and colder, my mind mercifully found solace elsewhere.

I sold my first book in October of that year. I was sitting in a chair near the sliding glass door, across from the entertainment reporter of our small, local Atkinson, New Hampshire, newspaper giving her an interview about the book when the sirens sounded. A police cruiser, followed by an ambulance, tore past the house.

"What the hell-?" I said.

This had always been such a quiet neighborhood, and within minutes, a small crowd had gathered on the front lawn, the onlookers all focused on the main road.

"Let me call the news desk at the paper," the reporter offered. "Maybe they know what's happened..."

I hear that sound often in my dreams, even after all this time. I'll be lying in bed, sweating outwardly, burning up in my subconscious, when I'll be with him again, in 1997, in his apartment, beneath him. He's less lost in my dreams, less sad and mean and pissed off at a world that failed him. He tells me he really did like me, and sometimes, he even kisses me. The dreams all end the same, however. I'll hear the deafening clatter of metal hitting wood and I'll wake in my bed gasping for air and haunted to the core.

A few days after the accident, Danny's sister and her husband showed up to sift through his stuff. For the better part of that week, they carted everything of his not of value to them out to the trash. His clothes, his furniture, everything. One frigid late October afternoon, when the sun was setting low and its light had the bent and angle of Autumn, I walked out with my garbage and saw the ugly harvest-gold couch jutting up through bags of trash at the dumpster's open maw.

They say Danny lost control out on the main road, that he was speeding and hit the tree going eighty miles an hour. But if you look at the tar, there are no skid marks, no signs he did anything to avoid the collision that stole his life. I think he simply decided that this was the time and the place when he'd had enough of living.

Every time I hear a siren or the roar of a motorcycle's engines, Danny's face comes to me, especially in May and now, in the fall, when the days are crisp and short. I want to smile when I think of him in these moments. Sometimes, I want to cry. But I do neither.

Still, I do miss him, and part of me will always wonder what might have been.

PLAIN BROWN WRAPPER
Thomas Roche

Baker's hog rumbled rough and violent between his legs as he roared up the dirt trail. He eased down the tight little alley and into the cramped little space in the back. It gave a shudder as he leaned on it—gotta check that intake.

Not yet, though. Baker'd been running hot and heavy since Fresno, and he needed a fucking squirt. He put the fucker on the side stand—he wouldn't be long—and unlocked first the left saddlebag, then the right. Out of each came a plain brown wrapper—matching Swiss Army surplus backpacks, crammed so full they bulged. He slung one over each enormous shoulder and ambled down the alley, which was barely big enough for his hog and barely big enough for his shoulders. He always parked in back.

He hit the front of the store and passed the big crackling neon sign, listening to the pink tubes' electric fizzle. BOB'S ADULT. Under the integrity-challenged neon was a long sheet of butcher paper running the length of the front window, on which someone had scrawled DVD-VIDEO-PREVIEW BOOTHS. HEAD CLEANER. EXCELLENT EUROPEAN MAGAZINE SELECTION. WOMEN AND COUPLES WELCOME. Behind the butcher paper was a big black vinyl backdrop, shrouding the interior of the store.

The clerk behind the counter looked all of nineteen, pretty behind his pimples, noticeably faggy. His eyes lit with terror when he spotted Baker.

"Can I check your bags, Sir?" asked the clerk in a meek voice that sounded more like a whimper.

"No," said Baker, without even looking up or taking off his glasses. It was dark in the store, but he wasn't about to take off his shades, not when there was probably an APB out on his ass. He was taking too much of a risk even stopping here, but he'd been thinking about the ripe melons on Annamaria, his sweet *mamacita* waiting for him in Cabo, ever since he left Fresno with his saddlebags stuffed with retirement funds. If he didn't get his weasel greased he was gonna fucking kill something. He might anyway, but without a good greasing it was a definite.

"Bathroom?" he growled at pimple-face.

"I'm afraid they're out of order," the clerk said weakly.

Baker took off his wraparounds, tossed the clerk with his nastiest mad-dog.

"Try again."

The clerk swallowed. "Past the video booths. Brown door. Um. It's been acting up so don't throw paper towels in the toilet."

"Much obliged," said Baker, putting his shades back on.

Normally Baker would have just pissed on the counter if a clerk told him the bathroom was out of order. That was the sorriest gag in the business, and he was having none of it. But he had business to do here, however brief it might be, and he didn't want to draw too much attention to himself. Though he was well aware that a six-two ex-linebacker bad-ass biker motherfucker carrying two massive brown backpacks which might or might not be stuffed with half a million dollars, he figured he could at least attempt to be discreet—for once in his life.

It was four in the afternoon—well past lunch hour—but there's always a certain type hanging out in squirt shops. As Baker threaded his way through the racks of videos and magazines, he took stock. "Jesus fucking Christ," he muttered out loud. Maybe he should just ask for directions to the center of town and try to find an actual female to polish his knob. This was some sorry shit: One decaying businessman who looked like he hadn't slept in a week, a couple of high school kids making fart jokes and giggling at the box covers, and a stoned-looking loser leafing through PREGNANT MAMA magazine. There was what appeared to be a migrant farm worker from the nearby orchards—Baker knew from experience that those fuckers give the most amazing head—but the guy made a beeline for the door as soon as he saw Baker. Baker wondered if he should change his image—apparently he was being mistaken for INS.

It was like trying to get laid at a BMW rally. Baker was about to figure he'd be stuck pumping his thing in the *pissoir* like some businessman on his lunch hour. Then he saw him.

Not like Baker was a connoisseur or anything, but he could appreciate the effort required to sculpt your fucking body like that. If it wasn't for his six years in Folsom—and the weekly piss tests, which meant he had nothing to do if he wanted to make parole—Baker never would have done it himself. Baker was all about power, pushing for that four bills on the bench-press, reaching it the day before his parole hearing. This guy was all about that and more—he looked like fucking Marlon Brando after a tour through hell with a Russian trainer named Olga. Army Airborne, current or past; that's what the jarhead cut said, not to mention the DEATH FROM ABOVE tattoo. The guy wore tight blue jeans cuffed halfway to his knees over his big heavy boots, and a skintight Army-brown T-shirt with Lucky Strikes rolled up in the sleeve. The shirt was so tight that Baker could see every fucking muscle group clearly defined, a body of knowledge it bugged him he knew, but he'd had to take anatomy classes to avoid Anger Management. Now, he stared at this guy's body with a new kind of mad-dog, something the guy seemed oblivious to. When he was this desperate, Baker didn't really give a shit who he got his suck-jobs from—but if he had to do it, he knew he'd be able to appreciate the sight of this guy's jarhead bouncing up and down on his fucking pole.

But that wasn't gonna happen. Airborne was here for the same reason as Baker—he wasn't going to be sucking anybody's cock.

Baker elbowed his way through the cramped hallway, his backpacks scraping the cum-spattered walls. He laid out his joint and Airborne's sculpted body came right into his fucking mind where a minute ago there'd been the firm round tits of Annamaria, his Cabo *Mamacita*. Airborne's tits replaced Anna's, and Baker's cock stood straight out and hurting, piss-full. Baker had to stand there holding it, trying hard to think about nuns and Nevada Mike's dysentery attack for about ten fucking minutes before he could get it soft enough to take a good long hose into the filthy bowl of the toilet, never putting his backpacks down—half a million green is a lot to trust to the floor of a squirt-shop shitter, and in a place like this even the rats were larcenous.

He started to get hard again the second he was done pissing. Airborne was probably gone; Baker knew he should just do his business. It took him like three strokes to shoot his fucking juice all over the toilet seat. He didn't stop to wipe it up. He tucked his thing back into his leather pants and hosed the jizz off his road-filthy hands. It rinsed off halfway between brown and black.

Baker tossed a few paper towels into the toilet, just for laughs.

He went back into the store and stopped dead when he spotted Airborne. The fucker was wedged into the tiny gay section, holding a video box in each hand as if he were trying to decide between boxes of chocolate. Baker could read the boxes: ANAL RECRUITS 12 and MUSCLE STUDS 14.

Baker had the motherfucker figured all wrong.

He edged down the aisle just opposite the fag section and reached out, grabbing BIG COCKS LITTLE SLUTS. He shot Airborne a mad-dog and the fucker took his own sweet time returning it, but when he did there wasn't any question what that fucking look meant. Face to crotch to chest, then face again, eyes narrowed and lips slightly parted. Baker reached into his front pocket for his roll and tossed Pimple Face LITTLE SLUTS with a wadded-up twenty.

"Preview," he growled.

"Booth twelve," said Pimple Face nervously. "Let me get you your change.

"Don't bother," said Baker, and gave Airborne one last look before heading toward the corridor.

The booth was big enough for two, but there was only one chair, a

127

cracked leather recliner that looked like it'd been lifted from Archie Bunker's living room. The booth's second resident was expected to kneel. Went without saying.

The recliner's footrest had been sheared off at the struts.

The booth was lit by a flickering fluorescent tube; he could see the floor glistening, well-defined streams of joy juice tracing paths from the chair to the screen. Baker crammed his plain brown bags behind the recliner. The door hissed closed and the light went out with a fizzle, replaced by the blue glow of the big screen, the same color as the ocean outside the Cabo villa where he was gonna fuck Annamaria until he pumped her full and she swelled with a little Baker.

Baker settled his ass in Archie Bunker's chair as the advertisements started amid a haze of static—phone sex sluts, triple-X websites, whatever. Baker found the plastic panel and hit fast forward. He got to the first scene and watched as some blonde slut, five feet in high heels, started wrapping her big fake tits around the twelve-inch pecker of a guy in a police uniform.

Baker heard footsteps. His cock started to swell, but it was so soon after he'd shot his load that all he got was an ache shooting through his crotch. He unzipped his pants, took it out and wrapped his hand around his soft meat just as the door opened.

Airborne stood there, backlit by the flicker of the corridor light.

Airborne looked Baker up and down, stepped inside and closed the door.

"Nice piece," said Airborne. "Is it gonna get hard?"

"Cut the bullshit," said Baker.

Airborne locked the door and squeezed into the little space between the recliner and the screen. With the two of them in there, both bigger than Terminators one and two put together, there wasn't much room to move. Airborne got on his knees, not seeming to give a shit that he was kneeling in spooge. He planted his pretty face in Baker's crotch and Baker guided his half-hard cock to his parted lips as Airborne unzipped his pants.

"Don't squirt on my boots, motherfucker."

"Relax," said Airborne, and wrapped his lips around Baker's joint.

He was raw from the endless throb of the hog between his legs and the fast jerk in the bathroom. He looked from the video screen—Fake Tits was taking it up the ass, the policeman not even bothering to make a pit stop in her snatch. Airborne's lips were thick and full and his tongue worked wonders. Except Baker couldn't get hard.

He was fucking hotter than hell—the jerk hadn't done anything to satisfy him. But his cock just sat there in Airborne's bobbing mouth, half-soft and useless.

"Tough day at the orifice, faggot?" Airborne quipped as he took his mouth off Baker's thing.

Baker went ballistic. He slapped Airborne across the face and grabbed his hair. "Shut up and suck," he growled, and went to force Airborne's face back down onto his cock. He wasn't paying enough attention, though, trying to focus on the bouncing titties of the bitch on the screen getting reamed. He wasn't paying attention at all, which he should have known is a bad fucking idea when you slap someone with a Death from Above tattoo.

Airborne planted a good one right in Baker's belly. Normally he would have taken it and laughed, but with his mind on his crotch he wasn't thinking straight. He saw stars and slumped forward just in time to catch Airborne's fist in his fucking jaw. If it hadn't been so cramped in there, Baker would have grabbed the guy's hair and head-butted him while he planted his knee in his crotch. But that's not how it went down, and next thing Baker knew he had Airborne's knee in *his* crotch, and a big muscled arm around his throat.

Airborne stood up, dragged Baker off of Archie Bunker into a half-standing position and laid another good one right in his balls again. Then it was one, two, three in the belly until Baker went slack and dropped to his knees.

Everything was spinning as he felt Airborne yanking first one wrist, then the other, up into the small of his back. With biceps like Baker's there wasn't far for his arms to go, but when he heard the clicking sounds and felt the cold metal around his wrists, he knew he was fucked. And if he hadn't known, he would have figured it out when he heard the click of a hammer behind his ear.

"First rule of unarmed combat," said Airborne. "Never let your guard down.

"I'll fuckin' kill you," growled Baker.

"Yeah, yeah," said Airborne, twisting his fingers in Baker's long hair and shoving he barrel of he revolver into his mouth. "After you swallow." Baker crossed his eyes and tried to make out the caliber—thirty-eight, probably, but where had the fucker concealed it?

"Feel free to shoot on my fucking boots," said Airborne, and took the gun out of Baker's mouth, a long stream of drool glistening from tongue to muzzle as the gun took its place against Baker's skull. "I'd consider it a compliment."

Baker would have continued putting up a fight. Even with his wrists cuffed behind him, he might have been able to jump to his feet and sucker-kick the motherfucker right in the face before he pulled the trigger. He might have.

Except that his cock was fucking hard. Harder than it had ever fucking been.

"Now, suck," growled Airborne, and shoved Baker's face down onto his piece.

Before he knew what was happening, Baker had taken it in his mouth. He'd gone six years at Folsom without ever polishing a single knob, though he got nightly suck-jobs from a long succession of punks. Now, though, he was on his knees with Airborne's dick in his fucking mouth, and his own cock was swelling like there was no fucking tomorrow.

Baker started sucking.

He wrapped his lips tight around Airborne's shaft and bobbed up and down as the moans from the video screen grew louder, Fake Tits whimpering with every hard pounding thrust the guy gave her in her ass. Baker's tongue worked around the guy's underside, and he pushed his face down onto the guy's cock until the head spread the tightness of his throat. He'd been deep-throated plenty and he'd always wondered how chicks and faggots did it. Now, as Airborne gripped his hair with one hand and held the gun close with the other, Baker knew he was about to find out. Only when Airborne forced his cock into Baker's throat, he only gagged a little, his throat closing around the thick hard flesh—and then his own cock fucking surged as Airborne began to fuck his throat.

Baker leaned forward and felt his cock against the edge of the leather recliner. Airborne pulled him harder onto his cock and Baker opened up wide, sucking harder between firm thrusts down his throat.

"Cum in my mouth," Fake Tits whimpered on the video screen, and Airborne let out a laugh as Baker sucked him. "Right from the ass to the mouth," said Airborne. "You gotta love a bitch who'll suck your pecker fresh from her chute. I bet you'd do that, motherfucker, wouldn't you?"

Baker wanted to say, "fuck you," but his mouth was full of cock. He rubbed his own against the edge of the recliner and it felt like he was going to fucking cum already. He grunted as he ground his joint against the rough, ruined fabric, and Airborne seized his hair to pump his face up and down on that big, fat cock, no longer interested in having it down his throat. Airborne was going to shoot.

Baker had never tasted cum before.

Baker heard a bestial groan from the video screen, and Airborne moaned "Yeah, there he goes. Right in her fucking mouth," just as a hot stream of jizz erupted down Baker's throat. He didn't even know he was doing it. He just...swallowed.

Another stream, and Baker leaned forward harder to suck it right out of Airborne's cock. The sharp taste filled his mouth. Baker shoved his cock hard against the cracked leather. He shot just as Airborne gave him another spurt, and his groan of pleasure met the thick, fragrant stream.

"You missed my boots," said Airborne, pulling Baker's head off his cock.

Baker looked up at the motherfucker with hatred in his eyes, his mouth drooling come and spit. Airborne reached over and hit STOP on the control panel. The screen went blue, flooding the booth with the color of Cabo San Lucas ocean.

Airborne pushed Baker off of him and got out of the chair, leaving Baker wedged into the corner with his wrists still cuffed behind him and the barrel of a .38 pointed right between his eyes.

And a badge flashing in Airborne's other hand.

"Fresno P.D.," said Airborne. "You want my badge number?"

Baker opened his mouth to say something smart and found that the taste of come still filled it. He shut his mouth and looked at the blue screen, the last fucking blue he was ever going to see except for denim coveralls and blue fucking toilet cleaner. And hello to fucking Folsom and four-and-a-half bills on the fucking bench press.

Airborne zipped his pants, put his badge back in his jeans and put his booted foot up on the edge of the recliner. He pulled up his pant leg and stuck the revolver into an ankle holster. Baker could have just reached the motherfucker with his boot, but what was the point? Sprawled on his ass like this, he wouldn't have been able to get any purchase; he would just have pissed Airborne off. And Baker knew he had to put this guy out cold to get the handcuff key and make it out the back door to his waiting bike.

Then the handcuff key landed in Baker's lap.

"You give me ten minutes, Baker," said Airborne. "Then you head south. I'll call it in. Far as the CHP is concerned you're making a run for Nevada."

"What the fuck are you talking about?" said Baker, eyeing the key in his lap, laying cold against his soft, raw cock.

Airborne leaned over and yanked a plain brown backpack from behind the recliner.

"Retirement plan," said Airborne. "Mexico's cheap; you should be able to live pretty good on a quarter-mil. Otherwise, it's back to fucking Folsom, *cabron*. Do yourself a favor: go down there and hook up with some *hombres, maricon*. You're too good a cocksucker to go to waste."

Airborne shouldered the backpack and squeezed out the door, shutting it behind him.

Baker wrestled his way to his knees, dumping the key in a pile of spooge. It was so slippery he had to try for most of the ten minutes before he could pick up the key and get the handcuffs unlocked. He tossed them in the recliner and zipped up his leather pants, his cock smarting from rubbing against the cracked leather.

Baker picked up the second backpack and slung it over his shoulder.

Thomas Roche

He looked once at the screen, reached out and hit PLAY. The Cabo-blue screen fizzled into one last shot of Fake Tits' upturned face, wide open mouth, taking the last stream of hot jizz on her extended tongue.

"Thank you," she whimpered, staring wide-eyed and cum-spattered up into the face of the guy towering above her, who had stripped naked but still wore his cop hat and aviator sunglasses.

The motherfucker smiled, a broad white-toothed grin as he looked down at Fake Tits' dripping face.

"You're welcome," he told her. "You little cocksucking whore."

Baker hit STOP and said hello to Cabo blue again. It was about an hour to Mexico, and Anna was waiting.

"Son of a fucking bitch," said Baker, and slammed the door behind him.

LONG HARD RIDE
Adam McCabe

I could tell that he wanted me from the first glance. It wasn't a casual look that dismisses a guy because he's wearing dirty jeans and carries a string of tattoos down his arm. No, it said that he was interested.

I was surprised. Usually those little weekend bikers don't associate with the hardcore bikers. They'll go back home to the suburbs on Sunday and leave the roads to us. Not that I didn't give him a look back. He was about six foot and blond with a slim build. He barely looked big enough to control the bike between his legs. I knew those little blond boys tended to have a lot between their legs though.

I tried not to think about him as I walked into the truck stop. I'd been riding hard since daybreak, trying to make a good day's ride before the rain broke. The skies had been threatening all morning with dark clouds and an occasional drop or two. Now it was looking like a downpour and I didn't feel like getting beat to death in the rain or pulling over under an overpass to stay dry. The truck stop would suit me just fine. Those truckers lived in style, compared to bikers.

I stepped into the darkened air of the truck stop. I could smell the smoke of a thousand cigarettes, even though the building was supposed to be non-smoking. I just smiled as I saw some kindred spirits sitting in the corner, nursing a coke or a cup of coffee.

I headed towards the back where the showers and bathrooms were. I needed a good scrub after a morning's ride. The grit on my skin chafed and I wanted to wash it off if I was going to be here a while. This storm didn't look like it was going to let up soon. I cursed under my breath, thinking that I might have to fork out the money for a room to spend the night. That wasn't something I'd planned on.

The bathroom was empty. I made my way through the room to the back where a small door connected a hallway of showers to the bathroom. Rain pounded on the roof, keeping time with the drip from two of the showerheads.

I stood outside one of the stalls and stripped

I smiled as I thought of the kid outside. He'd enjoy this view, I thought. My body was in good shape, even though I'd recently turned 35. I was tall, toned without much in the way of fat on me. The tattoo he'd been eyeing ran all the way up my arm over my shoulder and onto my back. It had been a bitch to get inked, but the end result was worth it. The dragon looked as fierce as anything I'd seen on the road.

I didn't have much hair on my body, except around my dick. It hung low today, even though that boy had made it twitch for a few minutes. When hard, my cock was about eight inches, and thick as an exhaust pipe. There weren't a lot of men out there that could match me for size.

The stall had a soap dispenser and I started lathering up. The scent of the soap smelled great after the exhausts and pollution of the last few hours. I breathed it in and exhaled slowly. Nothing beat a good ride after a storm, when the air was clean and you were too.

I let the water beat over my skin until I felt relaxed. Five hours in the same position could stiffen you up, and not in a good way. I cranked off the water and reached outside the stall for my T-shirt to dry off with. I hadn't come prepared for an overnight stay.

I grabbed the shirt when a voice startled me. "Wanna use a towel?"

I opened one eye and saw the boy from the pumps standing just outside my stall. He was still dressed, but he held a towel in his right hand. The other hand hung down by his crotch and I wondered if he'd been using it to rub himself while he watched me shower. Longs strands of blond hair fell down into his eyes, so I couldn't see exactly where he was looking, but I had a good idea, all the same.

"Thanks." I took the towel, and my hand grazed his. I could feel the tension between us and my cock started a slow ascent, betraying me as I stood there.

"No problem. That rain came up suddenly."

I nodded, shaking my dark hair all around. The water spilled out of it, and some landed on the boy's shirt.

"I thought I'd take a shower and get a place to stay for the night. It doesn't look like it's going to be letting up soon at all." He peeled off his shirt. I peeked from under my matted, wet hair. He was toned with two flat hard pecs and big nipples. No hair at all, just a hint of the summer's tan.

I finished drying off. "I might have to do the same." I stepped out of the stall and handed his towel back to him. He didn't move at all. I slid by him, letting my cock brush his leg for a second. I felt the heat of his skin and my dick started to respond. I tried to will it back into position, but it had been too long since I'd fucked a guy.

He smiled. "Hang on. Maybe we could get a room together. Save some money. I'm not exactly a rich man." He dropped his pants and stepped out of them. His cock was a nice size; his pubes were trimmed back to nearly stubble. His ass was firm and round. We stood face to face, and he pushed his half-hard dick against mine. The trimmed pubes scratched against my leg. He thrust himself against me a couple of times, and then let his hand slide over my shaft. I could tell by the expression on his face that he was surprised at how big I was. It scared some guys off, but he didn't seem to mind.

He brushed those muscled cheeks up against me as he stepped into the stall down from where I'd showered. "Would you mind holding the towel?

I stood there and watched him soap up that tight little body. My cock was standing at attention and throbbing by this point. I'm not a guy who likes to be teased and I thought about stepping back into the shower to give him what he needed, but I decided to wait. Some of the guys in the truck stop might not like the thought of two guys fucking.

I slid back into my clothes and went out front to wait. The clouds had grown heavier and the rain came at a steady pace. I looked to the guy at the counter. "Hey, tell that kid in back that I went over to get a room." I jerked my thumb in the direction of the hotel, trying to act more casual than my cock felt right now.

He nodded and went back to the NASCAR race on the tube. I took off at a trot and got to the hotel office without getting too wet. I paid for the room and headed upstairs. The rain was coming down hard now, a constant pounding on the flat roof above my head. I could see the kid running over to the hotel, and I nodded. He saw me and headed for the stairs.

I opened the door and stepped inside the room. It wasn't much for $40. Just a bed with an old paisley spread, one lamp by the bedside and a sink and counter in the back. I left the door open a crack, and the kid came into the room without knocking. In the half-light of the room, he looked young, probably no more than twenty or twenty-one. I usually didn't do kids like this. They were trouble.

He shook his head, and drops of water shot from his hair. He went in the bathroom and came back with a towel around his shoulder and no shirt. Those big brown nipples looked ready to eat. He smiled and turned toward the mirror to finish drying his hair.

I walked up behind him. I could see his face in the mirror and for a second, he looked scared, like maybe he hadn't done this before. I couldn't believe that, since he'd come on so strong, but stranger things had happened.

He began to turn around to face me, but I put a hand on his back and forced his torso down to the counter. He didn't struggle much, and with my free hand, I tugged down his pants. He wasn't wearing underwear and I heard his cock slap the counter as he moved to stand up. I didn't release him though. I wanted to make sure that he wasn't about to get away.

I spat on his ass and rubbed it with on my fingers as I spread his cheeks. I slid two fingers up him to start. His ass rose up to meet me, starting a hard pump against my hand. The fingers slid in easily and he moaned softly as I pushed in to the second knuckle.

I didn't wait for long. About six thrusts later, I pulled out the fingers and grabbed a rubber. I'd come prepared, but I'd never expected anything like this. I rolled it down over my throbbing member and slid my cock inside of him. He groaned so loud that people beyond our paper-thin walls could hear. I didn't care. His ass took me in and I could feel the heat of his tight little hole.

I leaned down over him, so that my chest nearly touched his back. His shoulder would come up from time to time and brush against my chest hair. The room was silent except for the muffled noises next door. I could hear a couple talk beyond the walls. I grunted from time to time, and the boy's groans had turned to a growl.

I slid arms under his and grabbed him in a full nelson. He couldn't escape, though he didn't much seem like he wanted to. I pulled him away from the counter and moved with him towards the bed. I was still inside of him, and I made him hop a bit as I shoved my cock up to the hilt. From this angle, I could see his cock pulse as he felt all of me inside of him. He couldn't touch it, but I could tell he wanted to. It looked like it might go at any time. I figured all that fucking had hit his prostate and he was getting ready to blow.

I moved him over to the bed and forced him down on it. His ass stayed up in the air, and we started at it again. He bucked his hips up so that we met time and again. The slap of my balls against his ass was enough to get me off, but I wasn't ready to let go. I let him out of the wrestling hold and slid my hands under him. I grabbed on to his cock and started jacking him with me still inside of him. The groans grew louder again and I could hear the people on the other side of the walls complaining, but they didn't pound on the wall for us to stop. Maybe they got off on it too.

A low growl came out of him and he started to spurt. All over the bedspread. I continued to pump his cock until he slowed to an ooze of cum. I pumped him a few more times for good measure.

Before he could try to get me to stop, I rolled him over so that we were face-to-face. His eyes were soft and warm. I could tell that it had been a while since he'd shot his wad. I pulled his legs over my shoulders and kept at it. I figured he was young, he should be good for another round or two.

He opened his eyes wide, as he realized that I wasn't going to stop. He started to say something and thought better of it. I wasn't the type who'd stop just because the other guy got off. We kept up the pace for a few more minutes. He pulled my face to his and kissed me long and hard. His tongue darted inside my mouth and found mine. The two battled for a few seconds. I wasn't in the mood for romance and intimacy. I wanted to fuck—and hard. I drove my cock deep inside of him, and he moaned around my tongue. The vibrations of his mouth on mine made me want him more. I stayed there for a few seconds, letting him feel all of me pushing deep inside of him. While I remained motionless, I felt a stirring against my abs. He'd started to get hard again. I smiled and pulled my face back a minute. "Ready for more?"

He didn't speak, but gave me a grin that let me know that he was. I started banging his ass again. The pace was faster this time, more insistent. I wanted him to know that I wanted it. I wanted him. His mouth fell away from mine, and I could feel him tracing the outline of the dragon on my shoulder with his tongue. Occasionally, he'd take a bite on my skin.

My hips pulled in and out and continued to push inside of him, faster and faster. I could feel my balls tighten up in the sack. I wasn't going to last much longer. I wanted to make sure that he felt my load, so I pulled out. I stripped off the rubber and threw it aside.

I timed it just right. I turned back to face him and the first shot of cum hit him across the chest. It shot out in thick hot streams, coating his front with my jizz. I watched as it landed on him and slowly rolled down his side.

He took a handful of it and slid it on the thick shaft of his cock. His other hand reached around and grabbed a handful of my ass. He squeezed it, and I clenched my cheeks so that he could feel the rock-hard muscles of my ass. I watched as he jacked his cock again, pounding his meat insistently while he stared at me. I could tell that he wanted a chance at my ass. But that wouldn't be happening tonight.

He stroked his shaft and I could see the tension in his face. The corners of his mouth drew up and he shot a second load. The cum didn't shoot far this time. It oozed thick streams of milky liquid down his shaft and into his trimmed pubes.

I lay down next to him. We didn't bother to wash off. We just fell asleep in each other's arms. The maids would clean up the mess in the morning.

TAKE IT LIKE A MAN
D.L. Tash

S hit!

I look at my old Chevy station wagon. Steam hisses from under the hood.

I just knew the radiator would never make the trip.

Unfortunately, I was right.

I get out. Damn! Stuck here in the middle of Nevada, nothing but nothing for miles, with a dead car and eighty bucks in cash.

I knew I shouldn't have tried it. But Lonnie begged me. He's doing a show in Reno, in a small art gallery there.

If there's anyone worth taking a risk for, it's Lonnie. He's tall, slender, really handsome and kind of aesthetic: a poet and an artist, who throws pottery in his spare time. He's the kind of man I've always liked: artistic and upscale and very well educated.

And a marvelous lover.

So here I am, Mr. Midwest City Boy, stuck somewhere in the Nevada desert on Highway 50, which has the nickname, "The Loneliest Highway in America."

With a busted car and almost no money.

I look down the deserted highway. No traffic in sight.

Behind me there is a rise, so I can't see anything that way at all.

I begin to wonder how long I could be waiting for someone to come along.

I hear the sound coming before I see them. It sounds like a truck. But as it gets closer, I get more nervous. There is a growing roar and has a bass rumble to it that I can feel right in my scrotum.

The sound gets louder. For a moment I think maybe a jet is approaching at really low altitude, flying down almost on the ground.

I hear they do that in Nevada.

Then I see the wide flash of dark and silver on the road, coming up over the rise.

My gut tightens.

Bikers.

And there's a whole lot of them.

Oh, shit! Here I am, Mr. City, driving from the Midwest to meet my (hopefully) new boyfriend in Reno, and there are a bunch of motorcycles coming at me, pouring like a wave over the hill: big, dirty-looking bikes, ridden by big, dirty-looking bikers.

I can smell the motorcycles even over the stench of boiling antifreeze from my Chevy. It's the dank, musky odor of oil and gas and leather and hot tires and hotter metal.

The bikes are spread at least six abreast, filling the entire two-lane highway.

These are no dirt bikes, or those big ones with all the side-bags and windshields, like the cops drive.

These are choppers. Big, mean, kick-ass, outlaw choppers, filling the air with their deep, throbbing roar.

Being out in the middle of nowhere, alone, with a broken car and very little money is bad enough. Try adding sixty outlaw bikers, just looking for trouble, to the mix.

Now add to that the fact I'm gay. I have a momentary flash of my battered body being dragged along the highway, chained to a bike, bouncing along behind them, leaving little bits of my flesh and bones in their wake.

One of the bikes moves closer to my side of the road and slows.

It pulls up a few feet from me and stops.

"Got a problem?" The biker asks.

His arms are huge. That's the first thing I notice. Massive arms, with big biceps and triceps and covered with tattoos.

He's bearded, with a long black ponytail hanging out from under what looks like a Nazi helmet.

He has on a Jean jacket. The arms of it are cut off, like you see in the movies and the handlebars on his bike are very high. His chest is massive and smooth.

He looks at me through his very dark sunglasses.

"Look's like your car took a shit," he says in a gravelly voice.

I nod, clearing my throat.

"Yeah, it did," I tell him, trying to get my voice as deep as possible and get a bit of a swagger.

"Just took a shit, just like that," I say deeply.

The guy nods.

"Get your stuff and I'll give you a ride to the next town."

No way. I don't ride motorcycles. They are called "donor-cycles" for a reason!

And this guy is twice my size, on this huge, chrome and red chopper, and traveling with a bunch of other equally vicious-looking men.

I figure it's safer to walk.

"You don't have to give me a ride," I tell him, trying to put a slight 'regular guy-like' drawl into my Midwest collegiate accent. "I got somebody who should be along soon."

I think to myself that was a smart move. I'll make him think that at least there would be potential witnesses if he decided to do something.

But he shakes his head.

"Stay out here if you want," he says, "But it's gonna be over a hundred and ten in the shade today and if ya look, there ain't no shade."

I look around.

If you wanted to film a movie set on a near-dead planet, a wild, desolate place almost entirely devoid of life, you'd come here. You could see hills off the distance, and sagebrush, and sand. The narrow black ribbon of road ran like a crooked line through the scene.

And that was it.

The biker was becoming impatient, since his friends were roaring off into the distance.

"Fuck, kid, are you coming or not?" he asks.

I nod. I grab my knapsack out of the steaming Chevy and lock the doors.

The biker looks at me and nods.

"Name's Kurt," he says.

"I'm Tommy. Thomas Burke," I tell him.

Kurt points his thumb behind him.

"Hang that on the bitch bar and let's get going."

I look at the back of the big bike. I assume he means the sissy bar, like on the banana seat bike I had as a kid, and I slide my knapsack over it.

Kurt shifts his massive body a little forward and I manage to straddle the motorcycle without falling. The back sissy bar was too tall, so I couldn't just swing my leg over. But I finally manage to get on the bike.

On the back of Kurt's jacket are embroidered the words THE BRETHREN, and underneath, in quotes, "Take It Like A Man!"

Kurt doesn't wait for me to get settled, but guns the motorcycle and takes off.

If you've never been on a motorcycle, it's an unbelievable experience. The vibration of the engine just rattles through your body so hard you can feel it in your teeth. And the wind isn't just rushing by, it tears at you. My shirt is whipped hard in the wind.

I manage to find the little metal pegs for my feet and try to get comfortable.

God, I can smell Kurt's sweat, mingled with a melange of motorcycle odors: Hot oil, hot metal, gasoline, hot rubber and his black leather pants.

I don't dare touch him. I certainly don't want to impart the wrong idea accidentally.

But the fact is, I'm getting turned on. The vibration of the motor comes right up through the leather seat, right into my balls and ass and up my prick.

My seat is raised, and I can look over the driver's shoulder and see the speedometer flirting with eighty miles an hour.

Kurt's hair whips my face, and I smell his sweat and oil and the scent of leather in it.

Oh, shit! I'm getting a hard-on.

I try to sit back, but the bar is in the way. Beside, when I move back, so does he, using my body as his seat-back. He relaxes that big, muscled, tattooed, sweaty body back into mine.

Apparently he doesn't notice my hard cock, because he doesn't slow down or anything.

We come up on the rear of the pack of bikes. You hear about a pack of bikers, but it doesn't begin to describe the reality. Imagine about sixty bikes, not driving in perfect formation, but in a constantly changing mass, weaving in and out of each other's way. Every bike is different, and every biker.

Now put all these on a highway at seventy miles an hour, only inches apart, with the roar of the engines and the smell of exhaust almost too much to bear.

We make our way through the pack. Several of the drivers look over at me. A couple of them nod slightly.

One of the motorcycles has a woman on the back, a hard-looking but pretty blonde, who looks over at me and smiles.

I wish she wouldn't do that. If her husband or boyfriend or whatever he is got jealous, I could end up dead.

Nineteen is way too young to die.

Then the bikes begin to slow as we enter a small town.

Hump, Nevada doesn't really even deserve the name of town. It's a wide spot in the road, with a gas station, two bars and a handful of weathered houses.

The bikes pull up in front of one of the bars, its front so dilapidated you can barely see the letters painted on the old facade. It just reads "BAR."

Kurt motions me to get off the bike. I try, but catch my shoe on the edge of the motorcycle seat. I yell as I fall face-first into the gravel parking lot, almost taking the bike down with me.

Harsh laughter erupts. I get up, trying to dust myself off.

"Maybe ya better stick to Chevys!" someone says and that sets off more laughter.

I blush as I get my knapsack. Kurt is laughing too but he winks.

"You ride bikes long enough, you learn how not to do that," he says.

I nod and smile.

"Thanks for the ride," I tell him.

Kurt nods.

"We're headed to Virginia City," he tells me. "We're going right through Reno, if that's any help."

"How did you know where I was headed?" I ask.

"Shit, there's nothing else out here," Kurt snorts. "A few cow towns and mining communities and that's about it. You're either going to Reno or over the pass to California."

I nod. Somehow, I thought the closer you got to California, the greener it got. But instead, the landscape went from flat prairie to desolate desert.

"I'll call a tow truck, but thanks for the offer," I tell him.

Kurt nods.

"See you around," he says.

I look over at the bar from the gas station's door. Another group of motorcycles are arriving.

Well, the gas station owner will tow my car into town for four hundred dollars. Then repairs take even longer, and all the parts have to come from Salt Lake City or Reno. So it will take a week or more.

And cost around five hundred bucks for the repairs. If I'm lucky and it's just the radiator.

There's only one bright bit of hope in the batch of bad news.

The service station owner offers me two hundred dollars for the Chevy, as is.

Damn. It's worth a lot more than that, but I'm looking at a thousand dollars or more to get it towed and repaired, and a week's stay at a motel on top of that. And it's located down the road about six miles.

My eighty dollars isn't going to cover it.

So I sign over the car and take the cash.

I walk over towards the bar. The new group of bikers look me over, in my khaki slacks and moccasins, and my Midwestern checked shirt and farm-boy haircut.

Yeah, I obviously don't belong.

But I head into the bar anyway. Kurt offered me a ride, and I guess I have no choice but to take it.

The place is pretty packed. Men are everywhere, but *men* doesn't describe it.

They were bikers. They wore leather and denim and heavy engineer's boots. Some wore T-shirts and others wore nothing but tattoos on their upper bodies. Knives hang on almost every belt, and some of the belts are made of chain—not ringed chain, but the flat drive-chain off a motorcycle.

Hair is everywhere, most long, some short, some heads shaven clean but still bearded. I see hairy chests and arms and backs and under-arms.

But it is the smell that is the most noticeable thing.

You can smell the beer and men's bodies and perspiration and oiled leather and the myriad of motorcycle smells, oily and metallic and acrid.

And underneath it all, a deep undertone of old sweat and sour urine.

It is mildly disgusting and totally arousing.

I walk through the crowded bar, looking for Kurt, the biker who offered me a ride.

I don't see him so I sit at the bar and order a beer. The bartender brings it and looks at me oddly as he leaves. Hell, I'm as out of place here as a nun at an orgy.

"You don't look like a one percenter," I hear. I turn to see the speaker, this wizened old guy beside me, in full leathers, with a black leather Harley cap.

"A what?" I ask.

He laughs.

"A one percenter," he repeats. "The one percent that can't be tamed. Bikers."

I smile wanly.

"No, I think I'm a ninety-nine percenter," I tell him. He laughs, showing a mouth full of bad teeth.

But at least he doesn't kill me.

I look around and finally see Kurt, but the blonde biker chick sees me at the same time. The girl has her shirt off and some guys are feeling up her small breasts. She has on tight leather pants and her hips swing as she approaches me.

"Look, a new guy," she says, sliding into my arms and kissing me.

Yeah, I've had sex with a woman a few times. It's not my preference, but I kiss her back, hoping no one notices my discomfort. She puts my hand on her breast, and I feel her, her nipples small and very erect.

I hear a zip. Damn, she's pulling her pants down. The bikers in the bar start shouting encouragement. She's almost naked right here in the bar, and you could cut the testosterone with a knife.

"Fuck her!" someone yells, "Get you a handful of that bitch!"

That seemed to be her cue, because she takes my hand. And while we are still kissing, wet and sloppy, she slides it over her hard belly and over her light pubic hair.

Shit. I really don't want to have sex with her. Hell, I'm not sure I can even get it up, with everyone watching.

But what am I supposed to do? Announce to a bar full of bikers that I'm gay?

The girl is spreading her legs for me and she pulls away from my mouth and moans.

"Touch me," she says in a deep, whiskey-soaked voice. "Fuck me, please."

Well, I don't have a lot of choice, so I slide my hand down to cup her pussy.

I never get there.

I hit cock.

I jerk back and the bar explodes in laughter. I stare at the 'girl,' with her big cock sticking out, fully erect and beautiful.

"Aren't you going to fuck me?" the guy asks, in his normal, deep voice.

I stare at his cock. I love cock, the taste, the texture, the feel.

I realize what I want to do could be dangerous, but I do it anyway.

I fall on my knees and take his cock deep in my mouth.

That gets a cheer from the bar, and I get a mouthful of leather-tasting sweaty cock, hard and wonderful.

I run my tongue under the ridge of him, tasting salt and oil and his harsh but wonderful musk.

Men all around me start going for each other, kissing or just feeling each other up. Soon, I'm not the only man going down on someone.

I can't believe the erotic charge I'm feeling. I've always been—yeah, kind of ashamed of being gay. But here are all these men, very real, very masculine men, getting it on with each other.

A slender guy is pushed up against the bar with his pants pulled down, showing his tight, hairy little ass. One of the big bikers just unzips and pulls his cock out.

He finds the guy's asshole and slides up inside of him.

I watch as I suck cock, licking and sucking this hard, beautiful prick. I take his balls in my hand and slide a finger up to his asshole.

He moans as I slide inside.

"Yeah," he says, in his feminine voice. "Go for it, City Boy."

I always thought of anal sex as really dirty. In fact, I've never had anal sex, either way.

My boyfriends have always been "nice" guys, and we made do with oral and hands.

But here I can smell ass on the air, and I want some of it.

So I fuck his ass with my fingers, as I suck and lick his cock.

He sits in my barstool, spreading his legs so I can suck his ass too.

"Ream it!" he says. "Suck my asshole."

I do. It tastes greasy and dark, but the masculine, hard scent is such a turn on and his tight ass feels so nice. I slide my hand up, slipping my fingers around his prick and running them along the greasy tip, making him groan in pleasure.

That certainly gets my prick harder.

It's getting rougher now, as big guys half screw, half wrestle with each other. Pants and shirts are coming off, and these muscled, tattooed guys are almost naked and fucking everywhere.

I never imagined something like this in my most erotic fantasies.

I smell leather and motor oil and familiar after-shave. Kurt is there. He pulls me away from the 'girl's' cock and pulls me up, smiling coldly.

"I felt your hard-on," he says. "Now I want you to feel mine."

He pushes me down in front of him, holding my hair in his tattooed fist. I get the feeling he wouldn't take no for an answer. I wouldn't want him to anyway.

And that really makes me hard.

I unzip his jeans and pull out his hard, slender prick. I have a flash, just a really brief thought, that it would be perfect shoved deep up my asshole.

Then I take him into my mouth and start sucking him.

I love to suck cock. I love feeling the guy tighten as I find the right spots and the feel and taste of his prick as I turn him on more.

The metallic, harsh taste of another man's come in my mouth is the best of all.

I slide my hands around his hard, muscled ass. I can feel his tightness and strength as I cup his hard ass cheeks through his jeans.

"Get up," he says. He drags me to my feet and kisses me.

I've kissed a lot of men. No, I didn't say slept with. I haven't. Just kissed.

But I've never been kissed like this, by a heavily bearded men, his whiskers rough on my face, his mouth tasting of cigarettes and jerky and beer, his strong tongue probing my mouth without hesitation.

"I want you to fuck my ass," I hear myself say.

My God! I didn't really say that, did I?

But I did. I want his hard, slender prick way up inside of me. I want his hard body, redolent with oily garage smells, slamming into my ass, filling me with that cock. I want to feel the leather of his pants and the rough denim of his jacket on my skin, and his hard prick fucking my virgin asshole, hard and deep.

I don't know what I expected, but being pushed face down on the bar wasn't it. I felt my pants pulled roughly down, then I feel a spit-wet hand on my asshole.

I feel a cock at my asshole a second later.

And I was so aroused I can't even think.

The feeling of a cock being forced into your ass is the most erotic feeling imaginable. And a guy who just takes control makes it so much better.

Kurt just pushes in, slowly but without a pause. I yell as his cock pulls me open, almost ripping me apart. Then he begins to fuck me, with long, deep strokes.

Shit! I am so turned on! But it hurts too and I begin to moan and cry.

Kurt laughs.

"Take it like a man!" he says.

All around us, men are fucking and sucking and drinking beer. Some are just watching the action; others are getting blowjobs as they check out the scene.

It is like a scene out of a religious pamphlet on what happens to homosexuals after they die: Getting ass-fucked for eternity by big, dirty, vicious bikers.

Only it feels more like I am in heaven.

Kurt pushes way deep inside my ass, so deep I can't breath, and yells as he comes, filling my ass with his load.

Then he steps away, and another man takes his place.

I try to straighten up, but the new man pushes me back down on the bar and unzips his pants.

"You're riding with us, ya gotta pay," the biker says. "We're gonna drag your ass to Reno, but you're pulling our train tonight."

"What?" I ask.

"Pull a train," the guy repeats. "Getting fucked by every guy here, at least whoever wants some. You get a train lined up behind you, and your ass is the caboose.

A wave of fear and excitement flows through me. The thought is exciting, but also scary.

Because I'm the bitch at the end of it.

My cock is throbbing. I have never been aroused like this, never once. I feel the guy push into my ass, deep and hard, and I cry out in both pleasure and pain as he pushes way deep inside me.

I can feel his hard prick fucking me, jamming deep inside and then pulling back for another stroke.

There is a roar as someone drives their bike right into the bar. There is shouting and greetings, as more bikers arrive.

Someone grabs my hair and sticks a cock in my face. I don't know or really care whose cock it is. It is big and tough and not real clean, but I suck it eagerly into my mouth, tasting the manly stench of it.

Oh, Jesus! I have never been so turned on. I had always thought of 'gay' as being just like one of the girls.

But here I am, just like one of the guys. Big, rough guys, men who don't play the little emotional, romantic games, but just see what they want and take it.

And I want them to take me. I want to be fucked and made to suck them and do whatever else they want.

The guy grunts and comes off in my ass. I am burning and sore when he pulls out, but a few seconds later, I feel yet another cock at my asshole, and it slides inside of me, longer than the others, and deeper yet up my battered asshole.

My mind goes gray, from pain and pleasure. I feel cock after cock fucking my ass, and the come flowing out of my asshole and dripping down my balls and cock. At some point, Kurt slaps me to get my attention, and gives me a spoon of coke to snort.

The party goes on for hours. I must have been ass-fucked by thirty different guys. My asshole is on fire and I'm in a lot of pain, but inside I feel truly satisfied.

Because as I look around, men are fucking men, dancing with men, totally uninhibited and totally comfortable. They were men, tough men, real men.

Gay men.

A fight breaks out, complete with smashing furniture and knives drawn. Finally, the fight goes outside and both men come back in, bloodied and battered and smiling.

I began to realize my interpretation of "Queer" might need a little adjustment.

Kurt comes back over.

"How ya doing now, kid?" he asks.

I smile.

"Pretty damned good," I tell him. He hands me a big mug of beer.

"You get any yourself?" he asks.

I shake my head. I have been so busy being fucked or giving head to guys, I haven't really given myself much thought.

"No, I didn't," I admit.

Kurt nods, reaching down to touch my prick.

"I can take care of that," he says with a crooked grin.

Imagine. Here I am, in a bar full of the biggest, toughest-looking and most fearsome men I have ever seen, all of them drinking and fucking and sucking. Big-muscled men, with massive thighs and arms and hard asses and tattoos and piercings everywhere.

And they are completely unashamed or embarrassed that they aren't "regular" guys.

That simple observation probably says more about me and my assumptions than it does about them.

Kurt begins sucking my come-dripping cock, hard and deep into his mouth, running his big, thick tongue over it, half sucking, half jacking me off. He runs his greasy hand over the tip, then licks and sucks me again. His big hands find my balls, squeezing and pulling at them, spreading all the men's come on them, making me even hornier. He sucks deep on my prick, sliding rapidly up and down on it.

I can feel his beard and his strong lips and my own tightening balls as I get ready. I yell as Kurt makes me have a really hard ejaculation.

Kurt sucks my cock deep into his mouth, sucking every last drop of come.

Kurt stands up and spits my jism into a coffee can on the floor expertly.

"Let's have another beer," he said.

The party goes on late into the night. I watch the wild scene all around us, a wild orgy of men. Sexy, masculine, sweat soaked, real men.

Fucking other real men.

We finally leave the bar, getting on the big choppers. Their roars shattered the desert night.

We head out of town, me on the back of Kurt's chopper. My cock is tired but happy and the vibration of the bike is both soothing on my ass and arousing to my cock. I move up against Kurt and felt him sit back against my body and cock.

A few hours later, he drops me off in Reno.

Well, it's been a while since that day. I met with Lonnie and he was everything I thought he would be.

We're still together, almost thirty years later.

But I have never forgotten that afternoon and night I spent with The Brethren.

I was just nineteen when I first realized that the word "Gay" encompassed a much bigger world than I had ever imagined.

And I took it like a man.

ROAD KING
John Scott Darigan

*W*hen the night was over and he drove the Harley back to his car, *Anthony Gardella realized that he, like everyone, wore a mask and what lay hidden beneath the surface could only be revealed slowly, like peeling back layers that cover a heart. He began to comprehend a minor shift in his perception, the confirmation that he was always moving toward the core of himself and what he would become. This night was the start of his unmasking.*

It was near the end of August. Anthony had just spent two long hours in a gay pub, talking through a breakup. He was twenty, body tight from years of hockey and lacrosse, a college Junior at Union, and a few months into the Albany gay scene with a fake ID.

His introduction to gay life occurred when he mistakenly assumed he had met the man he was destined to spend his life, with on his first night in a popular dance bar called RAGE. But Anthony fell out of love almost as quickly as he was overcome with the excitement of finding it, and the desire that had been present in June, had eluded him by summer's end.

Anthony left Russell sitting on the brownstone steps of his building on Willet, facing Washington Park. Russell was not pleased with Anthony's decision, but at twenty-eight, had entered the relationship with both eyes open: acutely aware of an age difference and the prob- ability of Anthony's inevitable wish to explore other men.

As he walked to his car, Anthony realized he regretted nothing. Russell would always be important to him and forever associated with the words "first love." He sincerely hoped they might find their way to the next stage in the relationship.

Post-break-up sex partners.

He thought of their better days together: a sweaty fuck on a queen- size bed at dawn, Anthony's hands gripping the headboard, on his knees waiting for the head of Russell's dick to enter his expertly double-fingered hole; the night they climbed over the red-brick wall that surrounds Victoria Pool in Saratoga and skinny dipped after hours; barbecuing on the roof of the apartment building where they had a perfect view of Albany's skyline, high-rises below a plethora of summer stars. The roof was where Russell practiced topiary. Misfit shrubbery of various shapes and sizes in pots cluttered the area: A

Mickey Mouse head missing an ear, a sagging Ionic column, a decapitated giraffe.

Anthony unlocked the car door and felt a sudden breeze whip along the avenue and heard the angry rustle of leaves in nearby trees that lined each side of the street. He felt the coming storm and something slightly uncertain in the air, like electricity crackling just below the dark cloud-filled sky.

He closed the windows and threw the car in drive.

The first drops to hit the windshield were massive and when Anthony was on the ramp to Interstate 87, they grew closer together. He switched his wipers on, each arm squeaked as they traveled back and forth across the glass. And then the sky, as if pried open by two hands, released its deluge.

A trailer truck sent arcs of spray out from its rear wheels. Anthony passed on the left and for a moment lost control as the car hydroplaned. In that uncertain split-second, when he knew the car would either veer off or regain its hold on the road, Anthony held his breath and wondered what it would feel like to die.

Layers and layers of rain continued to pound the car. Visibility was extremely poor, so he pulled into the rest area between Exits 9 & 10, a few miles away from his parents' home. The parking lot, like the interstate, was quiet: a Wal-Mart truck, a U-haul, and a red Honda Prelude. There was also a Harley-Davidson motorcycle illuminated by Anthony's headlights, parked under several tall pine trees. He pulled the key from the ignition, switched off the lights, and the motorcycle was again ensconced in darkness.

Anthony ran fast to the men's room. He was completely soaked when he stopped and sheltered under the overhang above the entrance. He stood there for a moment and listened to the sound of the wind, the rustling trees, an impossibly loud clap of thunder, and water like a waterfall that fell from roof to ground.

The bathroom was empty. Anthony positioned himself before the urinal and unzipped his tight, well-worn blue jeans. In mid-stream, he heard the door open. He wanted to turn his head, glance back to see who had entered, but his position made it difficult to do without being completely conspicuous. He had heard from friends in Albany that this particular rest area could be a hot spot for casual sex. Married men who left their wives and children safely tucked away in bed were known to frequent the place. There was even a raid a few years back that proved quite embarrassing for more than a few area business executives and men of high-standing in the community. He waited, thinking the man would sidle up beside him at the urinal, but there was no sound of wet shoes moving across the floor, no slamming of a stall door.

Anthony put his cock back in his pants, turned around, and walked to the sinks. He saw a man wearing black leather chaps over a pair of jeans and a black T-shirt standing with his legs spread shoulder-width apart, his arms crossed at his chest. He was tall, about six-foot-four-inches, and had short black, close-cropped hair, a dark complexion.

He was staring at Anthony.

Anthony washed his hands and tried not to appear nervous, but couldn't stop looking at the reflection in the mirror on the wall above him. The man had not moved an inch. Uncomfortable and a little frightened, Anthony crossed to the towel dispenser and dried his hands.

The man's eyes followed his every move.

"Can I help you with something?" Anthony asked.

"*C'est possible.*"

The voice was brusque, deep. French. Anthony had forgotten a great deal from his four years of study of the language in high school, but could easily translate this simple reply: *It is possible.* He wondered how he could help the man who looked to be in his early thirties.

"*Tu parle le Française?*"

"*Je prefere Anglais.*"

"*Bien sur...*Of course," the man moved from his fixed spot. Pointed-toe black boots carried him across the floor with an air of absolute authority. Anthony had never encountered such confidence before. It was as if this stranger owned the space and Anthony was intruding. His biceps bulged in the T-shirt that was soaked to the skin. The man stood at the urinal and unzipped his pants. Anthony heard the steady flow hit porcelain and waited.

For what, he wasn't sure.

He knew he could walk out, get back into his car and drive the few miles home. But he also knew his parents were sleeping soundly and not expecting him at any specific time. Now considered an adult in their eyes, there was no more waiting up or the imposition of curfews.

When the man finished, he turned around with his pants still open. His cock was impressive and growing larger, as was Anthony's straining for release from inside his underwear.

"My name is Eric," the man announced as he closed his pants, just as two men walked in to use the facilities.

Anthony bolted for the door and found that the storm had slowed considerably in the few minutes he'd been inside. He walked back to his car. Instead of climbing in, though, he moved to a water-soaked picnic table underneath the trees, close to the Harley.

Eric followed, approached him.

"It's not smart, parking your bike under trees like this."

"I like to take risks. You?"

Anthony averted his eyes, marveled at his uncomfortable reaction, uncertain how to proceed. He looked around; his car was the only one close by. The vehicles he'd seen before had taken off and the two men in the bathroom were about to, near the opposite end of the rest area.

Anthony looked at his watch, it read: 12:04.

"Is there somewhere you need to be?" Eric asked.

"Just home."

"Ah. Then go."

"Where are you headed?" Anthony didn't want to appear too interested, but knew once the question was posed, he'd given himself away.

"Home also, eventually. To Montreal. Have you ever been?"

"Yeah, once."

A memory of a last-minute road trip with his friend Wayne: a night of bar-hopping and a sex club accommodation where Anthony wore a towel, allowed men he'd never met grope him, where he walked into rooms with small TV's that played non-stop gay porn. He and Wayne found one where a guy wore a Venetian Carnival mask and was on all fours, waiting—a fifteen inch black dildo and a tube of lubricant strategically placed on the bedside table. Anthony locked the door and he and Wayne fucked the guy for a half-hour, and then put the dildo to good use.

Eric's hands were huge, his fingers thick. He put an arm around the back of Anthony's neck and pulled him in for a minute-long kiss. His tongue was strong and Anthony let go of himself for that moment, knowing he'd follow Eric anywhere that night.

"Come." Eric mounted the seat and motioned for him to do the same. The gleaming chrome-and-metal cycle was large, menacing—a bit like its owner—the perfect bike for his considerable frame. Anthony saw the words, ROAD KING emblazoned on the bike's right side.

"Where to?"

The engine was leaking oil. Eric reached down and dirtied his finger, wiped it on Anthony's cheek, and laughed. In any normal circumstance he would have been livid and walked away. But here, Anthony did nothing, and felt his dick get hard again.

"I drive from New York. On my way to friends in Saratoga," Eric said.

"You're not far."

"I know. Come with me. I want to see you naked."

Blood rushed to Anthony's head, he looked away.

"Now," Eric said, "we leave your auto here."

He offered Anthony his helmet, then turned the ignition. The sound

152

of the bike was deafening, louder than Anthony had expected. He yelled to be heard over the scream of the motor, "I—I can't." But Eric's steady and intense gaze was impossible to refuse, and Anthony climbed aboard, straddled the seat behind him. He wasn't sure where to put his arms and hands and let Eric roughly position them, first to his chest which was hard and well-developed, and then around his waist. Anthony could feel Eric's cock. It was in raging hard-on mode and was thick—much thicker than Russell's. Eric moved Anthony's hand inside his jeans. He wasn't surprised to find Eric's crotch sweaty and that he wasn't wearing underwear. Anthony couldn't get the image out of his mind of taking it in his mouth and maybe giving it a temporary home in another part of his body. The bike jerked forward. Anthony held tight, and in seconds they were back on the road.

This was his first time on a motorcycle. He always heard of terrible fates that could befall those riding. But this ride, although fast and dangerous, was undeniably exhilarating. He could feel the power of the wind and see the beauty of the rain that came down in tiny sprinkles, as he rode off into darkness.

They turned off at Exit 14 and kept going until Eric parked at a house down a side road near the thoroughbred racetrack. There were two SUVs and a pickup truck parked in front. The garage door was open and Anthony could see two more Harleys inside. He heard music. It sounded like a party.

"Come on. Don't be afraid."

Eric stopped when he realized Anthony wasn't following.

"Trust me. You will only do what you want."

"Seriously?"

"I promise."

Anthony was curious. He knew there was a lot more going on in the scene than what he'd been privy to in the downtown Albany bars. But he was also apprehensive, wondered what lay in wait behind the front door as they approached.

Eric pressed the lit doorbell. "I just realized I don't know your name."

"Anthony."

"Nice to meet you."

The door opened and a good-looking guy, also wearing tight leather pants over jeans, stood at the threshold. Anthony followed Eric inside and watched as the two muscular guys hugged briefly like straight men. Eric's friend, Tim, introduced himself and offered a firm handshake. Then he smiled at Eric, as if the two were in on some private joke.

There were seven guys altogether in the room, several holding drinks. It felt like everyone was watching Anthony, and the stares made him think of a National Geographic special he'd recently seen that showed wolves on the hunt.

Anthony walked into the kitchen. He was comfortable in party scenes, having attended several that often went out-of-control at his fraternity house in Schenectady. He made himself a vodka-cranberry in a large red plastic cup, and went heavy on the vodka.

He moved through a sliding glass door to the empty, privacy-fenced-in, backyard. He strolled around the lit swimming pool that was shaped like a kidney. Eric came out and offered him a joint. They shared it.

"My friends like you."

"I like some of your friends."

Eric laughed.

"This is a club. They'd like you to join."

"What's involved in the initiation?" Anthony finished his drink in one greedy swallow and put his cup down on the lawn. The alcohol tasted good and gave him the buzz he needed.

"You catch on, fast, *non*?"

"*Oui*." Anthony said. He held Eric's face in both hands and kissed him.

When they finished the joint, Eric and Anthony returned to the house and found it empty. The music was still on, but there was no one in sight.

"Where'd they all go?" Anthony asked.

Eric moved him to a door that, once opened, revealed painted wooden steps leading to the basement, a room aglow in red and black light. It was an entry into another world. Two of the guys wore leather masks, the jeans were now gone, and a few cocks stood at attention. Anthony was intrigued to see someone bound and hanging in a sling. He had once rented a video with Russell where he saw some porn bottom getting fucked in one by every guy in the room, and it looked to him as if everyone here had ambition to do the same.

There was an old Harley chopper in one corner of the room and Eric led Anthony in that direction, pulling his shirt off along the way. Someone came over and touched Anthony's nipple. It was Tim. They kissed as Eric pulled Anthony's Nikes, his jeans, and underwear off. Anthony leaned on the bike for support and felt the throb of Eric's thick dick in the crack of his ass. On the other side of the bike, Tim was brandishing his own cock for Anthony to suck.

Anthony took it in his mouth, as Eric's fingers worked at his hole. He closed his eyes and enjoyed the poking, prodding, and sucking.

When he opened them again, he saw the sling-guy getting fucked in the ass by a gray-haired man who was late-thirties, maybe early-forties. His dick was even larger than Eric's, and for an uncomfortable moment, Anthony thought he was Mr. Sherman, his fourth-grade teacher. The guy in the sling was moaning loudly, definitely in a state of pleasure and intense pain. The force of the fucking he was receiving was sending him swaying to and fro.

Anthony heard Eric whisper to Tim that he should "go first, and open him up" and then Eric's tongue was in his mouth as he felt Tim's hands on his ass cheeks and the sudden slide of a lubricated cock. Anthony usually needed to go slow, and the force with which Tim was fucking him was too fast, too soon. He tried to wiggle his ass away from Tim's cock, but Tim was holding tight and giving him a pounding. Anthony lost his balance, but Eric was there to catch his stumble and held his face tightly to his chest.

"You fuckin' take it, boy," Eric whispered in his ear.

Anthony felt and heard the slap of skin and leather on the back of his ass. And then someone's tongue was licking his balls. There were three men lavishing him with attention he never imagined receiving. Tim took his cock out and came on Anthony's ass. The explosion of cum landed all over his back. Someone had a white gym towel handy and Anthony was wiped clean. He opened his eyes and found Tim's mouth waiting for a kiss.

"You're fuckin' hot, you know that?" Tim said, and walked away to explore the gray-haired man and the sling.

Eric asked: "You ready for me, Anthony?"

Anthony nodded and closed his eyes. He once again held onto the bike and his face must have been close to the gas tank, because he suddenly smelled a strong whiff of gasoline. It gave him a kind of high.

Anthony cried out when Eric pushed the head of his dick into his ass. Tim was about the same size as Russell, but Eric's beer-can cock was ripping him apart. Eric noticed his discomfort and moved very slowly to compensate for the thickness. When he saw Anthony was still incredibly uncomfortable, Eric lay down on his back on a workout mat and a leather- masked man helped Anthony mount Eric's dick, which went a lot better. Anthony sucked the masked man's dick as Eric's hands lifted him up and then back down as he rode the entire shaft.

This went on for five minutes or so, and Anthony felt himself getting close to coming. He opened his eyes and silently communicated to Eric that he needed a break. Eric pulled out and his condom came off. He found another quickly and rolled it on. Then he pushed Anthony back down to the mat and positioned him on all fours. Anthony bit into his left arm when he felt Eric pushing back in. The masked man had Anthony eat his ass, but Anthony had to take several breaks while Eric pounded him unmercifully.

Anthony yanked the guy he was rimming closer, then pulled away from Eric, to start fucking the freshly rimmed asshole. The guy was too surprised to hesitate and Eric watched for a while before he gave his cock to the guy to suck on. Anthony liked being the top here. He liked seeing the guy he fucked choking as Eric shoved his dick down the guy's throat until he gagged.

The gray-haired man took a break from the sling and wandered over. He started touching Anthony's ass and in no time at all had two fingers in the hole, but when he started to put his monster-sized cock in, Anthony stopped, turned around, and gave the guy a contemptuous look. Eric laughed and then started kissing the gray-haired man and Anthony at the same time. Three tongues were moving in and out of three different mouths.

Eric fucked Anthony once more and Anthony came all over the aerobics mat; then Eric pulled out and came on Anthony's face. Finally, like he'd seen in the video he rented with Russell, all the guys stood around the sling-man and everyone came a second time on the guy's face and chest. Eric caressed Anthony's balls when he came and he shot his wad into the guy's open mouth—which seemed to impress everyone.

Completely spent, the guys moved upstairs, took their leather off, and jumped into the swimming pool. Afterwards, phone numbers were exchanged, and Anthony collected a few. Tim disappeared, then came back holding a pair of leather pants.

"These used to fit me, but don't any longer. You should try 'em on."

Anthony stripped off his jeans and pulled the tight pants up to his waist. They fit like a tight black glove. His cock hung out for all the world to see. Eric kissed him hard on the mouth and said, "Your first pair of chaps. Sweet."

"Nice ass," the gray-haired man said and smacked it with palm of his hand. "Next time, that ass is mine, boy."

"Only if you give up yours," was Anthony's reply, coupled with a wink. The gray-haired man smiled and passed his phone number along as well.

Anthony and Eric spent some time in a bedroom after everyone but Tim left. Red numbers glowed from a clock on the bedside table, it read: 3:55 and Anthony said, "I better get back."

Eric let Anthony drive the Harley back to the rest area, his arms wrapped around his waist. Anthony loved how both the bike and Eric felt. He never could've imagined wanting a motorcycle like this and wondered how he'd explain this newfound interest to his ultra-conservative parents.

The chaps were amazing. They looked great and would remind Anthony that he'd unearthed hidden treasure that night. A random rainstorm and a chance meeting had opened up a whole new chapter in his life. He wanted to tell someone, but knew Russell wouldn't want to hear it at this point. So, he'd wait until he had a friend that he could confide in, and maybe bring along for the ride next time.

The car was waiting where he left it and the parking lot was completely empty. Eric gave him one last kiss and Anthony promised to call and maybe even visit. Then, just as quickly as he'd appeared, Eric was gone—as the dark was turning into day.

Anthony made it home in less than ten minutes. He was in bed and sound asleep before Eric was back in Saratoga. The chaps were safely tucked away on the top shelf of his closet. Right before he closed his eyes and drifted off, Anthony felt a rush of excitement pulse through his body as he thought about the next time he'd get to wear them.

STORM RIDER
Cecilia Tan

Stormclaw settles his sunglasses onto his face. Although the wind is his ancient friend, road gravel and dust are not pleasant in his eyes. Leather creaks as he swings his leg over his mount. The bike rocks contentedly under him as he kicks the stand back end settles onto the tires. His hair is wound into a long braid, coiled against the skin of his shoulder like a black asp hidden under his jacket collar. It has been a long time since he has gone riding, but the time has come to resume his searching, his hunting. The Dragon bucks under him as he revs the engine, the roar out of chrome throats pleasing him. And then he is off, onto the road, heading west.

The sun is still in the sky, an hour or two from dropping behind the mountains. Stormclaw feels the heat on his face, the wind whipping across his bare chest, his leather-clad legs fusing to the machine under him. The sun is hot like a kiss, the wind like a lover's hand sneaking into his jacket, the rumble deep in his groin something else.

He pulls up to a roadhouse, angling the Dragon between two other bikes. The peeled paint on the thin walls once touted some brand of beer. He stares at the lettering, the images, doubting himself. I used to know how to do this, he thinks. Once upon a time.

Inside he pulls off his sunglasses. The light is dim, smoke-tainted. Two men are sitting at the bar in road-dusted denim, a few others sit at tables in the gloom, against the walls. Stormclaw takes a stool corner-wise from the two at the bar. The bartender, an over-thin man in an under-washed T-shirt, leans his crooked elbow on the bar in front of him. "What'll it be? Draft?"

Stormclaw nods, remembering the taste of beer, the earth turned to grain turned to ambrosia. The bartender puts the mug down on the wood, sloshing an inch out of the glass while the two bikers at the bar snicker. Stormclaw feels the disdain coming off all three of them as they stare at him. He takes a drink of the beer. It's mostly water. One of them spits out "Pretty boy."

Time does not pass in an orderly stream for Stormclaw. He has a sudden flash of the future—he gasps and shudders. He is sitting in a corner, a dark corner, his back to a wall, his hand around a sweating beer glass on the table. Under the table someone is sucking his cock, the tongue circling the swollen head and then the hot, wet mouth plunging down all around him, swallowing him. He blinks. Not yet.

That is not happening yet. First, they threaten him. "Pretty boy," he hears again.

He pulls off his gloves and puts them down on the bar, saying nothing. He takes a larger gulp of the beer and lets his jacket fall open. They are almost laughing openly now, like wolves that can't believe a wounded sheep has wandered into their den. "Jesus, look at you," one of them says. "What are you, some kind of faggot?"

Stormclaw lets a small smile onto his face. "No. I'm a fairy."

That does make them laugh, but nervously. Stormclaw's eyes do not smile and they are not sure what to make of him now that he has spoken. An edge of fear does not stop them, though. It spurs them on. "Fairy boy! What do you think you're doing, coming in here?"

"What do *you* come in here for?" Stormclaw replies. He is starting to distinguish between the two of them now. The one doing the talking has dirty red hair, a tooth missing, chapped lips. The other one is taller, quieter, browner. His face is sour.

Red answers. "We grab a brew, cocksucker."

"You want me to suck your cock, is that it?" Stormclaw's voice stays quiet, and yet all three men at the bar hear it.

Red moves fast, but Stormclaw moves faster. The man tries to grab him, lunging across the bar, hands open, but Stormclaw is off his stool, turning aside. The bartender retreats—not his fight—but Brown comes on then, too. Stormclaw lets the man grab him by the wrist while Red rushes in, as well. They both end up face down on the bar, one of Stormclaw's hands on the back of each of their necks. He speaks into the space between their two ears. "If you really want to fight, we'll have to go outside."

But they are weak. They are blubbering. The bartender is on the phone. Stormclaw walks out of the roadhouse in disgust.

His erection is pressing against his fly. He feels the awkward fold of the denim as he mounts The Dragon. The sun is setting and he rides toward the ball of fire, still searching. He is remembering how to play this game, now. The wind buffets the front of his body and he aches for hands to touch him, arms to hold him, somewhere wet to quench the burning tip of his firestick. That is, after all, why the name 'faggot' applies to him as well as 'fairy.' Silly humans.

The sun slips below the mountains as Stormclaw comes to rest at another roadside bar. Many more bikes here. Music comes muffled through the cinderblock walls. The wind has been tugging at his braid like a playful lover and wisps of his jet-black hair frame his face as he steps into the dimly lit room. Bar on the left, pool table on the right, small tables scattered about. His skin is still electric from the wind, despite the leather armor wrapped around his legs, his jacket. He takes a seat at the bar and waits for the challenge to come.

It takes longer this time. This group is smarter, more cautious, but as the liquor flows and evening slips into night, the young wolves of the pack crave excitement. Stormclaw does, too, his eyes meeting those of a man at a table near him. The man pops his cigarette into an open beer bottle with one finger and despite the loudness of the music, Stormclaw hears it sizzle. Before the man stands up, he lights another cigarette, the click of his lighter snapping shut coming as his chair scrapes back. The man is on his feet coming closer. Two friends of his are hanging back, waiting.

"We don't get many of your kind in here," the man says, and calls him a name Stormclaw does not recognize. Then he reads it as the bitter scent of cigarette smoke on the man's breath reaches him. He thinks Stormclaw is an Indian and Stormclaw wonders if perhaps he is, in some sense. "Any man wants to drink in here needs this."

The man pulls up his sleeve to reveal the blue veins of his wrist, running under skin scarred like the surface of the moon, pocked and lined by ancient wounds.

Stormclaw keeps his eyes locked on the other man's as he eases out of his jacket. His adversary has a scraggle of beard, no moustache, his eyes are blue. Stormclaw can also make out some kind of a tattoo on the man's neck, behind his ear and hiding under the man's short, brown ponytail. Now bare-chested and bare-armed, Stormclaw turns his right hand palm up to show the perfect skin of his wrist. With his other hand, he snatches the cigarette out of the man's mouth and holds the burning tip close to his flesh. Scragglebeard has a smile on his face, a light in his eyes. Stormclaw sucks on the anticipation in his mouth. "How long can you go?" he asks of Scragglebeard.

His adversary snaps his fingers and one of his cronies, a smooth faced blond, steps forward. Scraggle gets another cigarette, lights it with practiced puffs. He climbs onto the stool next to Stormclaw, puts his right arm onto the bar, and with the cigarette hanging from his lips, pulls Stormclaw's forearm onto his knee. "On three," he says, poising the burning end above Stormclaw's wrist. Stormclaw does the same and waits for the count. One, he feels the throb deep in his groin, two, he inhales, three...

The pain moves over his skin like pins and needles, the intense burning centered on his wrist sending out shock waves to every extremity. His cock pounds inside his jeans as the circle of energy he has created flows through them both. They are staring into each other eyes, teeth bared and jaws clenched, each wondering whether the other will quit first.... Stormclaw decides to see what will happen if he gives in. He pulls his arm away and let's out a whoop that sounds more like a cry of joy than pain, and then he begins laughing. All three of the men facing him break out into laughter, too. Stormclaw wants to throw them to the ground, tear the clothing from them and fuck them until his skin grows raw. But he just takes a drag on the cigarette, taps the ash from the end, and says "Two out of three?"

"You are a sick fuck," Scragglebeard says. "See if you can beat Jerome." The blond climbs into the chair and Stormclaw eyes him hungrily. "On three," Scraggle says, still in control.

The second burn makes Stormclaw's blood surge through his veins. The pain intensifies as time goes on and he ignores the smell, his eyes narrowing to slits as he lets the agony cut like daggers into his torso, his legs, so many parts of his body coming alive and struggling to keep still.

"Fuck you, fuck, fuck!" Jerome is screaming, still too proud to stop himself, "Sick motherfucker! Give up already!" But it is he who gives up, clutching his arm to him. The bartender is there with ice wrapped in a bandanna and Jerome is still swearing as he doubles over, pressing it to his wound. "You fucking tricked me!" It is not clear who he is referring to, Stormclaw or Scragglebeard. "That was way longer than...!" Perhaps the ice numbs him to silence. Scraggle pushes him off the stool and takes it for himself.

"We're tied," Stormclaw says to him.

The man motions for two whiskeys. The bartender puts down two shot glasses and fills them. Stormclaw never sees the bartender because his eyes never leave his adversary's. They drink in unison, tipping back their chins, their eyes still on each other. It is not so different now, Stormclaw is thinking. An age ago, he used to ride a black horse and drink ale with highwaymen. The whiskey adds another layer of fire to his insides. He wants to grab the man by the hair, and force his tongue into his mouth, press his erection against his leg...but he knows he won't. Stormclaw will play the game instead, which is just as good. Maybe better.

He is about to speak when he feels something wrong. He closes his hand over Scragglebeard's wrist. Stormclaw is the only one inside the bar who can hear the roar of the engine igniting. "Jerome is stealing my ride," he says softly, his grip tightening. Scragglebeard just laughs and Stormclaw leaves him there, knowing he is on his own.

In the parking lot, Jerome is throwing up gravel as The Dragon spins in a tight circle, the rear wheel squealing across the shoulder of the roadway, Jerome cursing and working the throttle with twists of his burned right wrist. He fights the bike up onto the surface of the road and up goes the front wheel, he loses his grip and falls back against the sissy bar. The next thing he knows he is lying on his back on the pavement. Stormclaw drags him into the gravel as a truck dopplers past. In a way it is a shame what he must do now. Stormclaw knows better than to trust highwaymen. He reminds himself of this as his knuckles are meeting the flesh of Jerome's face. He beats Jerome senseless and leaves him slumped over the hood of a car with little or no memory of what happened to him.

The Dragon comes when Stormclaw calls, and they race into the night, the wind turned chill now, and he has left his jacket behind. His hair streams freely behind him. He is trying to remember when his mount became a motorcycle. Sometime after they left the old country, and the old dangers. Stormclaw liked to seek out the new dangers, the new thrills. Yes, he remembers it now, searching for those who ever escape the mundane, safe life of hearth and blood family. He used to do it quite often. He is remembering now, the feeling of the wind in his hair, the hum of the motor through the pegs under his boots. His appetite has been whetted by the men he has touched today, whetted and far from slaked.

He is hardly aware of the bike pulling into another parking lot, until the moment when they come to a stop. He comes to, examining the adobe-plastered wall in front of him, a mural painted so large on the side he's not sure what it is. The Dragon has brought him into a small city, it seems. The doorway is in front of the building: glass, metal-framed, but curtained. Stormclaw pulls it open, pushes the curtain aside, and soaks in the scent of air-conditioning, liquor, and men.

The interior is divided into four quarters, separated by archways, bars along each side. Stormclaw walks in and keeps walking, up three steps to the back level, until he has reached the far wall. Eyes followed him as he made his way, but he does not look around at the men there until he has settled himself into a stool, his back to the bar, his elbows resting behind him. He knows he must look close to his elemental state, hair wild and flowing, torso bare, eyes crackling with gathered energy. The music here pulses subtly.

Two stools over from him a man sits, head to toe in leather, an unlit cigar in one gloved hand. He is not looking at Stormclaw. He is looking at another man, a younger man, positioned across the room. The young one has raven dark hair and Stormclaw is curious as to why this one is, like him, dressed in jeans and chaps, boots, but bare-chested. Ravenhair drifts close to the man with the cigar, they exchange looks, maybe even words, and suddenly Stormclaw feels desire and understanding blossom through his body like a gulp of whiskey. The man has put down the cigar and is kissing Ravenhair, bending him back like a young willow in a spring wind, one hand in the small of his back and the other caressing him with leather-gloved fingertips. Stormclaw's mouth opens in disbelief.

He has found faery kin. Humans, they are obviously humans, but...there has always been much he has not understood about mortals and their ever-changing ways. He accepts this and leaves himself open, as always, to whatever may come his way. "You, boy," the man says with the cigar clenched in his teeth. Ravenhair is kneeling now, on the floor at the foot of the man's stool, his hands clasped in the small of his back. "Looking to have some fun?"

Stormclaw nods.

"Then say 'yes, sir' and join us."

"Yes, sir." Stormclaw feels the words come over his tongue and sinks to his knees as well. Unlike Ravenhair, he continues to look up. The man is speaking and he wants to watch the man's lips and tongue while he explains. He talks for some time, Ravenhair answers and Stormclaw does, too, with "yes, sir" and then adds, "teach me, sir."

Other men have gathered around and Stormclaw feels their desire stoking his own, like rising heat whipping a thundercloud to new heights. He reaches out and begins to kiss Ravenhair, his lips electrifying the boy's, locking them together for a long moment until hands pull them apart. Then they are on the move, into the other half of the back level, through the archway, to a wooden frame standing in the center of the floor. Short lengths of chain hang from the crosspiece, and Stormclaw finds his wrists bound in the air. He is chest-to-chest with Ravenhair, their mouths again close enough to touch. "First one to cry out is the loser," says a male voice in his ear.

He understands it is a contest but he is too in-the-moment to think about whether, in the future, he will win or lose. They are dragging his pants down to his ankles. His firestick pokes hard and hot against Ravenhair's, equally erect and straining. And then the lashing begins.

Stormclaw feels the first strike of the leather cat-o-nine cross his back like the first bite into a sour summer fruit, a rich and intense pleasure. He draws breath waiting for the next blow to fall, and as he exhales he feels Ravenhair's breath on his shoulder—they are like one animal, tensing and then letting go, and then gathering themselves again. Breathe in, tense for the strike, then let go as the pain rains down around you. Stormclaw leaves his mouth hanging open as he presses his cheek to Ravenhair's, his eyes closed in ecstasy, wondering if in his life he has ever felt such an exquisite sensation as being whipped in this manner.

The whips continue to do their work, and Stormclaw feels the sweat prickling across both of their skins as they press together. Ravenhair's jaw is clenched tight now, and Stormclaw rubs against him, the boy becoming more rigid even as Stormclaw feels himself melting with each impact. The men are talking to them, or to Ravenhair, it seems, but Stormclaw is beyond hearing the words. He hears only voices, some encouraging, some chiding, all washing him with sensation. His back is on fire now, each strike of the leather feeling like sparks flung from a struck coal. Stormclaw arches his back into it like a cat into his master's hand, and then thrusts against Ravenhair's skin. The blows are coming faster now, harder, and Stormclaw feels the scream building inside his partner. He does not understand these mortals, how they reach their limits, how they decide that experiences must be finite and must end. He pulled his arm away from the cigarette, but he did not have to. Ravenhair is coming to no damage, and yet Stormclaw senses the peak coming, the moment of no return.... The whip tears at him from shoulder to ass and he presses his groin against Ravenhair as the scream begins.

Stormclaw soaks in the primal sound as the whipping continues. Ravenhair's chest is heaving against his, as he refills his lungs and cries out again. Ten strokes, ten more strokes, he hears the voices of the men counting them, the grunting of their assailants; as they have saved their hardest, most savage strokes for last. Stormclaw finds his legs giving way under him, his arms straining in the chains as he squeezes his eyes closed tight and drinks in the burning pain, which is gone as quickly as it comes. Hands are running over his back now, and words of praise, and he opens his eyes and is surprised to find tears spilling from them. He gulps in great breaths of air as if he has just surfaced from the bottom of the sea. No one seems surprised by this. And he realizes he has won.

He is exchanging handshakes and smiles—and words, too. He's not sure what he's saying but his mouth can take care of itself. Then the man with the cigar sits him down in a corner, in a chair, and drapes a jacket over his shoulders. Stormclaw leans back and enjoys the burn of his skin. He feels it radiate through him, out his chest, the tip of his cock glowing red-hot.

And there is Ravenhair, on his knees, crawling toward him. Cigarman is laughing, smiling and approving, and then there are Ravenhair's eyes, peering up from the dark space between Stormclaw's knees. He licks his lips, and then places them on the hot shaft, so tender at first, his tongue exploring. Then he sucks and pulls the apple of Stormclaw's cockhead into his mouth. Stormclaw's head falls back. How many years has it been since he was touched this way? How many lifetimes? His sense of time, weak as always, cannot tell him. A long time. And it seems a long time that Ravenhair sucks him, head bobbing, one hand stroking Stormclaw's balls, letting Stormclaw's cock deeper and deeper into him.

This time it is in Stormclaw's chest that a scream begins to build. Yes, that's right, he thinks to himself, that is what I had forgotten. That is what I wanted. For desire to be finite, to find that end, to have the longing burst and explode and ebb away for a while. Almost mortal. How many ages has he been quiet at home, quiescent, his hunger dampened by his never-changing state? His state is changing now, as he feels the welts on his back crackle as he arches forward, his blood quickening, everything building like the thunder that is his birthright, suddenly ready.

Suddenly cracking. His voice pours out of him, as his essence pumps into Ravenhair's mouth. He grips the boy's head, cradling him even as he savages him with two, three, four thrusts.

Stormclaw falls back in slow motion, his eyes opening and closing as he shakes his head from side to side, and then it is over. He blinks. Ravenhair is grinning from the floor, a bit of come smeared on one cheek. Stormclaw grins back. He gives another shake of his head. "Thank you," he says, remembering his manners.

Later, as he rides The Dragon east, toward the sunrise, he will look down to see the scars on his wrist are healed.

THE FIRST MARK
TruDeviant

When I came to San Francisco from the dismal suburbs in the late seventies, I was fueled by a mixture of anger and horniness. I wasn't yet twenty-one, but I ran around drinking and drugging, looking for the escapes from a stifling childhood that an urban landscape provided. I was rarely carded at a bar. In those crazy days, not many places cared how old you were.

I walked the streets South of Market dreaming of wild things. Ever since I discovered a thin portfolio of Rex drawings in the Taste of Leather store on Folsom Street, I wanted to do wild things. I thought Rex's drawings were much more intense than the Tom of Finland drawings that were already proliferating in all the other sex shops. And in my mind I added details to those drawings, nasty details that I thought Rex should have penciled into them.

I hung around with a guy named Sam. He was a cab driver with a bleached Mohawk, but he didn't look like Robert DeNiro.

He was forty-two. He took me to punk rock clubs. He had an abnormally huge cock. He showed it to me while we were hanging out in the crowded Ladies Room at the Mabuhay Gardens during a raucous Avengers concert. Mabuhay stuck out along the row of strip joints on Broadway in North Beach. It was a mediocre Filipino restaurant by day and the hottest punk club in the city at night. We saw all the local bands there: The Dead Kennedies, the Zeros, Leila and the Snakes, and the Cunning Stunts (obviously an all girl band). And Sam made me go with him to see the Pretty Pedophiles, fresh from the U.K., with their one and only single, "Elevator Hater."

Sam and I never had sex. He liked boys. No, he *loved* boys. Fourteen year olds. The more they got him into trouble, the more he tried to take care of them. They were always nasty little bastards from bad homes whose parents didn't give a shit about them. But Sam did, each one causing him more grief than the last. Eventually, he had to leave town because of them. The little fuckers.

Maybe that's why Sam liked me. I was a nasty bastard more often than not. Had I been six years younger, I would've had him.

We went to record stores. He stole Fleetwood Mac and Eagles cassette tapes and recorded the Clash and the Sex Pistols over them. He gave them to me with color Xeroxes of young brown boys cut out of National Geographic magazines.

After Sam left, I became a lurker at the biker bars, the leather queer bars South of Market. With spiked black hair and pale white skin, I hung around at the Eagle, the Brig, the Watering Hole, and even caught the tail end of the scene at clubs like Black and Blue and the Barracks. I spent hours watching these guys. Sometimes, I made fun of them. After all, I wasn't supposed to like anything that was so popular. Probably I was jealous of the fact that they belonged to these motorcycle clubs, jealous because I would never belong.

At the Eagle bar, I ridiculed the men for liking that disco shit. I liked the punks. I got a boner from the anger, the strange high of pessimism and simple-minded anarchy in the music. I just couldn't figure out how these guys could be into kinky stuff and listen to that syrupy, slicked-up, gospel-slut Donna Summer on Sunday afternoons at the Eagle patio. Where was the edginess, the risk, the wildness these men were supposed to be craving? Those beer busts had the gossipy air of a church picnic to me.

But still, I went to those bars and clubs and watched men. They talked to me. I was not rude, but fairly unresponsive. I covered my public shyness with a low-key observer's stance. I started to wear boots and a leather jacket, but hovered on the edge of things. I didn't grow a moustache and I didn't get a motor bike. I began to notice that a lot of these guys had little fetishes in addition to wearing cow skin, but I sensed that few guys were seriously twisted in the way I knew I was.

A few of the older guys asked me to join their clubs, but I didn't join things. I wasn't a group kind of guy. And I was afraid, not of them, but of the razor-sharp desires that were poking out of my chest. So I stayed fascinated by the whole thing. I lurked, I watched, I waited, and things started to come to me—

A lawyer with a Harley. From the deep South. A big man. An inch taller than I was, which made him six foot five inches. Open face. Drew the attention of the whole leather clad crowd. The way he filled up his leather completely. As if it were part of his flesh.

I knew from the general reaction to him that he was a stranger to the Eagle. He offered me coke and a ride to his place. He was twitching under his cool façade. It was more than the coke. He was like a poisonous snake glittering, well fed and stranded in the middle of freshly tarred asphalt in summer. He spoke lies, but I didn't listen much. His eyes told me all the truth I needed to know. He said he wanted to fuck me at his new house. But I saw right past that.

He sped all the way home. From behind him on the bike, I hugged his massive chest because of his reckless road etiquette. He stopped and put his boots down on the concrete driveway of his two-story Victorian on Dubose Triangle, revving the motor for effect.

New cream-colored paint coated the outside of the house. Prissy décor flourished everywhere inside. The onyx ashtray on the coffee table easily cost more than three months rent for me.

He handed me an Anchor Steam beer from the fridge and gestured at me to follow him upstairs. Off came his jacket, vest, and shirt. He flaunted his tedious muscled vanity.

I laughed at his flawlessness. He moved fast. Pushed me down on the edge of his king-sized bed. He was on top of me and held me down by the arms. I smelled my beer foaming on the plush beige carpeting below. For a few seconds I thought I'd been wrong about him, so I didn't struggle. But then he started to talk to me. Right into my ear. Some kind of goofy talk in this tiny Mickey Mouse voice I could hardly believe was coming out of this stud's face.

He told me how Daddy wanted to fuck me. And that I should be his good boy.

Fuck that shit. I elbowed him hard in the gut. Knocked the wind right out of him. I laughed louder than before and wormed my way out from under him. I fell onto the dense carpet, soggy with my beer. He was gasping above me.

Under the bed a few inches from my nose was a pair of handcuffs. I grabbed them and stood up. They were the real deal. Like cops carry. They were so heavy in my hands. I was rock hard instantly. He saw the look in my eyes and he let me put them on his wrists clumsily.

"Please—hit—me," he said with difficulty, facedown in a goose-down pillow.

He rolled over on his back and pinned his own arms under his massive frame. He didn't have to ask me twice. I crouched over him. Still fully dressed. My dirty boots on his fluffy beige sheets. I started hitting him hard with open palm. His chest first until it was bright red around the thimble-like nipples. Then his face. Just as hard.

I squatted down on his leather crotch and felt his fat bone hardness between my asscheeks. And I started slapping him back and forth until his nose and his mouth were bloody.

His eyes never left mine. As soon as I knew he'd shot his load, I hopped off him and headed out of there, not forgetting to fling that onyx ashtray into the beveled mirror above his fireplace and grab another beer.

I didn't even mind that I hadn't shot my load, because there had already been an explosion somewhere inside my head. I replayed my little conquest over and over in slow motion, as I headed right back to the bar.

*

Sometime after that, I fell into a new place called Chaps. A swarthy bartender in his late twenties got most of my attention. His name was Gunner. I overheard him telling some guy that he used to be a cop. I saw that now he pretended he was an outlaw. He wore thin leather chaps over fraying jeans behind the bar. Bulging out in front and back. Keys on the right. Coal-dust eyes that never seemed to register the person across the bar from him as anything other than someone who would stare at him. I could see that some of these guys came into the place just to get drunk and gawk at him more than at each other.

His confident swagger repulsed me, but I studied him carefully, looking for any sign of something that could get me what I thought I wanted from him. It came at the end of the night when he was a little tired of babysitting the older drunk guys who sat there pickled under the cigar smoke halo they made around him. I felt a certain weakness in him as he told them with a forced smile that they had to drink up and get out. He put one boot up on the sink and stuck his ass back as he bent over the bar to talk to the owner.

It was then that I could tell he was waiting for someone. Someone who'd surprise him. Someone who would really give him something the boys in his motorcycle club couldn't.

The next Monday night I waited outside in the alley behind the bar. I found his motorbike easily. By now, I'd seen him on it a few times. I knew he'd be coming out of the bar in minutes, so I unzipped my jeans and pissed some of the beers he'd been serving me that night all over his chrome and leather. I watched my piss make crooked lines in the road dust that clung to the painted metal. By the time I was done, I was hard. My left hand rubbed my cock and my right hand jiggled two beer bottle caps I'd picked up off the floor of the bar.

In my mind I was watching him sit down on his bike. I invented the expression on his face as my scent soaked through his jeans, making his asshole moist and even more pungent.

I decided not to wait for him to finish up in the bar. I knew he was alone inside. My mood was ripe. I crammed my hard-on back in my jeans and went around to the bar's front door. I banged on it. He opened it wide. He recognized me and said nothing. He looked down and saw my thumbs hooked in my pockets and my fingers framing the hardness under the tight faded denim.

"Left my keys in there," I said looking intensely into his bloodshot eyes and then into the brightly lit barroom behind him. I'd felt the hopefulness in him and then I'd seen the hardness cover it up in a second. I moved inside. He said, "I didn't see any keys," but he shut and locked the door.

I walked over to the bar.

"How about a beer?"

He regained his bartender pose and said, "Sure, you can drink it while I finish up. I'm almost done."

He swung a section of the bar up and went behind. He handed me an ice cold one and opened one for himself.

"You don't say much, do you?" he smiled and gulped half the contents. He'd noticed that I hadn't been social with the other clientele. There was a lot about this guy not to like and it was turning me on.

I leaned over the bar and stuck my tongue right in his open mouth while he was talking and put my hand on the back of his head. He kissed me back for a few long breaths. The air whistled softly coming out of his nose. I could tell he'd been drinking quite a lot. He tasted like beer, smoke, and I could smell a hot day's worth of sweat.

I tugged on both his arms and pulled him up onto the bar while he sucked my tongue. Then I yanked him hard so he slid off the counter into my arms. He was unsteady when he landed on his feet, so I moved back and let him fall halfway to the floor. One of his hands grabbed my bouncing bone, which I'd freed while downing the beer, and he plopped down in front of me.

I bent over and slapped his face hard as he looked up at me confused. He put both hands flat on the dirty floorboards and raised himself up on his knees. I stepped on the fingers of both his hands firmly, but not with all my weight, while he looked up at me. I was rock hard again.

He was mine already. He wasn't going to fight me. He wanted that bone and a lot more.

I slapped him three times hard again in the face. He moaned, got dizzy, and put his forehead down on the floor. I started to piss on him. A steady stream that I aimed mostly at the frayed material that barely covered his ass. He was still dazed from the slaps. I released his fingers and knelt with my shins on his shoulders, my bone-tip touching his back. Quickly, I reached down to his drenched butt and ripped open the worn material until it hung in tatters around the edge of his chaps. The flesh was not dark like the rest of him. It was white and hairless, like a fish belly. He grabbed onto my boots at the ankles and I start smacking his pale cheeks. His head was trapped there against the floorboards, my legs pressing down on him.

I slipped my leather belt out of my jeans and looped it around his neck. And pulled him, crawling, along the floor to the pool table. I stood him up and shoved him over onto the plywood cover that protected the green felt below. His chaps were torn at the knees, his cock was hard, and thought that I'd have liked it better if he was less willing to let me have my way with him.

Even so, I was happy to slip a dry finger in his moist asshole. It was clean and very tight. I was sure he'd kept himself ready for a long time under that bullshit tough-guy attitude.

"Looks like I found my keys, shithole," I said as I jingled the clump that was ringed to his belt loop. I kept my belt tight around his neck the whole time.

I noticed the supply closet door to the side of us was wide open with a bare light bulb shining down on an assortment of brooms and mops. I spied a big roll of black duct tape on the shelf and I left him for a few seconds to get it.

He was still a bit dazed and stayed put. Quickly, I hopped up on the table in front of him. I taped his arms down to the plywood, sticking them straight out from his body, twisting and overlapping long strips of the sticky stuff. He put his chin on the plywood and kept his eyes on my bone. When I was done with his arms, I crouched down and dangled it half-hard in his face. He opened his mouth, but I inched back and slapped a long piece of the tape between his lips and wrapped it around his head. That's when he started to struggle, but it was too late then.

I moved around to the other side of the table where his butt was exposed on the edge of it. I used more long strips of the tape to anchor his boots to the legs of the pool table. That spread his ass apart nicely. He started jerking around, but the hard, uneven surface of the plywood slowed him down.

I decided to give him something else to get upset about and undid my belt from around his neck. I hit him hard and fast with it, the pointed end making thin, arrow-shaped welts rise up on his pearly cheeks. He was making all kinds of sounds through the tape, but it only spurred me on. I didn't stop until he was sobbing and through resisting the blows. Then I stuck my finger in that hole again. It was still wet and willing.

I'm sure he expected me to give him the best fuck I could throw up his ass. I knew he was hurting as much from being down flat on the plywood as he was from my belt. The rugged edge of the board was pressing splinters into his crotch and thighs.

I jumped up on the table and yanked the tape from his mouth. He yelped and kept his eyes closed. I knelt with my knees beside his ears and I pressed my piss hard-on against those sore lips. I smeared a little clear liquid on them before he opened and tried to suck the head, but he couldn't lift his chin up. It just didn't fit like that.

I thought about letting him up and having him suck me off, but I was already done with him. I felt like doing things to him that I didn't know if I could control. I wanted him to bleed more than from his scraped up knees.

Since I had to piss again, I let it go full force in his face. He opened his mouth as best he could and slurped some of it. He looked good that way. Eager to take what little I was giving him. I pushed out the last squirt of hot piss. I was limp as week-old celery by that time, so I zipped up. He looked confused and grateful, but started to struggle against the tape. With the aid of my piss wetting the tape, he'd pull free in a few minutes.

"Gotta go," I said and slapped his stunned face a few more times.

He still said nothing, but as I walked out and shut the door behind me, I relished the thought of seeing his expression the next time I showed up there. I congratulated myself for doing such a good job of warming him up for the next guy who might just stick around and give him that fuck.

After a few months I got better at figuring out which city biker dudes would enjoy being truly abused. I was growing more comfortable with the idea that what really turned me on was hurting men. I wanted to make them suffer to a degree that neither of us had explored before and I learned quickly to create the right circumstances to facilitate this kind of interaction. And I learned to tell which few of these guys wanted to be put down as far as they could take it and a little bit more after that.

Early one warm morning at dawn, I was hanging around in the parking lot across the street from this after-hours fuckhole called the Headquarters. A glossy-eyed guy with safety pins in his ears and lips stumbled out of the place to the distorted roar of "Love Comes In Spurts" by Richard Hell and the Voidoids.

Once he got a big gulp of the outside air, he straightened up and sat on his stripped-down bike with a banged-up personalized license plate that said, TRENCH, in yellow letters on blue.

He was very small. He didn't even see me standing there at first, while I looked at the sloppy tattoo of a chain snaking out from his ripped up Black Flag tee shirt. It stopped abruptly on the back of his shaved head. A few years before, he could've been one of Sam's boys. He was just sitting on his bike, aware that he couldn't do much driving at this point in his high.

He looked over and saw me leaning there against the cyclone fence that ran around the lot. I unzipped my jacket and put my hands in the pockets of my jeans. This pushed up the bottom of the leather and made the top part of the jacket flare open to show my bare chest. He didn't look away, so I walked up to his bike and stood in front of him. He just kept staring at me, jerking one leg up and down nervously, expectantly with his mouth already open.

I pulled my hard-on out of my open fly and pressed it down. I really did like to show it off sometimes. He licked his chapped lips and looked back and forth from my bone to my boots. I let loose the reservoir of beer in my bladder.

I pointed a finger down at my wet boots. He slid off his bike and got his belly down on the asphalt. He started tonguing them, caressing the sides of them with his fingers. He was a dedicated bootlicker. The bottom of one of his Doc Martens was kissing the worn front tire of his motorbike as I made sure his tongue covered every square millimeter of my engineers. He put both hands on the top of his head and he licked old dirt out of the creases where the metal ring held together the leather bootstraps at my ankles.

When he was done with that, I lifted one of my boots up and shoved the toe of it right into his open mouth. He used his lower teeth to scrape a wad of dirty pink bubble gum that was stuck there. He chewed on it a little and smiled up at me before he spit it out. Then he showed me the blood on his tongue that came from flicking it across a piece of the smashed beer bottle glass that I'd stepped in near his bike.

That really made my bone jump in my hand. My other hand toyed with the beer caps that were still in my jacket pocket, so I took one out and bent down to pick up the wad of gum. He was already kissing on the toe of my other boot, so I put the bottle cap on the ground with the name Budweiser showing and pressed the bubble gum onto it. Then I straightened up and stepped on it with my free boot until the cap stuck on the sole. I told him to look up at me.

"Stay that way," I insisted and steadied myself by holding onto one of the handgrips of his handlebars. I rested the bottle cap against his forehead, almost dead center, and started jerking myself nice and slow. I pressed his head back and he pushed his head back at me with equal force while sucking the heel of my boot in his bloody mouth.

He was shaking and the sweat was dripping down his face with the tears. Little mewling sounds came out of his mouth and when I pulled my boot off him the bottle cap stayed there imbedded in his flesh against his skull. I shot all over his face and his skinhead. He came too, grinding hard against the asphalt, both of his hands now gripping my boot.

I bent down once more and it took longer than I thought it would to pry the bottle cap off him. He smiled in delirious gratitude, my spunk dripping onto his lips. That thin serrated circle of blood was one of the most beautiful things I'd ever seen and as I walked away from him, I knew that after I'd slept a few hours and the stores were open, I'd go find myself a knife.

LOSING CONTROL
D.D. Smith

These busy streets are home to so many mislaid souls. It's easy to be ignored. Easy to get lost among the tourists in shiny leather boots and ridiculous cowboy hats. Starry-eyed hopefuls are fashionable fakes eager to be discovered. They're molded and adorned with rooster feathers and snakeskin, glimmering in rhinestones, or brushed to perfection and embroidered with a well-known emblem.

I offer Granny High-pockets a twenty, a nod, and a smile. I'm hoping the cash will get her to the mission, and watch as she pushes her shopping cart uphill. How does she do it? She's not wearing shoes. *Jesus Saves* written in permanent marker on the soles of her feet. Maybe the preacher will give her another pair of shoes, a blanket, a bowl of soup. Maybe he'll give her more than a useless sermon to get her through another night trapped in hell on these heartless streets. I don't know.

I only know I'm tangled between the concrete and steel, captured somewhere between the rusty pick-up and the Mercedes parked in the tow-away zone. My image is faded, reflecting in the glass of the novelty stores filled with phallocentric tributes to Elvis boldly painted on velvet, and a larger-than-life-size cardboard cutout of Hank Williams leaning a little too far to the right. Everything in this town is larger than life, and nothing is ever what it should be.

A powder-blue sky filled with heavy clouds lends an uneasy feeling. A storm is coming to Music City. Soon it will wash away the crowds, drown out the twangy guitars, and give new energy to the lonesome melodies in the voices that echo from the doorways of the bars. From a distance, the endless shades of weathered gray concrete and black asphalt look like an inland sea of troubled water. It's dark and mysterious, constantly churning with dirty white caps. The scraps of debris float along the gutters. This peculiar image stands in stark contrast as business goes on as usual. The buildings emerge from the murky depths. Blood runs thick in the streets, faces yell, and women eloquently curse with a southern drawl. Bottles break, knives cut the air, bullets fly, bodies scatter, and the sirens blast. The cars speed by like boats trapped in a strong current, swept away on a blind voyage, searching for a safe harbor.

Today, the sun is behind me. The shadow reminds me that I'm here, but I'm alone. Everybody leaves me, and I know I shouldn't give a damn—but it's the story of my life.

It always struck me funny how I was attracted to certain smells, and how those smells can sometimes take me back to some past incident. I'm gripped by the scent of new tires, burnt rubber, high-octane fuel, and the smell of steam rising from the blackened pavement after an intense summer rain. French fries—and I'm inhaling them in the backseat of mom's old 2-door Impala. I'm comfortably wrapped in a quilt. We're on the way home from the lake. The wind is on my face. The sun sinks in the sky, and The Stones are number one for the second week in a row. Suntan oil—I catch a whiff of the warm buttery tropical blends of coconut mixed with the sweet smell of sweat and my cock is throbbing, stoked, pumped, and needing to be pressed between the folds of a muscular ass, bronzed and fuzzy, juicy as a ripened peach in the hot Georgia sun. It makes me think about a former lover.

Work, work, work—way too much work makes Seth a dull boy. I'm throwing myself into my work, staying occupied and trying not to think too much. Business is good, but twisting glass linear tubes 16 hours a day, 6 days a week has pushed me past the limit.

Saying goodbye to Phillip last September fucked me up. I stayed with him too long. I'll never forget the day he walked into the studio— knew I'd fall for him the moment I laid eyes on him. Seven years, and I'd like to say it was easy to love him, but it wasn't. He was so guarded, and hard to reach. I couldn't break through his wall of defense. What he wanted—sometimes I still don't know. He could only tell me what he didn't want. There were times when I could get past it. I was forever searching his eyes for something more. Part of me wanted to fight what I felt, and the other part wanted to reach out and hold on to him forever. I could never let him go. I needed to believe in him, in us.

I was obsessed with making it work. I often wondered what would happen if I stopped making the extra effort. I'm too structured, too predictable—I can't take a shit without checking my schedule. Obviously, I needed more, a promise, a plan, anything that would suggest a future. I couldn't find a way to get that from him. Perhaps I needed too much.

I should've known better. He could never figure out what he wanted to do, to be. He was always too busy trying to be something he wasn't.

His occupation changed constantly, changed like his clothes with the change of the seasons. Changed like his mind. He went from hair stylist to bartender, poet to construction worker, and a hundred other jobs in between. When he left me, he was working as a repo man and singing in the clubs. He could sing me to my knees, sing me to tears, sing me to sleep. The passion in his voice could make me forget my name.

He could've quit the day job, but he was too proud. I made more than enough to take care of both of us. He wouldn't listen. Instead, there would always be another writer's night, another struggle to find his reason for being, another diversion that took him away from me. Fucking bars and clubs—JEEZ! The name alone indicates what will happen if you hang out in one too long.

Me—well, I never wanted to be anyone else. I never needed to hang out in the clubs to find anything. I think I always knew that I'd be a creative type. Change, I couldn't get used to it. Ironic—I know, and me a sculptor.

Our relationship was an arcane concept, ambivalent life imitating art. I think I was constantly transforming damned flirtations into ever-changing affairs of the heart, mind and body. And maybe Phillip found pleasure in that. He's the only man that I've ever known who could tear my world apart, put it back together—and make me love him for it.

Night after night I'd lie down with the hope of finding him. Maybe I'm too difficult, too critical. I'm never satisfied with the way things are. Even during lovemaking, I pushed him too far. Perhaps he was trying to keep me interested by being unpredictable. Our relationship was an insane attempt to alter an existence that always produced the same results. No matter how hard I tried I knew it would happen anyway—I knew an end would come.

I wrapped my world around him, tried to make him feel safe. Maybe that's how I wanted to feel—I don't know. I think I thought I could control his changes, as long as I was with him. Thought I could protect him and right all the wrongs in his life, and mine too. Phillip was a test for me, a constant work-in-progress. I would study his face, watch him sleep, listen to his breathing, and still it would happen—that hollow feeling, the lonely emptiness, wondering why at times I couldn't understand him, and then suddenly realizing I couldn't control a damn thing.

Now—he's gone forever. The bars and clubs took him from me. Son-of-a-bitches beat him with an iron bar and left him lying face down in the street. They left him broken, bleeding, and choking. When I got there the lights were screaming, flashing to the brightest violent shade that smashed against the bricks. They lifted him from the pavement. I stood there in silence, and stared at the dark crimson lake that formed tiny rivers and filled the cracks in the sidewalk. Watched as his life washed the filth and indifference away. I stared into his eyes, and gripped his hand. I had to make him know that I was with him, never leaving him, not letting go. He squeezed my hand tighter when he heard, "Phillip, everything will be all right. You'll be all right." I tried to comfort him, help him through it. I hoped he'd believe me. I wanted to believe.

All possibility was lost as I watched his pupils grow larger. The cold black darkness of death consumed the warm ocean blue. I heard him struggle for his last breath, and watched him slip away as they made a great effort to put him back together. Some of the pieces were gone. Death had a face, absent of color, silent and unforgettable.

Muthafuckers took his boots and the watch I gave him for his birthday. They wanted his leather jacket, and he wouldn't give it up. They didn't know him. They were just a few kids having too much fun. Instant assholes—just add alcohol. Their so-called fun went too far and took Phillip from me. I loved him, I tried, and they didn't care.

Now, I have nightmares. Vivid recurring dreams are filled with horrible images that wake me at 3 a.m. In them, he's elusive, and looking as if he's ready to tell me one of his deepest secrets. He's smiling and always offering gifts that are never quite right.

I need a distraction, something to look forward to, a promise of something—anything would be an improvement. My situation could be too fragile for any dalliance with the unexpected, but these are uncertain times and I don't have time to waste. I need to move on. That's why I have to do it. I have to taste the unpredictable, do something that I wouldn't normally do.

Somewhere along the way it stopped being about creating and making money, and started being about an effort to find peace in an intolerable existence. I'm tired of forever searching these streets for his face. Tired of hearing the music and not hearing his voice make it sufferable. I feel helpless, and abandoned. I want him here with me, and he's not coming back. Getting over it. No, it doesn't make sense. I'll never get over it. I need to take it further, outside myself, somewhere that I'm not afraid to let go. I know what I've got to do.

What got into me? Most likely too many late nights watching master craftsmen create those high-speed thundering monsters of chrome and steel. Holy shit! Those guys have a fucking gift when it comes to twisting metal and constructing rumbling rockets for the open road. The strength of the steel, the custom paint, the chrome, the leather, the power, the violence in the thunder shakes me to the core. Those dominant machines take on a life all their own. They grab you by the balls, shake you, and force you to notice them. They are the angry shouting sons of the modern day masters. Who wouldn't want one? Six months later, $80,000 lighter and I'm the proud owner of a brutal mechanical devil of the highway.

Nashville can kiss my tired ass. YES, I am so outta here! I'm heading out for Bike Week. I should be in Daytona late tomorrow night. I can't wait. Shit is packed and sitting by the door. I figure I'll be back in a couple of weeks. Thought I'd take some scuba lessons, and do some deep-sea fishing. Maybe I'll get lucky and figure out what I'm looking for, and if not, that's okay too.

Tonight? I'm set with a couple bottles of brew, a club on rye, my favorite chair, and a few movies. I've got Easy Rider for the road and a few porn flicks to thrust me into oblivion. I'm ready and set. Research, entertainment, and sleep—no doubt.

I'm nodding off into a neon dream. Strange surreal shit, clouds, electric humming light. I'm floating, moving fast, faster. A snake, it's chasing me. I'm running through tall grass, lightning speed. Fucking HUGE! A giant anaconda is close behind. How in the hell is that thing keeping up with me? Okay, think rational thoughts—change the dream. If I slow down, the snake will slow down. If I slow down, the snake will slow down. If I slow down.... Son-of-a-bitchin'-thing is biting my neck! I can't breathe, can't fuckin' breathe! I can't get away. Gigantic spiked teeth are sinking into my flesh. The pain, goddamn the pain is excruciating! It burns, damn-it it BURNS! Ripped skin, warm blood, I feel it...FUCK! I feel it, hot-wet heat trickling down my chest and back. I can't see anything but more rapid flashes of glowing atomic red, neutron-orange, cool argon-blue, mercury-green, fading to pale proton-yellow, and finally a blinding white light.

Am I dead?

"Seth, where are you going?" She's calling after me. I'm running, running as far as these too-tight-mirror-polished shoes will carry me into the tobacco field. I'm hiding among the towering stalks bent with heavy green leaves. I won't go. I'll hide. Oh fuck! Big worms, huge and ugly, and velvety bright green. Thick fuckin' worms from hell!

"I don't want to go to church. I can't! Those people hate me...I'm not goin'...not goin'!" I answer but keep running deeper into the field. Southern Christians like their sermons, sex, and coffee the same—bitter and hard to swallow. I smell cow....oh no...SHIT! Damn-it, it's all over my shoes. Mom will be pissed, and she'll give me that look...that look.

Mom's gone, she's gone. We put her in the ground five years ago. For the love of lilacs and pink roses—why didn't she stop? She didn't see it, didn't hear the whistle, running late, she was running late. The train, it was too fast. Damn-it! Goddamn-it ALL!

WAKE UP! Wake the fuck up—it's over. SHIT! What a fuckin' nightmare—I can barely breathe. I gotta get up! I can't take it anymore. Sheets are soaked with sweat. I'm wet. I'm cold, too cold. FUCK! Turn up the heat. Clock ticking. Trains, sirens…working girls are shaking their tits at the cars and laughing on the corner. Crazy bitches.

Awake again at 3 in the fuckin' morning. It still pisses me off. They piss me off. Mom's gone, and all they could do was stand there and smile their sad smiles, spewing halfhearted sympathies. They didn't care about her, didn't care about me. That's why I stopped going to church with her 12 years before the accident. The things they said, "She's in a better place…at least she didn't have to suffer."

What the fuck do they know? I'd rather that none of this happened—thank you. I would rather have her here with me—thank you! I knew what they were thinking. They were thinking—*She's gone, and now we won't have to hear her talk about her son, the starving artist, the neon sculptor, the queer who can't live in his hometown. Thank GOD, she won't have to pray for him anymore!*

Fuck them! They didn't know her, and they damn sure didn't know anything about me. Mom wasn't even in the ground and they were asking what I'd do with the farm. Insensitive ASSHOLES! I should've announced in the local paper that I'd be converting it into a retreat for gay artists. Yep, that would've pissed off a few neighbors. Instead I hung a sign and made them pay dearly for their bad manners, and what they wanted all along.

At the funeral they were watching me, watching Phillip to see if he would put his arm around me as they walked away. He didn't do it, wouldn't do it. A train, "She got run over by a damned old train." Isn't that the way the song goes? Fuckin' artless redneck shit! Pisses me off every time I hear it. Phillip pisses me off, and he's not here. I can't stand country music.

Mom could have been anything, done anything. She dreamed of being an actress. She'd recite line after line of Shakespeare as we worked beside each other in the fields. She loved to dress up in chiffon and silk scarves, sing show tunes, and entertain me. I'd hold my breath and hold a flashlight, her spotlight. She was a star. I was captivated with her magic as she'd dance and sing her way toward me across the weathered boards. We had TV, but couldn't get anything on it worth watching that far out in the sticks.

We worked hard every day, chopped wood all summer and fall just to stay warm during the winter. I'll never forget finding her under that steam-cloud that filled our kitchen. She was busy frying country ham, cutting out buttermilk biscuits, and being Mom. She was fraught, trying to keep that 100-year-old house filled with heat, food, good smells, and love.

One winter it was so cold that we found ice forming around the electrical outlets. We laughed about that until we cried. She kept crying. She pretended they were tears of laughter, but I knew she was covering up the strain of being overwhelmed.

She'd smile and hug me. Her long golden hair would brush against my face, and I'd breathe in Chanel No. 5. Those are the moments that I wish I could hold on to forever. Those were the times that made life bearable on that 150-acre sweat-equity farm in the middle of Nowhereville. Mom taught me the meaning of determination, and she was the source of my hope.

How she got the money to send me to college that first year—I'll never know. Mom always could pull a rabbit out of her ass when I least expected it. She was resourceful. She amazed me. I don't know why she stayed on the farm. We paid it off two years after I graduated. I begged her to sell it and come live with me. Now, I wish she'd listened, wish she hadn't been so determined to hang on to the old place.

Determination seems to be a way of life for me these days. Determined to keep going, to wake up another day, to find a reason—a reason to hope. I need to stop thinking about it, lots to do. Daylight soon.

Over and over again, the images of the men in the porn flicks are going through my mind, images of massive cocks and no body hair. Slick and smooth—those guys must have sprayed on some kind of exfoliating mist. Stuff probably smells like a special blend of citrus and the ass of a skunk.

I grabbed a mirror, and looked, and thought about it. The basic equipment is better than average. Not massive, but my stuff ain't bad. No one EVER complained. It works, it's mine, end of story. Still, recently the porn flicks have emphasized these guys with great cocks and huge balls. They do look bigger when bare.

Makes me think of the guy that sells a copy of his cock as a dildo. Picture the size of a guy's ego who sells a reproduction of his cock as a sexual aid on the Internet. Does he wake up one day thinking he'll beat the meat and figure out how to make a mold? I guess that's one guy who can say, "My cock has been in thousands of holes around the world—without requiring medical attention." Talk about bragging rights—I reckon. I have no idea if the thing vibrates or not. Of course it comes with a complimentary tube-o-lube. Life does have its simple pleasures.

Anyhow, I've thought about shaving. I discussed it with Phillip a few years back. He thought the idea was silly, even laughed about it. I'd catch myself fantasizing, wondering if it would feel more intense to rub my shaved groin against his warm and very well rounded ass. I wanted to feel him beneath me, his muscular thighs closed. Thought about soft music, candlelight, heated oils, and gliding over him with naked balls. To think of his full lips firmly wrapped around the base of my naked cock, watching him suck as the head swells, my hands tangled in his thick auburn hair, controlling him, watching his move-ments…well, the thought still makes me very hard. DAMN! Actually, makes me want to cum. Is that sick?

Okay, I've decided to shave the cock hair.

I wonder how difficult it is to shave this stuff? Scissors and trimmers first. Time to clear the jungle and find the long-tailed monkey. Nope, it doesn't come off that easy, not the way stubble does when I shave my face. It bunches up and fills the razor, slides up the razor, slides under the razor, and every once in a while…SHIT! It catches in the razor.

I've spent at least an hour shaving hair off my balls, not an easy task. In fact, it's much like shaving a jellyfish with two marbles inside. I've discovered that for the effect to work, I need to shave my belly to the navel, and the tops of my thighs.

Fuck-it, everything has to go! I can't decide if I look like a porn star or a professional swimmer. I can't just shave the obvious places—oh, no, that razor must go right up to the sensitive, puckered little edges of my asshole. Otherwise some rather long strands of pubic hair will form an odd little backdrop to those wrinkled surfaces of my balls and that will look bizarre.

Finally finished, a quick glance in the mirror. Oh my, I'm HUGE! Well—I look huge. Those professional fuckers have the right idea. Okay, time to shit, shower, and shine.

It's startling what happens after shaving your crotch—besides, of course, feeling naked. These silk boxers feel incredible, and walking around is different. The hair below serves several functions, one being to reduce friction not only when two bodies meet, but also between surfaces of your thighs and the suspended elements of your private life.

I feel my newly naked upper thighs sliding back and forth along my balls, and the slick fabric makes that feeling even more pronounced. Now, I can't think about anything but sex. Something tells me I'll definitely be riding a thundering monster all the way to Daytona, and I ain't talking about my bike.

*

One last look in the mirror and I'm ready to hit the road. I look like a born-again barbarian wandering the false dream kingdom of *the saved* with too much time on my hands. Looks like I'm up to no good, like I have something to hide. (Yes, I'm hiding hairless balls.)

It's amazing how a few hundred dollars of dyed cowhide can change me. Phillip's leather jacket feels good. I can still smell his scent, smells like orange blossoms, cinnamon, and ginger. I feel powerful wrapped in leather, like nothing can get through this armor. Maybe I don't care if it does, and I find strength in that.

I'm feeling cynical today. I don't give a damn about anything. There's something inside my head that drives me away from this monotony. There are secrets in my life I can't run from, can't disguise anymore. In a perfect world, all of the secrets disappear. This is what I need, for months I've been too far away from me.

Five miles down the road and Nashville looks small in my rear-view mirror. The only thing I see behind me is the city skyline. It resembles an ocean liner sinking below a thick wave of trees. A dark ribbon of freedom stretches out in front of me. The wind whispers in my ears, calls out to me, taking me away from my home. It leads me away from a painful every-day world, a hell that haunts me. I'm afraid—and I don't know why.

I'm blinded by the unknown, my face toward the sun. This feeling is familiar. I'm warmed by it. Changes are brewing.

I think of Phillip. I can feel him with me now, his arms around me, holding on tight. He'd love this—high speed on a lonesome stretch of highway, and feeling the thunder between our thighs at dawn. Making love with him in the morning always brought the thunder. I know he's not really here, but I feel him and it shakes me. I think I understand him now.

Loving someone when they're gone is tough, and I don't know how to let that go, let him go. I'm clinging to a heavy metal demon, wanting to let go of this life. I'm glad I don't have to talk, explain it, or feel anything...but numbness. Freedom. Having the balls to let go of it all. Can I do it? I don't know.

Monteagle Mountain...going down. It would be easy to lean into one of these curves and just keep leaning. Plow into the face of a rocky hillside with all the jagged edges. I could slam into it, full force with all of the fury of hell inside me. Living hell, that's what it is, what I'm going through. Life sucks with both lips and I don't think I can make it any better.

Chattanooga...famous for its...don't even fuckin' think about it! How can I not think about it? Trains, fuckin' trains! Once I get out of this state—I'm free. Twenty minutes and I'll be in Georgia. Kickin' through the gears hard and heavy. Feeling the strength of a painted and chrome-plated evil spirited horse as it races uphill and carries me across the state line. Passing cars and trucks at high-speed. They stare, but they don't know. I want to scream, "If you can't help me, get the fuck outta my way. Get in my way—and help me die!"

I need a break. Lot lizards are crawling in and out of the trucks as I cruise through the parking lot. A couple of them walk by admiring the bike. They stare while I fill the tank with fuel.

"Nice bike." One smiles and looks back at me through heavy mascara and lipstick bleeding from the corners of her lips.

"Nice ass too!" The other laughs, wide open-mouth, minus 6 front teeth. She jerks the cumbersome glass door and flips back her lice-infested hair.

"Thanks!" I grin and twist the gas cap. They have no fucking idea. I don't care what they think of the bike or my ass. I nod as I push the hot beast to an empty space in front of the windows. I stare at my reflection. I look like a tough bastard, and the bike is—well, fuckin' singing in the sunlight.

I'm starving, and feel the pain of emptiness in the pit of my stomach. I hate standing in line. Waiting, fucking waiting. The cashier is too slow and obviously can't make change. Fuck-it! I don't give a shit about a couple dollars. Keep it. I gotta piss, NOW! Finally, relief. Damn! This feels better, stretching and holding my naked balls. Shake, shake, shake—and put the cock away. Glance at the graffiti on the wall, "Nadine is a bitch, but she gives good head." Nasty fucking sink. Looks like some asshole used it as a cum receptacle and shot off all over the fuckin' mirror. Where are the paper towels? Fuckin' great! Just drip dry.

There's one stool left in the corner facing the grill. The lot lizards are behind me, still staring at my ass. The waitress slaps a menu on the counter. She has thick lips, a sour expression, and way too much make-up for daylight. I scan the menu and make a quick decision, one I'll most likely regret. "Watcha want?" Nadine asks while chewing gum and untangling one of maybe ten gold chains around her neck.

"Cheeseburger, fries, and something brown and fizzy to choke it down and cut through the lard." I grin and try to be charming. She doesn't notice, and snatches the menu while looking over my shoulder at the lot lizards.

The toothless one is talking loud. I can't help but overhear the conversation.

"I prayed that God would make me ugly. Prayed about it, you know. I thought maybe then I wouldn't have to fuck these horny truckers anymore!" She snorts and drops her fork on the floor.

Jeez...what a silly fuckin' whore! Maybe God does exist, 'cause I think he answered her prayer. She just doesn't know it yet. I tried to ignore it. Ignore her and her loud empty mouth. I gotta get outta here. Eat this greasy heart-clogging shit and hit the happy trail.

Pine trees as far as I can see. Three lanes of asphalt remind me there are always three sides to a story—their side, mine, and the right one. Change lanes, change your mind, and stumble on a new point of view. Billboards stand tall in the red Georgia clay. High dollar signs that try to tell me what I need, and I don't buy it.

I've discovered the magical source of all frustration and despair. Now I'm ready to go to the next level and battle the vicious satanic demon from hell with a hard-on, and a fierce bike that gets me off.

I feel Phillip's hands all over me, can't forget the few things he said in the heat of passion. I feel like I'm on fire. I'm carried along by something that's strong, wild and brave.

I'm counting on the wind. It will blow these cares away, blow them behind me. It could carry this heartache to the clouds, hold it until the burden is too heavy, and wash it away over the ocean, or some distant land. A cleansing rain of tears, coming down hard. They are lost in a forgotten sea of sadness. I don't want to hurt anymore.

Florida state line. I'll be in Daytona before 6 tonight. I'm in the land of palm trees and pines. Spanish moss is clinging to the branches of live oaks. That smell....yes, I'm definitely in the Sunshine State. I smell decaying black muck, the stench of rotting leaves, putrid fish guts, decomposing animal carcasses, stagnant water, rotten eggs, alligator shit, something—it's awful.

A straight stretch, two lanes, and not another car in sight. I'll take my hands off the handlebars, just cruise a few miles. "Look Mom, no hands." Maybe that's the problem, my life has been too safe. I let the fear of consequence keep me from following my instincts. I wanted to be with Phillip forever, but I could never say it.

I could die here. It would take a few days for them to find me, if they found me at all. It would be better this way. I could make a wild dash through the trees and hit the largest one with everything in me. I'd die with metal bars at my throat, my head badly bruised, my body twisted. I'd die like Phillip, choking, bleeding, broken, and wearing his leather jacket.

Jacksonville...Florida's Business City. They're taking care of business from the car. Cell phones and laptops are necessary. Traffic is crammed and jammed coming and going. How do they do it? How do they find the time to think? They just do. They change lanes without using signals, take what they need when they want it. They don't bother to ask. Heads behind the glass, preoccupied with financial planning, day care, retirement, the health-care nightmare. Work smarter, not harder. Steal, lie and cheat—it takes money to make money. It's the lifestyle of the rich and shameless. Some would gladly stomp on my face if that would give them an extra dollar. Inconsiderate of others? Maybe. I've been too lost in my own world to notice.

Wake up. I need to wake up to life. I know this life isn't all about me.

St. Augustine…

I have to make time for it. Make time for the fort, the lighthouse, folk singers in the streets, paintings on the sidewalk, tales of ghosts, fried clam strips and key lime pie. I'll have a beer with the rowdy crowd at the round table in the smoking section. I want to sit with the sinners and suck on cigarettes. I want to hear the maritime stories that Captain Webb exaggerated a hundred times before. History, I need to go back and see what I've missed.

I've walked and searched the streets of Nashville for too long. I've been lost in the darkness, hoping someone safe would change my life. Nothing is safe, no relationship comes with a guarantee, and someday may never come.

I've finally arrived. Daytona welcomes me with open arms. Other bikers smile, wave, and offer a thumbs-up as I ride down the strip. The biker chicks lift their tops, and shake their tits. The tourists shuffle down the walkways wearing ridiculous straw hats. They're carrying plastic bags filled with things they don't need. They're weighed down with cameras around their necks. They're on a sightseeing mission strapped in sandals that wear blisters on their feet. It's outrageous, and I'm looking forward to losing myself in the madness.

First things first. Go to the hotel, and drop the baggage. I need to square things away with the sweet little lady behind the counter. She smiles through eyes of wisdom. "You've made one helluva trip. Nothin' like the ocean to put things in perspective. Changed my life. I came here 50 years ago and couldn't leave it."

"Yes, I think I could use a little of that." I sign the receipt and quickly push it across the counter.

She grins and pats my hand like an old friend, holds me there for a moment, looking into my soul. A subtle suggestion that makes me realize I need to slow down. "Well honey, you never know…what might be waiting for you."

"Thanks." I grip the key card and lay down the pen.

My room is cozy. A chair, sofa, a table with fresh flowers and fruit. A large mahogany bed is filled with pillows in rich colors. Candles are placed in highly decorated ornamental stands. The view is breathtaking. I open the door and walk past the gauze curtains. Out on the lanai, palm tress and tropical foliage smell like heaven. The waves whisper a rhythm, call to me, call my name as they tumble to the shore and rush back. There is something spiritual about this place. It lures me to the water's edge.

The sand feels good between my toes. I rest back on my hands and dig in with my fingers. What can I do? I give up—I have to let it go. I close my eyes for a moment, lift my chin to the sky, and listen.

The sun is behind me. The light touch of mom's golden hair brushes against my cheek. It fills my heart with hope. A warm ocean of soothing blue, the color of Phillip's eyes. Tears of sadness are now tears of joy. I taste the salt on my lips. The soft breeze kisses my skin. It reminds me that I'm just a small part of this world. Dolphins play in the waves. Seagulls soar and call from above. I feel mom and Phillip—they are with me. They will always be with me.

I can't stop the tears.

What's in my pocket, in Phillip's pocket wrapped in a handkerchief? A thin gold box, a case decorated with 2 doves adorned with mother of pearl and coral inlay. A heart of brilliant cut diamonds surrounds the doves—it sparkles. Where did this come from? Is it a cigarette case? Can't be—Phillip didn't smoke.

A small card in Phillip's handwriting tucked inside..."Happy Anniversary Seth." Two gold bands tied together and secured in white velvet. One engraved *Forever Yours* and the other—*Mine Forever.*

N M 466-CPA
Mark Wildyr

Most guys at least *claim* to have gotten laid by the time they collect their high school diplomas, but Ivan Catlow was the exception. Ivan Catlow, that's me. Something strange was going on inside my head, and it wasn't just raging hormones; it was more the *way* the frigging things were cavorting! Like when I determined to lose my virginity, what did I do? I invited my best friend to go fishing up on Fenton Lake. Strange as it sounds, there's a half-assed explanation.

Walt Haber is good-looking and funny, and he kinda acted like he wanted to do something a year ago after we took our dates home. At the time, I froze up and let the opportunity slide right on by; I was too blessed shy. Shy! That's me. So shy I can't stand at the urinal and piss with the other guys. Now there we were with only an hour left before heading back home to Albuquerque, him flicking a fly rod and me nursing a hard-on and too backward to approach the handsome shit.

The sight of Walt, twenty yards ahead of me, muscles rolling with every cast, was more than I could stand. I tore open my britches and lobbed it out. Old Billy Cock pulsed in the clear, clean mountain air, hot and hard and ready. Slowly, I stroked him, afraid, no *hoping,* Walt would look around. In my mind's eye, I saw his handsome, lopsided grin as he traded a fiberglass rod for a flesh-and-blood one. He came to me. Our cocks kissed. Our lips met, and—

"Unghhh!" I shot off all over my shirt and sneakers. Suddenly ashamed, I fled, afraid now that he *would* turn around and catch me flogging my pisser. Still exposed, I rushed into the bushes, hoping those leaves scratching my wilting cock weren't poison ivy. Halfway around the small lake, I washed off and stuffed myself back in my trousers. The experience had been exciting and scary, but really it was only what I'd been doing since I was fourteen, with an element of danger added. But face it, old boy! You're still a fucking virgin.

I mooned over Walt casting his fly on the far shore until a car door slammed, waking me from my reverie. A healthy, active curiosity sent me to investigate the red Mercury SUV sitting at the far end of the parking area. The hood was warm, but there was no one around. With nothing better to do, I set off through the forest to see what I could find. Five minutes later, muffled voices with a sort of furtive air caused me to stop walking and start sneaking. Easing up a wooded rise, I halted abruptly and forgot all about Walt Haber.

The hunkiest, buffest, most beautiful stud I'd ever seen stood facing my direction, legs spread, hands on hips—one still clutching a black leather biker's jacket, while a good-looking dude felt up his crotch. The look on the youth's face was almost belligerent, but he put up with the groping. He didn't even flinch when the guy slid his trousers down around his knees. Wow! What a fucking cock! And he wasn't even hard! The other guy, who must have been in his late twenties and was kinda sexy himself, grasped the stud's shirt and started skinning it over his head. That's when the hunk rebelled.

"Shit, Miles," the voice came up out of those big balls, "leave my clothes alone. Get on with it!"

"Vince, a deal's a deal. You agreed, so stop stalling."

Vince sullenly lifted his arms, flaring his ribcage like a cobra's hood. Miles tugged the muscle shirt over the dreamboat's head to reveal a broad, smooth chest that didn't look like it had a hair on it. Man, he had shoulders out to there! A large black and red tattoo decorated a beefy bicep. I could cum just staring at all that bronzed flesh, I thought. Vince flinched when Miles sucked on one of the dark nipples and batted the guy away when he went for the second.

"Man, I don't even know if I can get hard," the hunky vision sulked.

"Don't worry about getting hard," Miles said confidently. "I'll take care of that!" Kneeling before the Greek god, the man sucked that big cock into his mouth and tongued it until it started to grow. And grow. And fucking grow! Old Vince must have been packing eight inches, but that only told half the story. It was fat, man, *fat*! But it didn't bother Miles. He worked patiently until he had more than half of it down his throat.

It finally got to Vince. He put his hand behind the other man's head and pulled it into his groin. I never thought of the bump and grind as truly sexy until that moment. The guy's handsome muscles bunched and rolled as he threw it to the man kneeling before him. Things were really getting interesting when Miles suddenly stood. They had another little tiff about Vince lying on a blanket spread out on the ground, but the biker eventually gave in.

Vince was totally naked when he lay back on the blanket. That fucker must have modeled for Adonis! Broad shoulders, small waist, and all kinds of interesting flesh between the two. Good hips, strong thighs, that fantastic cock, and a set of balls a stallion would have envied. Probably about twenty-one years old. When Miles finally bent to his task, I shifted my gaze to Vince's exotic face. Ethnic. Black hair. Brown skin without blemish. Rich lips. Cleft chin. And ears that lay close against his head. The eyes were big, but they were closed so I

189

could only guess black or brown. Shit, I was about to cream again.

Suddenly Vince's eyes flew open, and I thought I was caught flat-out, but that wasn't what it was. He grabbed Miles and flipped him over. Lying right on top of the dude's face, Vince began fucking. Instead of panicking, Miles stroked his lover's smooth buns. Those big thighs drove Vince's groin like a pile driver. He *had* to be rupturing the other guy's throat. I was willing to bet the whole eight inches were buried down Miles' esophagus. And when Vince came, I *knew* he was up to the hilt. He froze, groaned, and then jabbed with his whole weight behind him. He froze again, his head thrown into the air, and then he slowly ground in and out, obviously shooting cum from those big stones.

Finally, he rolled over on his back and covered his eyes with an arm. A fine sheen of sweat covered him from head to foot. Miles sat up, apparently no worse for the wear as his eyes roved his buddy's muscular form.

"Fuck, Vince! You're the best looking Mexican I've ever seen."

"Spaniard," Vince muttered. "I told you a hundred times."

"Whatever! You're the best-looking hunk of any kind of man! You are really put together. Fuck me now, okay?"

The younger man had been sitting; now he was standing. He was just towering over Miles, his flaccid cock right in the man's face, the hostility back. "I made a deal, motherfucker! And I stuck to it. That's the end of it!" he announced and commenced collecting his clothing.

Vince was half dressed before I retreated back the way I had come, pausing behind the Merc to scan the New Mexico license plate…466-CPA.

I was a hormonal mess again when I reached the other side of the lake. Walt packed away his gear, blissfully ignorant of how close he was to being sexually assaulted. I drove all the way back to Albuquerque with a prominent bone, but old Walt was oblivious to it all. Shit, he was a good-looking fucker!

The next week I obsessed over what I'd seen Saturday at Fenton Lake. When those images weren't in control of my mind, I was fixated on Walt. I had steeled myself to make a move when my best bud blandly informed me he was getting it on with Melissa and how fucking great it was. Defeated, I made the proper 'no shit, cowboy' noises and slunk home to jerk off.

Totally frustrated, absolutely screwed up, and a little around the bend, I remembered the license on the Merc and called a friend who worked a summer job with a law firm. He was only a gofer, but he had a better chance of coming up with the information I wanted than I did.

He thought it was a girl's license plate and promised to call the next day.

I flogged old Billy Cock that night, dreaming of running across Vince in that SUV one bright afternoon. Or maybe riding tandem on his cycle. I was convinced by the jacket and the tattoo that he was a biker, and I pictured me mounted behind him, my legs clasping his thighs, hands circling that narrow waist! He'd pull them down on his big basket, and we'd…. About that time I came all over the bed.

I hung around the house damned near the whole day before my friend called with the information that the plate belonged to some guy named Miles A. Bierne. Shit! It wasn't Vince's car, it was the Miles guy's. Nonetheless, I tripped down to the library and dug out the Criss-Cross directory, which gave me the guy's address and revealed that he was a lawyer and a homeowner. It didn't list a wife. A lawyer, for Chrissake! He'd see me behind bars if I tried anything. What the fuck do I do now?

Hormones won out over common sense by the middle of the following week. I dialed the Miles dude's home number on my cell phone from the privacy of my own bedroom. I recognized the baritone when he answered. Sounded manly. Lawyerly. Sure didn't sound queer. Quickly, I hung up. After fifteen minutes, I tried it again, but chickened out when he picked up the receiver. Two minutes later, my phone rang, and like the dodo I am, I answered.

"My caller ID says you just phoned my number?"

It was him! Miles A. Bierne, Attorney at Law! Sucker of Vince's King Kong! Panicked, my voice squeaked.

"I…uh…this is a friend of Vince's. I…I lost his number."

"A friend of Vince's you say? What's your name?"

"Uh…Dick."

"Is that a name or a description?"

Flustered, I blurted it out. "I saw you up at Fenton Lake. I saw you suck his cock!" I said in a rush. "His big cock." What the shit did I have to add that for?

"Really big cock," the man agreed equably. "Get a bang out of watching us?"

"I…uh…No!"

"So why are you calling me…Dick."

What a dumb-ass alias to come up with! "Vince's address… telephone."

"He is something, isn't he? Beautiful fucker. How old are you, Dick? You're young, but sound like you've got a pair of balls on you."

Stupid me answered him, "Eighteen. And yeah, I got a pair of balls and everything that goes with them."

"I'm sure you do. Are you hard now? I am. Your voice sends shivers down my back."

"M..my voice? Aw—"

"It's true, Dick. Damn, that name does something to me. Take it out of your pants. Describe it to me. Straight? Curved? Cut?"

Son of a bitch if I didn't pull it out and answer his questions. "S...straight. Well, maybe curves up just a little. Cut."

"Slender or fat?"

I shrugged before realizing he couldn't hear that. "Kinda thick, but not—"

He laughed. "Yeah, not like Vince's. Very few are. How long?"

"Six inches...or so," I added so I didn't sound like a dork who went around measuring his cock, which I did, of course.

"Is it hard now? Are you stroking it?"

"Mmmm," was all I squeezed out of my larynx.

"Meet me!" he said suddenly. "Right now! I want that cock. I want to suck it, swallow it, lick your balls."

"Unggggh!" I moaned.

He laughed again. "Too late. Was it good?"

"Gotta go!" I said in a rush and hung up. I sat for five minutes with the mess drying on me before I moved. I couldn't believe I'd talked to a *lawyer*, while I jacked off. Shit! Shit! Fuck, it felt good!

I dithered for an entire week about what to do, but before I could screw up the courage to act, my cell phone rang on the way back from the swimming pool.

"Thought I'd hear from you," Miles A. Bierne, Esquire, opened.

"Uh," was my brilliant reply.

"Where are you?"

"San Mateo Northeast."

"Meet me at the Banana Bar. Fifteen minutes," he said and hung up.

Shit, who did he think he was, issuing a royal command like that? The king, I guess, because my jalopy headed straight for the teen hangout.

The lawyer was even better-looking up close. In fact, he looked like some college jock rather than a professional man. He couldn't have been more than a couple of years out of law school. Anyway, I found myself in the passenger seat of his Merc SUV with hardly a protest, not even when he pulled out of the parking lot and headed...I didn't know where.

"You're a good-looking stud," he observed, cutting his green eyes over at me. "I halfway expected a pimple-faced nerd, but you live up to your voice."

"My voice?" I squeaked inanely.

"Sexy," he explained. That brought a snort of laughter from me. "You don't think you're sexy? I do." He paused. "Are you a virgin?"

Hell, no!" I lied. "What makes you think that?"

"Intuition," he said, giving himself wise airs. "You sound like an innocent novice, but it takes balls to do what you did. Call me out of the blue like that, I mean." He gave me a sideways look. "Balls or desperation. Which is it?"

"Desperation," I admitted before thinking.

"So you're a cherry?"

I leaned back in the seat and stretched my legs. "To everything except my right hand."

"No jacking off with buddies? No getting it off kissing a girl?"

"Nope. Closest I came was busting my balls while talking to you."

"Glad I'm the first," he said, groping my groin.

Miles drove straight into his garage with his hand still on my prick. We made it no farther than the dining room before he turned. His lips on mine shocked the hell out of me. I never considered kissing a guy. It was nice, but better was his package grinding against mine while he swabbed my throat.

Miles A. Bierne, Esquire, blew the shit out of me right there on the floor under his dining room table. He sucked my tits, stabbed my navel, nibbled my balls, spanked my buns, and did something I never even imagined. He pushed my legs flat against my chest and ran his tongue up and down my crack. Each time he stroked my pucker hole, I thought I'd cream. Finally, he zeroed in on the thing and had it vibrating like a sounding board. Then his tongue penetrated me, and I had to grab a table leg to remain on earth. He tongue-fucked me for five minutes, and when his lips closed on my dripping, throbbing, hungry cock, I had to take a look because there was still something in my asshole. It was his finger. He played me like a string instrument for fifteen minutes, drawing me out, but never letting me hit crescendo. Finally, I went over the edge and came like a fire hydrant! The old balls poured out gush after delicious gush. When it was over, I didn't have a nervous system left. Miles laughed at my helplessness and my inability to speak coherently.

"I've ever had anyone react quite like you did," he laughed. "Most guys try to act all macho, like they put up with it but didn't really get anything out of it."

"Like Vince," I gasped. "But he liked it. I could tell. He liked it."

"Yeah, tell me about it. It was my throat he was fucking with that monster dick. By the way, you're not going to tell me your name's really Dick, are you?"

"Naw," I owned up. "Ivan. But guys call me Ive, you know, like 'I have'."

"Okay, Ive, I enjoyed sucking your cock more than most. It's as good-looking and sexy as the rest of you. It's an exceptional cock. Hard as hell. Drips like a leaky faucet when you get hot and bothered. Big, but not too big. Old Vince actually hurts when he rams his home, but yours fills me up pleasantly."

"Uh, about Vince."

"I'm disappointed. I thought I could make you forget about him. You're hot for outlaw bikers, are you?"

"Is that what he is?" I asked, secretly pleased at the confirmation of my mental characterization of the hunk.

"Biker all the way. Outlaw about fifty percent. Can't blame you. I really dig macho studs like Vince...and you."

"If I'm so macho, why am I still a virgin?"

Miles ginned again, something he did really well. "You're not. You busted your cherry right down my throat. By the way, you taste great...macho."

I probably blushed on all four cheeks. He laughed aloud.

"Tell you what, Ive, you fuck me as good as I think you can, and I'll tell you how to get in touch with Vince."

I frowned. "I don't know about that. It, uh..."

"Seems nasty?" I nodded. "You can wear a condom if you want. There's nothing like it, Ive. It's the gay man's vaginal sex."

"And you'll put me in touch with Vince if I do it?"

"No, I'll tell you how to get in touch with him. And you can't tell him I told you, either. You'll have to find some way to stumble across him." Miles considered me a moment. "But what are you going to do when you find him? Are you ready to suck his cock? He's sure as hell not going to suck yours." He laughed at my stricken look. "If you think he's going to sit around and jack off with you, forget it. That stud quit masturbating five years ago. I happen to know he fucked his first woman when he was sixteen."

"I'll figure out...something," I hedged, my mind a total blank. All I knew was that I *had* to find him. "If he's so macho and likes girls and all...if he's a *biker,* how did you get him to let you blow him?"

"He owed me, and that's the way I chose for him to pay. And bikers are human, too."

"And he agreed? He's gay?" I asked.

"No, it's more like he's an undiscovered bicycle, a bisexual who hasn't come to grips with it yet."

"Why wouldn't he fuck you, if he owed you?"

"Unfortunately, that's not the deal we made. And it violated his self-image. If you want him to fuck you, you'll have to find a way to make it okay from his perspective."

"I don't' want him to fuck me!" I flared. "He just—"

"Got under your skin. I know the feeling. He's been getting to me for ten years now. His mom and dad came to work at our house and brought along the prettiest kid I'd ever seen. Looked like an angel, acted like a devil, and probably made me the way I am today. All through high school, I figured I'd fuck his trim little ass. Then my dream changed when he started packing a full groin. When he turned biker, he was even more irresistible. I sucked my first cock thinking about Vince. Took my first one up the ass dreaming of his prick."

"Man, you've got a bad case of the Vince. Worse than me."

He grinned again and stroked my smooth chest. "Yeah, but I'm getting over my disease. You're in the contagion stage. When it really hits you, you'll go crazy. I won't be doing you any favors telling you how to get in touch with him."

His words and his hand playing with my nipples were getting to me. "But you will, won't you?" My cock started crawling up my belly.

He fingered it gently. "You fuck me, and I will."

He stripped and stretched out on top of me, his big cock nuzzling mine while he plumbed my throat with his tongue. Then he started down my torso, caressing and tasting every inch from my lips to my groin. I liked my nipples being sucked, and enjoyed a tongue in my belly button. For a minute, I thought he'd decided to blow me again when he swallowed my cock and rode it up and down a couple of times. But he was just priming the pump.

"Get on your knees," he ordered, drawing his legs against his chest. My wet cock throbbed against his crack. "Rub it up and down me."

Shit! Even that felt good. I centered myself, and his legs went around my waist, pulling me forward. My old cock slid in like it belonged, and I forgot all about dirty and condoms and all that crap. All I could think about was the silken cocoon sheathing my cock.

"Fuck me, lover," Miles whispered.

Man, I fucked! For the first time in my life, I fucked, going at it like a rabbit until he brushed my fevered brow and told me to slow down and enjoy it a little. When I lapsed into a gentle, languid thrust, I felt every inch of my cock sliding in and out of his butt, my thighs on his buns, my balls slapping his flesh. I even felt my bush mash against him on every down stroke.

"Beautiful!" he murmured. "Harder now."

So I gave it to him slow and hard, pulling all the way out and plunging back to the hilt again. Crap! That felt even better. Then I started getting that drawing-up feeling and stopped, afraid I'd cum. He understood, allowing me to rest while he played with my torso and stroked his hard cock. Then those legs drew me to him again, and I let him establish the rhythm. Miles knew what he was doing. It must have been thirty minutes later when he shouted, "Now, lover! Now!"

I leaned into him, my nose almost touching his, and rode him hard. I fucked. I bucked. I...came! All of a sudden, my nervous system went haywire and shot cum into his channel. He got it at about the same time, and his ass grabbed me and milked another gallon of sperm out of my exhausted balls. Shuddering through an orgasm that came once in a bazillion years, I finally collapsed atop him, a mass of boneless protoplasm.

"Beautiful!" he panted into my ear. His sweat mixed with mine. His jism smeared my belly and chest. My half-hard cock still rested up his butt.

"Didn't...know...was...like...that," I gasped.

"It isn't always," he acknowledged, recovering faster than I did. Well, why not? I did all the work. "I knew it would be special with you, Ive."

When his anal muscles expelled me, that was the signal for the magic to fade. Suddenly ashamed at my nakedness, at what I'd done, I bounded up and looked around for escape. He halted me with a single word. "Vince!"

Miles regarded me a little sadly. "I'd rather keep you for myself, but I've been bitten by the Vince bug, so I know how it is. You know the San Mateo Custom Van Shop? He works there."

"He *works?*" I asked. "I thought bikers just...well, biked."

Miles laughed in genuine amusement. "Of course, he works. Bikers need to eat and drink and keep a roof over their heads like everyone else. And they've got to pay for their toys. Very expensive toys. Not all of them deal drugs, you know."

"Guess not," I muttered, ashamed that I'd allowed my parents' prejudices to frame my thinking.

"Anyway, Vince is a paint artist. He customizes vans, cars, bikes, anything. He wants to work on the Merc, but I tell him he'll ruin my lawyerly image."

"Have you got with him since Fenton Lake?"

"No. And I never will again. I forced him into it, and Vince doesn't like to be forced. He's got this macho image of himself. Nobody forces a *man* to do anything." Miles shrugged. "I was getting nowhere the other way, so I called in a debt knowing that would be the end of it. In a way it was a mistake because just being around him is sort of a thrill."

"How did you force him? You represent him? Get him out of trouble?"

"Vince Arello lives life on the edge sometimes. A lot of bikers do," was the only answer I got. "What are you going to use as a lever? Are you willing to suck that big cock? Take it up the backside?"

My answer was a shrug. "He's Hispanic?" I asked, remembering their exchange at Fenton Lake.

"Spanish, he claims. His father was a real Spaniard, but his mother's a local Chicana. His dad was as handsome as Vince except not as dark."

I dithered for a week, driving by the van shop until I finally caught sight of Vince Arello tossing his denim-clad leg over a Suzuki Intruder 1600 with customized modified ape-hanger bars. Unfortunately, I was headed north, and the motorcycle roared off to the south. That quick glimpse of the Spanish houri was enough to motivate me. The next afternoon I barged into the San Mateo Custom Van Shop, asked about a paint job for my twenty-year-old Ford Mustang, and found myself in the back of the shop standing before the *sexiest* human I'd ever seen.

"What did you have in mind?" Vince Arello asked in a deep, vibrant voice. Did he know it turned people queer and drove them crazy?

"Ah...uh..." All I could see was the muscles playing in his arms as he wiped his hands on a rag. The tattoo, a snarling wolf, lunged dangerously with each manly movement.

"I've got pictures of some of the work I've done," he suggested. "Like to see them?" The voice gave me a hard-on; the Adam's apple working in his throat about made me cream.

"Uh...yeah, sure. Yeah, I'd like to see some of your work."

Fiery red flames dominated most of the photographs of vans and cars he showed me. One number was a plain paint job with a border around it like a Navajo blanket. Actually, it was pretty nice.

"See anything you like?" he asked, meaning one thing.

"Yeah," I breathed, meaning something totally different. Damnation! Was every move he made so fucking graceful? "This one." I pointed, to a photo close to his hand so I could brush it 'accidentally.' Hard, but satin smooth. "It's not quite what I want," I added, looking at the paint job a second time. "I want something unusual. Something totally different."

"Gotta give me a direction," he said.

They were brown. Those eyes I couldn't see the other day were big and brown and hid behind long, sable lashes.

"Well, Vince...it is Vince, isn't it?" He nodded. "I don't want flames. I don't want red or orange. Toned down, but distinctive." I shrugged helplessly. "Hell, I don't know what I want. Uh...haven't we met somewhere before?"

He frowned down at me from his three-inch height advantage. "Don't think so. What's your name?"

"Ivan. Ivan Catlow." I took the plunge. It came out through a dry, frightened throat. "Have you ever been up to Fenton Lake?"

He looked at me sharply. "A few times."

"A couple of weeks ago? I was up there fishing with a buddy, and I think I saw you. You were with another guy. In a red SUV."

"Yeah," he said impatiently. "How about I come up with some ideas? You touch base next Friday, okay?"

Disappointed, I left after agreeing to stop by Friday. He hadn't even batted a beautiful, brown eye when I called him on Fenton Lake. What do I do next?

What I did was come back the following afternoon and park around the corner until Vince got off work. About six the Intruder shot out of the alleyway and turned south on San Mateo with my Mustang a block behind. Why was I stalking him? I had no idea, but I sure got a charge out of his black-jacketed figure leaning in and out of traffic.

I am not an expert at tailing, and he made me before we got to Central. He cut into the Wal-Mart lot and parked at the south end away from the cars. I drifted to a stop in the middle of some traffic and then pulled into a parking space. He shot back up the tarmac and screeched to a halt at my window.

"You following me, Catlow?" he demanded, his thin nostrils flaring.

Out of total confusion and abject fear, I blurted: "New Mexico 466-CPA!"

"What?"

"That was the license plate on the SUV at Fenton Lake."

"You son-of-a-bitch, you spied on me, didn't you?" His flesh turned dark as he flushed.

"Y...yes. Well, not you. The other guy!"

"The *other* guy?" he asked in disbelief.

"Man, the way he worked on you. That was something. And when you turned him over and fucked his—"

"Shut your mouth!" Vince snapped, but there was confusion in his eyes.

Sensing a way to survive this fiasco, I babbled on. "Look, man. I'm a virgin. Been wanting to get my ashes hauled for a long time. When I saw that dude swallowing your big cock—"

"Shut the fuck up!" he hissed. "No shit, you're a virgin? Good-looking dude like you oughta have chicks hanging all over you."

I shrugged, halfway between cool and consternation. "I'm shy, Vince. I get in a tussling match with one and get all hot and bothered, and then I just chicken out. I'm so fucking frustrated, I figured maybe that guy I saw sucking you would do something for me. That way, I'd start with a guy, you know like when you mess around with your buddy. Get over being shy and work up to the big time."

"Man, you're fucking crazy. A real life virgin, huh? I'll be damned. You want me to set you up with a gal?"

"Wouldn't do any good. I'd just choke up again."

"Not with this chick. She'd take it out and put it in for you. She'd get a kick out of fucking whitebread like you."

"Just tell me who NM 466-CPA is. After I see him a couple of times, maybe I won't be so bashful. I almost didn't recognize you in the shop. I mean it was the other guy I was looking at mostly. But when I figured out it was you; I thought maybe you might go see him again. So I followed you. Sorry."

"You were looking at him, not me?" Vince put a question in his voice. "I don't know, man. Let me think about it. I'll see you on Friday."

"Yeah. Uh, and Vince, when you talk to him…that guy, please don't tell him about me."

His cycle roared to life. "I don't talk to him anymore."

Figuring the game was up and that I was lucky to escape with my teeth, I almost didn't contact Vince on Friday, but the urge to stand face-to-face with Apollo one last time was too much. Late in the after- noon, I parked in the alley and walked into the back of the shop. Vince was cleaning those magnificent hands and arms with linseed oil. A van with a fire-breathing dragon stood drying a few feet away.

"Catlow," he called on spotting me. "Thought you'd forgot."

"Naw. Had things to do. Come up with any ideas?" I played the game.

"Yeah, think so. Wanta show you something I did. You got a few minutes?" I nodded. "Let me wash this stuff off," he added.

Fifteen minutes later, he came out of the rest room looking like the national treasury of a first world country. Hip-hugging black chinos showed his groin to its best advantage. Black muscle shirt with a blue linen over-shirt unbuttoned and hanging loose. Gold chain. Linked watchband. Big ring with a colored stone.

"Get on!" he ordered, throwing a long, muscular leg over the Suzuki, the sight of his trim butt robbing my knees of strength. I stumbled aboard clumsily. My legs clenched his thighs, not in a sensual embrace, but from fear as he roared off! Vince was an organ donor, he rode without a helmet…which meant my cranium was at maximum risk, as well.

We picked up I-40 West and left the city behind, jetting down the four-lane past the volcano cliffs. He abandoned the freeway at Paseo de Vulcan and hammered south. Long after we left civilization behind, I spotted a small adobe in the distance. Turning down a twisting, rutted lane, the handsome biker carved the road and did a breathtaking powerslide into a small, dusty yard.

"This your place?" I asked, bailing off the hard-tail and trying to support myself on shaky legs, the result of fear, excitement, and crotch-testing the rear of his saddle-seat during the ride.

"Yeah," he acknowledged, unlocking the padlock on the door to a small structure beside the adobe house. Inside, he swept aside a tarp exposing an old Model-A with a truly amazing paint job. It wasn't flashy, it was spectacular. Basically, it was a series of blues that subtly changed hues four or five times from front to back. The paint had such a deep, metallic luster that you felt you could put your hand through it.

"Perfect," I breathed sincerely. "With a red and orange checkerboard stripe."

"Orange and yellow. Muted, different degrees of intensity."

"Let's do it!" I said, carried away by my enthusiasm. I hadn't really intended to get a paint job up until that point.

"Great." He slung the tarp back in place. "You got time for me to shower and change before we go pick up your car?"

"Yeah, sure," I agreed.

I searched the fridge as he headed to the back of the little house and was sucking on my second beer when he came out toweling his head. He wore nothing except a blindingly white towel around his middle. His dark flesh made an alluring contrast.

He paused in front of me. "You sure you want that guy's name? You know, Mr. NM 466-CPA?"

"Why…why wouldn't I?" I mumbled, trying vainly to keep my eyes off of his groin. His cock was clearly outlined against the terrycloth.

"Maybe I can suggest a substitute," he said slyly.

Well aware that he was challenged by my pretended interest in Miles and not him, I didn't know how to answer. I didn't need to. He released the towel and let it fall to the floor.

"Geez," I breathed.

"He doesn't have one like that, I can tell you."

"He…he doesn't?" I quavered.

"You want a man, then you want me."

"But…"

"Not buts," he said, walking up to me. That fantastic cock was right in my face. All I had to do was lean forward. And then what? I leaned forward, and that was all there was to it. He smelled fresh from his shower. His pubic hair was fine and curly and tasted of rinse water as I ran my tongue through it. His cock began to harden beneath my chin and poke against my throat.

"V…Vince?" I mumbled.

"Call me *Lobo*," he said, placing his hands behind my head and moving me to his big balls. "That's my outlaw handle. *El Lobo Moreno*. The Brown Wolf."

"I don't know what to do next," I said around a big testicle.

"Lick 'em," he said. "Don't worry. I'll tell you exactly what I want."

"But," I mumbled, talking and licking at the same time. "I want to cum. That's why I wanted to find that guy."

"You're gonna cum, Catlow. You're gonna cum the best way there is," he declared huskily. "Hope you don't have anywhere to go this evening. Tonight you're *Lobo* meat."

"Mmmm," I replied, a big ball in my mouth.

It would probably have been easier to perform my first blowjob on a cock about half that size. On the other hand, nobody else could have motivated me like this sexy, Spanish biker. He made love to me with every part of his being. His torso brushed my lips, his belly tickled my tongue, his legs excited my hands. He took me to bed and made it last. I tasted, felt, licked, and explored every inch of him before I started trying to take that monster cock. I was never able to get much more than the big glans in my mouth, but I wrapped my hands around the rest of it, and worked on the bulbous end until he came like a soda fountain spewing phosphate. My instinct was to get out of the way when he started spasming, but his big hands held me to him, and I took his cum. Some of it escaped me, and when he was through his orgasm, he had me lick it from his chest.

He suffered my naked, hard cock against his leg while I held his dick in my mouth as it slowly softened. Even then it was a mouthful. I moved to rise, but he held me where I was. I didn't mind; I liked my head on his belly, my leg thrown over his, my cock pulsing against his flesh, leaving a pool of pre-cum.

"How was it?" he asked.

I pushed him out of my mouth long enough to answer. "Wasn't exactly what I had in mind, but it was great, Vince…uh, *Lobo*."

"Truth! First blowjob?"

201

"First. I swear."

"You still want Miles?"

"Miles?" I played along.

"The guy you saw sucking me?" He pulled me up to look me in the eye. "Tell me. Do you want *Lobo* or the other guy?"

I could pretend no longer, even if it ended the charade. "*Lobo*," I answered leaning my brow against his. He took the hint. His lips closed over mine, and I discovered that I had never been kissed before. For a moment, I thought I was cumming against his leg. I moaned and moved my hips. I felt it down to my toes.

"Man, I gotta cum," I panted when he released me.

He grinned lazily, about tearing my heart out of my chest. "Get me hard."

So I sucked that monster back to life, and when it was sniffing around in the air, he twisted his body. Now he lay atop me.

"Oh, no!" I said, beginning to panic. "I can't take that! You're too big!"

He silenced me with another kiss, and then slid slowly down my torso, sucking my nipples and trailing his tongue down my belly. He tugged at my pubic hair with his teeth and licked my balls while I pulsed against his forehead. Still licking my sensitive flesh, he raised my legs and moved into position.

"No!" I said, stiffening my legs. "I can't take it, Vince."

"How do you know? You ever tried?"

"N…no. But…but…"

"You wanta see me again?"

"Yes," I said fervently. "If I let you fuck me, we can see each other some more?"

A momentary frown flickered, but cleared when his big cock brushed against my crack. "We'll see one another. You gonna be my bunny boy, you know, warming my back on the cycle. You gonna be *Cachorro*, my wolf pup, until you're sick of me."

When he penetrated me, I thought I'd died. Then I thought I'd gone to heaven. Once the pain was gone, the incredible fullness, the feel of that magnificent shaft stroking my channel about drove me crazy. He eased all eight inches into me, and worked over me slowly, gradually increasing his tempo, the harshness of his thrusts, the intensity of his lovemaking. The wolf hugging his muscled arm danced menacingly with every movement. I'll swear I heard it bark! Just before he came, Vince Arello leaned forward and kissed me deeply, fucking my mouth and my ass simultaneously. When he shot, he raised his head into the air and howled. His big hand grasped my cock and pumped me half a dozen times, fulfilling his promise. I came the best way there was, with his big prick delivering jism up my ass while my cum soaked both of us. I howled right along with him!

I saw *Lobo* the rest of the summer, and never got over the 'Vince bug' as Miles had called it. He turned me so thoroughly queer that I forgot all about Walt or women or anyone. He had spoiled me for everyone else. He not only turned me into a faggot, but into a biker, as well. At least, he converted me into the male equivalent of a biker chick. Everyone soon grew accustomed to *Cachorro's* package plastered against *Lobo's* handsome butt as we rode from one biker's rally to another or roared along on a cross-country. Strangely, nobody seemed to mind. I was treated decently by everyone. The fact that Vince fucked some of the unattached biker bunnies occasionally, gave us enough cover to satisfy the rest of those crude, hairy, oil-stained dudes. It hurt a little when *Lobo* went off with one of the women, but he always came back to me once he busted his balls. And he never failed to enthusiastically give it to me afterward in the privacy of our own tent, explaining how much better it was with his *Cachorro* than those bitches.

But what about when I leave for school? Well, I switched to UNM, so I won't be going away. Just finished my first semester, and we're still going strong. And if he gets tired of me, I'll have to deal with it somehow. There's this long-limbed swimmer who lives in my dorm who just might make things easier. He rides a bike, too. Isn't that cool?

THREE-WAY CYCLE
Felix Lance Falkon

The big BMW coughed as it rolled to a stop, then settled down to a rough idle that shook cycle and riders, reverberating across the empty street. A lonely traffic light, swinging overhead, bounced scarlet glitter off the chrome and polished black of the motorcycle, but barely outlined the three black-leather-jacketed men who sat astride the throbbing machine.

MARK, the middle of the three riders, loosened his grip on the driver's lean waist. He slid one hand down to rest lightly on the driver's thigh, at the same time arching his back and pressing his bulging crotch against Stony's rump. The throbbing motorcycle between Mark's powerful thighs was triggering an answering beat in his balls now.

Stony's gauntleted hand dropped on Mark's, pulled Mark's hand forward and down to touch, then grip, the long bulge that stretched from Stony's crotch almost to his knee. Mark felt Stony's big cock swell under Mark's fingers as it strained against tight Levi's. Mark probed with his fingers, setting off another stiffening surge in Stony's hot meat.

Mark saw Stony turn his head, heard him ask, "Like th' ride?"

"It's a quick way to get to the main event," said Mark. "Sure, glad I found you guys again."

"Again?" asked Ray, from behind Mark.

Mark glanced back over his shoulder, saw white teeth gleam in the darkness. "I saw you two at the Tool Chest, but you left 'fore Jimmy— the guy showing me around—told me you were cruising together, not each other. He guessed where you'd probably go next, and—" but the rest was drowned in the roar of the BMW as they leaped forward, under the now-green light. Mark grabbed Stony with both hands and held on tight.

STONY braked the cycle to a skidding stop in the carport, then steadied it as his passengers got off. He propped the cycle on its stand, unstraddled it, and turned to Mark and Ray, who were eying each other warily: Mark, big and powerful, strong-jawed and rugged; Ray, clean-cut and handsome, very much the lithe young athlete. Tousled hair lay across Ray's forehead; the single light bulb in the carport ceiling accented the smooth line of Ray's jaw, the sweep and flare of his almost snub nose. Stony watched Ray run a frankly appreciative look down Mark's body.

Mark turned to Stony and asked, "You always go that fast?"

Ray laughed, stepping back a pace as he did, then moved forward again. "Sometimes, Stony and me, we don't wanta mess around with th' preliminaries, and like you said, get t' th' main event."

"Yeah—well—yeah, said Stony. "Th' idle on this hog needs adjusting. You two wanta go inside? I'll just—"

Ray licked his lips, glanced from Mark to Stony and back to Mark; Stony watched Ray for a moment, then let his eyes drift to Mark's muscular frame as the trio stood in the cool night air.

"Motorcycle can wait," Mark growled, looking grim and hungry as he stood, thumbs hooked at his belt buckle, blue eyes glittering, booted feet planted well apart on the concrete. His jaw thrust forward; his broad shoulders hunched, then dropped as the powerful muscles slowly relaxed.

Stony said, "Then both—" but stopped, realizing this magnificent stud, if he didn't mind being watched, might even—"Motorcycle can fuckin' well wait," said Stony, digging his door key from a tight pocket. "Come on."

RAY, once inside, turned from closing the door behind him to see Mark shrugging his broad shoulders out of his leather jacket. Mark tossed his jacket aside and stood for a moment while Ray and Stony looked him over.

Mark's tightly stretched T-shirt covered a splendid body-builder's torso. Even through the cloth, Ray could follow the line of the pectorals, the ripple of stomach muscles—but mostly, his eyes took in the breadth and depth of Mark's chest. Mark tensed his arms; sudden shadows marked the swell of his triceps. A deep breath tightened his stomach and emphasized the taper of his torso down to the wide, black leather belt.

Mark dropped to his left knee, flipped open the buckle of his right boot. Before the big man could shift to the other foot, Ray knelt and reached for the battered leather. Mark froze for an instant, then leaned back and shifted his right boot forward. Ray's fingers touched rough leather, loosened the leather strap. As he worked, Ray smelled the leather-and-sweat odor of the big man and the stronger, virile scent of Mark's feet as Ray worked off first one boot, then the other.

Mark scrambled to his feet; Ray was still kneeling, looking up. Mark grabbed the bottom of his tight T-shirt and pulled it up and over his head with a smooth, slow twist of his thick arms. Looming above him, the kneeling Ray saw a hard, sharply defined washboard of stomach muscle appear, stretched from narrow, belted waist to the broad arch of Mark's heavy-boned rib cage. Above that, the powerful chest spread into swelling lats and tensed pectorals to the full width of Mark's thick shoulders.

Ray stood up slowly. Mark tossed his undershirt aside, dropped his hands to his belt. Mark's pectoral muscles made a smooth, hard sweep across his chest—like marble; no, granite—Ray thought to himself as his gaze ran across the lightly freckled skin, over chest and shoulders and bulging biceps, up to the thick neck and strong-jawed face under a mane of jet-black hair. Black too, were Mark's eyebrows, and one was raised in wordless question.

Ray licked his lips, felt a hungry grin spread across his own face. He shook off his own black leather jacket, let it fall without taking his eyes from Mark. Ray's hands fumbled at his own belt, jerked open the buckle, and shoved his tight-fitting jeans down his legs. A couple of kicks and a jerk freed his feet, and Ray stepped out of tangled trousers and boots and socks, legs bare, stiffening cock swinging free. Ray jerked his own T-shirt off, tossed it across the room. Watching Mark, who stood less than a yard away, Ray slowly ran his hands down his own naked chest and flat stomach to stop, thumbs crossed, almost but not quite touching the base of his fast rising cock.

They stood, staring, for a long moment: naked Ray, big, muscular Mark in trousers and nothing else. Ray's gaze darted over the splendid physique before him, dropped to the massive bulge at Mark's crotch, rose again to study the broad chest, the powerful band of muscle that crossed it. Ray's gaze shifted to Mark's shoulders, rough-hewn chunks of hard muscle—like living granite, he told himself. He moved a pace closer, raising his right hand to touch, then grip the Mark's big, warm left shoulder. A hint of a smile touched Mark's hungry blue eyes. Ray started to smile back—and without warning, Mark's strong arms locked tight around Ray's naked torso, squeezing the young athlete tightly to Mark's chest.

From collarbone to waist, Ray felt warm nakedness pressed to his own; from waist to ankle, rough cloth over hard muscle and swelling basket rubbed against Ray's bare skin. Ray's head was caught between Mark's neck and shoulder; his nose took in the warm, clean smell of Mark's dark hair. A thick arm tightened around Ray's back, pulling him closer. Mark's other hand slid down Ray's spine to stop at his bare butt, there to press hard, driving Ray's hips and hardening cock and hot balls into Mark's cloth-straining basket.

Just as abruptly, Ray was free, standing just inches from Mark, looking up to meet Mark's twinkling eyes. The scrape of rough cloth on the tip of his cock jerked Ray's eyes down. His cock, now proudly erect, pointed straight out, bridged the gap between their hips, and just touched Mark's basket. Ray noticed Mark's hands were well away from Mark's belt buckle now. Ray lifted his own hands slowly, touched the brass buckle, and unfastened it. A quick pull opened the fly, half-disclosing a set of balls and a thick cock that was erecting fast.

Trembling with eagerness now, Ray jerked Mark's trousers wider open. The youth dropped to his knees, dragging the Levi's down Mark's thighs and on down the bulge of his big calves. Ray was sitting on his haunches now, one hand sliding up the inside of Mark's thighs, the other clutching the big man's lean, hard buttocks. Ray's face was just inches from Mark's cock. The stiffening column seemed to reach out for him, an inviting mouthful of hot meat. Ray's hand gripped the base, fingers meeting surging hardness. The brick-red cock-tip was right at Ray's nose now. Ray opened his mouth wider, pounced with lips and tongue, and engulfed the end of Mark's throbbing cock.

Lips and tongue clamped tight, sucked hard. Mark's shaft was a mouthful, filling Ray from tongue to palate, from lips to gullet. Ray swallowed. Mark's cock stiffened harder, driven deeper by a jab of Mark's hips and thighs. Ray sniffed the musky scent of balls now. His tongue barely caught a hint of saltiness from Mark's cock-tip. Ray still gripped the base of Mark's cock with his right hand; Ray's left arm clamped tight around Mark's thighs, sensing every move of the big man's muscles. Ray's bare chest rubbed against Mark's thighs— touched and slid over warm, sweat-dampened skin all prickly with a sprinkle of close-cut hair.

Ray opened his eyes. He saw nothing but a furry blur. He pulled back along Mark's long prong until just the big glans was in his mouth, the corona clamped tightly between his lips. The blur resolved itself into a tangle of black hair at the base of Mark's virility. Jutting out from that tangle, coming too close to see properly, came a column of hard Mark-meat. Above the tangle, a washboard ripple of muscle went up and up, out of sight. Ray sucked, swallowed, sucked again, tonguing firm resilience. Ray twisted his head to the side, making Mark's cock press against the side of his jaw from the inside. Then Ray moved his head forward, taking all he could of Mark's cock. Ray pulled back quickly. He sucked in a mouthful, pulled back, sucked in, and on into a fast-bobbing rhythm of his head. He sucked harder, pumped his head faster; he was caught up in a pounding, lusty hunger for cock, more cock, and more—more—more!

MARK twisted his broad body a little to the left for a better view, a view down his rippling muscles, on down his torso, which tapered in to narrow hips from which jutted his shaft. Ray's mouth was around the end of that shaft now, sliding back and forth along it. Mark curled his hips forward, thrusting his stiff prong still deeper into Ray's tousled head. Mark saw the outline of Ray's eyebrows, knitted in concentration, just above his wetly gleaming prong; saw Ray's nose and lips, stretched wide around Mark's cock, guiding it into Ray's mouth. And at the very tip of the body-builder's cock, Ray's tongue squirmed and licked and rubbed back and forth and around. Suction drew, relaxed, pulled again at Mark's shaft. Now and again, Ray's teeth just brushed, gently scraped the hot meat, awakening in Mark a surge in the roots of his organs, an answer to the youth's lusty hunger.

Mark took a deep breath, feeling muscles tighten across his broad chest. He looked up from Ray, and glanced around the comfortably untidy living room. In a corner nearby lay a pile of cushions. A few feet away, Stony—the driver during the wild motorcycle ride—lay sprawled in a chair. He had stripped, and his rigid shaft and balls were in full view. Stony's cock was as impressive as it had been in tight Levi's at the bar—even more impressive now that it was hard, the big glans thrusting out from its sheath. Stony's balls were big: the better to fuel such a weapon, Mark thought to himself. The body attached to that big prong was lean, with a thin skin that displayed in clear relief every muscle of Stony's well-knit build. There was a confident, easy grace about the motorcyclist that told of long practice in handling that lithe body. A touch of silver on Stony's head and in the crisp fur on his chest and arms also hinted at plenty of experience with wielding that shaft.

As Mark watched, Stony picked up a pipe and started to fill it with tobacco. Stony glanced down at tousle-haired Ray, who was sucking lustily away on Mark's cock, then looked back up to meet Mark's gaze. There was, Mark noted, just a hint of excitement in Stony's cool gray eyes.

Mark looked down his body again, down at Ray's lips, sucking eagerly along Mark's cock. Ray's head was darting back and forth, back and forth, almost a blur of bobbing motion to Mark's eyes; definitely a blur of suction warmth along Mark's out-thrust shaft. Mark tensed his own powerful thighs; his hips were actively thrusting with a beat to match Ray's hungry mouth. Inside, deep in the roots of his shaft, Mark felt an expanding warmth that was rapidly coming to a boil.

Mark put his right hand on Ray's bobbing head, his left, on the youth's shoulder. Mark let Ray suck his cock for a few strokes more, then, without warning, Mark pushed down and away with both hands, at the same time jerking his hips back. Mark's cock was free.

"Hey—don't!" Ray tried to pull himself onto Mark's hard-on again.

"Hold your horses," growled Mark. He brushed away a grab by Ray, then pushed him again, so that Ray was off balance, falling back.

Mark dropped atop him, forcing him back to the floor and pinning him there with all the weight of his own body. Mark wrapped his thick arms around Ray's chest, and hugged Ray to him with all the strength of his thick biceps, eagerly savoring the pressure of Ray's squirming nakedness against Mark's own. They lay thus for a moment: broad chest on chest, hip on hip, legs entwined, stiff cocks squeezed together between hard stomachs. Big Mark relaxed his grip a little. Ray slid his arms around Mark's chest and hugged hard. Mark felt strong hands clutching his back, stroking the big muscles there, pressing hard again.

Mark began to rub himself against Ray's naked body, sliding bare skin over skin, pressing bulging chest muscles over the strong planes and smooth, hard contours of Ray's athletic physique.

Ray was breathing hard, his body slick with sweat. Mark felt Ray slide easily as he squirmed in Mark's grip. He put a hand on the rug on either side of Ray's shoulders, then straightened his arms in a push-up, so that chests and stomachs separated, and Mark's naked body touched Ray's only at their hips—where cock rubbed against hot, throbbing cock—and along their legs. The big weight lifter dropped himself onto Ray with a breath-expelling thump. He wriggled from side to side, rubbing the sweeping breadth of his thick pectoral muscles across Ray's chest, savoring the feel of bare skin sliding under his nipples, just conscious of the nudge of Ray's teats pressing up against his own nakedness.

Mark propped himself up on his arms again. He grinned down at the very-out-of-breath Ray for a second, then looked around the room. Stony was sitting on the edge of his chair, gray eyes intent on the naked bodies on the floor. Stony's cock was completely erect now, a superb shaft of man-meat reaching halfway up Stony's lithe torso.

As Mark grinned knowingly at Stony's obvious fascination, Mark saw Stony try to relax. He picked up a matchbox with one hand, fumbled on the chair-arm for his pipe with the other. Pipe in mouth, he picked up a pipe cleaner and tried to strike a light with it on the side of the matchbox. Unsuccessful, Stony took a look at what he was doing, scowled, and tossed the things aside. Mark grinned more broadly as Stony abandoned any pretense at appearing calm and leaned forward, frankly interested now in the naked wrestlers on the rug. Still smiling, Mark turned his own attention back to the clean-limbed young man he was lying on.

"Well?" asked Mark. "How ya doin'?"

"It's almost like getting raped," Ray panted.

"What d' ya mean, 'almost'?" Mark dropped himself onto Ray's sweaty chest again. He took a deep breath; the young athlete smelled hot and sweaty, yet fresh, as if he had just come from the sea.

A crushing embrace squeezed hot, sweat-slick bodies together again. Mark's head was right over tousle-haired Ray's. Mark bent down and touched the blunt tip of Ray's nose with his lips. A slippery squirm brought Mark's lips to Ray's. Hungry mouths touched, pressed hard. Mark slid himself down Ray's wriggling nakedness to bring his lips to Ray's left teat. He kissed the dark nipple, drawing a sigh from the youth. Mark's teeth took Ray's right nipple and bit hard.

"Wow !" Ray yelped. "Again—that's it—aahhh!"

Mark moved on down, sliding his powerfully muscled torso over Ray's clean-limbed body until Mark's chest lay on Ray's thighs. Mark's elbows and forearms clamped Ray's slim hips between them. Ray's stiffly jiggling cock was just under Mark's head now. The bodybuilder slowly bent down and touched his tongue to the head of Ray's cock.

Sharply indrawn breath—a gasp of surprise—made Mark look up, along Ray's naked body, to his face. The youth had propped head and shoulders up with his elbows; his face was aglow, eyes sparkling under the low sweep of tousled hair across his forehead. Mark saw that the muscles of Ray's torso and arms were taut; *the long, smooth muscles of a swimmer,* Mark told himself. A faint sprinkle of gold accented the tanned hide.

"You mean—you mean you aren't just—" Ray paused, licked his lips.

"Just?" Mark snorted. "Watch." He parted his lips, bent down, and in one gulp engulfed half the length of Ray's waiting cock. He clamped his lips tight and swallowed hard.

"Take me, man, suck me!" said Ray.

Under Mark's chest, he felt Ray's thighs tense. The iron-hard cock jerked in Mark's mouth. Mark raised his head slowly until just the broad tip was inside—a tip just the right size for sucking: a live chunk of meat that his lips and tongue fitted onto easily—a hot, barely salty chunk of Ray. Mark curled his tongue around the edges of Ray's glans, to the right, to the left, and up to the cleft that led to the opening at the very tip. The bodybuilder swallowed again, with an extra squeeze and rub of his tongue that brought a twitch from the youth's responsive shaft. Still sucking, Mark lowered his head down on the hot cock, down and down until the shaft filled his mouth. Mark twisted his head to the right on the next stroke so that the upward curve of Ray's shaft was sideways in his mouth. Slowly, Mark twisted his head to the left on the return stroke, so that his lips and tongue traced a spiral on the youth's now-throbbing cock.

Ray wrapped his legs around Mark's powerful chest. Ray's hips jerked up, relaxed, jerked up again, jabbing his cock up and up again into Mark's mouth. Mark felt young Ray's hands grab his head to pull him even further down onto Ray's cock.

Mark continued to suck, going down—up—down again at the same steady, relentless pace. Under him, the youth squirmed and squirmed again. Ray's sweat-slick body jerked; he gasped aloud. He thrust his slim hips higher, lifting Mark's chest and shoulders with them. Mark rode the bucking youth easily. His hands gripped Ray's hips, his forearms braced along Ray's tense thighs; all Ray's struggles got him not an inch deeper into Mark's jaws. But Ray's cock was harder with every stroke, quivering, swelling, the broad glans surging to full size. A few more seconds, Mark sensed, and...

So, with the next upward stroke of Mark's sucking mouth, he kept on going, up and off, leaving Ray's cock waggling in empty air. Ray grabbed with both hands at Mark's head. Frustrated by Mark's strength, Ray grabbed next for his own cock; Mark easily slapped the youth's hands away. Gradually, Ray. subsided until he lay panting on the rug, cock quivering but unfired.

Mark rolled over to lie alongside Ray, still facing him. The panting youth followed him with his eyes. "That was—was close," said Ray. He reached over with one hand to touch, then stroke the muscles of Mark's chest. In a moment, Ray sat up, twisted toward Mark, and bent over Mark's crotch, saying, "Now let me—"

Mark watched Ray's mouth close on his own hot shaft, felt the wet suction take hold again. The big man lay still for a couple of minutes, watching Ray's head bobbing up and down, feeling lips and tongue slide along his prong. Then, before his glands began to respond, Mark jerked his cock free and pounced on Ray again.

This time the bodybuilder took Ray from the side, lying across instead of along the youth's supine body. Mark grabbed Ray's shaft with both hands, one gripping it at the base, the other wrapped around the barrel, half-way between base and tip. Mark took a second to glance up; Ray was watching, bright-eyed and eager. Mark looked down at the waiting cock, then went slowly down on it again.

After a few long strokes, Mark raised his head so that only the tip was clamped between his lips. With the hand that gripped Ray's shaft in the middle, Mark started to stroke up and down—fast—so fast that his hand was an out-of focus blur and the cock vibrated furiously between his lips as he sucked.

In seconds, tousle-haired Ray was gasping and squirming again. In seconds more, his hips jabbed upward, his hands groped for Mark's head and thick shoulders. In a few seconds more, he would—

—but again, Mark jerked up and away before Ray could erupt, leaving him to slowly relax and catch his breath. Then Mark went down on Ray again, this time with fast, hard-sucking, head-bobbing suction. Again, young Ray responded, muscles tensing, cock throbbing.

"Please, all the way. Don't stop; that feels so good!" panted Ray, but again, the big weight lifter pulled up just in time.

Twice more, Mark went down on Ray. Twice more, he left the youth gasping, on the brink, cock jabbing empty air. Mark lowered himself onto Ray's warm, naked thighs again; slipped his mouth down and onto the hot, hard cock. This time, Mark sucked slowly, spiraling down, licking and rubbing with his tongue at the throbbing mouthful of man-meat, pulling slowly back to the tip, going down again. This time, Mark kept on and on, while Ray bucked and squirmed and panted under him; kept on while Ray tensed, went rigid, jerked, and went rigid again. Mark went down, all the way, and just sucked. Ray was still now, muscles hard, with not a quiver of his athletic frame except for the wild jerking of his cock as he pumped out jet after jet of semen. Mark swallowed, and a big, hot mouthful of man-oil went down his throat. Mark sucked again. Ray's cock was still spurting, pumping the youth dry, pumping surge after swirling surge of hot cream into Mark, straight down his gullet.

After what seemed an erotic eternity to Mark, the volcano in the base of Ray's prong subsided, the eruption quieted, the jet of ball-juice slowed to a trickle. Mark sucked hard. Ray spurted once more. Mark swallowed, then rose to his feet.

On the rug, Ray lay quiet, eyes half-closed. Mark poked him in the ribs with one bare foot; Ray grinned, sleepy and satisfied.

STONY looked up from his partner, Ray, to the big, powerfully built man who stood over Ray. Mark's blue eyes studied Stony, who felt his body go warm under the appraisal. The expression on the Mark's face shifted from calm interest to frank hunger. Stony glanced down his own lithe, naked body to the long cock that stood proudly up from his crotch. He twitched his cock once, then looked up to meet Mark's gaze again.

The big bodybuilder slowly lifted his arms in a muscle-rippling stretch. His six-pack stomach pulled in, relaxed. His chest lifted, its muscles tensed into sudden, sharply defined relief as his pectoral muscles slid up into a curving V that linked breastbone and shoulders, then thickened into a solid trapezoid as Mark's arms dropped to his sides again. Mark stepped over Ray and walked away from Stony to the far end of the room where he opened the door to the bedroom and bathroom. Stony watched the big man stride away, watched muscles in the broad back tense and relax as Mark's weight shifted from one leg to the other. The strong, lean buttocks relaxed, tautened, relaxed. Not much chance of getting in there, Stony told himself, but still—

The big weight lifter was back in a moment, now with a bottle of mineral oil. He splashed some on his right hand, started to smear the gleaming oil on his hard stomach and on down to his crotch. Mark glanced down at Ray as he stepped over the youth again, still resting on the rug, and stopped finally at the pile of pillows. Mark sloshed a little more oil on his right hand and spread a gleaming sheen over his chest. Mark's gaze met Stony's; he beckoned with a toss of his head.

Stony, long-cocked Stony, found himself scrambling to his feet. He tried to walk casually as he crossed the room to join Mark by the heap of pillows, somehow managing to keep from throwing himself at the superb specimen of muscular virility who stood waiting there for him.

The big bodybuilder carefully put down the bottle of oil. He stood for a moment, not quite posing but still looking like he'd just stepped off the stage of a physique contest. Stony stopped a pace away and stood, waiting, while Mark looked him over for a moment. Abruptly, Mark stepped forward and clamped both arms around Stony's chest.

And a fraction of a second later, Stony locked his arms around Mark's muscular torso. They held each other tightly, while Stony felt all the strength and power and lusty virility of Mark's Herculean physique in his arms, pressed against his own nakedness. Their lips met for just an instant, separated again. Mark shifted his arms; Stony savored the feel of skin sliding over oiled skin. Still locked in each other's arms, Mark and Stony sank to the floor and rolled onto the soft pillows.

Stony's wiry strength was no match for the power of Mark's great muscles; Stony was pinned, on his back, with the big bodybuilder squirming on top of him. Stony felt his long cock squeezed between their bodies, felt a hand—Mark's—grab Stony's shaft. He responded with a hip-curling thrust that drove his cock into those groping fingers. Stony groped too, found Mark's thick spike, and explored it for a moment before a shift of their wriggling bodies pulled his hand away.

Their legs were entwined now, pushing and rubbing. Mark, on top, worked his knees between Stony's. Another move, with cocks rubbing against each other between flat, hard stomachs, and Stony's legs were together again, with Mark's on either side, straddling him. Mark raised himself on his arms for a moment; Stony reached up, let his hands stroke across the hard, powerful chest and shoulders that loomed over him. Mark's skin felt slick with oil, stretched tight over bone and massive muscle. Stony moved his hands further down to touch the deep corrugation of Mark's stomach muscles, the sharply defined valley between obliques and hip. And there, pressed together, were cocks— Stony's own long weapon, Mark's sturdy shaft. Stony grabbed both, squeezed them together, felt both throb and swell in his grip.

Without warning, black-haired, strong-jawed Mark dropped down onto Stony's chest and pulled him into another muscle-straining embrace. A squirm, a wriggle rubbed their naked chests together. Mark, irresistibly strong, was nibbling on a teat, now rubbing his splendid chest across Stony's lithe body, yet again raising his shoulders on stiffened arms so Stony had room to reach down and stroke their hot prongs.

Marks thighs straddled Stony's. The bodybuilder sat up, still astride Stony's hips, sat there a moment while Stony ran his hands over Mark's great, muscle-bulging thighs and on in to fondle Mark's big, warm bails where they lay on his flat belly. Mark squirmed forward, still straddling Stony's body, until he sat on Stony's chest. Stony bent his head forward, opened his mouth. Mark shifted a few inches closer, and Mark's thick cock slid into Stony's mouth.

Though the angle was awkward, the motorcyclist sucked hard, nodding his head with the fastest, most vigorous beat that he could manage. After a few seconds, though, Mark moved himself back, pulling his cock from Stony's mouth, moved on back until he was kneeling astride Stony's hips again. This time, Stony's cock was behind him, standing stiffly erect just behind—and pressing against—the weight lifter's hard, muscular buttocks.

Stony looked down his naked body, down to where Mark's big balls lay, and then up, examining the naked Hercules who sat astride him. Hard, warm thighs clamped Stony's hips. Soft pillows supported his naked body from below, soft enough to let him curl his hips upward, sliding his hard cock against Mark's butt.

There was a tense, hungry look in Mark's eyes now, as he worked himself a little further down Stony's body, pushing harder against Stony's cock with his butt and then rubbing up and down against the upright shaft.

So close, Stony thought to himself as he lay there, under Mark. A guy with a build like this, Stony went on to himself, couldn't be anything but trade—but he had pounced on Ray, pounced on the youth's cock and sucked him dry. Still, Stony told himself, sucking wasn't the same as fucking, even though—

Stony interrupted his thoughts and boldly said, "It would be better inside." At Mark's puzzled frown, Stony licked his lips and said, "My cock. Inside—inside you. Mark, stud, lemme fuck you."

"You sure you want to?"

"Hell yes!" the motorcyclist said, then held his breath.

"Well—" Mark looked grim for a moment, his black eyebrows lowering in a scowl, and then he reached slowly for the oil.

Stony resumed breathing while the big bodybuilder oiled his hand and reached behind. Stony felt cool, slippery fingers grip his cock, slide along the shaft. Another slurp of oil went to Mark's ass; a few drops felt cold and wet on Stony's balls. Mark rose on his knees, still straddling Stony's hips. He let Stony's weapon snap erect, and then slowly—very carefully—sat back and down onto the long prick.

Stony lay motionless, scarcely daring to breathe. His cock-tip slid between the cheeks of Mark's butt. He felt it hit resistance and slide past its goal. Mark raised himself again, settled down slowly, guiding Stony's shaft into place. Stony's glans touched a tight opening. He jabbed upward, felt the opening close tighter. Stony pushed up harder, felt Mark pushing down. Stony's glans began to penetrate, opening the way for the shaft that followed.

"Take—it—easy!" said Mark. "You got a big 'un there," he panted, as he slowly lowered his hips, gradually impaling himself on the virile length of Stony's prong.

Mark's hole, like a tight-fitting O-ring, spread slowly around the big glans that capped Stony's cock. The ring snapped past the rim of Stony's glans. He was in! His cock drove on and on into the unbelievably soft yet tight inside of the big weight lifter's ass. Mark impaled himself further, further, and Stony felt his cock drive in deeper, still deeper. Hot gut gripped almost the full length of Stony's shaft now—just a few inches more—a little more, and Mark settled down with a sigh onto the hilt of the motorcyclist's prong.

For a few seconds, Mark just sat there, motionless. Stony watched him, studied the superb hunk of muscle and manhood impaled on his cock. Mark tightened his thighs, raising himself, then settled down again. On the next stroke, Stony pulled back with his hips, then rammed them up and his cock in as Mark settled down again.

"Don't; just let me ride you," Mark rumbled.

"I'll try, but you've got me hot—so hot—" Stony put his hands on Mark's thighs, felt the powerful muscles tense and relax as the big stud slid up and down along Stony's cock.

And as Stony watched, Mark tensed the muscles of his tapering torso. He raised one arm, sucked in his hard-muscled stomach, tightened his biceps in a physique pose all the more exciting for being done by a muscle man while Stony was fucking him. The sight: a splendid muscleman; the feel: a tight ass gripping Stony's prong; together, they turned the motorcyclist on. Mark dropped his arms, holding them a few inches out from his sides, and just rode Stony's cock with a rolling stroke that sucked Stony toward climax, that pulled his lust nearer to boiling eruption with every second.

MARK, big, powerfully muscled Mark, felt the impaling thrust of Stony's magnificent prong as a burning flame of ecstasy, warming Mark's body with every stroke. Mark looked down, down at the lithe body he straddled, down at Stony's sharply defined physique—Stony whose muscles were tautening, as he neared climax. Mark became aware of his own rampant cock, bouncing in empty air. He grabbed it and began to jack off furiously as he slid himself up and down along Stony's cock—up and down along the cock that jabbed and probed and fired the reservoirs of his lusty virility, deep in the base of Mark's sturdy cock and big testicles.

RAY sat up and ran his fingers through his tousled hair. He glanced around the room and saw Mark, body gleaming like polished granite, sitting astride Stony, bouncing slowly up and down. Ray's eyes widened as he realized Mark was impaled on Stony's cock. Ray scrambled to his feet, trotted across the room. He spotted the vibrating blur of Mark's hand on Mark's own cock. Ray dropped to his knees beside Mark and bent down. He grabbed Mark's cock in one hand, opened his mouth wide, and went down, engulfing the sturdy shaft.

STONY, on the bottom of the pile, was almost ready to explode. Pressure was building up in the roots of his virility now, heating his body, making every muscle tighten. Stony pumped harder with his hips, meeting every descending thrust of Mark's body with an upward thrust of his own. Another stroke—another—and a liquid blast detonated, erupting up and out, spurting Stony's man-oil up and into the tight, hot ass that gripped Stony's cock.

MARK felt Stony's cock ram upward, driving up and in to its very hilt. Hot ball-cream spurted up into his impaled ass. He gasped aloud, felt his own powerful body go rigid in a muscular spasm. Mark ejaculated his own geyser. His sperm gushed out through his sturdy prong and straight into young Ray's hungry mouth.

RAY felt a torrent of hot ball-cream fill his mouth. He gulped it down. Sucking hard, he felt Mark's thick cock shoot squirt after squirt of the bitter cream. He swallowed again, feeling the slippery load go down, sucked on until he had drained the bodybuilder dry; until, with a sigh, he finally released Mark's still-hard cock, then collapsed in a heap with Ray and Mark.

CLINGING ON FOR THE RIDE
Stephen Albrow

Clinging on to his leather-clad torso, I get sped off into the night. Moonlight all around us. We bob and weave through three lanes of traffic, buzzing a cop car and spitting smoke into a hundred station wagons' faces. The spider tattooed onto the back of his jacket seems to be crawling towards me, like it's moving in for the kill. I bury my face into the thick black leather and inhale the scent of Troy's perspiration.

A sudden screech of tires, as we head off the main track and start scooting over cornfields, really churning up the mud. I squeeze my thighs real tight around Troy's legs and strengthen my grip upon his torso. My body's getting jolted all over the place, as he revs up hard up enough to bust through the half-broken fencing that shields the cornfields from the highway beyond.

Quiet. Deathly quiet. Not another sole on the open road. Just the sound of Troy's engine working overtime, as we power towards our destination. *Not that he's told me what's going on tonight. Not that I have a clue where the hell that destination's gonna be. I'm just clinging on. Just clinging on for the ride. Troy can take me wherever he wants to. He's the stud with the beast between his legs and I'm just his latest willing patsy.*

Faster, faster, plenty more revs and a fat jet of smoke from the streamlined cylinders. Troy hollers something about the bliss that comes with freedom, as the speedometer hits close on twice the legal limit. His long, greasy hair trails behind him in strands, riding on the wind and catching on my face.

Clinging on, that's all I'm doing. Just clinging on for the ride. A smell of oil, as Troy kick-ass overtakes a truck, then freewheels down the ravine towards the truck-stop diner where the Spiders hang out. A flash of purple neon in the window advertises HOT FOOD and BEERS AT REASONABLE PRICES. It doesn't tempt Troy, though. He revs straight past the diner building and heads on into the woods out back.

Thick trees and close-on black, but somewhere in the darkness glows an orange-yellow pyramid of flame. Troy slows the bike down to walking pace, as he zigzags through the undergrowth and overgrowth. I hear a burst of laughter, as an empty beer bottle gets thrown onto the fire and cracks into shards. Someone shouts out that Troy is coming, then as the bike comes into full view someone spots that I'm riding pillion with him.

"What you got there, Troy?" says a hairy motherfucker in oily denim.

"Troy's brought us one of his toys to play with," shouts another voice, coming through the pyramid of flame.

There must be close on ten of them here, but in the flickering firelight, I can't be sure. Parked all around, in between the trees, are the metal machines that brought them to the secret destination. Every so often, illuminated by flame, I catch a glimpse of leather, or a chain and crucifix, or some denim, or a T-shirt with some metal band's name emblazoned on the front. The air is fragranced with sweat and oil, plus the pungent odor of burned-out rubber. Someone passes a beer to Troy. He lets me swig first from the dirty bottle, then he drains the remains in a single swallow. I feel the heat from the fire burning my neck and my face, as Troy leans forward and begins to kiss my lips.

As Troy's tongue shoots in and out of my mouth, I hear the sound of his fly zipper getting tugged open. He grabs my hand and places it down the front of his jeans. The rest of the gang all whoop and holler, as I tighten my fingers around his shaft and don't stop beating until that slab of meat is good and hard.

"You better hurry along, fella," someone shouts. "That pretty, little mouth of yours has got a lot of horny Spiders to satisfy."

A loud smash, as another empty Bud bottle gets tossed into the flames. Troy stops kissing me and gets to his feet, then he pushes his dick between my lips. It's so sudden and unexpected that I choke upon his crown, which goes darting in and out of my lips with a seemingly unrelenting vigor. *Jesus, you should hear that bunch of bikers all laughing when they spot me gagging on Troy's bulky dickhead!*

"Troy's a meaty cunt, fella," one of them shouts at me.

"I don't think the cute little city boy can handle that much prick," shouts another, making the whole bunch of them laugh some more.

I take the comments as a challenge, puckering my lips around Troy's meat, then letting him slam his full length deep inside me. He's fucking my mouth at incredible speed, so I reach around his body and cup his buns in my hands to try and slow him down just a little. His pants are falling further down his thighs each time that he slams his pecker in and out of my mouth, leaving me free to grope his naked butt. I feel the thin layer of perspiration that's wetting his butt cheeks, as I dig my fingertips into his flesh. The harder that I dig my nails into him, the easier it is for me to control the speed of the blowjob. After an overly frantic start, I get him to settle down a touch. He allows me to guide his prick in and out of my mouth by working his butt back and forward with my hands.

Slow, sensual sucks. The gentler speed allows me to focus the blowjob on the parts of his prick that are most sensitive to my touches. I push his foreskin down his shaft and flick my tongue against his spunk-slit, then I work my tongue right around his crown and force it down the folds of his hood. A spasm in his dickhead makes it clear that he likes to be licked there a lot. I push my lips back and forward in tiny thrusts, so that I'm stimulating that sweet spot at the base of his crown over and over again.

Hollers from the watching crowd, as Troy lets out a hearty, climactic groan. A globule of spunk smacks the back of my mouth, so I hurriedly gobble up Troy's full length. His syrupy seed slips down my throat, as contractions make his prickhead expand and contract in the tight confines of my mouth. I swirl my tongue all over his tumescent cock, while bobbing my lips up and down his shaft to heighten and prolong his climax. He ejaculates in spades, which I like one hell of a lot.

The click-click-click of a zipper getting ripped open, then the rustle of denim as some jeans fall down. Troy withdraws his prick from my mouth and gets a high-five from some of his fellow Spiders. He turns around and pisses into the fire. I watch as his pee hits the center of the flames, and then a body steps out in front of me.

"Open wide, fella."

A fat dickhead slides between my lips, then pushes four inches along my tongue. A thick patch of pubic hair tickles my face, and then a hairy scrotum slaps into my chin. The second cock is short, although it has more than enough girth to get my lips really stretching wide apart. A squat cylinder of beef, it begins to jerk in and out of my gaping mouth in fast, aggressive thrusts.

An intense gaze watching over me. Looking up into the eyes of the guy now fucking my mouth, I see that he's staring right down at me. He's watching as his prick shoots back and forward between my lips. He's liking what he sees.

"This guy sure has got a pretty mouth," he tells the rest of the group, then he plugs his full length between my lips and starts to pull my hair. "Suck me, baby," he yells out loud, then he uses his grip upon my hair to make my mouth bob up and down his shaft.

Lips stretched; tongue darting back and forward; titillating the open crown of a circumcised dick. Pre-cum drips into my mouth, as my hair and head get yanked back and forward. Someone yells for the guy to hurry up. *They're waiting in line to fill my mouth with prick. Zipper after zipper is getting tugged down.*

I close my eyes and become an empty vessel, ready to be filled by a succession of cum-squirting cocks. *The Spiders are in town!* I hear the angry purr of an engine, as another biker motors up and another erection gets in line. He asks what's on the menu tonight and someone shouts out that it's one of Troy's toys.

A jet of spunk hits the back of my mouth, as the circumcised prick reaches orgasm between my lips. I flick my tongue out and lick the guy's scrotum, as he drains his sac in my mouth.

"Me next," someone shouts, then just for a moment I have two dicks inside me, both at once. The tip of one erection penetrates my lips, before the circumcised cock has finished ejaculating. My tongue makes a meal of the two juicy cockheads, then the short, squat cock vanishes and I'm sucking on a piece of rubber.

The bitter taste of spermicidal cream. A long, thick cock that presses deep between my lips. Once again, I'm gagging on excess inches, so I bite into the guy's shaft, making it clear that he should push no further. He does what I want. He's different from the others.

I look up at the big fat bear whose dick is deep between my lips. *Long beard, thick sideburns, handlebar moustache.* I run my hands all over his beer belly, as I slowly push my lips up and down his shaft. He pats my head and tells me that he likes what I'm doing. His prickhead grows a little thicker, as it repeatedly pushes in and out of my mouth.

In and out. In and out faster, as the bear begins to thrust his hips back and forward. I grip my fingers around his buns, then he tells me to make a play for his asshole. Without hesitation, I dig my middle finger as far as I can inside his back passage. The teat of the condom balloons in size, as the bear spills his load inside my mouth.

They're waiting in line to fill my mouth with prick. Zipper after zipper is getting tugged down. First another long prick and then a short one, then two more long ones and then one that's fairly average. My mouth is fast running out of saliva, so I take another shot of spunk, before asking for a beer. Troy walks over and hands me a Bud, which the Spiders all watch me drinking. They like how I work the rim of the bottle in and out of my mouth, like it's just another erection that's been waiting in line to party with my lips.

The click-click-click of a zipper getting ripped open, only this time it's my own. First my pants are tugged off, and then my boxer shorts. Troy lifts me up in his powerful arms, then he waits for the bike to get wheeled in. He lays me out across the saddle, my butt poking up for him to fuck. He spits in his hand and uses the moisture to wet my crevice. His finger pokes in and out of my hole, then his dickhead slots inside me.

A burning sensation in the depth of my anus, as Troy's prick powers deep inside my butthole. Anal spasms. A groan. A sudden breathlessness. A shadow falling across my face, as another body looms in front of me.

An oily T-shirt with a skull logo. I close my eyes and wait for the dick to slot between my lips. *Clinging on, that's all I'm doing. Just clinging on for the ride.*

There's an all-pervading odor of oil and perspiration, as, there in the darkness, Troy and his buddy proceed to shaft me from front and back. I hear noisy squeals coming from behind me, as another butthole gets fucked at speed. *Orgy.*

Gang-bang. I open my eyes and see that the fire has gone out. *Everything is black now. Everything is kicking off. Dicks that have already lost spunk inside my mouth revivify and turn their attentions to other waiting orifices.*

The Spiders are in town! Orgy.

Gang-bang. Leather and denim hit the floor, as bodies bend over kick-ass machines. Buttholes wait to receive hard meat. But I'M sucking on the hardest meat and I'M getting fucked by the hardest meat.

Two thick pricks shoot in and out of my body, pumped back and forth with the kind of rapidity that you'd expect from a pair of guys who like to work their speedometers right to the max. They're slamming their dicks inside me, then they're pulling them right back out again. *And they're slamming their dicks inside me, then they're pulling them right back out again.*

And they're slamming their dicks inside me, then they're pulling them right back out again. I feel the friction in my mouth and my anus, as the unrelenting force of the two-way fucking sparks fires within my body. I'm swimming in a sea of testosterone, pumped high on oil and leather. My dick is throbbing with pent-up sexual tension and Troy notices how stiff I've gotten. He grabs my shaft and starts to jerk my erection back and forward between his fingers.

Meaty fingers tightening around the accelerator. Working through the gears. Revving up. Burning rubber. My foreskin chafes my bulbous crown, as it's jockeyed back and forward. *And don't forget that they're slamming their dicks inside me, then they're pulling them right back out again.*

In and out. In and out faster. A dick in my mouth and a dick up my ass. They're fucking me so hard and they're fucking me so deep that I swear that those two prickheads are touching somewhere in the center of my body. Each forward thrust makes those swollen crowns collide. Somewhere in my guts, they're touching one another. Somewhere in my guts, they meet.

And I long to yell, as the sexual tension becomes too great, but *how can I yell with a massive boner ramming in and out of my lips?* All that I can do is suck on meat and focus on the feelings that are causing my dickhead to start to throb. I'm fucking Troy's fingers. I can feel them around my swollen cock. My dick shoots in and out of the hollow in his hand, as he jerks his fingers back and forward. *And don't forget that they're slamming their dicks inside me, then they're pulling them right back out again.*

Then, all of a sudden, the throbs in my cockhead reach a level of intensity that sees me start to blow. *A spasm in my crown and I spit out some spunk. Another sudden spasm and I spit out some more.* Troy grabs my cockhead and squeezes hard, his fingers smearing through my juices. *Another spasm and I spit out some more,* then Troy slams his full length deep between my buns.

Friction burns. A scream from the guy who is fucking my mouth, as I bite into his cockhead to relieve the sexual tension. I get nasty with the biker's chunky crown, using lots of teeth on his foreskin, so he retaliates by jamming his prick in deep. Troy's full length remains plugged within my sphincter, his crown throbbing fit to burst. He fucks in and out of my asshole in thrusts of barely an inch or more, till the throbs in his crown become orgasmic; at which point everything turns to liquid.

Warm sensations deep inside my body. Somewhere in my guts, two prickheads meet. My tongue darts all over a full, thick shaft and after a little more oral stimulation both of the prickheads inside me are firing. *Full length in front. Full length in back. Spitting out spunk for all that they are worth. I'm clinging on, just clinging on for the ride, as they shoot their loads inside my body.*

Cum continues to drip from my prickhead, as, simultaneously, a pair of cockheads withdraw from my mouth and from my asshole. I open my eyes and see the erection in front, as it eases out of my lips. It takes an age for the biker to pull his knob-end out of the depths of my guts. Then he drops to his knees and kisses my lips. His wiry whiskers scratch my face, while his tongue pushes deep inside my mouth. I can still taste the spunk that he spent inside my mouth and I figure that he can, too.

A hand slaps hard into a naked butt cheek.

"Time for us to go, fella," Troy says to me, so I stop kissing the other guy, then jump off the bike and rush to find my clothes. My pants and boxer shorts are lying over by where the fire once burned, illuminated by the last few dying embers. The biker bear is getting topped nearby. He jerks himself off, as a dick slams in and out of his anus. As I dress myself, I watch him reaching orgasm, spilling his seed upon the ground.

Meanwhile, Troy is waiting for me; engine revved and ready to go. Clinging on to his leather-clad torso, I get sped off into the night. The metal machine drifts in and out of the trees, then past the truck-stop diner and out onto the open road. The speedometer needle heads right off the dial, as we motor along the freeway. I feel the wind in my hair and a glow in my body, then I'm overwhelmed by a sudden sense of total freedom.

Pure, unadulterated liberation. Shooting along the freeway, gripping onto my lover's body. I kiss the spider on the back of his jacket and smell the oil on his T-shirt. He pulls on the handlebars and lifts the front wheel of the ground, as we head back across the cornfield towards the pick-up point where he found me.

"There you go, pal," Troy says to me, as we finally reach the end of the line.

But I don't want to go. His body feels so warm. *Clinging on, that's all I'm doing. Just clinging on for the ride. Just clinging on so tightly that he can't put me down.*

He waits, but I'm not budging.

"Okay," he says, when I fail to make a move, "let's take another ride out someplace."

Clinging on, that's all I'm doing. Just clinging on for keeps.

SADDLE UP!
Troy Storm

The big guy's rugged face broke into a huge grin. "You don't know what the fuck I'm talking about, do you?" His meaty fist looped up to slug into my shoulder and knock me sideways. "And you've got the reflexes of a sleepy kitty cat."

Poking a finger, he traced a line down my nose and over my mouth and chin. "But you sure are a pretty piece of work. I don't mind saddling you up at all." Leaning back, he gave me a thoroughly unnerving look. "And I don't think any of us in this mixed herd of biker cattle has an outfit that fits anywhere near as good as that hide wraps around your sweet ass."

He turned me around and patted my butt. "I'd give a couple of left nuts to be shaped so tasty."

"Will you stop the fuck whatever it is you're doing," I shouted, totally all shook up. I jerked my head around. Sure enough, I had caught the attention of a couple of bikers camping nearby. But since neither Jake nor I seemed ready to precipitate my outburst any further, their attention shifted away.

"C'mon, P.T.," he snickered, and before I could squirm away, the big guy had me in a friendly headlock and was knuckling my short-cropped scalp. "Ease up. Don't get so huffy. Sooner or later the gang'll accept you. You're already riding with me, right?"

The heavy leather vest covering his big chest pressed solidly against my cheek. "My name is not Pretty Thing," I snapped. My shoulder was jammed against his broad back and, automatically, my arm went around his hips to steady myself, the firm, solid butt cheeks inside his pants supporting my forearm like living marble globes.

With my head pushed down, dead in my line of vision was the huge bulge of his crotch. It could have been the density of the black hide that caused the material to punch out so lasciviously, but I noticed that though the other wrinkles in his pants shifted and flexed as he moved, his distended crotch remained solid.

He must have a dick and balls like a pair of fucking fists.

I wriggled free, my ears stinging, my chest pumping, gulping air. "What the fuck were you talking about then?" I stormed...quietly.

"Well, it wasn't about how my nuts fit inside my drawers," he smirked.

"I didn't say that," I insisted, but it had been something smart-ass and close to what I thought he had meant by the term he had used.

"My hot 'boxer' is the kind of engine on my bike, nerd. But, don't worry, just keep strutting around in those tight britches and I don't care if you don't even know my name, much less whether I straddle an in-line or stacked." He reached for me again, but I jerked back out of his way.

"Will you stop that," I pleaded, adding, "Jake," firmly, to impress on him I was more than aware of his name—even if I didn't know what the fuck an in-line or stacked was.

I was more than aware of the rest of him. But I had been hoping my interest wasn't that obvious, not having a clue as to which way he swung. The way Jake blatantly teased, he must have had a clue how I swung, but I often wasn't sure what the fuck he meant by his cracks. And it was getting my leather knickers in a double helix.

Jake squatted beside his sleek BMW R80 GS, to polish the dust off the bike, his big, muscular frame contrasting sharply with the lean machine that he drove with the loving ease and sureness of a well-ridden mustang.

Like I hoped he might soon be riding me.

Jake and I were work buddies. We worked in the warehouse division of a wholesale food outfit, hustling gigantic pallets of food-stuffs in and out. Jake was a good-looking, outgoing, friendly stud who had the ladies in the warehouse switching their comfortable pants for red-hot miniskirts in hopes of catching his eye.

And catch his eye they did: the eye of a big, lovable guy who treated them as if he were their collective, protective big brother. And he treated the guys in the warehouse like he was one of their oldest and best pals.

I fell for him like everybody else, and did everything I could to get in tight, to the point of telling him I was a secret biker enthusiast when I found out he rode a motorcycle and ran with a motley crew of guys and gals who took off into the countryside each weekend, sometimes for overnight camping.

Sure enough, eventually, he invited me to saddle up behind him and ride off into the sunset.

And there we were, off in some God-knows-where desert hellhole with no facilities and getting colder by the minute as the sun sank like a leaden orb behind a deformed saguaro cactus.

Jake's buddies and buddy-ettes weren't too bad. He took me around to say 'howdy.' There were pairs of guys, too, but none of them struck me as even remotely gay.

I endured a few joshing comments about my too-good-looking, too-fitted leather outfit, but also some nice words about how Jake had better watch his beer intake, 'cause his work buddy was looking a damn sight better in them fancy duds.'

"You ready to peel off them fancy duds and crawl in here with me where we can bump beer bellies?" Jake grinned another night-chasing grin over the small campfire he had put together to warm our pre-packaged dinners.

I was feeling cozy and malleable, and had pretty much decided Jake was just a cock tease and nothing was going to come of his smirky double-entendres. So I decided to tease back.

"You mean in that shrink-wrap two-man sleeping bag you call a tent? Either one of us pops a boner and the other one gets his nuts strangled." I tried to copy his smart-ass tone, but the thought of being wrapped together with Jake was making my crack about popping a boner a reality and not a joke.

"Well, finally, now we're getting down to brass balls." A heavy eyebrow quirked as he slid into the slim, elongated tent leaving his head sticking out. As he shifted around, clothes began to emerge, and when his underwear was thrown out and added to the pile, my leather pants really got tight.

I peeled, facing the other way, and, with my boxers and T-shirt still on, wriggled in beside him, back to his front. Something hard and spongy nosed into my butt and dragged up past my waist, instantly pumping my pecker to rock, but when it continued on up I realized he was drawing a knuckle up my back.

"If you take off your shorts and your shirt, they'll air out overnight and won't be so randy tomorrow," he purred sexily into my ear. "I promise I'll be a good buddy and not lay a…" He thought for a second. "Lay anything anywhere you don't want me to."

I stripped off my shirt and shorts awkwardly and tossed them outside. A couple of times my bare skin brushed his, igniting my midsection even more.

Jake shoved an arm under my shoulder and pulled me back against his muscular body. His massive dick punched into my butt and rode up. "We gotta snuggle close to conserve heat," he explained hoarsely. His other hand snaked over my hip to slide into my crotch and grip my hard-on. "Heck yeah. I was hoping you had a fire going, just like me." He began to milk my dick.

It took about ten seconds to realize I was about to blow a load. "I'm gonna cum," I gasped.

"Shoot that muck, sweet cheeks," he muttered, rubbing his dick up and down my ass crack in counterpoint to his beating me off. The damn tent was beginning to steam.

"I don't wanna make a mess." I slithered out of his clutches, slid out the top of the tent and dove back in, head-first. When I fitted my face to his crotch, he got the idea.

Sliding us both down inside the tent, I heard a muffled grunt and, immediately following, felt my rock-hard rod thrust down his throat.

Jake's dick slapped at my face. His big nuts knocked against my Adam's Apple. After wiping my face back and forth over his meat pole, and taking a tentative measure with my stretched lips, I realized there was no way I could possibly deep-throat that sucker.

But I could suck like hell on the finger-sized pisshole yawning at the end of the giant knob and that seemed to satisfy my stud biker buddy just fine. In about two minutes he was writhing underneath me, his big chest heaving, the grunts and garbles around my swallowed meat coming quicker and quicker.

I shoved his hairy low-hangers aside and rammed my fist into his bunghole, sinking in a goodly number of digits. "Aaaaaah!" He yawned his throat, ingesting my meat up to the pelvic bone as I used my other hand to keep his monster beef steak's snout planted solidly against my pursed, vacuuming lips.

The first shot of his cream blasted straight through to streak down my throat and squirt into my belly, immediately followed by a series of firehose gushes. I guzzled and gulped, forgetting about my own imminent orgasm, overwhelmed at the copious protein drink slaking my thirst.

He continued to pump, his mouth lax around my dick, his hips jutting forward with every explosive delivery.

My body was buried deep inside the narrow tent, the heat from Jake's crotch and my guzzling mouth sucking out all the oxygen. Popping my fist out of his suctioning butthole, I grappled for the inside tab of the double zipper and jerked upwards, parting the bottom of the tent enough to feel a wash of reviving night air sucked in to replace the heated air squeezed out.

The clotted cream he was delivering abated, his hose shrinking from humongous to gigantic, but enough for me to wrap my lips around the monster and shove it in.

"Ummm um, really nice" I felt, more than heard, Jake mumble as he inhaled past my mouthful of meat. He returned to vacuuming my nuts dry.

Tightening my lips around his throbbing column, I felt the throb of the thick veins pulsing on the surface of the thick flesh. My arm slid under his leg where I gripped my forearms around his butt, pulling his hairy lower abs into my face and drawing the rancid scent of his heated crotch and freshly ejaculated spooge deep into my lungs. I settled in to receive his expert blowjob.

I sure as hell wasn't settled long. Jake's mouth was like a devouring meat grinder. He gnawed and chewed and pumped his head up and down my swollen rod at a blistering pace. His hands rubbed all over my nuts and butt and inner thighs, stroking and slapping, and marking his territory with scraping nails.

The more he sucked the bigger my dick thickened until I felt it would explode inside his mouth; until I begged it to explode inside his mouth. But he was a devious son of a bitch with the abilities of a male houri and the instincts of a champion cock tease. Just as I was ready to give my desperate load up, he pulled back and adjusted his rhythm just enough to keep me dancing on the edge.

Awe-fucking-some. I was stretched to the outer limits of my bearability, sexed beyond best. And the biggest surprise, other than my massively grown meat pole and rock-hard, swollen, cum-stuffed nuts, was the more he danced me on the edge the more of his prodigious dick I was able to get down my throat.

Soon, I had half of big daddy in, ecstatically devouring its throbbing rebirth while at the same time so close to blowing my own load I could hardly hold it back.

When Jake finally allowed me to rocket off, it was the greatest wad I had ever loosed. My entire insides spurted happily out my porker as Jake replenished my liquid loss by pumping a second, powerful volley of cream down my gullet.

So fucking cool: getting it and giving it at the same time. We hung ten for about two minutes, pumping out and scarfing down. It was amazing, even after the exhaustion of letting loose the biggest blow of my life while ingesting the biggest stick of my life, I was ready for more.

"Yeah? More?" He revolved me in the narrow tent and we sucked face like we had sucked dick. He licked my nose. "More still? How about giving it to me up the ass?" He twisted around and spooned against me.

I couldn't believe what I was being offered, but there the hairy melons were, nuzzled against my instantly red-hot, ready-to-puncture piston. And there the condom and lube were, being handed to me over his shoulder.

"Where the hell do you keep...?" There was barely enough room in the tent for us, much less for the niceties of proper butt-fucking.

229

"Never mind, young one. Just try to keep up with us older, more experienced dudes. Now that I've made available the gates of Paradise, make me proud that you know how to swing 'em wide."

It got kinda messy, squirming on the rubber and then greasing it and his ass up. He was snickering and I was flat out laughing. Not normally my attitude when boffing, but Jake was so hot and so easy and so fucking funny, I had the feeling that if my dick hadn't been stuffed down his throat while we were 69-ing, he'd have been cracking jokes

"Okay, stud bunny," he purred sexily, when we were ready for the big time. "Start your engine."

"Speaking of which," I said, snuggling up to his proffered backside. "I think I've figured it out about your boxer. In-line pistons…" I shoved my dick up his butt. "And stacked." I rolled him over face-down, and humped up onto his back.

It was good to hear him chuckle and snort as I pounded away, driving my bone nuts deep into his ass. The melons clutched at my piledriving, in-line rod, lubricating it to a frenzy of fucking.

"Oh, shit, yeah, man." His muffled sighs into the feather-stuffed pad lining the floor of the tent spurred me on. I recognized I was being given special access to Jake. I needed to make him rumble with pleasure, to make him invite me back into his saddle and into his tent.

I also knew what was probably going to be expected of me. Very soon.

My butt jackhammered up and down. I dragged my teeth over his back. My hands pawed up and down his sides. His dick was mashed underneath and his tits were also inaccessible. I realized what I wanted to see was Jake's face while I fucked, and I wanted access to his hot, leather-loving bod.

Next time he'd be on his back.

If there was a next time.

From what I had heard about the leather boys and the 'cycle gangs, if they weren't already shacked up together, more than likely it was a quick get-off they were after. Why had Jake let me fuck him first before he fucked the daylight into where the sun didn't usually shine— which I knew was coming, once I had finished carving my way deep into the heart of his melons?

Whatever. Who cared? The more I gave it to him, the more he seemed to want, and the less time I had to think about what might or might not be. All my energies and all my concentration were focused where my dick was punching: in and out of his tight ass, trashing his prostate, choking his colon, rupturing his rectum.

I was one giant dick and he was one giant butt.

And when I hit the giant cum shot, it all but blew out my nuts. From a solidly pounding man with one thing on his mind, I instantly became a gasping, mewling, wheezing totally wrung-out, totally emptied, totally thrilled guy who had just experienced the best fuck of his life.

We rested a bit, twisting around inside the small enclosure so I could snuggle against him, licking my way up onto his chest and sucking in one of his big, thimble-sized nipples. His breath evened out contentedly and I almost went to sleep, suckling like a hungry calf.

He kissed me on my damp forehead. "Goodnight, sweet cheeks, don't let the big bad bikers around here bite that sweet, tender ass of yours."

I drew my hand down his front, loving the feel of his tight abs under my palm. "If you're talking about you, biker buck, you can bite anything you want." My hand hit a drizzling boner the size of my forearm. "Holy mackerel, you done gone fishin'. We gotta get that thing in the frying pan. Where do you keep them rubbers, and they'd better be extra strong."

"No, no, come on, man," he protested. "I appreciate the gesture, but I am so damned pumped up, I'd rip your butt wide open."

You gotta love a guy like that. I was suckered in—sometimes the mouth is bigger than the butthole. "Are you saying my sweet tight ass can't take that l'il ole sausage you're bouncing off your tummy?" I grabbed it. My fingers didn't touch. Sweat popped out. Everywhere, except my asshole, which was as dry as my mouth. "C'mon, Jake, do this for me. I need you inside me, man. All the way." I stroked the massive, throbbing log. Prelube gushed into my hand. I greased him up, hoping at least the rubber would slide on without too much trouble. Where he was going to put it after that, I knew was going to be a hell of a lot more trouble.

"Don't tease, man," he growled. "Okay, so I guess maybe I deserve a little of my own medicine. I like teasing you. I like seeing you blush. I loved the fucking blowjob. I gave good head, too, right? I don't need to wreck your hole."

I crawled on top of him. "Rubber up. I ain't leaving 'til the dick done come home."

He protested, but more and more feebly. We finally worked the rubber over him.

He stuck in a tentative finger. My butt almost bit it off.

Jake snarled. "You shit, you're asking me to shove a full grown man's third leg up a cherry butthole." He stroked my face. I was sweating like a sonofabitch. "Okay. Why don't I just tease that little cherry for a while. Maybe one of these days...."

231

I was upended yet again and flipped. He stuck his face between my legs while I faced his rubber-clad dick. I am not a man turned off by latex. I went to work slurping the slurpee while he played around with my ass and I tried not to think about what was to come.

His tongue licked gently all around the bung button. He drew circles around the tiny, tight orifice with delicate fingertips. He blew, his hot breath cooling the steaming heat. His big thumb pressed against the pooching lips, urging entrance, smoothing the tight flesh, soothing the relaxing tissues.

I sucked on his meat, mesmerized by what was happening around my hole, my ears tingling from his delicate touch.

Fingers, tongue, moist pressing lips circled the forbidden entrance. Gently, fingertips pressed through, joined by more, knuckles knuckled in, until I was totally crocked at what was happening. He had three fingers up my ass, stirring. He could have shoved his whole fist in for all I cared, my ass was so accepting.

His fist wasn't what he had in mind.

Gently he pulled my slack lips from around his giant beefsteak, and revolved my body to pull me onto his chest—the small tent pitching gently from the action—my tongue dragging over his abs and furry chest, then entering his open mouth. He stretched my legs wide on each side of him, slipped his big hands between to cuddle my ass cheeks in his spread palms, and gently pulled me open.

His magic dick slid inside. Puncturing, spreading, penetrating, filling me up, up, until his meat nuzzled past my prostate. Still he fed me more. Even he seemed surprised at how my ass took him.

"You," he breathed heavily, "are fucking awesome." He urged my ass cheeks further apart with his hands and kept the driving meat coming. I was so full, a load spurted from my rigid porker to grease our fronts as I settled my ass onto his impaling stalk and he pushed further and further inside.

His chin slipped between my lips, the raw stubble sandpapering my stroking tongue. My ass ring tightened around the root of his bone. I pinched hell out of his nipples and twisted and tweaked as he snickered, bending his head to swab out my throat as his dicktongue licked into the depths of my ass where no man had gone before.

Once we locked together, we stayed. He flexed his orifice-filling appendage inside me, slowly at first, to test the elasticity, then increasing the frequency and building the ballooning pulses until his magic penis filled me up to my armpits and nuzzled the back of my throat.

I fired again and again, blanks, but so engorged and so sated all I could do was hang onto his tits and tighten my sphincter, and dance tip toe on the mountain top until with a grateful sigh a gush of liquid lightning oozed through me and I slid down the searing magna riding the boiling mass into a steaming sea.

I lay exhausted, my cheek welded to his soaked chest.

"That was…fun." I could barely croak.

He chuckled. "Yeah. Almost as hot as saddling up and taking off on my wheels."

His hips tilted, forcing his buried semi-soft forward. Abetted by my clutching colon it conquered whatever iota of asshole he hadn't already tamed.

His palms circled, polishing my ass cheeks. "Which do you think work the hardest?" he purred, the animal growl rumbling up through his smirking lips. "In-line pistons, or stacked?"

We're still running tests.

SHOOTING STAR
Daniel Ritter

In those days, I spent my summers working at my father's diner just off Exit 56. It's really a truck stop, complete with a shower in the back, but the sign said Ernie's Diner and everyone called it the diner.

The clientele was pretty much what you'd expect. During the day, we got traveling families, truckers wanting a meal and a quick shower, periodic groups of bikers. Every once in a while, we got someone who never quite recovered from the sixties, someone in tattered jeans and a T-shirt, crystals around their neck, who had all of their belongings and an air mattress in the back of a Ford Escort station wagon or, for the hardest cases, an old Westphalia.

It was the night shift, my shift, when things got interesting. When all of the normal people were sleeping, the night-owls came out to roost in the Diner: shift workers, long-haul truckers, people crazy enough to drive straight through, and bikers, the loners, the guys who don't ride with a gang anymore. Instead, they rocket through the night like a handful of shooting stars, stopping in the wee hours to refuel before resuming their erratic orbits.

He was a regular, if you want to call twice a month a regular. He'd come in about two AM and order three eggs over easy, bacon, buttermilk pancakes and enough black coffee to refloat the Titanic. He was an older guy, late forties, maybe early fifties, not as heavy as you'd think given what he ate but a burly man, built like a brick shithouse, as my dad would put it. His head was shaved and tattooed with a wolf's head and below the pushed-up sleeves of his road jacket, his forearms were canvasses, covered with animals, all predators. His black chaps outlined an impressive package. He looked fierce but he was an easier customer than some, easier than the family men who kept trying to make themselves look impressive for their mousy wives and gum-chewing daughters, or the retro-hippies who kept asking if the juice was organic. He sat, ordered, ate, and minded his own business.

So one Wednesday night when I heard the growl of a Harley-Davidson at the usual hour, I poured batter on the grill, tossed on a few slices of bacon, put on another pot of coffee and set the one on the warmer on his favorite table next to a full cup. He saw it and looked up at me.

"I've got your pancakes frying," I said, "unless you're planning on changing your order."

His face broke out in a grin. "Thanks, kid." He glanced at my nametag. "Del." He held out his hand. It was strong and callused, blackened with old grease. "Name's Wolf." He got his coffee and came back to the counter. "Your memory always this good?"

"Doesn't usually need to be," I said as I cooked. "We don't get many regulars."

"Don't suppose you do. I don't remember seeing you back in May."

"College," I said, a bit nervous. I didn't know what bikers thought of college kids.

"Where?" he asked.

"State."

"Not bad. What are you studying?"

"English." Translation: wimp. Maybe I should have waited for him to order and kept my mouth shut.

"English. So you're one of them smart kids." His voice was kind, though. "What are you doing working here?"

"My dad owns the place."

"Ernie's your dad?"

"Yes." I flipped pancakes and broke eggs.

"Your dad's a good man. You making him proud?"

What father was ever proud of a gay son? Still... "I do my best."

"It ain't easy," he said.

Something in his voice almost made me forget about the food. I filled his plate and looked hard at him as I set it in front of him, but by then, his face was normal. I picked up a rag and started wiping down the counter.

"What do you do when there ain't no customers?" Wolf asked, a smile playing at the corners of his mouth.

"Read."

"What are you reading?"

I set my book on the counter.

He put a thick finger under the author's name. "Mark Twain. I've heard he's pretty funny."

"He is. So what brings you through here every second Wednesday?" I asked, feeling bold.

"Had a friend in a nursing home out in Grover. Went see him every few weeks. Won't be going no more."

"I'm sorry," I said. "Cancer?"

"AIDS."

A chill ran down my spine. "I'm sorry. That's a hard one."

"Yeah. I'm negative," he said quickly. "I used to ride with him is all, years ago. I'll miss Jacks. He ain't the only one." He took a long sip of his coffee. "Sorry, kid. Don't mean to talk your ear off."

"That's okay," I said. "I just wish I had something to say."

"Nothing to say," he said, his voice level again. "Life ain't always kind." His eyes met mine. "Thought you'd understand better than most."

Maybe I did. Sure, it was different then than it had been when he had been my age, but I knew guys who were reckless, guys who chafed at the restrictions. I wasn't one of them, but I was too shy to be really popular. "I guess so."

"You're still young," he said.

"Yeah. I know guys, though," I said.

"Everyone does. You're lucky."

"How?"

"You got brains. It may not seem like much now, but it matters in the long haul. Me, I ain't got much upstairs but I do okay with what I got." He made a fist, muscle bulging on his forearm. "It gets me where I need to go. Good smarts can take you pretty far, too."

"Thanks," I said. "I guess right now, I feel like just another nerd." That was all my brains meant to me at that point in my life.

He looked me over. "You'll be good-looking once you finish growing."

I felt my face go hot. "I'm twenty."

"So? You think I looked like this at twenty?"

"I don't think you ever looked like this," I said. I was average height and skinny.

He laughed. "No, I didn't. I was a twelve-pound baby and just kept growing. But you got good bones, kid." He reached out and clasped my shoulder. "You just have to fill out a bit. Let me tell you something."

"What?"

"I met Larch when I was about your age. We was crazy about each other. Some of the guys used to tease us, called us the bride and groom because neither of us felt like fooling around much. I'd get mad and then someone would get hurt, but Larch, he was smart like you. He just laughed, said to me, 'Come on, let's fuck.' That always got my attention. Anyways, without Larch, I might have had the bed next to Jacks. I guess what I'm trying to say is that sometimes it's not so bad to be a little uncool."

"You still together?"

"Nah," he said, mopping up egg yolk with the last of his pancake. "Larch lost a tire at a hundred and twenty. They had to scrub him off two miles of road." He looked both sad and proud, then his eyes changed, darkened, as he swallowed. "You ever get a break, kid?"

I caught my breath. "Not really. But there's a buzzer in the back that goes off when the door opens."

"Get a lot of customers this time of night?"

"No." I started getting hard in sheer anticipation.

"What do you say we go in the back for a little bit?"

I grinned. "All right." God, I thought he'd never ask! I'd been afraid to. I was sure he'd laugh and I couldn't have stood it.

In the back was a battered couch, a television set, my father's desk and the safe. I closed the door and stood, watching as he stripped off his jacket and the stained T-shirt underneath. He had a hard body, not cut and polished like a weight lifter but solid and powerful with a generous sprinkling of brown hair. The art on his arms extended up across his chest, and I reached out, traced the head of a hawk that looked like it was about to bite his nipple. He made a low sound deep in his throat as I played with the steel ring. "What did that feel like?" I asked. I'd always been curious.

"Hurt like hell but it feels great now," he said. "You can pull on it a bit. Yeah. That's it." He pulled me in suddenly and kissed me hard and sloppy, tasting of eggs and coffee, and I felt the grief and guilt and need in him that hid behind bluster and leather. I ran my hands over his scratchy scalp, trying to ease the pain as best I could. I'm sorry, I thought. I can't say that I understand, but I know. And I did, I knew death, knew how desperate it could make you to live just a little more. His fingers dug into my ass as our cocks made friends through our jeans. I slipped a hand between our bodies, to the patch of denim framed by the road-worn chaps.

"You like?" he asked in my ear.

I licked my lips. "Yes."

He unbuckled his belt. "Want a closer look?"

"God, yes!" I dropped to my knees and watched as he unzipped his fly and took his cock out. He wasn't very long but he was solid and meaty, the finest thing I'd seen all summer. I feasted my eyes on Wolf's dick, memorizing every vein, every ripple, the rich pink above his circumcision scar that deepened to purple at the glans, how the head wasn't really much wider than the shaft, he was so thick. I rubbed my face on it, buried my nose in his crotch, inhaling deeply, fished his balls out of his jeans, felt the skin tighten at my touch, took each one into my mouth and sucked it.

"That's it, kid!" He moaned. "That's it." He reached into his pocket and handed me a small packet. "You don't have to take my word for it."

I was grateful because I wasn't sure I had the guts to ask. Still, I toyed with him a bit first, licked the shaft, flicked my tongue over that magic spot right where it met the head, and he rewarded me with a low groan. I kissed his swollen knob before unrolling the condom over it. I put it on the rest of the way with my mouth.

I tasted latex, smelled the musk of his arousal and the deep-sharp smell of leather. He felt thick as a baseball bat in my mouth. I hefted his balls in my hand, felt them pull up in response as he tangled his fingers in my hair and groaned. "That's it, kid! Suck me hard! Jesus, what a sweet mouth you have!" The truth was, though, he wasn't giving me a chance to do anything except hang on. The heavy muscles in his ass flexed as he fucked my face and I had to concentrate on keeping up with him. I grabbed him, dug my fingers in, and that only seemed to egg him on, but then he slowed, caught his breath as his nuts tightened and released, and when I worked his head with the back of my tongue, I felt the condom slipping on his precum.

"Alright," he said when he caught his breath. "You ever been screwed?"

"Yes," I said.

"You like it?"

Did I have a choice? Did I care? "I love it."

"Good."

I took off my jeans and braced myself on the back of the couch. I heard him replacing the condom, good, I'd sucked all the lube off the first one and I'd need all the help I could get. The head of his cock felt even bigger against my ass and I had to blow out hard to keep relaxed as he pushed in, resisting the impulse to fight. God, he was thick, but I stayed relaxed. It never quite hurt, just seemed like it was going to any second.

He rode me the way he must have ridden his bike, hard, fast and right on the edge of recklessness. My cock rubbed too hard against the old upholstery and I caught it in my hand to ease it; the heat from his fucking spread through my gut to my balls and my belly. His open zipper bit my ass and his leather-clad thighs pressed against the backs of my legs. I thought for a moment that this must be what it was like to be smeared over two miles of asphalt, being peeled away until there was nothing left but the friction and the blood that pounded in my ears. I knew then who I was to him, but I didn't care. I thought I'd come from him fucking me, knew that I wouldn't, then I heard him growling, felt his hips bucking as he spilled his grief and his living into the condom, into me.

He pulled out; I heard the snap of discarded latex. "Turn around, kid. Let's see what you've got."

I turned, my erection bobbing.

"Hey, not bad! Looks like you got more than brains."

"Thanks," I said. I might not have been the biggest guy on the planet in most ways, but I wasn't average height and skinny all over.

His big, stained fingers wrapped around my shaft, squeezing it hard as his thumb slid over the head. "Not bad at all. You make a nice handful, kid."

I laughed and it trailed off into a groan as he started working on me. We both watched as his big fist slid up over the head and down again, filling my crotch with a different kind of heat. My breath thickened in my throat as he jacked me slowly and exquisitely, the world narrowed to my cock and his hand, friction and pressure and another man's touch—this big, dangerous man who worked me like the throttle of his bike as his finger rolled my nipple under my shirt. I felt it building deep inside, stretching, stretching to the breaking point, then it snapped, pulling my come from somewhere in the backs of my legs and sending it shooting onto his chest, fouling the wings of the hawk.

We grinned at each other. I put myself back together. He grabbed a napkin off my father's desk, cleaned himself off, and put his shirt and jacket back on. "Good food here. I'll miss it."

Right. With his friend dead, he wasn't likely to be back. "Where will you go?" I asked.

"Dunno," he said. "Maybe California. Ain't been there in a while. Couple of good guys out there who probably ought to know about Jacks."

I got a sudden vision of a world of chrome and leather, the pungent smell of exhaust, the wind tugging at his jacket at a hundred and twenty miles an hour, nowhere to go and all the time in the world to get there. Not for the first time, I wished I were a bit bigger and a lot braver.

He grabbed me in a great, creaking bear hug. "Just keep studying, kid. Use your smarts. And don't be afraid to wave that dick around a bit. You got an asset, you use it, know what I mean?"

"Thanks," I said.

I didn't say goodbye or watch him leave. Instead, I found the condoms and tossed them straight into the Dumpster. My dad would be livid if he knew. I heard the Harley roar to life, heard tires squeal on the parking lot as he shot out into the night, onto a new trajectory, and wherever he was bound, I wished him luck.

TWO BIKERS IN A ROOM
AT THE MOTEL 6
Simon Sheppard

"Harleys are all about pussy. Big-time pussy." Duane smiled.

Trev didn't know quite what to say to that, so he remained cautiously silent and kind of smiled back.

Duane reached over for a pack of American Spirits. "Mind if I smoke?" he asked, not waiting for an answer before lighting up. He leaned back in the chair, legs spread, and blew smoke rings. Trev tried to figure out just what was happening. He looked again at Duane, sitting there just feet away wearing nothing but a black T-shirt, white off-brand briefs, and thick gray socks. The T-shirt had a picture of a flaming skull. Trev gave up trying. But he knew damn well how he'd ended up there, in a cheap motel room at three AM with a man who was going on about pussy.

He'd been heading for home, still had an hour or two to go, twisty mountain roads having given way to freeways with an endless procession of Dennys, Jacks, and Wendys, when he'd pulled into a non-chain coffeeshop for a jolt of caffeine. He'd been walking through the parking lot, helmet in hand, when he spotted Duane standing by his Harley Softail Fat Boy, the bike all chrome, fringed saddlebags, and just-waxed gleam. They stared at one another the way two men who probably aren't gay, but might be, do. After one long moment, Duane nodded. "Hey, bud," he said.

Trev figured *What the hell* and walked over. The man had a pug-handsome face, a longish ponytail, and when he smiled Trev could see he was missing an incisor. It was one of those stupid movie moments. There were cars all around them in the spotlit parking lot, hungry people coming, well-fed people going, but all Trev could see was Duane standing there, mid-thirties, maybe even forty, in jeans and leathers, smiling. It wasn't because the man was particularly good-looking. It wasn't because he was Trev's type—he wasn't that, either. He might even have very well been straight. It was just one of those stupid things that happen sometime, those times when your dick should know better but gets hard anyway.

"Can I buy you a cup of coffee?" Trev asked, hoping such a noncommittal invite would give nothing away.

"I got a room next door," the man said, gesturing toward the neighboring Motel 6, mute testimony to affordable lodging. "And I got me a fresh fifth of Jack Daniels in the room."

"I shouldn't drink. I'll be riding home."

"Just one." The man smiled that missing-tooth smile again. If this wasn't a flirtation, it was a passable imitation. "I'm Duane."

"I should make sure my bike's locked up." Trev walked over to his motorcycle, Duane in tow. Trev took the U-shaped Kryptonite lock from its mount, locked it through a spoke of the front wheel. He was acutely aware that Real Men used chains.

"Nice bike," Duane said. Trev stared hard, looking for a hint of condescension. The motorcycle in question, a Suzuki Bandit 1200, was sleek and powerful; from a standing start, it could most likely have left Duane's chromed-up Harley in the dust. But it was a sport bike, not a cruiser, and worst of all it was Japanese—a "rice-burner," the object of hardcore Harley riders' contempt.

"Thanks."

"Looks like it would be real fast." Not a trace of irony in his voice. Trev wondered if irony entered into Duane's life at all. "Real fast."

When the two of them got to the room, Duane hung out the Do Not Disturb sign, winked when he locked the door, then pulled off his big boots, unbuckled his ornate H-D belt buckle, and let his jeans fall to the floor like it was the most natural thing in the world to strip down to underwear in front of a man that he'd just met. Duane's legs were squat, muscular, and very white.

"All about pussy," he repeated one more time, as though neither of them had heard it before. "Must be why you ride a Suzuki."

"Um…" Trev said.

"Got me all the pussy I can handle. Course, I was married. Still am, really, till the divorce becomes final. But it just didn't work out. For one thing, she didn't like how much I was on the road. See, I repair and customize bikes for a living, and I spend a lot of time out scouting for old Harleys to fix up. That's where I just came from. Found a '66 Sportster that I wanted to check out before I bought it and had it shipped back home. So, Trev, what do you do?

"For a living?"

"Yeah."

"I teach."

"Kids are great." Duane smiled that missing-incisor smile of his.

"I teach college."

"You look kinda young to be a professor." Duane stubbed out the American Spirit and spread his legs wider. Trev couldn't help but steal a glance. Briefs well-filled, by the look of it.

"I'm a teaching assistant."

"What do you teach?"

Here it comes, Trev thought. "British literature, mostly." He probably should have said something butch, like economics.

Duane reached down and scratched his balls. The unselfconscious maleness of the gesture made Trev's cock throb.

"Yeah," Duane said, "she was jealous of me, which was screwed up because I let her fuck around all she wanted, which was with other girls, mostly."

"Double standard, eh?" Trev made his voice sound as sympathetic as possible.

"You know it, man." Duane tugged at his ponytail, then pulled off the rubber band. His hair fell to his shoulders, an unlikely halo. "Guys are only as faithful as we have to be, right?"

"You got it," Trev said, wanting to strike just the right tone of conspiratorial cocksmanship. He thought back to Barry, beautiful Barry with the perfect nipples and improbably big cock. They'd been together almost a year, back when they were both in grad school. But Barry had wanted their relationship to be open, Trev had resisted, and finally Barry left him, at first tomcatting around the bars, then settling down with the prof who'd taught them Woolf and Strachey. Presumably the teacher's focus on Bloomsbury made him less monogamously inclined.

"...get fucked up the ass." Trev's attention had drifted away, but that sure snapped him back.

"Huh?" he said stupidly. "The ass, you liked fucking her up the ass?"

"You sure you're paying attention?" Duane grinned and slid his right hand under his T-shirt. "No, man, I'm the one who likes to be fucked up the ass."

"Oh," Trev said stupidly. "Maybe I will have that drink."

"Help yourself." Duane gestured to the bottle. Trev got up to fetch a glass from the bathroom, rearranging his crotch en route.

"I discovered it when I was a kid," Duane continued, "that I liked playing with my asshole, liked the feeling. Becky and I tried one of them strap-ons, but it didn't do the job. A man's cock, that's what does the job." He pulled off his T-shirt. His torso was white and nearly hairless, with clear lines of demarcation where his arms and neck had gotten sun. There were two tattoos, one on each pec. On the left was a bird, a bluebird or something, done fairly crudely. On the right was a swastika.

Trev didn't want to know.

"Only thing is," Duane continued, taking a swig of Jack straight from the bottle, "too many fags want to kiss and shit. And most of 'em want to take it up the ass. I don't do that, fuck guys—I ain't a queer. All I want is to get fucked. But I'm sure you'd like it either way, huh Trev?" He reached over and touched Trev—who was not sure about the tack this was taking—briefly on the knee.

Trev kind of froze. A weak "So you think I'm gay?" was all he could manage.

"Dude, I'd bet the fucking farm on it. Why do you think you're here?"

Trev exhaled.

Duane leaned back, hands behind his head, his bushy armpits in stark contrast to his otherwise smooth flesh. "So how about it, professor?"

"You want me to fuck you? Just like that?"

"You're dick's hard, ain't it?" Duane rose to his feet, hands still behind his head, and walked over to Trev, who was sitting uneasily on the edge of the slightly saggy bed. The biker shoved Trev's legs apart with one knee, sliding his left leg between the seated man's thighs. Close up, Duane smelled like tobacco and white trash.

"Hey, uh…"

"Fuck man, just fucking relax." Duane took a little step closer, pressing in until his leg was against Trev's swollen crotch. "Yeah, you're hard, all right," he said. "So how about it?"

Trev looked around the room, at the TV on the dresser, the mass-produced prints on the wall, the Gideon Bible next to a little pile of condoms in the half-open drawer of the bedside table. Anywhere but at the well-filled pair of white cotton Y-fronts that hovered inches from his face.

"How fucking about it, Suzuki Boy?" Duane pulled the front of his briefs down and a big hard dick flopped out, pubes even bushier than armpits, cock even whiter than the rest of him, foreskin still half-hiding the swollen head.

Trev wanted to, he wanted to take that dick between his lips, down his throat, suck it dry. But he didn't. Some things were just more than he bargained for, and at times like that he got reticent, he got shy.

"Shy, huh?" Duane backed off and let his underwear fall to his feet. Wearing only socks, like in some cheesy porn video, he turned his back and slowly, deliberately walked back to the chair. His back was covered with tattoos, all the way down to his narrow waist. "Your fucking loss."

Yeah, Trev thought, *my fucking loss.* The biker's ass was beefy, muscular, and absolutely perfect. Without thinking, he reached out and touched it, touched the man's right ass-cheek.

Duane looked back, hair swinging around his shoulders. "That's it, professor. You want it, huh?"

Well, yeah, Trev did. He wanted that biker ass, that butt that was usually perched on a Harley but that could be his for the night. All he had to do was say yes.

"Yes." Just like that.

"Well, you'd better get your fucking clothes off, then." Duane raised the bottle and poured more whiskey down his throat. "If you're gonna fuck me." Unspoken: *If you're man enough.*

Duane put down the whiskey, bent over and spread his cheeks. His asshole had a surprisingly dark corona and a distinct pucker. Well-trained. Well-used, apparently. Trev reached down and gave his hard-on a squeeze.

"What're you waiting for, Suzuki-boy?" A taunt, a challenge, an invitation.

Trev stuck his thumb in his mouth, getting it wet with spit, and then pressed it up against the biker's hole. Duane's ass was hungry and very hot, nearly sucking in his thumb. He slid it further in, the slick tunnel opening right up for him.

"How you want it?" Trev asked, taking back his finger.

"Hot and heavy."

"I mean, you like being on your back?"

"All fours. That way you can't look in my eyes and get all romantic."

"Then get on the bed." Trev hoped the sneer in his voice didn't sound too forced.

The biker did as he was told, posing doggy-style, his ass offered for use. Trev pulled off his boots, jeans, and boxers. He left his socks and T-shirt on; he figured if he was going to be in cheesy porn, he might as well look the part.

"Okay, fag," Duane rumbled, "let's see how good you can fill me up." That was it, no more preamble, no foreplay, just Trev's dick inside a stranger's ass. And he could live with that.

Trev reached into the bedside table for a condom. Fishing around for lube, his hand met something cold and hard and metallic.

"Hey, professor. You gonna fuck my ass or what?"

Trev, startled, pulled his hand from the drawer. "Just looking for some lube."

"Over there."

Trev had to admit it: There was something about the whole situation that made him uneasy, though nothing disturbing enough to deflate his erection. Maybe his cock thrived on danger, be it riding his 1200 at 80 miles an hour down a freeway crowded with cellphone-talking SUV drivers, or riding the ass of a debatably straight redneck with "USA's the Best, Fuck the Rest" tattooed on his right shoulder blade. He unrolled the rubber over his thickish cock. He'd make it through this. He'd perform.

Duane reached over to the bottle of whiskey and took another swig. "Ah, that's better," he said. "Now let's get that prick of yours up my ass."

Trev squirted a big glob of lube in his hand and rubbed it down the crack of the biker's butt.

"Man, that feels great."

Trev's first two fingers found the man's hole and slid inside.

"Fuck, yeah. Yeah."

The inside of the biker was smooth and welcoming. Trev knelt behind him on the bed and positioned his cockhead up against the guy's asshole.

"Just shove it right in," Duane said, his voice suddenly soft around the edges. "I can take it. I've took bigger things than that." He looked back over his shoulder and smiled his missing-tooth smile. "No offense."

"None taken," Trev said, and he rammed his dick home.

"Unh."

Trev had to admit it—Duane's hole felt great. Actually, Trev hadn't fucked anyone in months, and his cock was happy to be plugging an eager ass again. He put his hands on Duane's smooth, pale hips and started thrusting.

"Faster, dude."

Trev speeded up his stroke.

"I said faster, faggot." Trev felt a sudden flush of dignity—*nobody's going to treat* me *that way*—but instead of pulling out and leaving, he grabbed hold of Duane's ponytail and slammed in hard.

Trev gritted out, "You take it, you fuck." Where had *that* come from? Virginia Woolf would have been appalled.

But Duane wasn't appalled, he was excited, and he started thrusting his ass backward, impaling himself on the younger man's hard shaft.

"That's it, dude. Screw my fuckin' ass."

Trev wasn't sure just how he felt about being bossed around by a man with a swastika tattoo—it was just as well Duane didn't know his last name was Cohen. But Trev did know how being up the biker's ass felt. It felt absolutely great. All the way in, he reached around Duane's smooth thigh and grabbed at the man's cock. Trev was pleased to note that it was hard as steel; he himself could never stay hard while he was getting fucked. Maybe he was just not enough of a bottom. Or maybe, unlike Duane, he just wasn't enough of a man.

"Let go of my dick," Duane said. "I'm not ready to come yet."

But Trev was ready for the whole thing to come to a climax. He'd been riding all day, and his tired thighs were starting to tremble. He looked around the motel room, at the leather jackets lying in a corner, at the half-empty bottle of whiskey, and suddenly all he wanted was to be back on the road, gliding through the freedom of curves. He speeded up, bringing himself to the edge of orgasm.

"Oh, man, that feels so fucking great that feels so fucking great," Duane moaned. But Trev didn't care anymore, if in fact he ever had. With one final push, he made himself shoot a load into the rubber, a jet so strong it was almost painful. He caught his breath and slid his dick out of Duane's ass, a load of milky cum filling the rubber's sagging tip.

Duane was silent for a moment, then said, "I gotta get off. Suck my dick."

"Listen, I'm not your wife."

"Fair enough," Duane said. He flipped himself onto his back and started beating off, long foreskin sliding back and forth. He reached his other hand around to his ass and started playing with his slippery hole. And within moments it was over, cum oozing out of his piss slit, pouring onto his belly.

Trev was already on his feet, looking for his pants.

"Hey, what's the rush?" Duane slid his hand along his belly, then brought it to his mouth, slurping off his own jism.

"Gotta get going is all. Have a long ride ahead of me."

"Stay for a shower and another drink." It sounded less like an invitation than a command.

"No, really, thanks but…" Trev could smell the guy's asshole on his cock.

"Oh, man…" Duane's voice sounded suddenly softer, less like a hard-bitten biker's than a disappointed child's. Trev looked into his eyes, and something—probably whatever drew him to Duane in the first place—led him to agree to stay.

When he got out of the shower and wrapped a towel around his waist, he found Duane still lying there naked, the cum almost dry.

"Pour yourself a drink and lie down," Duane said. Trev filled the glass with whiskey and lay back down on the bed. He hesitated for a moment, then began to stroke Duane's leg. The tracery of a scar ran most of the way down his thigh, even paler than the rest of his skin.

"Pins and rods. I've gone down so often that my body is held together with pins and rods."

Trev winced and took a slug of Jack Daniels. His towel fell open, revealing his just-washed dick.

"Man," said Duane, "you're a really good fuck. Thanks. Thanks a lot."

"No problem," Trev said, which seemed like a fairly stupid thing to say,

They lay around talking and drinking, telling each other things they might not have said to anyone they actually knew. If this all had been a semi-romantic cliché, they would have discovered that they weren't so different after all. But the more Trev learned about Duane, the wider the gaps between them seemed. It was, after all, only sex, just dick into ass that had brought them together.

Somewhere toward the bottom of the bottle, Trev slurred, "You know, I think I'm in absolutely no shape to get on my bike." But Duane was already on his way to passing out, eyes shut, breath slowing. Trev wobbled into the bathroom, took a piss, and made sure the motel room door was double-locked, in case some maid got over-enthusiastic. He crawled into bed beside the unconscious biker, drew his fingertips over the still-unexplained swastika tattoo, and fell fast asleep.

Around seven, Trev woke with a *Where the fuck am I?* start. Sunlight crept through the imperfectly shut drapes as he gathered up his clothes and got dressed. He was about to leave when he remembered the object in the bedside table. He carefully pulled out the drawer. There it was, what he knew it would be: a gun, a biker's shiny handgun, just inches from the Gideon Bible. Involuntarily, he drew in his breath.

"You like it?" Duane had woken up.

"It's just...I'm not used to guns."

"Don't worry about it. So you're heading out?"

"Miles to go before I sleep." Trev wasn't sure that Duane would even get the reference.

"Sit over here for a sec," Duane said. Trev lowered himself to the bed and Duane propped himself up and awkwardly gave him a hug. And then, astonishingly, the biker kissed Trev on the lips, softly but decisively.

Trev didn't know what to say, so he said nothing, just slowly stood up and walked toward the door.

"Keep the rubber side down and the shiny side up," Duane called after him, already lighting up a cigarette.

"Yeah. You too," Trev replied, closing the motel room's door behind him. In a few hours, he'd be hundreds of miles away.

THE FOUR FRIENDS
Don Luis de la Cosa

Prologue: A Motley Crew

Nuts Melendez woke up and felt his face. He was almost sure he'd left it somewhere until the tips of his fingers felt the delicate skin around his eyes. The whiskey bottle with about a shot and a half left in it leaned against the wall next to his head. He decided that was the best medicine for how he felt at the moment, and downed the contents before he even attempted to sit up. Nuts looked down and realized that there was still a mouth wrapped around his cock that had probably fallen asleep there around the same time he had. He chucked the body that belonged to the mouth in the shoulder and the mouth started working again like a generator sputtering in the cold.

Looking around at the floor in the clubhouse the previous night's party had left most people in similar states of dereliction. The other bros had gotten on to more varied mind-altering substances, and gods know whether or not all of them could accurately remember what exactly had happened. Not that it really mattered, but it would be great if someone could remember a story or two. The mouth on Nuts' cock was doing wonders for his headache, and he was sure that he would be terribly hungry the second he came. Nuts threw the now-empty bottle at the sissy maid passed out in the corner opposite him, hitting him square in the chest, knowing from experience that hitting him in the head would have no effect. Our man awakes, Nuts growled at him to fix breakfast, and the maid stumbled through a maze of bodies and empty bottles on his way towards the kitchen.

Nuts leaned back against the wall he'd found the whiskey bottle on and enjoyed the blowjob he was getting. This one wore a prospect patch stitched onto his right upper shoulder, and Nuts figured he might just be worth the trouble. Whoever he was, he'd obviously done this job before, 'cuz it was difficult for Nuts to hold on. Eventually, the prospect's technique won over Nuts' resistance, and spewing curses and bellowing like a bear, Nuts shot his load down the prospect's throat. The screams woke a few of the other attendees, who dreamt they'd fallen asleep in the woods, and the general stirring roused the rest, squinting at the brightness of the hazy sunlight filtering in through the windows. Coffee perking on the stove and toast, eggs, and bacon sent wafts of breakfast scents up everyone's collective nostrils and the haggard group, moving as a pack of hungry carnivores, aimed themselves for the eating space. Of course, every seat in the eating area had to be cleaned of spilled beer, stickiness, and hardened food that proved general evidence of the previous night's achievements. Out came the cleaning supplies and the prospects went to work while the members sifted through the empties for more 'hair of the dog.' By the time the maid came out with breakfast, everyone was at least able to see straight.

After breakfast, the crew managed to revert to their normal degenerate state. The rest of the day was spent patching holes, repairing broken windows, and ridding the place of colored pieces of broken glass, while everyone tried to piece together, by way of stories each could remember and inspecting each others' clothes, the events of last night. By the end of the day, there was much raucous laughter and loud music, and the ground floor of the clubhouse sounded like the party had never stopped.

Being a Sunday afternoon, everyone begged off another night of terrorizing the neighbors in favor of being able to wake up and go to work in the morning. True, they were quite possibly the worst hooligans in that section of town, but they still had to come up with money for beer and condoms. Or, at least, that was the main excuse to be heard just then. All the prospects left with the characteristic signs of fidelity, and with a roar that shook the Earth beneath them, rode off in a pack for their respective houses.

"Wuddya think about Bikini?" Nuts was saying to his companions.

"How do you mean?" responded Eagle.

"Well, I'm thinking he might just be worth the effort. I woke up this morning, and found his mouth still around my cock. When I hit him in the shoulder, he just started working again, and got me off before any of the rest of you even woke up." It was difficult to argue with this kind of logic. Bikini had been around for long enough now, and had helped enough of the bros out or performed favors similar to the one that Nuts had just described, that those with the power to do so now agreed on accepting him as a permanent addition to the tribe. The ceremony would take place on the following Saturday.

On his way home to the south end of town, Bikini was involved in a hit and run. He had been involved in similar incidents before, and so was more than prepared to deal with the aftermath. While coming around a long wide arc in the road, his speed, as always, was question- able. However, all reports later showed he was simply 'following traffic'—a smallish poodle-haired mixed breed of a dog and its master busy playing in the street. Bikini's dual shotgun pipes trumpeted his arrival, the ten year old boy, just back from Sunday school, was fairly occupied with his game of catch with his rat's nest of a companion, knew better than to stay in the street with oncoming vehicles approaching. His pet, however, due to its lack of an intelligent heritage, did not share his master's wisdom and continued chasing after the ball. Of course, even with his normally good eyesight, the decent breakfast and strong coffee Bikini'd gotten before leaving the clubhouse, he could not look around the corner, and so he had no idea of what was awaiting him and simply blasted through the curve as if it were the same curve he'd always blasted through without impediment.

Even though the animal considered itself more ferocious than the heartiest lion, its diminutive size assured that Bikini could neither hear the excited yaps that accompanied the excited bounding that were an animator's wet dream nor the hysterical screech of the youngster as he witnessed the horrific scene unfolding in front of his eyes. Bikini's front tire was about as thin as the underwear that provided his namesake, and almost split the living dust mop in half. Part of the fur got caught in the tread and was carried up into the 'bikini fender' and cleanly severed the head causing blood to spurt back and hit Bikini in the mustache and splattering on his goggles. Bikini licked his facial hair, hoping for a fresh bug, but was disappointed.

"Bijon Friz with a bit of Dachshund. Yeeech. Now I'm gonna hafta go eat some real meat to git this taste outta my mouth." Bikini smiled and pointed his bike towards his favorite steakhouse that, luckily, was only a few short blocks from where he lived. Once there, he reached inside his vest and pulled out the necessary implements to remove his fender. That done, he found the spigot he knew was on the outside of the building, and washed it clean of all the bits of fur, bone and sinew still stuck there, and replaced the fender. Bikini's mechanical dexterity had first reared its head when he was four years old. His parents had made the irreparable error of handing him a block of wood with copies of all the locks in the house screwed into it. Not only did he figure out how to undo all the locks, he also figured out how to lock and unlock every single one of them with a paperclip and one of his mother's hairpins he'd found lying around. He progressed on to exotic car theft and safe cracking as an adolescent—he was acquiring the necessary funding, you understand—and finally, his crowning achievement: a custom bike shop where his sole occupation all day was taking things apart and putting them back together again. Even at his present age, he still felt something like an infantile glee every time he managed to put a machine together and it worked.

"I love the smell of hot grease in the morning!" he was heard to say quite frequently when opening his shop for business. Of course, he could not have possibly expected that his skills would be put to such hard use as they would in the sequel. Bikini and Jimmy had partnered together on several heists, and by the time they both had found their way into the club, they were feared and wanted men.

Jimmy–No–Pants roared off towards the setting sun for the hour-long ride he knew was going to blind him. The road towards his house was almost straight West, with few variations, and since it was already late in the afternoon, the sun would be sitting at the end of that stretch of freeway making sure his retinas wouldn't survive the trip. He hated that part of the ride home. Even though there was plenty of open road to rip open the throttle between him and home, what good was it if you couldn't see at the end? Of course, part of why he lived there was because of its proximity to where he worked, and the fact that he could go home and eat lunch without having to worry about making it back on time. It was time to decide what was really the most important thing now that he was involved in the club.

Jimmy pulled into his favorite roadhouse on the outskirts of the city and ordered himself an extra spicy sausage and peppers plate, a large basket of fries, and a pitcher of beer with one glass. Thinking this hard was gonna require some extra energy. But then, between the first handful of fries and the second glass of beer, a flash of brilliance struck him:

"I can just leave town a couple hours later!" Jimmy smiled to himself proudly. He had always been good at logistics; it was how he managed to become the dock manager where he worked. But now he had a new problem: what to do about the remaining food and beer now that he didn't need to use his brain any more. As fate would have it, he didn't have long to wait for an answer.

A couple of rowdies up for a scuffle that night decided Jimmy looked like a good target, and, feeling the burn of the liquor in them, headed for his table. Sensing trouble, Jimmy checked over his shoulder, saw the three men heading towards him, grabbed hold of his chair in one hand and his beer glass in the other. Just to throw them off the scent, Jimmy filled his beer glass and took a sip as they were walking up to his table.

"Hey!" he felt their steps behind him, "we don't take kindly to them patches around here!" Jimmy could feel his attacker's hand falling onto his shoulder, and spinning out of the way as the lead man fell into the empty space, dropped an elbow on the back of his head, cracking his skull on the oak wood table and eliminating him as a threat. What remained of the beer went into the eyes of the man on the left, and as the now blinded man staggered back, Jimmy brought up the chair catching the third attacker under the chin, lifting him off the ground and laying him out for a solid hour. The fight was over before the owner could hustle over with his hollow-core aluminum Louisville Slugger. By the time the aging owner puffed and wheezed his way to Jimmy's table, the waitress had already brought him another mug.

"You awrite son?" asked the owner.

"Yeah, pops. Just wish one o' my captains could a' seen me defending my colors." Jimmy sighed his impotence. The owner rolled up a sleeve to reveal an insignia tattooed on his forearm the same shape as the patch sewed onto Jimmy's jacket. The two men clasped hands in the prescribed manner, further solidifying their alliance. Jimmy sat back down to his sausage sandwich and fries.

"I'll make a phone call," promised the old-timer. Jimmy finished his food hungrily. Scuffles always had a way of making his stomach feel empty. On his way out he made his goodbyes to his new friend and started up his scoot. Cleaning off his goggles, he checked the horizon and found it considerably less bright, then checked his watch.

"Just enough time to get to the docks and catch that shipment from Colombia." Jimmy smiled to himself. For being one of his 'days off', Sunday had managed to be rather eventful.

Juanito "El Guapo" Lopez had never lacked for attention. The run- ning game the rest of the club members played was to see how many times they could pinch El Guapo's butt while barreling down the road at 70 miles an hour. Of course, El Guapo was not a hapless victim in this exchange. He could speed up or hit the brakes to get away. But, other members had also realized they could set up a rolling blockade to prevent him from escaping. Juanito, being privileged with a modicum of intelligence had begun to recognize the preliminary maneuvers leading up to the rolling blockade, and the boys had to invent increasingly creative ways of assuring that it would work.

In the past months, El Guapo had become everyone's favorite fuck toy. He could swallow the largest cock in the clubhouse and not miss a breath. His tongue moved with a deftness normally reserved for mythic beings and legendary individuals. And, even given the endless parade of both known and unknown cocks making their way through that most pleasurable Arc d'Triomphe, Juanito's asshole, his was habitually the tightest among the entire crop of new recruits. The captains' favoritism towards this as-of-yet officially unaccepted prospect had inflamed animosities amongst several of the previous favorites, and their ire was something made known with a terrible conviction. But, just as he'd managed to recognize the ass-grabbing game, El Guapo had also managed to recognize when the deposed favorites were circling, like wolves for a kill. Many had been the time that Juanito had foiled a planned blanket party by managing to slip deftly by his would-be attackers. The last fouled attempt resulted in the entirety of the dining room furniture being upturned, broken, or otherwise damaged, several broken arms, two bent noses, and three concussions. As Juanito watched giggling from just outside the room, club leaders pulled apart the gaggle of grapplers, lined them up against a wall, busted them down a few notches, and whipped them soundly as the rest of the party looked on, then sent them all home without any party favors. After that night, the outright attacks on El Guapo ceased, and others' outward expressions of anger and frustration generally amounted to nothing more than a few extra swats here and a couple extra paddlings there. All of which in actuality more than excited our protagonist.

At a different party, several months after the dining room incident, a wager was made that Juanito with his delicate features would not out-last a several-years veteran while standing up to the practiced strokes of a captain's whip. The money was counted, the crowd assembled, clothes removed, and those who were not either plying or being plied with the whip took hold of their own weapons, and set to manualizing themselves in an attempt to loose the flow of collected desire, weighing heavy in their balls and straining to break free of its confines. Dozens of pricks brightened with the fire to burn Desire's incense.

The prospect presented his hindquarters. Compared to the veteran's they are infinitely more supple, many times more well rounded—owing to decades less of rough use. Mars' furious blush burns in the cheeks though the blows have only shortly begun to fall. The honed planks fall on the naked flesh, leaving fresh marks and extracting screams from both recipients. A storm of strokes heats the victims' skin, after infinity, the veteran collapses, convulsing, vomiting from the pain, blood dripping from his torturer's implement. Many of the lookers-on edge over to the now deposed champion lying prostrate in his own misery, and let fly their collective liquid emotion, drenching the shamed veteran in a blanket of sticky whiteness. As the audience collapsed on itself, Juanito continued his resistance, refusing to be outdone, and doing it all with a smile. The captains in charge of administering the wager called a halt to the proceedings, and, since they had also had a hand on themselves, washed Juanito's hide with their own juices. Money was exchanged, clothes recovered, bandages applied, and that was that.

El Guapo's true skill, however, was languages. It was because of this skill that, with the help of Jimmy-No-Pants, he had orchestrated the unimpeded flow of the cartel's number one export through Jimmy's distribution center. Of course, being able to massage state officials since he'd met the governor's son while they both did five years in the pen was a definite asset in his business dealings. There was generally very little that separated the degree of moral corruption that both sections of society lowered themselves to for sport, aside from which suit they put on to go to work. Hell, he'd been working in bathhouses and seen officials drop unconscionable amounts on his services. Knowing which councilman was spending intimate moments in which house of ill repute was also useful information.

"Information is free," Juanito was fond of saying. And if knowledge is power, then El Guapo was nothing short of godlike.

Snoopy had gotten his name for being able to sniff out the man in the room with the largest cock. Of course, few things were praised higher by the leaders of the organization than an enormous appendage, and, like elements being attracted to one another, Snoopy's own fan- tastic member must have drawn out the others in the room. Snoopy's gifts had been put to good use frequently in the previous months, and several times in conjunction with Juanito's extremely fine ass. Both were blessed with constitutions that allowed them to withstand the most extreme amounts of physical pollutions with good grace. Our leaders' inability to be decisive about which of these finest jewels to prefer sent them frequently into weeks-long debauches where every possible combination and function was attempted. This sort of behavior, as in the case of El Guapo, had instigated a controversy, especially since it had been Juanito who brought Snoopy with him to the club to begin with. In Snoopy's case, the dissidents were all previous favorites for their prodigious size, whereas with Juanito, all of the dissidents were previous champions of the most finely shaped category. However, these veterans had more than paid their dues, and were loath to relinquish their positions of authority to rank amateurs and unknowns.

The weeks following the prospects' initiation rites were to be a protracted libidinous debauchery, planned to be experienced entirely from the road, with little rest between riding and the further pollutions of one's soul requisite during such an adventure. Indeed, given the ire our new protagonist had inspired in the company, his safe arrival home that Sunday afternoon was miraculous. He had sped off with the rest of the prospects present at breakfast, and was the last of the four to deviate from the course. His residence was more or less in a straight line from the clubhouse, but, having been involved in the organization for some time now, he had been made aware that along the road that led to his place, there lived several of the very veterans whose anger he had managed to inspire. That being the case, and given that those very veterans had been harshly warned by their superiors against any deviousness aimed at this particular prospect, Snoopy pulled into his garage still in one piece. Of what each of the veterans who found themselves displaced was blissfully unaware was Snoopy's prior battle-strewn history and his superhuman ability to not only endure pain but to derive pleasure from it. The man had experienced no short list of broken bones, brandings, whippings, piercings, clampings, and every other manner of device all in the pursuit of pleasure. Short of first killing the man, and then making sure that his body was properly mutilated and strewn about, there was likely no good way to assure that Snoopy would not resurrect himself and come in search of revenge.

"Transcendence follows the separation of body and mind. Once you've allowed yourself to be subjected to every available form of physical pollution, your mind is no longer fettered to this particular plane, nothing can prevent you from both surviving the most depraved ordeal, or learning the secrets of the ancients." Given his long track record of doing precisely that, we are inclined to believe him.

Here, good reader, you must decide which road to take: to follow the pack leads to a very impure existence, and to deviate now could save your conscience. These four individuals will be the focus for the remainder of our story. Their trials and pitfalls will form the backdrop for their personal development, and we shall see, dear friends, how these men survive to tell the tale.

Crew Log: Eve of Departure/Into the Fire

Bikini, Snoopy, Juanito, and Jimmy all arrived at the clubhouse around nine o'clock. After filing through the sea of chrome and widely varied paint jobs, they found their way to the door of the house and were met by two lieutenants who bade them wait on the stair. As they stood there, the remainder of the crowd that had been carousing on the lawn, sitting on their bikes and obviously waiting for them, formed a human barrier behind them, and ensured that none of the prospects would attempt an escape. Of course, escape was likely the last thing on their minds at this juncture, and after the entirety of the crowd outside the house found their way to the bottom of the stairs behind our protagonists, the lieutenants let everyone in.

For the first time since they decided to join the club, all four of the friends walked into the main room and were terrified. They were well accustomed to entering the main room and witnessing all manner of debauchery and lewdness, hearing blasphemies and imprecations, but, tonight, all was serenely quiet. Everyone in the room sat perfectly still and, horror of all horrors, the main room was *clean*. It looked like no one had been there since the house was built. Easily half the size of the first floor of the house, the main room was capable of seating a hundred people comfortably. The front door entered onto it, and at the back opposite the front door was the kitchen. A hallway led off to the right from which one reached the dining area, the stairs that led to the second floor, and, at the far end of the hall, rooms where no end of deviousness was performed. From the kitchen, one could reach the back yard, where a mechanic's shop, pieces of motorcycles, kegs of beer both full and empty, and the dogs' realm occupied the space. Every last inch of floor space was occupied by members, both veteran and young, and all stood statue—as they awaited the final moment. At the center, stood an enormous bearded man with braided hair that fell between his shoulder blades. His hands were gloved and he stood behind a table covered with what appeared to be implements for piercing flesh. As the four filed into the room, the carousers that had formed the human barrier behind them filed in and took their places to watch the ceremony.

"Today is a very special day in the lives of these four men," began one of the captains as soon as the assemblage had accommodated itself. "Today, they leave the rest of the world behind as they become brothers to us all, and claim all the rights and responsibilities of brotherhood." Cheers went up as he finished the opening to his statement. On cue, four of the men in the crowd took the prospects by the shoulders and guided them to the chairs arranged especially for them in front of the table covered with piercing implements, facing away from the piercer towards the rest of the crowd. The piercer availed himself of two needles and a pair of medallions that hung from steel rings. He first arrived at Bikini's chair, and as he knelt to perform the operation, his captain continued with his oration:

"With these emblems of our company, we accept you into our fold. Guard and protect them, and wear them always. They will act as keys for entry, and seals of secrecy to the innermost privacies of our organization. Welcome, brother, to our family." Cheering and roars of contentment accompanied the needles piercing Bikini's nipples, and he accepted the new adornments with barely a shiver or complaint.

The rest of the new recruits acquitted themselves just as admirably, and after the little ceremony had been concluded, the festivities were begun. The feasting was legendary, and for dessert, the four friends had been stripped, smothered in chocolate sauce, topped with fresh fruits and whipped cream, the whole draped in a butterscotch dressing, and set on the table for all to consume as they pleased. A description of the ensuing scene would be far too extensive for the confines of our narration, and we leave it to the reader's discretion to imagine the feats accomplished at that table.

The rest of the evening passed in a similar fashion, once Bikini, Jimmy, Juanito, and Snoopy had all been relieved of their makeshift trappings, nothing short of wretched excess and mindless indulgence followed. The entirety of the organization, their minds bent from the events they had just participated in, and spurred on by potent drink and a host of other intoxicants, fell to debauching themselves in a manner that would have pleased Bacchus immensely, and shamed the most admirable of his adherents. By the end of the night, most of the floor-boards in the house had been mired by the jets of loosed seed from the company's participants. Those who roomed in the establishment retired to their beds, taking favored individuals with them, and none save the dogs remained untouched, though several made the attempt, and owing to drunkenness and the less-than-pleasant disposition of the animals, had failed miserably. We will leave it to the reader to decide who was the more fortunate in this case.

The following morning transpired very much the same as that fateful day when Bikini's acceptance was decided, though with many more participants. Slightly after noon, the entire company found themselves in a proper condition to mount their steeds and hurry off towards their next objective, the "southern corners" rally, set to take place by the end of the week. The plan was to arrive by Thursday night, at the very latest, in order to be somewhat rested for the events that were sure to transpire starting early Friday morning. We shall see in the telling, whether or not they achieved their objective.

Nuts, Eagle, Fuzzy, Hercules, Victor, and Scratch, the six captains, all took up positions at the rear of the pack, bidding the newly accepted recruits ride out in front after instructing them very specifically on the route to be taken. The road in front of them, their companions behind, and nothing short of the most perfidious adventures in store, our four friends kicked their bikes into first gear and set out for whatever might come. Trailing them, for sure, were the individuals with the most devious designs on their persons, hoping that, now that they were out in the open, and that freedom predisposed them to incredible dangers, simply disposing of the new recruits 'accidentally' would return their vaunted positions to them. The deposed favorites, however, under-estimated their adversaries, and we shall see how, in the course of things, these new brothers banded together even more tightly to overcome the terrible obstacles set in their path.

Don Luis de la Cosa

Crew Log: Day the First/Time of Departure

Jimmy was quite pleased not to be heading into the sun for once after leaving the clubhouse. Having the light and heat hit him from the right instead of burning through his eyeballs into the back of his head was more comfort than he'd been able to achieve without chemical intervention. He rode with Bikini on his left, El Guapo on his right, and Snoopy all the way over on the end. The air was warm on their faces, being late spring, and their entourage was two lanes wide and fifty people deep. On their way to the first night's destination, nothing of terrible import disrupted our colleagues, and they arrived happy to be on the road, expectant of that night's adventures, and very hungry. As soon as they rolled into town, Eagle blasted up to the front of the pack and took the lead. One of the reasons he'd been given his name was for his ability to spot food from far away, and he'd just managed to draw a bead on a prospective target. The crowd of chrome and leather followed him into what, from all appearances, was the only burger joint in town.

"Awrite gen'lmen!" screamed Eagle. "There's meat in there, and empty bellies out here, you know what to do!" At the very least, the employees of the establishment were ill prepared for what the fates had directed to their door. Every last reserve staff person was phoned in, the manager wasn't sure whether to call the police or quit that instant, and the poor innocents working the registers, the oldest of whom had just returned for a second year at the local university, found themselves overwhelmed with indecent proposals. The manager decided to stay, the customers were paying in cash after all, reinforcements arrived, and the exceedingly inexperienced front line found themselves much more seasoned at the end of the night than when they had walked in. Seeing that the newly arrived group had taken over the entire establishment, and that in all likelihood was not about to leave before closing time, the manager locked the door and drew the shades making certain that the secondary damage that was assured from this sort of invasion would be minimized by his preliminary efforts. It was half past nine, and if what he was expecting to happen actually did occur, there would be no leaving the place until midnight at the earliest.

One poor fellow, in a fit of laughter while he was pounding on the table, caught the right edge of his basket of fries with an open hand and sent the ketchup-covered mass splattering all over his neighbor.

"You idiot!" screamed the indignant recipient "Get over here and lick this mess off me!" Of course, the instigator was only too happy to oblige, and invite several tablemates to join him. The vision of all this

258

lasciviousness inflamed the desires of the entire company, and like-mannered events began erupting around the room. The staff, only somewhat safe behind the counter, began to sweat again, though they were very far removed from the battlefield. In fact from their entrenched positions, there was no safer place to be. Just as the happenings were reaching a feverish pitch, Scratch's booming tones were heard over the rest of the din:

"Brothers mine!" This was a customary address in their brotherhood, and only reserved for directing oneself at the whole of the company, "we must unburden ourselves of our desirous imaginings. A hotel awaits us, and let us not be so quick to waste our strength all in one place!" A general agreement was heard and the crowd just as quickly vanished from the dining area as they had appeared. Sighs of relief were heard from the workers, though their good cheer was short-lived as the throaty growl of above a hundred motors rattled the windows to the point of shattering several, and those behind the counter barely were able to shield themselves in time. The manager sighed. Midnight was no longer the target time to find himself leaving the establishment. No, with this development, his estimated time of departure had just advanced itself by several hours.

At the hotel, a completely different sort of reception awaited our wearied but excited travelers. Years of experience in hosting similar practitioners of the most unclean desires had seasoned the owner of that inn and the second he heard the cacophony of engines dopplering towards him, he was more than prepared for what was about to happen. In preparation, he started the outside showers he'd specifically installed for similar crews, and was quick to stack piles of towels close to the front door. He called and left a message on the pool cleaner's office answering machine to be sure to arrive late in the morning the following day, around eleven o'clock would be best so that it coincided with checkout time. He gave his maids the night off knowing that he would be needing them with full strength the next morning, but not before he sent them to air out the entire east wing of the motel, and especially open the doors that separated all the adjoining suites, knowing full well that if they couldn't be opened by key, they would be opened by force. The long-awaited crowd arrived, their names set down in the register, credit cards swiped and monies exchanged, and soon the east wing was alive with more action than it had seen since its construction. A whole host of infamies were performed there, the likes of which, the reader will have to permit us, it is better for us not to describe at this point, as there will be ample space devoted to these activities in the later stages of our narrative.

The four new recruits managed to arrange themselves all in the same room despite the besotted antics of their superiors, and began to devise a plan to arrive back at their homes in relatively the same state that they had left. El Guapo had been listening to the dinner conversation of the two groups he perceived the most dangerous: those that had lost their place to him, and those that had lost their place to Snoopy. In Juanito's case, there were four dissidents each of whom, he had managed to learn, took as their role model none other than Achilles.

Worm is beholden to Scratch for having relieved him of the burden of an ex-lover who it was simply impossible to convince that their time together had come to an end. The poor gent was an outstanding member of society, a prominent figure in the community, and, like many of Juanito's customers, had been known with a special regularity to frequent houses of ill repute. Of course, the details of the undoing of that fine individual included nothing less than murder, and by scant hairsbreadths, Worm had managed to escape the suspicion of the local authorities. However, such was the case that should Scratch release slight tidbits of information, the entire charade would fall entirely on Worm's head, for Scratch was a master strategist, and had so neatly enfolded matters that he appeared completely innocent from all angles. In exchange for his continued freedom, Scratch had gained the ubiquitous servitude of Worm without any hope of annulling the contract until one or the other of them expired. As such, the captain had subjected his possession to such perfidy that it is immodest to describe. Seizing an opportunity to not only gain an ally, but eliminate an enmity at the same time, El Guapo resolved that they should engage to find a way to cancel the debt between the two.

"Scratch holds a key very privately that releases the collar 'round Worm's neck. Part of the bargain was that, if Worm could find the key, he might relinquish his special responsibilities to his captain. One of Scratch's favorite games with Worm is to hide the key, and then have Worm search for it, taunting him the entire time with promises of freedom should he encounter the fabled instrument, and severe punishments for not accomplishing the mission. Scratch is such a man, however, as to never lay the key anywhere that it might be found by one so unencumbered by intellect as Worm. If we could but encounter the key, we might even be able to bring Scratch under our thumb," described the angelic orator.

"Manny and Fixx are brothers. Theirs is the repair shop behind the clubhouse. For their work, they are favored by all the members of the organization. In their more-than-colorful history, they have been known to accommodate the most inflated organs to have passed through the brotherhood since their acceptance. Their powers to satisfy even the most jaded and experienced of the brotherhood is legendary, but most frequently, they are to be found in Victor's bed. The well-known secret about the brothers is this: their father gave them their mounts before he died. He himself was a member of this brotherhood, after a falling-out with the mother, and he passed along his legacy to his sons. Their father and Victor were also lovers and Victor made a promise to their father to keep an eye on them as they progressed through the ranks. Being part of the heritage of the organization, their protection is very well assured. Their machines, however, are just as subject to disorder as any other, and, since they regularly fawn over them and coddle them the way one would an aged relative, their hearts quite practically bleed the second the slightest thing is mechanically wrong. All we have to do is loosen a bolt here, disconnect one end of a hose there and I believe that the hassle will soon come to an end. Their bikes will literally shake apart underneath them, and, if they survive, they will surely be in no shape to cause us any more harm."

"But they watch those machines closer than a hawk. How could we possibly hope to achieve our objectives? " asked Bikini.

"Just like every one else here, they drink themselves stupid nightly."

"Yes, but, you saw what happened the last time someone thought they were passed out drunk, and went near one of their bikes!" Shot back Bikini.

"Yes, though they managed to sew his finger back on. Anyway, that's not the point. What is the point is the fact that we have Jimmy here. And his knowledge of chemicals is without comparison. He's brought with him an entire saddlebag full of every manner of intoxicant he could manage to get his hands on before he left. We will make our attempt after Jimmy sprinkles their drinks with the most formidable stuff, and carry out our plans during their stupor.

"Mangú is the last of the veterans aligned against me, and he is likely the most difficult to subdue of all. Far from being able to over-intoxicate him, he has more than twice the tolerance of any of the champion drinkers in our group, and is unbeholden to anyone. Add to all that his prodigious ability to outperform the strongest and most resilient of men who walk amongst us (the very reason for Hercules' favoritism towards him), and you see why we are faced with a par-ticular situation. It is known, though, that on the occasion that he does reach the moment of release he will collapse unconscious, shuddering like a leaf and incapable of being roused for hours. During this period, we might, despite his Herculean strength, bind him in such a way as to convince him that his ire is perhaps misdirected, and that his energies would be better spent elsewhere."

Jimmy raised his hand in an attempt to stem the flow of verbiage barraging his brain.

"Apparently this is one adventure in which I won't be involved," he said.

"Quite the contrary," returned Juanito, "we will need your help for this attempt more than any other. We all know of Snoopy's generous gifts. But, even with his prodigiousness, we will need something to desensitize him so that he might resist the urge to release before the precise moment. In fact, your help here will be more necessary than in any of our other plans. We can't have our colleague getting too awfully out-of-sorts from a reaction to whatever it is you give him. It will require all four of us to carry out the bondage that I have planned for that man, and should we lack any of our company, we might not accomplish the task before he awakes. We will be able to plead the fact that he conspired to attack one of us, and, knowing the clearly-set-down rules for conduct regarding this behavior, he will be sternly reprimanded."

The four continued their deliberations long into the night, each contributing a part to El Guapo's plan until they had successfully plotted the undoing of all eight of their detractors. In the morning, they awoke refreshed, prepared, and more than hopeful that their first engagement with the enemy might be swift and victorious.

Crew Log: Day the Second/Cruising Attitude

Morning stirred not a single one of the crew until well past ten o'clock when the first wake-up call went out, and then a sudden urgency struck the east wing. Nothing short of a Manhattan gridlock was more disastrous to witness.

"Are those my pants?"

"No! They're mine!"

"How can you tell?"

"'Cuz, idiot, they're the ones with the liquid acid in the pocket. Now go wash the cum off your face!"

"What the hell did you get all over my boots?!"

"Just throw 'em on. We'll figure it out later!"

Suffice it to say that this was a shining example of the types of heated exchanges heard in the rapidly evaporating last hour before the crew had to be out of the rooms. Eleven o'clock was the checkout time, and that certainly didn't make for much time to have everyone showered and in their traveling gear, breakfasted and coffeed before they headed out for the road again. The four friends, in contrast to the others, had been out of their rooms since nine and were already toweling themselves off from a leisurely shower before planning on enjoying an uneventful breakfast.

The scuffling, grumbling, half-awake contingent stumbled out into the lobby of the hotel at 10:59. Luckily, the man who had checked them in was the same who checked them out. He had also, in preparation for their hasty morning departure, set up a canvas behind which, several of the members had already managed to find relief from the heaviness in their bowels, and several more were on his to join them. They also found one half of the dining area set aside and prepared for their arrival with the very breakfast for which they had all been searching.

The next stop was to refuel the bikes, then get back on the road. Once everyone had managed to safely pull onto the freeway, the morning game of grab-ass with Juanito was played. Most players acquitted themselves admirably, scoring at least three or four times. However, once Juanito had managed to jockey his position next to the rest of the friends, and tucked himself neatly in the midst of the four, not even the rolling blockade could manage to satisfy their desire for sport.

Some of the dissidents noticed the greener's insolence, and decided it was an appropriate moment to make their first attempt on El Guapo's life. It was Mangú with a contingent of three confreres, muscling their way through the crowd. Juanito got the attention of his wingmen, and motioned for them to check their mirrors. They recognized the threat, and then followed him into a full-tilt boogie through the traffic on the road. Juanito's bike was a machine he'd carved out of imagination: shorter wheelbase, drag bars, rear set controls and incredible suspension, making his beast the more maneuverable ride. Mangú's was the heavier fat tire in front and back, and wide handlebars version, making it more difficult for him to follow the flitting, never in one place for more than a second. Bikini, Snoopy, and Jimmy all rode machines closer to Juanito's than their pursuer's and managed to shift in and out of tight spots with equal acuity. Eventually, they had maneuvered themselves into a traffic situation where the cars they raced between closed off the space to get through just as Mangú and his cohorts roared up beside them. If their bikes hadn't been so deafening they probably would have heard their adversary roaring as he was forced to jam on the brakes; one of his followers' front tire just barely nipped his back tire and it caused a wiggle that almost turned the entire parade into a frightful heap of torn steel and twisted bodies. Mangú smiled to himself once he again had control of his steed. This little one would be much more difficult to dispose of than he thought.

At lunch, there were hard stares and much grumbling over the morning's events. But, it was impossible to create a wholesale impediment to the group's collective spring fever, and challenges came tumbling out that later would have to be met.

"I'll bet I can fuck twenty asses in a row!" screamed one of the lieutenants. That was Honey Bear; a seemingly endless supply of sticky goodness, and no matter the time of day or his condition, always difficult to extract. His most recent achievement before lighting out on this journey had been fifteen in a row, all of whom had to retire early citing soreness and muscle cramps from maintaining the same position excessively long. Even after the fifteenth man had cried for mercy, Honey Bear had still not yielded his product, and a horrible sequence of ministrations had been necessary to relieve him of it. Again, money was laid out, shouts and challenges to his boast were heard, and the selection of individuals for the line was scheduled for the dinner hour.

As soon as lunch was over, the captains called for everyone to saddle up, and the four friends all headed for the bathrooms. No one was privy to what went on behind closed doors, but the four strode out smiling, and found themselves mounting their respective steeds and speeding off behind the pack just as the others were starting to point themselves back towards the open road, which was precisely where they wanted to be. From the rear position, each of them could watch for any of the number of dissidents sure to be making still more attempts on their lives during the ride.

Having now been on the road for the equivalent of one full day, the pack had ridden into a much warmer climate than the one they had left. Now, heavier jackets had come off, scarves and neck protectors had been packed away, and one less pair of socks was necessary. Much of the protective insulation had been shed just outside of the diner where the society had stopped for lunch, and now, well-muscled arms brightly painted and bearing signs and arcane symbols came into view. The assembly now rode with either only a vest or a light shirt. All, that is, except for the four friends for they, you see, had a plan.

Just as our protagonists were gliding through the slipstream to approach the rear end of the pack, Manny and Fix decided to have their first go at the friends. They dropped back to the same row the friends were in, and, not realizing their mistake until it was too late, made a grab for Juanito. But, both Juanito and Snoopy had exchanged jackets with Jimmy and Bikini, and the second the two brothers dropped back to their rank, had swung outside and blasted up towards the front of the pack. Once the two brothers had recognized their error, they also had to change their course, and give chase, but, what they hadn't learned was that Bikini had been busy during lunch time, and managed to turn the spark plugs out juuuussst enough that they began misfiring horribly and the engines completely quit once the brothers tried whacking open the throttle to catch up with the speeding adversaries. The brothers had to drop out and sit in the emergency lane fiddling with this and that until they could figure out precisely what was going on, then hurriedly try to catch up. After years of experience in the club, however, they knew the route well, having traveled to the same party every year since they could ride.

The rest of the day until dinner was uneventful, and that night at dinner, the selections for Honey Bear's challenge were to be made. The six captains huddled together as they ate, everyone watched, poised, in anticipation of the result, and no one discussed anything else during their own meal. Several side bets were made on which members would make it onto the list, and money again was exchanged. Finally, after a full hour of consultation, the captains turned to their followers and gave the report.

Mender, Flathead, Switch, Beetle, and Kid would form the first contingent. The captains had selected them since this would be their one-year anniversary of acceptance into the club. Next, they chose a group of five veterans who had been disgraced in one form or another and were in desperate need of redemption: Banger, Mauler, and Trailer (the man who'd lost in competition to El Guapo months before,) had been chosen for past transgressions; Manny and Fixx were surreptitiously added to the line for falling out of the group that afternoon. Next, the captains wanted a crop of tried and true champions to round out the parade in an attempt to prevent Honey Bear from attaining his goal, in which figured Mangú, Nahs, Thor, and the twins Gemelli and Gemelo. Finally, the captains selected from the most recent crop of recruits, amongst which, of course, figured Juanito, but also Gino, Carlo, Tony and Clyde—all of whom, to be sure, would have been prize possessions in anyone's stables. These twenty individuals having been read off and generally accepted, those who had wagered on the list and lost gave up what they owed, the victims were allowed to follow Eagle off to the lodgings early for the evening to allow them to prepare for that evening's festival, and the rest of the assemblage finished what beer and food was left on their tables before following the rest towards the hotel.

Bikini, Snoopy and Jimmy watched the crowd. They noticed Mangú and Worm sitting in the midst of another four members, whispering, and pointing, drawing faint diagrams on the table with their fingers the way a sports coach works out an offensive plan, and they decided that they had to enact their own preemptive strike.

"Those are the ones aligned in opposition to me," began Snoopy. Bikini and Jimmy were apprehensive to begin talking about things until Juanito could be present, but they decided that they had better begin planning before anything else went wrong, and Juanito could be brought up to speed later.

"That one to the left of Mangú is Spyder. He's famous for spinning webs to trap unsuspecting individuals, and relieving them assiduously of the entirety of their savings. He has perfected the craft over time, and there are few who are keen enough to be able to spot his deftness in maneuvering. He, however, is easier to dissuade than possibly any of the others. We simply have to convince him that there is a bigger prize involved in attacking someone, or something else. Since Nuts happens to be the owner of several key properties in town that businesses and developers alike would pay their eyeteeth for, we should have no trouble whatsoever convincing him of the absolute value of focusing his attention on this much bigger catch.

"That one to the right of Worm is Gerlach. He comes from a long line of Samoan warriors. There is very little that can be done to him physically, he easily outweighs the largest of us by at least fifty pounds, and can lift and carry a whole bike on his own. However, he has a severe allergy to leather, which is why he always wears a textile jacket. Tonight, all we have to do is make sure that we switch his jacket for a leather replica of it: which I had made before we left town, and he'll not only be publicly humiliated, but they'll have to call an ambulance to rush him to the emergency room where he will have to stay for an entire week.

"In front of Gerlach is Vince. He's a really bad character. Few crimes exist that he has not perpetrated. His web of murderers, thieves, cons, rapists, and safe houses is nationwide. There is literally no state in the union where he would not be able to melt into the shadows and be protected. However, he is only as strong as his weakest point, and that is his phone and his list of safe houses. Lose either, or both, and he is absolutely valueless for he keeps none of the information in his head in the event that he is asked who he knows. We would be able to torture him beyond recognition before anyone could arrive and identify the man we were assaulting. Victor was particularly fond of Vince until we came on the scene...."

"And how!" chuckled Bikini. He was forever unable to pass up the opportunity to make a joke.

After they all settled down, Snoopy continued, "We came on the scene because of his ability to procure the finest asses, and the best nose candy there was to be had in the entire state. Between Jimmy here and Juanito, we've managed to disrupt the entire flow of business for Vince, and he would really like to be back in a powerful position once again."

"He's got a beef with me too?" Snoopy nodded and just hung his head.

"I thought you would have figured it out by now." But he hadn't. Now there was only one thing for it.

"Ah, well! If you're gonna make an omelet, ya gotta break a few eggs!" spouted Jimmy.

"Last is Ammo, the graybeard next to Vince. He signed up for the Marines around the time of Vietnam. After that he also toured Korea, and did a stint in Panama for which he was promoted to the appropriate rank to command troops in Desert Storm. He's seen more combat time probably than any other military man you'll come across. He's been shot, tortured, starved, knifed, beaten, had his skull cracked twice, and metal plates cover the areas that were broken. His limbs have been twisted, broken, and generally mistreated for a good portion of his life and none of his fingers are straight. There is very little available to us in the way of frightening him off, or physically roughing him up that hasn't already been tried. However, truth be told, he never can pass up a fine ass. And one of his favorite activities is a hot ash scene with the finest cigars his government pension check can buy him. This may in fact be the easiest of all to effect. All we have to do is make sure that whichever cigars it is he is carrying are laced with a copious amount of inhalable poison and that, as they say, will be that. Fuzzy is the man who generally supplies his habit. Making sure that we intercept the next exchange and make the proper adjustments will be crucial."

Just as Snoopy was finishing his discourse, the remaining captains decided it was high time to rally their troops and prepare themselves for that night's entertainment. The collective filed out the diner's double doors, again rattling the foundations of the locale where they had spent the last hour, as they conducted themselves towards the lodgings for the night, and a unanimous heavy sigh was heard from the wait staff as they watched the last of the ranks disappear from the parking lot.

The dining room looked worse than the trailer park next door the last time a tornado rolled through it. Chairs were overturned or broken, plates had been used for other nefarious purposes besides eating, and utensils were bent, stuck in walls, and several had even managed to get lodged into the ceiling. Broken glasses, empty bottles of hot sauce, and smiley faces drawn with ketchup covered the floor, the tables, and any surface that could have possibly been vandalized, had been. The manager still wasn't sure how most of the damage had happened, but he knew that not enough hours existed between now and when they were supposed to reopen to repair and restore his establishment.

At the hotel, a string of suites had been reserved, each with a set of doors that led to the adjoining rooms so that each member of the club might be able to wander from room to room and enjoy himself as he saw fit. It was decided that, since Honey Bear's challenge had to be met, and likely it would draw the largest crowd, he should be stationed in the middle suite, it being the largest of the four. Next to Honey Bear's arena would be housed the drinks and other intoxicants: a huge collection of whatever mind-bending substance the pack had managed to carry with them or acquire as they were on the road. Jimmy figured prominently in this display, and his contributions were well appreciated. As he was setting up, he noticed Fuzzy with a pocket full of cigars:

"That seems to be a larger number of cigars than one man can smoke in an evening!"

"Ah! They're not all for me. Ammo requires a steady supply of them to keep him happy. He says inhaling cigar smoke is much easier than napalm or tear gas, and probably has less deleterious effects. Given his experience, I'm not likely to argue with him. I just wish I could be watching the excitement in the next room instead of waiting for him to get around to being done with his current diversion!" returned his captain.

"Well, you could always leave them with me, and I'll make sure he gets them when he returns."

"Now that is a wonderful idea! They have to be kept just so, and be exceedingly careful not to put them anywhere they will get soaked, broken, or otherwise damaged. The damn things are more expensive than anything you have on this table. If it wasn't for the fact that I get them for free, it would be impossible to keep this arrangement going."

"Not to worry. I will be sure to keep these prize possessions in perfect condition." Fuzzy turned over the smokeables to Jimmy, and, as most everyone was busy watching the festivities in the adjoining room, no one was busy watching Jimmy lace the cigars with poison. This was a particularly nasty chemical mixture that had a habit of disintegrating a person's intestines slowly over several days, causing immense pain and suffering the likes of which were incomprehensible. But, being that Ammo was given to smoking two or three cigars in a night, this might take even less time than was originally planned.

In the next room, Honey Bear had made it through the first two contingents of asses without so much as a quickening of his pulse. Ten good men lay groaning on the floor as they recovered from the assault provided by the challenger, and still, none had been able to impede him. Next in line were the twins, and these two, though they were skilled in a 'butterfly' technique, proved no more of a match than their predecessors, and fell by the wayside, incapable of continuing. Likewise, Nahs and Thor. Though Mangú, from his resilience, lasted nearly twice as long as his compatriots, he too was eliminated from the ranks, as Honey Bear finally began to show signs of being taxed. Sweat appeared on his brow, and as he entered Gino, he had to bite his lip to force back the desire to let his seed flow freely. Carlo also tightened his sheath around the sword that impaled him, and this brought a quick scream from the invader. However, Tony and Clyde were not so easily vexed, Tony required ministrations at least as long as Mangú's, and Clyde certainly put up a decent fight, causing Honey Bear to withdraw from the environs for a scant few moments as he breathed to himself. He plunged back into the fray with renewed vigor, and left Clyde panting amongst his confreres. Juanito was sure to be the most difficult one. He easily accepted Honey Bear's girth, but the grip that he was able to exert, and the variety of sensations he was able to produce created an impossible situation for the would-be conqueror, and the club's newest favorite became the proud recipient of Honey Bear's discharge. Still and all, the judges decreed that the challenger had met his challenge, he had arrived at the twentieth ass, and that was well enough for them. Those present who had kept a hand on themselves during the entire display far outweighed the number of those who had not, and now those same members found their way *en masse* over to the tangled heap of recipients who had been unable to resist the challenger's ministrations, and showered them with the product of their desires. The required money was exchanged, the usual grumblers complained about losing money—again—but everyone in the end found themselves satisfied.

The major event for the evening concluded, there was much revelry, and since the adjoining rooms fall outside of our focus, it is difficult to recount the perfidious nature of the goings on therein. The reader can rest assured, however, that there were no end of infamies late into the night, and that again, as the day before, they barely made it out of their rooms on time.

Crew Log: Day the Third/Excess Baggage

Ammo was discovered dead the next morning. His mini-torch lighter was still in his left hand, the cigar he was about to smoke in his right hand, and his boy asleep in his lap. They had dragged pool chairs up to the roof in order to have an encounter under the stars. After satisfying their burning desires, they had relaxed into the chairs, and slept. In the morning, waking with the daylight, Ammo's boy had reached over to stroke the hair on his chest, and found him cold, his limbs frozen stiff. Apparently, his body had simply quit on him, and there was, sadly, no help for it. Being the most practical, the captains strapped him to the back of one of their bikes, made arrangements to have his bike shipped back to the clubhouse, stuck a beanie helmet on his head, and made for the open road. Ammo would be taken care of that night, in a special ceremony. Likewise, Gerlach had to be carried out on a gurney, being that in his early morning daze, he had unquestioningly donned the leather replacement jacket that Snoopy had thoughtfully supplied him with, even managing to place his keys, wallet, and shades in the same pockets as they had been in his original jacket, further confusing the issue.

At breakfast, the four friends huddled together to discuss their experiences so far and bring Juanito up to date on the rest of the situation. After briefing him on the additional hazards, less one since this morning, they regaled each other with stories of the night before.

"None of us thought you'd be able to topple Honey Bear."

"Please, he was easy. You should see what it takes to deal with this one!" He indicated Snoopy.

"Woulda been difficult for me to see anything last night," grimaced Bikini, "Since Mangú was busy, Hercules had me bent over the sofa for more than an hour!"

"Y'know, I heard they make drugs for that!" came back Jimmy.

"For what?"

"Well, either way, actually, to make him come faster, or to help you not get so sore. And, of course, there's a huge number of painkillers for the next morning. But nothing you'd wanna take before jumping on yer scoot."

"Speaking of which," broke in Snoopy, "I have some news that may be of general interest to the group: I managed to accost Spyder last night." There was a collective '*ahaaaa*' from those assembled.

"Go on, man! Don't keep us here waiting!" Juanito, for all his subservience to his leaders, could be drastically impatient.

"I supplied him with some key information about Nuts' prize possessions."

"You mean his nuts?" laughed his cohorts.

Once they had quieted down again, Snoopy continued. "Asshole! No, those key properties I told you about last night!"

"So what happened?" asked Jimmy.

"I practically had to pick his jaw up off the floor. Apparently no one in the club is aware of this, and they all thought that either he just had money or he made it someway none of them could conceptualize. The point here is, that it seems Spyder is hard at work."

"This, my friends, is an unprecedented boon to our cause," started Juanito. "We should make a consolidated effort to ensure the continued success in his pursuits." The friends toasted each other with fresh-squeezed juices.

The discussion continued in like manner until Nuts announced it was time to mount up. The pack ambled towards their bikes around nine in the morning, and rumbled through the main street of the two-blink town before erupting out onto the wide-laned pavement once again. The four friends found themselves two lines up from the absolute rear of the pack, an unfavorable position because it was now easy for their adversaries to make a run at them and cause them all manner of problems. Mangú decided to initiate the harassment, in order to repay them for their having disgraced of him earlier that week. He steadily dropped back through the ranks until he started to approach Juanito's vicinity. Once there, he was first to open that morning's game of grab-ass with the new boy. Deciding that the brothers Manny and Fixx most likely had communicated the deft costume change that the friends had effected for yesterday's ride in order to avoid complications, they had neglected to attempt the same sort of deception this morning. To the left of Juanito was Snoopy, on his left, Bikini, and to his right, Jimmy. On the other side of Jimmy was Worm, and Mangú was attempting to wedge himself in between Juanito and Snoopy. In front of the line of four friends rode Fuzzy, Vince, Spyder and Manny. As Mangú continued to try to muscle his way into the line, Fuzzy and Spyder took notice of the goings on and began to regulate their positions in order to prevent any of the friends from escaping what was sure to be an almost assured destruction.

As their adversaries drew the circle around them tighter, Jimmy checked his rearview mirror, and saw that the line behind him— Gemelli, Gemelo, Clyde, and Thor, none of whom had quarrels with any of the friends—rode farther apart than the rest of the lines. He decided that as long as there was a 'Hail Mary' type of chance, he'd take it, and managed to squeeze the brakes and fall back just as Worm was about to swing into his lane, slashing with an enormous blade, aiming for Jimmy's underarm. Juanito perceived immediately what was happening when he checked over his own shoulder and followed suit. Snoopy and Bikini were not far behind. Once removed from those perilous environs, the friends blasted past their adversaries in time to see them collide into an enormous heap of twisted flesh, torn metal, and see the entire pile ignite from the spilled gasoline on the freeway. Unfortunately, they took with them the twins, Thor, and Clyde, none of whom could have possibly predicted their fate. The friends, however, felt no remorse. The larger society would survive, and in effect there were four fewer people to worry about since grumblings were heard at breakfast about their consternation over all four of them had fallen by the wayside before Honey Bear had reached Juanito.

Since the leaders of the organization were at the front of the pack, they never noticed the explosion, or the loss of their extra members, until news of the loss was reported at dinner. There was a general feeling of grief, and it was decided that in honor of their fallen comrades, a general company discharge was in order to honor the dead. No challenges were issued during dinner, and all were not surprisingly subdued. The reader should remember the condition that every other establishment (and the attendant staff) had been left in, and consider that such was not the case this evening. Indeed, even the collective exit was comparatively quieter than on other nights. No hotels were to be found near the dining establishment, though Eagle had spotted a campsite not more than a quarter of a mile from the diner. They headed towards camp, and the first to arrive were parked and setting up sleeping arrangements as the last to leave the diner were just pulling out of the lot.

The four friends again had lagged behind, finding their way to the bathroom, and had recruited Honey Bear to their cause. Before they emerged, bellows that would have frightened a raging rhino were heard resounding from the far stall. All five of them made a dramatic exit, and their faces barely contained their smiles. They wound their way towards the campsite and found the rest of the collective well into readying themselves for the ritual. The captains had picked a location far from anyone else in the campsite, and in the center built an enormous pyre on which Ammo was being laid out by Fuzzy and several attendant veterans. The members of the clan surrounded the fire pit, facing each other, each man with his dick in his hand, slowly working his way towards an erection. Once they were sure that they had reached a quorum, Fuzzy began his speech:

"Tonight, we bid farewell to our brother, Ammo. May he ride unencumbered wherever he may be. His spirit will be with us through the rest of our earthly travels. We hope that he finds rest for his tired bones. If ever a man was deserving of the long sleep, it was this one. RIDE ON BROTHER! BLAST OFF INTO THE NIGHT!—and with that, Fuzzy, who had been carrying a lighted torch, set fire to the final resting place of his friend and lover, and soon, the flames consumed the lately fallen warrior. Fuzzy smoked one of the bunch of cigars that

Jimmy had laced, unaware of the danger that such an act put him in, but, not one of the new recruits dared to warn him off.

Hercules, having lost Mangú was particularly distraught. He could barely address the crowd, though his speech was dramatically similar to Fuzzy's. One by one, those who would eulogize the dearly departed stood forward and did so, finally ending the orations as Ammo's body disintegrated into hot ash. As a final gesture, the entirety of the company, all whom had been steadily themselves during the laments, now stepped forward and gave their final release into the flames, burning their incense on the altar to their heroes. The company found solace in each other's arms, and heavy drink, and soon, the mood of the place was much less morbid. More logs were thrown on the fire, Jimmy's display case was brought out, and different members took advantage of the opportunity for sadistic practices the likes of which are probably better left to the imagination. In the midst of it all, Scratch and Worm were at their game again, though Scratch had thoughtfully added a new element to the equation: the fact that the key might be lost in the forest, and therefore wholly unable to be found. Bikini, that indefatigable scout had observed Scratch during the previous two nights, and knew precisely where the key was to be found. He had pocketed it himself, and made it his objective to liberate the poor tortured soul once most of the brothers had drunk and expended themselves so much that they would be ill prepared to stave off sleep any longer.

Fuzzy and Hercules, in order to distract themselves from their losses, had recruited several of the younger veterans, as well as several of the crop of new recruits to occupy their minds. Each captain had four attendants on his blanket, and perpetrated no end of infamy. Just at that point, Fuzzy found Nahs' ass stuck to his face while Gino rode his dick as if it were a wild bull. Honey Bear's enormous engine plumbed the depths of his ass while Banger's expert hands worked the two dicks that were not being put to use. Hercules had managed to reconfigure the situation so as to create a more voluptuous experience for himself. He sat astride Snoopy's fabulous prize, who had Carlo, in turn, astride his face. The one called Kid sucked Hercules' dick while Hercules planted his mouth on Carlo's stiffened member, and so as not to be left out, Mauler attacked Kid from behind. All ten of them rolled, worked, and stroked late into the night, making certain that each person had taken a turn in every position.

Nuts, Eagle, and Victor, the three captains, had decided to sport with Juanito, Jimmy, and Bikini. The tribal elders were convinced that some sort of foul play had been involved in the Honey Bear incident, and, though they had all separately made sufficient use of Juanito's faculties, an agreement was made that the facts had to be set straight, and Juanito had to be put to a test. Nuts and Victor, those with the two most prodigious members among the elders, laid themselves on the ground so as to be blade against blade, hilt against hilt, and Juanito was made to accept their combined girth. As he worked, Jimmy's talented mouth was set to work on his cohort, in an attempt to further confuse the issue. Bikini's post was to suck Jimmy's balls as Eagle, whose purpose was to observe keenly the goings on, invaded Jimmy from behind. In no short order, the elders, under Juanito's care, began to show signs of waning; they clutched the dirt, convulsed, howled liked demons, banged their heads against the ground and released into that gilded sheath into which their swords had been slid. Jimmy, Eagle, and Bikini had barely begun their exercise when the two elders had reached the pinnacle of their excitement.

"I am certain that a good deal of trickery is being used against us!" swore Nuts.

"Agreed," returned Victor. "The last time I came that fast I was thirteen years old! What are you that you have that sort of power? I am not convinced that he could possibly perpetrate that same exercise on the whole group!"

"That sounds like a challenge…" broke in Eagle, still toiling away at Jimmy's backside, with Bikini under them both. "I say we make it tomorrow night's adventure!"

"I say why wait?" continued Victor. "What better venue could we possibly have than this? Besides, tomorrow night we should have reached the Southern Corners fairgrounds, and we run the risk of engaging unwanted attention from other organizations."

"Victor's right!" Eagle answered. "Besides, it will take everyone's mind off of the recent misadventure."

"Your foresight is magnificent, Eagle!" screeched Nuts, and clasped him on the shoulder. From behind his back he drew a hollow horn, which he trumpeted to gain the attention of everyone present. Everyone except for those in the blankets containing Hercules and Fuzzy's montage turned their heads and listened to their new instructions. A ranking system was quickly devised, copious amounts of lubricant dispersed, logs added to the fire, drinks passed around, and before the entirety of the entourage began its slow and steady march through that fabled arch, Eagle's cry was heard signaling his release. How long the entire operation lasted, or what the company's general condition was afterwards, are details unavailable to us. However, one thing is for certain: Juanito emerged, once again, the victor.

That night, the clan stayed where they lay, unable to reach their sleeping arrangements even should they have an inkling to do so. The following morning, they all woke with the daybreak, though it was impossible to tell at what time they slept, all felt rejuvenated and ready for a fresh day's adventure. Again the general confusion about whose pants were where and which person's cock ring had found its way onto a branch eight feet off the ground ensued, though camp was generally broken down in a reasonable amount of time.

Mauler and Switch, two roughnecks who had spent an incalculable amount of time in the wild busied themselves cooking the collection of rabbits and wild birds' eggs they had managed to acquire either the night before or this morning. The fire still burnt strong enough to sear the meats well, and Flathead produced his famed Evolution engine coffee machine. In less time than it takes to tell the tale, breakfast was ready, and everyone lined up to get their share. Just as the line was being formed, Bikini strode out of the forest.

"Anyone seen Scratch and Worm?" he questioned, the slightest hint of vile glee played across his lips, under his mustache.

"They seem to be missing..." reported a veteran whose name he didn't know. Just then, Worm appeared, spattered with blood, mud, and filth. He washed himself inconspicuously, put on clean clothes, and made his way to the breakfast line. Eagle saw him walk up and decided that before they broke camp, he would wander into the forest towards the direction that Worm had come from and see what he could see.

By the end of breakfast, our protagonists began hearing the lilting voice of wild wolves, as if they had focused in on a hunt. Eagle, finishing his second cup of coffee, decided to make a dash for the source of the sounds, since they had come from the same direction where Worm had emerged. He quickly retreated, green in color, and aimed steadily for his machine, started it up, and rode off towards the freeway, saying that if any of the rest cared for their lives, they would do the same. Bikini and Worm found each others' eyes with a look of shared knowledge, dropped their plastic breakfast plates in the fire in the hopes the smell would keep the animals at bay for few more minutes, hopped on their steeds and escaped with all due haste.

Crew Log: Day the Fourth/Estimated Time of Arrival

Everyone in the crew made it safely to the highway, save those lost during the evening. Even Flathead's coffee machine had been salvaged prior to their hasty departure, as well as the mysteriously placed cock ring.

The morning's ride was mostly uneventful, though the southern heat was much more evident than it had been originally. It was practically impossible to stay dry between the humidity and the sun; it was lucky they were out on the open road, otherwise, each man would be bathing in his own sweat. Luckily, the lunchtime diner was an air-conditioned establishment that understood such things. As our remaining heroes filled their bellies, Bikini and Worm found themselves seated across the table from one another. Vince spied them speaking in hushed tones, and availed himself of the opportunity. He approached their table and commandeered a chair.

"That was one helluva ballsy thing you did back there," he started.

"Wut're you talking about?" asked Worm, trying his best to wriggle out of a bad situation.

"Getting rid o' Scratch like that. That worked out pretty neat. I gotta tell you, I'm not sure I could've done it better myself."

"Huh?" Worm was simply at a loss for intelligent answers. "You mean, you were looking to get rid of Scratch?

"Aw, he was a bastard! But, then again, he was supposed to be, I guess. But, shit, I also owed him for something similar for a lot longer than you. Seems you've done us both a favor without really meaning to, and you helped him, hmmm?" Vince tilted his head towards Bikini.

"Uuuuuhhhhh, yeah. I found the key." He offered the key to the veteran who took it and reached under the table. There was a click, and suddenly an iron manacle appeared in front of Vince.

"Funny thing about collars, they're not always somewhere you can see. What do you want for your help, little man?" asked Vince, again indicating Bikini. The new recruit gulped down his fear, swallowed some orange juice and made a decision.

"You and Snoopy no longer have an axe to grind," came back the junior bravely.

"Done!" The two clasped hands in the prescribed manner. The contract had been made; it could not be broken. Vince went back to his circle, and the rest of the four friends rushed over to join Bikini and hear the news. Before Bikini's cohorts managed to sit down, Hercules announced it was time to leave, and the four friends, trailing Worm, adjourned to the little boys' room. By the time the company had all started their engines, and the leaders of the pack had begun to pull out of the driveway, animalistic screams accompanied by the rending of steel and snapping of wood filtered through the door and competed with the bestial growl blown back from the parking lot. The four friends emerged jubilant, arm in arm with their newly conscripted ally. Following the example of their superiors they erupted out of the lot in time to see the last of the clan disappear onto the freeway.

Every one of the captains wore a somber face for their fallen comrade. Scratch—for all his puppeteering—had been a good leader, and a solid friend. He would be missed. For the second half of the day, the captains all rode together at the front of their ranks.

When the restaurant's clean-up crew made it into the bathrooms, they all stared in wonder at how they'd managed to bend the metal dividers and bind them together with Vince's former collar, but that, again, is a different story for a different time.

The secular society, now composed of Juanito, Bikini, Jimmy, Snoopy, and Worm, rode the rest of the afternoon without incident since the whole of those dissenters dangerous enough to prevent them from arriving at their objective were no longer amongst the ranks. Triumphant, they pointed themselves in the direction of the campsite where the weekend-long fetish festival was to take place. The leadership had planned the route such that they arrived a few short hours after lunch, with plenty of daylight left before nightfall. The welcoming committee was at the gate making sure all who entered did so with a smile.

The plot set aside for their company was ample, but now even more so due to a smaller clan. The remaining company now found they had plenty of space to set up camp with space left in between tents. Jimmy set up his regular post: a pharmacopoeia of pain relievers, pleasure pills, and things to make your brain go boom.

Dinner was the traditional Hawaiian-style pig roast, something Gerlach was more than irate about missing. The welcoming committee offered each club with more than 100 members registered for the party those benefits. After dinner, all the half-empty bottles of liquor, hip flasks, and hidden containers stashed in the bottom of well-worn saddlebags appeared. Bones, gristle, and empty pineapple shells lay smoldering amongst the coals. Nuts, Eagle, Fuzzy, and Victor sat in a remorseful huddle passing around some of the "Flathead Homebrew" that Manny and Fixx extracted from a still based on an old flathead engine. Flathead had gotten his name one night when he chugged down an entire bottle in less than five minutes. Of course, Flathead had never really been the same again, and it had taken him an entire week to remember his name, but that, as the reader should be aware, is another story.

The drink loosened their tongues, and the remaining leaders began recounting collective remembrances of their dearly departed comrade. Realizing an opportunity to both eulogize their friend and brother, and potentially instigate a calamitous debauchery, Eagle proposed that the whole of the group should contribute to the story-telling.

Victor, having had the closest confidence with Scratch, began the orations in this manner:

"Our fallen brother, since we are unable to offer you the glorious send-off that is customary for our clan, we choose to represent you, and pay homage to you thusly. Your memory will be extolled here in the present company, and your spirit laid to rest as our crew shows respect for your adventures. Roll on, our brother, wherever you may be! " With that, Victor opened the circle for contributions, and a light breeze nudged the coals to life just as Mauler dropped a load of freshly collected wood on top of them, enough so that a hearty flame blazed brightly in a few short moments. Nuts made the first contribution:

"Our dearly departed Scratch, in a fit one day for an opiate fix, found his way to salvation through some truly unorthodox means. One of our other brothers, who we called French because none of us could pronounce his name; beautiful man, physically I mean, and even after all the rough use we put him through, he still had a most beautiful ass. Anyway, French had gotten himself into an accident that was just a fender bender, and was in such a condition that he had to be put in traction. There was really nowhere to stick an I.V. into his arm either, or most other parts of his body for that matter, because they were covered in plaster. Fast-forward about two months. French should have been coming off the painkillers, but the doc okayed the refill on his prescription, so we kept getting it for him. So, like I was saying, Scratch was all in a tizzy about finding some form of opiate that night. Nobody had any, a problem which, I'm sure if anybody here shares, Jimmy will be more than capable of remedying."

Jimmy waved and nodded. Everyone cheered their approval of the new alliance. "So, in the middle of a company dinner, right around the time Sissy was bringing out the ice cream, French starts screaming, as if the pain is taking him over. Fuzzy runs upstairs and slips a couple of the suppositories into our patient and eventually he starts to calm down. Scratch figures, why let him have all the fun, and launches himself towards the infirmary, and slams the door shut. Immediately, a variety of sounds are heard expressing pain, then pleasure, then confusion and disillusionment as French finally comprehends the true purpose of Scratch's visit. Scratch comes back to the table, his face filthy, and the rest of us incapable of comprehending what precisely happened, though our overactive imaginations surely made up the difference. As he sat back down, he smiled broadly, showing exactly how much of a mess his face was. As everyone else returned the smile, he made the following comments: "Is there anything better to taste than an ass? How could you hope to compare the finest dish, its flavor, what greater pleasure exists than to kiss that favored gate? What greater sight than that beautiful flesh-colored star? What better feeling than to be firmly ensconced in that human sheath? Wouldn't you agree?" And the entire

278

company, spurred on by this inquiry, spent long hours extolling the virtues of that very same opening, heating their brains to such a degree that once Scratch, now feeling the effects of the drugs he'd ingested, stood on the table and showed his ass, the entire company disengaged from their discussions, and it was that night that the old furniture got trashed, and we had to go shopping the next day for replacements." The inheritants of Scratch's legacy clapped and laughed. Somewhere in the back, one of the crew was busy getting off, and from the screams filtering out of the forest, several others from different campsites had had similar ideas.

Fuzzy, dripping homebrew from his soaked beard and mustache, decided now was the time to add to the mix, and related the following tale: "Our annual enema contest grew out of one of Scratch's stunts. I had issued a challenge to him after a night when we had all become particularly unhinged. That morning, in a bit of sport with another former captain, I had taken three bags full of liquid, all of which were shot through a pump that had given the probe the finest tingling feeling. Scratch, not be outdone, revealed that he had been developing a much heartier machine. True to his word, he produced the device from its hiding place in the closet. He'd attached an Evo engine from a recently wrecked Softtail to a water pump from a similarly acquired Vortec engine, bolted the whole thing onto a spare sporty frame lying around in the back yard and even given the damn thing a kickstarter. The drag bars connected to the front end controlled the vibration and, finally, since it would have been unallowable to be out-styled by anyone else, a steel three inch in diameter butt plug which sat squarely in the middle of the rigid seat." In the midst of Fuzzy's discourse, as soon as he stopped to take a breath, the sound of some unfortunate's flesh being whipped floated over from in between the trees. These, however, were fairly close, and Hercules mandated that several of the veterans should stand guard at the back of the pack while the eulogizing carried on.

"Since I had already taken a good deal that day, I was more than prepared for a second adventure, though I was plainly unaware of what Scratch's new invention was capable. He greased the probe for me; I prepared myself, and accepted the challenge. Once astride the beast, he started the engine, goosed the throttle just to give me a taste of what I was in for; it shook my insides more than I had ever been shaken, and I convinced him to let the warmed water flow. As it trickled in, he slowly rolled the throttle backwards, increasing the vibrations until I though I might be ripped in half. As the vibrations became more forceful, so did the flow of water, and it was plain that the experience I'd had in the morning was no equal to this present endeavor. At the end of one quart, he shifted gears, the frame began to bounce, and several lieutenants had to be called in to support the machine as we forged ahead. The second quart lodged itself comfortably inside me, though the vibrations from the machine certainly had caused me no end of difficulty in maintaining my composure. By the time he shifted into third gear, my dick was stuck to my belly, and I was searching for a support, anything to hold onto what was solid, thinking it would be some sort of comfort because my teeth had suddenly begun to rattle. I passed my previous limit as he shifted into fourth gear, and halfway through this final ordeal, I was no longer able to maintain control over myself, and had to somehow escape the torture. I leapt from the machine, Scratch killed the throttle, and I barely made it into the bathroom across the hall. I returned still buzzing from what I had endured. Everyone cheered once I rejoined the group, but for three days following I had to simply lie in bed praying the buzzing in my skull would stop.

"Well, once I had taken the ride, everyone else thought it was a great idea, and a line formed out the door longer than I've seen at any roller coaster, all to see just how long they could last. No one made it any further than third gear, though we still have the machine, and people are still trying. There was really nothing quite like that ride...." Fuzzy stared off into the distance wistfully, and a collective sigh was heard. Then he suddenly brightened up: "Hey! We still have the machine! I move that we reschedule the enema contest for immediately after our triumphant return from this event!"

A roar of approval went up from the crowd. In a different corner, another man was heard releasing his flow as he was satisfied by his partner. Several men fell to pawing at each other, and stroking already stiffened appendages in the hopes of finding eventual release. Jeans bulged, leather strained, sweat broke out, and the heat of the moment as well as the warmth of the fire tested the limits of even the most faithful amongst them. By the end of the storytelling, it would have been nigh impossible to contain the passionate discourse between individuals. Not that anyone would have wanted to if they could anyway.

Just then, with all of the watchdogs at their post, and with nothing remotely related to a warning, someone in the throes of passion from another camp fell out of a tree on top of several crew members near the fire. Their reactions were still not slowed; they had not been into the drink for yet long enough, though, done all in good time. For now however, they were able to defend themselves against the unforesee-able onslaught. The intruder was pushed into the flames out of pure reflex; being a largish bear-type, his body was well singed before he escaped his fate. Several crewmembers had ready lengths of rope and an appropriately hideous ball gag. Once thusly restrained, the marauding meteorite hung suspended from a branch much sturdier than the one that hadn't supported him. Hercules began his commemorative story.

"This event stemmed from nothing out of the ordinary. Scratch and I got into some light play; we hadn't even involved heavy restraints. After loosening me up first with his tongue, then a well-greased dildo, he then inserted an inflatable butt plug. This was terribly exciting for me because, not only had I just healed from a significant tear, but, the inflatable butt plug continues to be one of my favorite toys." Several cheers from members who shared his predilections went up momentarily. Hercules continued on with his adventure: "I doubt the possibility however, that any will be capable of replicating the style and deft improvisation with which Scratch remedied the following situation. The specific plug we were using was the same one he'd taken on the road with him the weekend before, and by way of getting jostled this way and that, had developed an air leak in the bulb he squeezed to inflate the instrument. I was in fits, all the time he's been massaging my entrails, he was also been steadily pumping my cock in and out of his mouth. This whole affair had entirely retarded the process, and neither one of us was prepared to yield the day to an unexpected technicality.

"He pulled the knife from his belt, sliced off the bulb, created an alternate valve from I'm not entirely sure what, attached the handheld tire inflator that uses CO_2 cartridges, and began to inflate the device. While he did so, he continued to stroke my erection, the pleasure and the pain: my cock was bursting, I'd already missed coming once by scant seconds, and it took a great deal of time to work back to the climax once again. He finally decided to restrain me because I was flailing wildly, yanks some rope from his road bag, bound my hands and my feet to the same posts, presenting my ass for easy access, and continued inflating the device. As I was straining against the cord, he positioned himself so that I can suck him at the same time as he did the same to me. The device growing inside me, we were both thrown into fits of ecstasy. Spanking me while he's coming, one of his unintentional strokes strikes the plug, which tickled just the right spot in my intestines, and I exploded, filling his mouth with more juice than I though my balls were capable of producing. After, we both collapsed on each other, and in commemoration of the day, we enshrined the inflatable plug in my room for special occasions. This trip, however, being the fifteenth such trip he and I made together, I had remembered to include the device in my bags, for some extensive play once we arrived here...."

Hercules' voice trailed off and several of his normal detail of boys rushed in to support him. He quickly straightened up, however, and got back his normally stoic face. The second he was once again composed, several of those seated around the fire, having been steadily stroked during Hercules' entire discourse, suddenly shot the contents of their inflamed scrotums into the fire. That incense burned on the altar with a hiss, and their screams sounded off like fireworks in rapid succession. In a darkened corner, almost immediately following the men at the front, an entire group screamed its release at the same time, almost emulating a grand finale presentation. The burning of much incense in Passion's temple, and the exclamations of the men's ejaculations yanked Hercules back to the present from his reverie. What greater eulogy to his fallen friend could there be than to do exactly this, ride free, give himself over to passion, and celebrate what had been an exceptionally bright existence with those same activities that would have pleased him most? Yes, this was the way to properly remember his lost comrade, and Hercules would make sure that, if no one else, he would burn brightest during the celebration.

Several of the previously faithful were beginning to mill around Jimmy's table, starting to make selections for the evening. They knew that, if they wanted to be in prime form for what they expected to happen at the end of the story-telling, they had better start now otherwise they might miss it. Since Jimmy's table was close to where the unknown intruder hung, the already sore-looking captive was the recipient of random whipstrokes, poking and prodding as club members filtered by. Several other members decided that the smell of burning cum on the fire was pleasurable for them and decided to aim their ejaculations into the flames in the interim as more of the last bottle of Flathead homebrew was passed to Hercules in an attempt to soothe his nerves.

Fuzzy, Nuts, and Hercules all fell to commiserating, and Eagle, his foresight as sharp as ever, predicted they would call for the following story, and so began his own part of the eulogizing of their confrere.

One more man leapt forward just as Eagle was about to begin and jettisoned an enormous flow into the flames, causing them to his and spit in their own fashion, and Eagle to smile as he remembered his friend: "Body modification night had always been popular in our house. In fact, it's become such a ritual, that there is rarely an event that goes by where some sort of body modifying doesn't go on." More laughter and eruptions of cheers. Eagle was not swayed from his task: "The particular night, however, that I am about to recount, will be more than memorable for those as yet uninitiated, and a jarring, pleasurable memory for those who shared the experience.

"Most of your will recall Scratch's predilection for getting pierced. I sometimes think that his skin was nothing more than something to hold all the metal together, but, this was something few of us knew about, and most weren't expecting. He'd had his chest pierced verti-cally, and the holes gradually stretched until the size was something like single-gauge barbells three inches long." Here, everyone started to grab for their respective pectoral region and groan in pain. Their gasps and exclamations sounded amazingly like the ejaculations hitting the fire. "Anyway, his final objective was to be able to toughen the skin in that region so as to be able to do hangings from flesh hooks. Well, for several years he worked on the area, having himself regularly flogged on the chest, and the barbells stretched, increasingly over time. Well, finally, one day, he decided that he had trained and stretched far enough, making it possible to accomplish his goal. So, he began to experiment with different hangings, trying to *stretch-out* the process." Everyone chuckled at Eagle's wordplay. "He wanted to be able to hang for what was sure to amount to at least half-an-hour or more. Since he was starting at the end of a calendar year, he had plenty of time to practice, since body modification night generally happens in the middle of the year. The first attempt was a success; he lasted more than five minutes before screaming out in absolute pain and exclaiming that he was close to losing consciousness. As the months passed by, however, he was increasingly closer to his goal, and about a month before our annual body modification night extravaganza, he clocked more than half an hour hanging. The date arrived, the group assembles, and general depravity ensued. There are sharps boxes conveniently located in every section of the room, the floor is covered with disposable absorbent material, and it would have been easy to confuse the clubhouse for something like a slaughterhouse, or a horrific biological experiment gone awry: Men bent backwards over benches bound to posts with peacock-like arrays of needles jutting from their stomachs, or what looked like delicate stitching sewing its way down their backs, necks, arms, nipples pierced by five needles, dicks nailed to boards, scrotums similarly stretched, tattooing happening in the back room, and fire play outside right next to the brothers' shop. That night, Scratch took us all by surprise.

"After a while, most people had begun to take breaks from their long night of playing, and losing blood. Sissy kept sugary drinks going around, and while the moon was still high, a general announcement was made that a show was about to take place in the back yard. Scratch took his place under the enormous oak tree that had been got split in half a year earlier by the lightning storm, and, since the barbells had been replaced by flesh tunnels, the hooks glided in smoothly, easily finding their resting place. They had been attached to a spreader bar that was hoisted by two different people through a pulley system hung on a sturdy branch thirty feet off the ground. As the slack was taken out,

Scratch laid back, relaxing into such an experience, or, at least, as much as anyone is able to relax into the experience. While he was being hoisted, very few other people noticed the fire bearer on the side, heating several brands, and grinning wildly as he did so. I wasn't quite sure what he was up to, but I was sure it would be a spectacle to witness.

"Scratch's legs were also bound to a spreader bar, something none of us could really comprehend at the time, though no one could have possibly missed his erection. His cock was literally stuck to his belly, pulsing with his heartbeat, stiffened from the excitement. Once he was three feet off the ground, the fire bearer began to shoo people out of the way, until he reached the front of the crowd and managed to lay hands on Scratch. He grabbed hold of that shaft, brandished his metal to convince the crowd that it was extremely hot, and stuck the piece to Scratch's flesh, sending smoke, the scent of searing flesh, and his screams towards the heavens. Luckily Scratch's hand had also been bound and there was only so much that he could do to extricate himself from the position he was in. After the branding took place, Scratch just hung there, limp, as if the life had gone out of him, and after about ten minutes, the other participants let him down slowly so that someone could catch him, and apply the appropriate salves to the new wound." By now, every other member of the crew besides the captains was squirming in their chaps. None of Scratch's previous partners had ever really taken the time to inspect his cock that closely, besides which, he generally wore a latex sheath that covered not only his shaft, but his balls as well. That being the case, few and far between had been the persons who actually had the privilege of seeing the marks Eagle had just described. Almost assuredly, however, the wolves had paid it no mind.

Eagle's story concluded the eulogizing of the recently defunct captain, and Juanito and Bikini could not wait for the storytelling to end so they could get into playing out in the open instead of sneaking around in the dark corners of the campsite. The invader was bound hugging the tree he had been suspended from, and the already singed skin of his back flayed until it bled then was splashed with hydrogen peroxide for a further burning effect. He finally fell unconscious and was attended to by the medic on site for what his bearers described as "one helluva fall." The four friends found themselves intertwined as the remaining captains consoled themselves in each other's company. The rest of the company, incapable of containing itself any longer, degraded into general depravity, and the flames dancing in the center did not produce as much heat as the friction among all those bodies. Jimmy's table was emptied by the end of the night, enough rubber to supply a tire factory was put to the test, and by dawn, enough new histories had been created that another volume the same length as this one would be necessary to recount them all. Exhausted, the company retired, or more precisely collapsed on itself, and not a single one of them stirred before noon. The four friends had rejoiced of their own accord, having not only survived, but surpassed all expectations and eliminated all possible obstacles to their future success in the company. At last, relaxed, elated, and spent, they slept.

Epilogue: Watch Your Step and Thanks for Flying

The following day, the serpentine weave of bodies typical of the previous three nights stirred, slithered, and eventually untangled itself. The members looked around the campsite, attempted to comprehend the mess of implements of ass destruction, realized that an explanation would be futile, and instead decided to go in search of their boots. Again, Flathead's coffee machine made an appearance and Banger and Switch composed a fitting breakfast out of gods know what because no one remembered them either hunting or stopping at the food store on the way into fairgrounds. No matter, all were happy to eat anyway.

After returning the campsite to a general sense of order, those still in a condition to do so, those not too hung over, recovering from whippings/piercings/suspensions, or unable to walk straight, entered the party with high hopes for new adventures. Peace strings were tied, iron and attitudes checked at the door, and shades appropriately donned. United, they strolled through those hallowed gates, and what happened there I know not what, and perhaps, it is better not to attempt an explanation, but rather allow the reader to construct the scene of his own accord.

MOBY
M. Christian

Yessir, the good folks around these here parts are particularly struck by the telling of a good tale. Some like to say that it's 'cause we've not—how shall I say—'misplaced' how to sit a feller down and spin out a damned good yarn. Others though, they like to gesture towards those there damned high and awfully wooded peaks and say that it's got more to do with the fact we all got shit-poor teevee reception.

Like any collection of folks—that is, folks who knows the how to put the right collection of words together to spin out a handsome yarn, or got more than snow on the local tube—we've got a few we like to tell a bit more than others. Like the one about how Old Uncle Conti done helped Miss Oleander birth her seven little young-uns in the middle of that awful thunder and lightning show we had back in '60; or that time Crazy Jeb got too big a taste of the 'shine and went on his rather reckless excursion with Huge Henry, Mr. Larkin's bulldozer; or even when Old Jeb at the Dry Goods found himself at the business end of a shotgun in the hands of that no-good eldest Barnaby boy, and how he done turned the tails on that no-account without being able to see his wrinkled old hand in front of his dead blind eyes.

But there's no one we like to chew the fat about more than that Beast of the Highway, our Monster of the Road, the Legendary Creature of the Blacktop.

Yeah, that's him, that's the man—if 'man' could be quite the word to describe him. It'd be more accurate to call him a force of nature, or like a tiger someone done educated enough to stand up on his hind legs, a cyclone wearing size sixteen boots, a motorcycle-riding fiend from the deepest, darkest depths of your wildest nightmares. That's Moby.

Moby, we like to say, ain't just big, 'cause that makes anyone who'd never had…funny, but I was just about to say 'the honor to see him,' but you know that sure is not right, 'cause anyone who done see Moby sure as shit not call it anything like an 'honor.' No sir. But anyone who has laid eyes on him would have to say that 'big' just ain't the right word. Three little letters just ain't enough to describe the heights of the man. They say—and I can neither agree with such nor deny for I've never seen such a thing myself—that Moby ducks his head so as not to hit a sun hanging low, on its way to setting; or that he's said he's able to reach up and tie a peaceful-looking cloud into a righteous twister with just the twirling of his finger. Yeah, I know that's tall for even a tall tale, but I'll tell you friend, I have seen Moby myself and I can not only say that it was not any honor, but that he's taller than even the tallest tale I or anyone else could ever tell.

Another thing that people who meet the Hog Rider From Hell say about him is—well, how could I say this, being we all in polite company? Let me put it this way, the man has a 'presence' that announces his imminent arrival even before the ground starts to do its shake and shimmy from his size-sixteens crushing down on the hardest-packed asphalt, crushing good cement to powder, cracking stones like walnuts. Moby—and to be right straight with you there really ain't no way to say this and retain civility—has a hellish fragrance. Wherever he rides, he leaves a rooster tail of reek, a hurricane of stink, a billowing cloud of stench. I've heard it described in all kinds of ways, from the sweat off a bull's balls—and I did say there was no polite way to say it—to May Tilly's septic tank on a hot Saturday afternoon in the middle of summer. And if you know the kind of seasons we have in these here parts, and you know May Tilly, you would know that he's truly a hideous proposition in regards to fiendish aromas.

The only thing said to be more potent than Moby's emissions is the strength that courses through the big-ass muscles that you can clearly see knotting and cording around his mountainous biceps and hydraulic thighs. Some say that he's strong enough to bend quarters twice, making two bits into four bits, just between thumb and forefinger. Others like to point out how he parks that roaring hog of his: no backing and forwarding for Moby, no sir. Instead, the biggest of the big and strongest of the strong, he instead finds himself the perfect old spot to put his chrome and grease-dripping machine and he just lifts it up in one brawny hand and drops it down right where he wants it—and what with the power of those arms and that stink, it's just about anywhere he reckons to.

Now Moby, he's quite a lot of other things—more even than his size, his aroma, or his brawn—but those are what you might call other kinds of observances, less on the great list that is the tales that folks like to tell about the biker. But there's another thing about Moby that's right there up on the top, even greater than his cloud-rippling height, his eye-watering stink, or his ground-shaking muscles. But for that one I've got to give you a little bit more than some homespun metaphors and back-porch similes. For that I've got to sit you right down—you comfy now?—and spin you a downright special tale, the one I like to tell more than any other about that leather monster, that motorbike hurricane, that beast on two tires.

For that I've got to tell of the time Moby came barreling down to our sleepy little town, needle tapping out a high-octane, fuel-injected rhythm against the top of his speedometer, rumbling engine like the four-stroke from hell. Fast? He was way more than fast, friend. You could even say he'd just left *fast* way behind, past blasting through *quick*, leaving *breakneck* in his dust.

That day is the one I'm talking about. The day he come through—and the day a certain officer of this here municipality decided that he'd had quite enough of this hog-riding, quarter-folding, reeking tower of a man. This, you see, was the day he decided to give Moby a speeding ticket.

Who knows why he done it? When we get just a smelliest bit tired of telling tales about Moby, someone or other will bring up that day, ponder over some 'shine and a smoke, just what did possess that certain Officer Langtry to take it into his head to bang his own motorcycle to life and take off in pursuit of the demon. Jeb over at the old Wicker place likes to say that the sun that day must have cooked his brains into something that may very well have resembled grits, while Miss Barlow is more akin to the theory that the only thing that could explain the whys and wherefors of that pursuit of Moby is that Langtry's family tree must have had some very shallow roots.

They say what they say, friend, but I can tell you for a fact that no one, least of all that officer of the law, knows quite why he did it. But he did it—he sure as hell did it.

Right up there with the whys and wherefors of Officer Langtry's darned earnest pursuit has to be another important element to this tale of his meeting with the Moby—in other words, why in the heavens above and hell below did that Harley Davidson maelstrom look behind, clearly see the flashings and the wailings of the law behind him, pull over, and—puzzle of mysteries, strangeness of weirdness—*stop*?

But he did. He did. Right over there in fact, at the fork where the main thoroughfare curls off towards River Road, by that very same gnarled old pine. That's just where Moby glided that chrome and greasy machine to the side of the road.

Who could say what Officer Langtry thought when that happened? More than likely a sense of some kind of professional satisfaction that it was his lights, his siren that did what no one else had done. That his own bike, his own authority, had reached out to the bad craziness that was Moby and reined in that wild biker bull. But just as there was a smile on his handsome young face, you have got to know that riding right along with him was more than a bit of the old stomach-clenching, jaw-tightening thing you and me and everyone on this whole darned world call *fear*.

But Langtry was *Officer* Langtry, more than he was young and handsome, and for him that was enough to relax that jaw, calm that stomach, and steady his racing heart. He had his badge, the authority invested to him by his good little town, this right honorable state, and this glorious nation—and he wasn't going to let no legend, no big, smelly, or even strong, biker blast through his quiet little world without paying the price for his reckless disregard for those laws of town, state and country.

And with that authority in him like a good belt of something smoky and well-aged, but with a kick like a mule who woke up on the wrong side of the barn, he glided his own two wheels up next to the biker, killed the engine with a quick twist of the wrist and dismounted.

It would be honest to say that at that moment in his young life on this planet Earth spinning through space, that officer of this here town, state and Good Ol' Wonderful country, and even with the badges and nifty uniforms and let's not forget that pearl-handled, brushed chrome Smith and Wesson dangling there at his hip, Officer Langtry couldn't have been more terrified. This was Moby, people, and don't you forget it. His rough-hewn brows parted the clouds all up on high, tufts of them vanishing like the steam over the old sawmill the day they shut it down, his hellacious aroma curling every single nose hair in the vicinity and causing more than a few pigeons to drop from that summer sky in shock as he climbed off of his grease-glimmering motorcycle. Then, for it is said by more than just me, your humble story-teller, that there is nothing more important to Moby—not putting the fear of hideous death in the minds of the citizens of this region, not the destruction of road and all wildlife foolish enough to attempt to cross it, not...other even more fiendish activities I will not even dare to mention for there are ladies here at present—than that motorcycle. And so to put it aside from even the most casual of damage, heaven help anyone who would do such a thing, he demonstrated another of his Moby attributes and lifted it up off the ground with one mighty flex of an arm and put it down as neatly as a mother putting her youngest to bed.

Fear or no fear, terror or no terror, dread or no dread, Officer Langtry of the Town Constabulary, was invested with all the powers of the previously mentioned town, state, and wonderful country and as such he had a duty to perform, a higher order if you will, a task that no one in the history of this town, this state or even this here country had even managed to accomplish: he had to give the dreaded hog-driving beast of the End Times a ticket and that's what he was going to do.

And as such, there were—shall we say 'rituals' that had to accomplish the giving of a Motorvehicular Citation for Excessive Velocity On a Municipal Thoroughfare, Payable to the Officer himself or via the Local Courthouse, and Officer Langtry wasn't about to simply shake in his boots (even though he was) and twitch his hands (even though they were) and just, simply, only hand the huge, smelly, strong biker a Traffic Ticket.

And so, even through his shaking and twitching, hoping the fear he felt did not leak out through his manner of speaking, Officer Langtry walked forward, stuck his thumbs in the belt loops of his uniform pants and said in his best Law Enforcement parlance: "Do you have any idea of how fast you were going?" I should mention to all of you that to complete the aforementioned ritual correctly, there is the insertion of a word at the end of that there sentence to fully convey to the perpetrator to whom a law enforcement officer is speaking that they are truly in the presence of a formidable authority figure. But while Officer Langtry had those many levels of authority—and I will not try your patience by reciting town, state and country once again—he was still in the looming, mountainous, aromatic, Herculean and smelly presence of Moby and so, possibly wisely, did not conclude his statement of "Do you have any idea of how fast you were going?" with the word, "boy."

To this, and the absence of the word so often used by members of the law enforcement community, Moby replied with stony silence.

"Well, I'll tell you how fast you were going," Officer Langtry continued. "You were in excess of the posted limit by more than fifteen miles per hour. That's breaking the law, and there are penalties for the breaking of our laws. Harsh penalties, some might say."

To this additional commentary from Officer Langtry, Moby also did not reply.

"I say to myself that no penalty is too damned harsh that'll keep the streets of our fair city safe from reckless no-goods like yourself, who seem to think that every road is their road, or that stop signs are just a suggestion."

Again, there was only tall, strong, stinky quiet from Moby.

"That's right, you heard what I said. I opened this here mouth and called you a 'no-good,' and by the Lord Above and the Laws of this fine town, noble state, and great country, I stand by that statement, for Mister, I can tell just by laying eyes on you that I may in fact have been more than necessarily polite in my description."

Moby only kept his silence, eyes showing nothing but a steely glimmer.

Now your more perceptive-of-listening might be thinking that our Officer Langtry might be more than slightly putting his size-twelve official shoes over the line between what a law enforcement officer should be saying and what any person who knows of the biker called Moby would say. In this I would have to say that those who are thinking such thoughts are completely right in wondering such, for even Officer Langtry himself was no doubt engaged in the back of his brain wondering just such. But the words were there, coming out before he could even stop himself, one after another like bubbles coming up from a glass of cool beer, and just like you can't put your finger through the foam and stop them from coming up to the top, neither could Officer Langtry stop himself from saying the things he wanted to say, and probably many folks have wanted to say to that monster of the motorbike for a good many years.

"Just look at yourself, son. Take a damned long, hard look at yourself. You call yourself a man? A beast, more like. Big, sure as shit you're big. Strong—that too. Muscles all rippling and moving under that tight denim vest, calves like tree trunks under those jeans, chest like mom's old washboard, hands the size of one of Old Mrs. Gator's prize sows. And the stink, Lordy, don't get me started on your foul emissions. That's the worst of all, I say; the bottom of the barrel. Get rid of the reek—and once again I can only think of one of Old Mrs. Gator's hogs—and you might, and I do say 'might', come out the other end of such scrubbing and cleanliness to be a halfway respectable sample of … masculinity."

Moby stayed quiet as an owl flying across a deep night sky, but while he did not say anything, his face spoke through the raising of one eyebrow.

"It's not too late, son. You're still not on the other side of that hill. You could be something, do something with your life aside from pissing people off and scaring the local inhabitants. Clean yourself up some, get yourself some kind of respectable form of transportation, settle down with some…girl, I guess. Do you really want to go on down the road you've been driving, end up in jail for the rest of your years or maybe dead on the side of the road somewhere, like some stinking skunk too slow or dumb to get out of the way of two pair of radials?"

Nothing again from the biker, nothing but stone silence. But his hands, great monster mitts with fingers the size of extra-large sausages made from the best of Old Mrs. Gator's prize pigs, dropped down to his waist.

"Hold it right there, son—you just hold it right there. No sudden movements now. You keep your hands right where I can see them or you're going to find out, right personally, just how fast I can draw this here gun and put a .38 slug right in your well-defined chest."

But Moby did not stop, not at all, and all the time he was not speaking, he did not stop. Hands to his waist, thick, beefy fingers forward, a twist of the thumb to push aside a narrow strip of road-filthy denim then a pinch of zipper and down.

Down, as they say, and out.

Smelly, it has been said, by myself as well as many others who like to talk about the biker known as Moby, is the stink that follows, making even the foulest of smelling creatures run for cover. Strong, it has been stated, like a bear, like a bull, like a 4x4 truck, a locomotive, and any other thing that might come to mind when you think about things that can lift, push, of pull really heavy things. Big, he walked, birds and light aircraft were known to move out of the way of his towering immensity, that his shadow has been known to fall across county after county stretching far out yonder.

But I have yet to hear anyone else talk about Moby's...manliness.

There's no other way to say it, ladies and gentlemen, and so I have to beg your humble apologies for having to be so blunt about such matters but there really is no way to continue to tell this tale of Moby and Officer Langtry without using words that will no doubt offend some of us with their coarseness. I shall put my all into trying to use some terminology, shall I say, that will singe rather than burn the ears of some of my more sensitive listeners. To remove the shock of such words for you long before they happen to appear in the telling of this tale, I am going to put them out into the air right this very moment. You all ready now? Prepared and cautioned enough for this? Well, then here you go, in regards to the part of Moby that hangs well below his knees, I shall call it his: privates (because that part of a man is just that), wily (because I had a pal by that name), old friend (because I dare you to find a man who doesn't feel at least that fondly for that part of himself), dick (because I had another pal with that name), manliness (as I said before), and penis (because that's what it is).

And there it was, right in front of Officer Langtry on that warm summer day. In all its...well, now, I was about to use the word 'glory,' but that's not exactly what would be an accurate description of that there biker's privates.

Because, good listener, this intimate part of Moby's anatomy reflects much of what we've all learned about the man, and none of that anyone, least of all myself, would call by that Church-like word, 'glorious.'

You see, upon the opening of those greasy, torn-up jeans a powerful reek of oil, sweat, farts, and other foul body emissions wafted forth, befouling the otherwise ordinary smells of that day. Like an animal in rut he was, with that kind of aroma flowing out of his pants and out into the atmosphere.

Then there was that other aspect of the man, the muscles and lifting, the sinews and strength, the brawn and potency that was reflected in that awesome willy. Men know that sometimes the sprit may be ready to perform its duties but the flesh may be more than occasionally drunk and weak, but not for that biker, and definitely not that day.

Now if I were a coarse gentleman, not one of a refined disposition and the like, I would stroll off into perhaps a bit overly long description of the biker's manhood, going into some too-exact details such as how the veins along the length of it pulsed and quivered with primal juices of pure animal lust, or how the end was as big and hard as the ball on top of the flagpole in front of our beloved town hall, or how the entire flashy assemblage seemed to be as long and as steely hard as that very same flagpole. Or maybe I'd mention, casual like, how from the tip of that mighty manliness a gleaming bead of anticipatory emissions had started to form. But, like I said and continue to defend, I am not a coarse or rude man so I won't be saying anything as such.

Then there was the fact that, like the man himself, Moby's... extension was just such a thing. Big, you see, doesn't touch on the immensity of the organ that emerged from the man's fly. If you think of such things, kind of ponder how big something like that could get, I can bet you dollars to donuts that you will not even come close the prodigious measurements of that man. After all, he is not called 'Moby' for just the whale of his size, but rather the whale size of the last part of his particular moniker, the word that follows Moby—I speak of course, of 'Dick.'

Now as to what the long arm of the law thought about the appearance of that certain part of Moby's body...well, you could guess and would guess right that the man was rightfully shocked by the accusing arm of the biker's privates, jutting out at him from his fly. So, to the appearance and the appurtenance's owner, Officer Langtry—an arm himself of the law and what he hoped then and there was bigger than the penis of the dreaded Moby—coughed quickly and managed to sputter out: "You p-put that thing away right now, son, or I'll have your ass rotting in jail before you can say fucking 'Jack Robinson.'"

To this Moby maintained nothing but stony silence, though he did move, just a bit, to wrap one of those Mrs. Gator ham-sized fists around the thick length of his dick.

Officer Langtry still managed to say: "Now you stop right there. I'm only going to tell you once, put that damned big...hard...thing away. You do it right now or you're going to be spending more than just one night in my less than comfortable can...I mean 'jail.'

Quiet again, no words—not a lone one—from Moby, but the beast did move his fist up and down the length of his old friend, a bright gleam in his nasty eyes.

"I'm telling ya, you put that thing...that thing...away or I won't be accountable for what might happen," Officer Langtry said, licking his suddenly dry lips.

Still not a word from the huge biker, who was still lazily committing the sin of Onan standing out there in broad daylight on the main road.

"Yeah, you might not...know...what could happen," Officer Langtry said, words getting all soft and sensitive-like. Then it happened, folks, the thing that shocked him just as you're going to be shocked by my telling of it. You see, Officer Langtry was one of those fellers who thought he was right with himself, comfortable in the house of his life, you know? He knew just where everything was, and why it was there: His Ma and Pa, his work, what he liked to do on Saturday nights, his favorite sit down meal, his favorite stand up eating, the movies he liked, the tunes he listened to, the books he liked to read. But that sunny summer day, the day he pulled over the biker called Moby, he came to realize that while he knew what went where in the house of his mind he came to know, with a shock, that there was a whole other room in that house he didn't even know existed.

In that room there were two folks, Officer Langtry and Moby. Moby was just as he was there, standing with his dick out, hand around it, but here is the shock, what made that room so much more different than any other room in Officer Langtry's mind, because in that room Officer Langtry was there was well, but on his knees with Moby's penis in his mouth.

Now don't say I didn't warn you, don't you dare say I didn't prepare you for what I definitely said was a shock. Don't you go opening your eyes all wide or putting on some swoon or other. But I do understand just how much of a remarkable thing this is to hear and so I'll give you all a bit of time to sort yourselves into a state where you can actually understand what I'm going to be telling next.

Ready? You sure now? Well, then I shall continue.

So there they were, the biker and the cop, the biker with his dick out and all aroused like, and the cop who wanted nothing more in this big old world than to drop down to his knees and start sucking at that pole of manhood like a calf working his mamma's teat.

Now things would have been great, for the cop that is, for Officer Langtry, if that's what would have happened. Now I'm not one to say what anyone should do for pleasure and all that. I'm what you'd call a church-going fellow. But I don't think the Lord Above would fault one person for doing something mutual and fun, for the lack of a better word, between himself and even another himself. God is Love, am I right? And love can mean lots of different things to different people. So I'm not saying that what Officer Langtry wanted to do to that big, smelly, strong biker that day was a bad thing. No, sir, I am not saying that. Because I know for a fact, as much as one man can know anything, that sucking on that man's penis was the only thing in this wide world that Officer Langtry wanted to do at that moment in time, and that his desire was good and true and free of any kind of game or cruelty. Officer Langtry, you see, had looked into that room he didn't know he'd had in the house of his soul and he realized that it was a room he wanted to spend a lot more time in, a room of love—even if it was a room of man with man love. It was still love.

But what happened next was not love, no sir. In no way. What happened next was the height of cruelty to man, an act of pure mean. Because you see, this is something else a lot of folks know about the biker called Moby, a thing right up there with his towering height, his awesome strength or his offensive aroma. You see beyond all that, Moby is one thing and one thing even more powerful than his muscles, greater than his height, even more overwhelming than his stink.

Moby, you see, is pure mean.

How mean is he? Well, I could go on for hours at a stretch telling you the various and sundry acts of cruelty this 'man' (to be polite) has enacted upon his fellow beings on this globe, but none would say it as well as telling you all what the biker did to Officer Langtry that day—a single action that would hurt that man most of all, rub him down deep in the ground and harm him in ways that no physical injury could ever do.

For, dear listeners, what Moby did that day was to smile his most vile of grins, fold away his hard and pearl-beaded manliness, get on his bike, kick it to life, and thunder off down the highway—leaving Officer Langtry there on the side of the road, mouth hanging open for the dick he'd never have. It was an act as mean, as cruel, as vile as someone taking a righteous bowel movement in the room he'd just that moment discovered within himself.

That's my story, people. Everything that happened that day between the two of those men, the peace officer and the biker. The honest man who discovered something new about himself, and the biker who was meaner than them most rabid of dogs. I wish I could say that things ended well, but to be honest with you, I can't say such. Officer Langtry, yes, did discover a new way to spend his Saturday nights, a new kind of physical affection to share with his fellow man, but that day still burns in his soul, that rejection and humiliation by the side of the road.

How do I know this? Well, friend I am pleased to make your pleasant acquaintance. Langtry's the name, Officer of the Local Constabulary. Who, after all, would know such details of that day better than the man who was himself involved?

And Moby? Well, to this day you can see his head towering over the tallest of trees, feel the thunder of his hog as he roars by, smell his deep beastly stink as he passes, and hear his bellowing laugh as he continues on his journey from one cruel and heartless act to another.

Tall, strong, reeking but most of all pure, absolute, horribly mean, is that biker, Moby.

Most of all. Most of all.

GANG MEMBERS

When **Stephen Albrow** climbs down from his Harley, he always heads straight for the quill pen and ink. With visions of his night-rides still churning through his filthy mind, he then pens erotic fantasies for a veritable kaleidoscope of porno mags, like *Torso, Cherry Boys, Beau, In Touch* and *American Bear*.

Barry Alexander lives in Iowa, but doesn't grown corn or raise hogs. The author of *All the Right Places*, Alexander's work has appeared in many gay magazines such as *In Touch, Men*, and *Honcho* and in several anthologies including *Casting Couch Confessions, Divine Meat, Fantasies Made Flesh, Saints and Sinners, Friction* 1, 2, 3, and 5, *Best of Friction*, and *Best Gay Erotica 2002*.

Chris Bridges is the proprietor of HootIsland.com, a site devoted to silly sex. His work has been published all over the Web, in the *From Porn to Poetry* anthologies, and in his own collection, *Giggling Into the Pillow*. He has ridden on a Harley before, but not to go anywhere.

M. Christian is the author of the critically acclaimed and best selling collections *Dirty Words, Speaking Parts, The Bachelor Machine* and (upcoming from STARbooks) *Filthy*. He is the editor of *The Burning Pen, Guilty Pleasures*, the *Best S/M Erotica* series, *The Mammoth Book of Future Cops* and *The Mammoth Book of Tales of the Road* (with Maxim Jakubowski) and over 14 other anthologies. His short fiction has appeared in over 150 books including *Best American Erotica, Best Gay Erotica, Best Lesbian Erotica, Best Transgendered Erotica, Best Fetish Erotica, Best Bondage Erotica* and...well, you get the idea. He lives in San Francisco and is only some of what that implies.

John Scott Darigan is the pen name of Stephen Soucy. John's work has appeared in the anthology *Straight? Volume 2* from Alyson books. Stephen will soon be published in a collection of Christmas-themed fiction from Haworth Press. He currently lives in Los Angeles.

William Dean is a columnist for the Erotica Readers & Writers Association and Associate Editor at Clean Sheets magazine. His online erotic stories have appeared on *Nightcharm* and *Suspect Thoughts*. He has stories in the anthologies *Desires*, From *Porn to Poetry* 1 & 2 and the forthcoming *Love Underfoot*.

Felix Lance Falkon, has been editing magazines for almost 45 years. He has sold two collections of his short stories, two novels, and an anthology of gay art to a paperback publisher; and he has published about twenty books himself, all but two written by other authors. He's ridden, he estimates, about a half-mile on a motorcycle in his life, and that hanging onto a football player who was driving the machine. He currently lives in the western suburbs of Philadelphia.

T. Hitman is a full-time professional writer who pens features for a number of national magazines, short fiction, a series of novels and nonfiction books, and television episodes for Paramount. His story pays tribute to Danny, a man who never knew how attractive he was and is based on factual events.

Don Luis de la Cosa is a freelance writer living in the Bronx, NY and is a long time participant in the leather scene. Previous writing credits include a novella-length story included in Michael Huxley's *Men, Amplified* anthology. When he's not busy putting pen to paper, Don Luis enjoys martial arts, anything related to Spanish language and culture, and of course, riding free on two wheels.

Jeff Mann has published a book of poetry, *Bones Washed with Wine*; a collection of essays, *Edge*; and a novella, "Devoured," included in *Masters of Midnight: Erotic Tales of the Vampire*. His work has also appeared in *Harrington Gay Men's Fiction Quarterly*, *Rebel Yell*, and *Best Gay Erotica 2003*.

Adam McCabe is the pen name of a well-known mystery writer. He was named one of the best American erotic short story writers in 2000. McCabe lives in Cincinnati with his partner who helps inspire his works.

Moses O'Hara was discovered floating in a basket down the Blackstone Canal. He was rescued by a small pack of wolves who clothed and educated him in the ways of the world. Later, after being voted "Most likely to make a killing in pornography" he moved to Los Angeles.

Rick R. Reed's horror fiction embraces the demimonde of urban Chicago, where serial killers, pedophiles and those who've bargained with the devil seek life's simple pleasures, including torture, pain, humiliation, sexual degradation, addiction and murder. His novels include *A Face Without a Heart*, a modern-day retelling of Oscar Wilde's *The Picture of Dorian Gray*, short-listed as best novel of 2000 by the Spectrum Awards. His other novels, *Penance* and *Obsessed*, together sold more than 80,000 copies. His short fiction has appeared in numerous anthologies including *The Crow: Shattered Lives and Broken Dreams*, *Dante's Disciples*, and White Wolf's *Dark Destiny* series.

Alexander Renault has published in several genres. His erotica has appeared in *Mind Caviar*, *Ophelia's Muse*, *Velvet Mafia*, *Scarlet Letters*, and the *International Journal of Erotica*. His monthly column, "Inside Out," can be found at *Beefyboyz.com*. He is living in rural Pennsylvania with his partner and their two Boston terriers, Boris Karloff and Bela Lugosi. Mr. Renault invites you to visit him at AlexanderRenault.com.

Daniel Ritter lives in the Midwest with a couple of parrots, and has written just about everything from reference work to poetry; His erotica has appeared in various places both online and in print, and he vehemently denies any rumor that the parrots are dictating it.

Thomas Roche is the editor of the late, great *Noirotica* series of erotic crime-noir anthologies, and the newly born online version of the series, *Noirotica.com*. His short fiction has appeared in the *Best American Erotica* series, *Best Gay Erotica* series, *Mammoth Book of Erotica* series, *Best New Erotica* series, and *Electric: Best Lesbian Erotic Fiction*, in addition to many other anthologies. You can visit his personal website at www.thomasroche.org.

Jason Rubis lives in Washington, DC. His erotic fiction has previously appeared in *Leg Show*, *Variations*, the anthologies *Desires*, *Guilty Pleasures*, and *Sacred Exchange* and a number of adult websites.

Simon Sheppard is the author of *Kinkorama: Dispatches From the Front Lines of Perversion*, and the award-winning *Hotter Than Hell and Other Stories*. He's also the co-editor, with M. Christian, of *Rough Stuff* and *Roughed Up*, and his work appears in nearly 100 anthologies. When he's not hanging out at www.simonsheppard.com, he rides a Yamaha Seca II; its not the biggest or fastest, but it gets him where he needs to go.

D.D. Smith is a freelance writer, voice actress, and painter from "The South." She writes everything from advertising to smut. Her stories and articles have been published in various on and offline publications. She enjoys recording erotic audio, exploring many aspects of human desire, and creating characters that connect to the reader.

Jay Starre has created nasty stories for gay men's magazines and anthologies including *Honcho*, *Torso*, *Men*, *International Leatherman*, and the *Friction* series for Alyson. From Vancouver, BC he was first runner-up in the Mr. BC Leather contest of 2002

Troy Storm has had over two hundred stories published in gay, straight and bi magazines and anthologies. His collection, *Gym Shorts*—hot tales of West Hollowood—is available from CompanionPress.com. Troy has six dead bikes in his backyard—typing is easier than working on gear shifts.

Cecilia Tan is a writer, editor, and sexuality activist from Boston. Her work has appeared in *Best American Erotica*, *Best Lesbian Erotica*, *Penthouse*, *Ms. Magazine*, *Aismov's*, and many other places. She says of "Storm Rider:" "I wrote this in a kind of fever dream I had one winter where all I did was watch my Lord of the Rings DVDs over and over. It is one of three pieces that go together in a triptych about searching for things both inside and outside of relationships."

D.L Tash is a former biker and spent much of his life riding the roads of Nevada. He now works as a freelance writer. He recently sold a piece to E.L. Publications for real-world publication, as well as having other stories and articles published on the Internet.

TruDeviant's stories have appeared in *Saints and Sinners*, *Sex Buddies*, *BUTT magazine*, *Love Under Foot*, *Bad Boys*, *Tough Guys*, *Black Sheets*, *Sex Toys*, and *Best BiSexual Erotica* 1 and 2.

A.F. Waddell writes multi-genre fiction, is a film lover, and lives in California. Works include the *Thelma and Louise* parody "Tina and Lucille" in *The Mammoth Book Of On The Road* (Carroll & Graf/Robinson) and "Cashmeres Must Die" in *Leather, Lace and Lust (Venus Books)*. For more, visit the web presence at afwaddell.com.

Greg Wharton is the author of the collection *Johnny Was and Other Tall Tales*. He is the publisher of Suspect Thoughts Press, and an editor for two web magazines, *SuspectThoughts.com* and *VelvetMafia.com*.

He is also the editor of numerous smutty anthologies including *The Love That Dare Not Speak Its Name*.

Mark Wildyr was born and raised an Okie and is now living in New Mexico, the setting of many of his plots. Mr. Wildyr has a keen interest in personal and sexual development and the interaction between diverse cultures. His erotic gay stories have appeared in works published by Companion Press, Alyson Publications, and STARbooks Press.

James Williams' first collection of stories, *But I Know What You Want* was published in 2003 by Greenery Press. Since then his work has appeared in the anthology *Dreaming in Color*, edited by Janet Hardy (Greenery Press, 2003), *Velvet Mafia #7*, edited online by Greg Wharton and Sean Meriwether, and *Blue Food*, edited online by David Salcido. His cursory history can be exhumed at www.jaswilliams.com.

wearing any underwear. "Excuse me," I said, having a hard time

, blinded by that bulge in his crotch. "but don't I know you?" "Ma

g kind of t   be

e with Ray   Go

hat loser?   in

I said. "Lik   s s

. nice body   e ɡ

kfully, he l   I

you up to t   an

. mistaking   he

'Uh, I coul   er

. blood raci   me

.acing with   e

)ut we go ɑ   b

e will see ι   iɪ

.ared?" he   ve

n privacy.   g

e—hard. I

back, traci   t,

.eezed it, ha

e it with m   b

ı.robbing, I   n

The sound of unzipping filled the small space. I don't know wh

.rst, but before I knew it, I had his rod in my hand, and mine was

want to do?" he asked, his tone challenging. I knew exactly, and